ᴮLUE-B

...reetcar's wheels hissed against their tracks, signaling
... Frowning, I squinted out the windows, trying to see
...many more until we reached First. But the trolley
... stopped at an intersection. Instead, it had squealed
...halt in the middle of the grassy median that held the
...ks. I looked around to check if any of the other passen-
...s had pulled the emergency stop cord.

The birthmark on my left shoulder suddenly itched and
...rned, like a warning. That's when I realized all the other
...ssengers were unnaturally still. Two old ladies near the
...nt leaned toward each other with their mouths open.
...e had a hand raised in midair to make a point, but it
...n't move.

My gaze swiveled toward Adam. His head was bowed
...e a man at prayer. His hand was still on my thigh, but he
...n't moving either.

I shook his shoulder. "Adam?" I whispered.

Nothing.

I waved a hand under his face.

Nothing.

"Shit."

By Jaye Wells

Sabina Kane

BLUE-BLOODED VAMP

Jaye Wells

www.orbitbooks.net

ORBIT

First published in Great Britain in 2012 by Orbit

A CIP catalogue record for this book
is available from the British Library.

ISBN 978-0-356-50075-1

Printed and bound in Great Britain by
CPI Group (UK) Ltd, Croydon, CR0 4YY

Papers used by Orbit are from well-managed forests
and other responsible sources.

MIX
Paper from
responsible sources
FSC® C104740

Orbit
An imprint of
Little, Brown Book Group
100 Victoria Embankment
London EC4Y 0DY

An Hachette UK Company
www.hachette.co.uk

www.orbitbooks.net

For Dad.

"To live in the hearts we leave behind, is not to die."
Thomas Campbell

The St. Charles streetcar lumbered its way toward the Garden District like a mourner in a funeral procession. The rocking motion should have soothed me, but I was pretty sure I was beyond ever relaxing again.

Adam sat next me. His warm hand on my leg helped dispel some of the chill. He wore his trademark brown duster and heavy boots. The goatee and muscled frame added to his general air of menace, but the mage's real danger lay in his ability to wield magical weapons.

In addition to being my partner, he was also my... boyfriend? No, too high school. Lover? Ugh. Consort? Meh.

I guess when it came down to it, he was just my mancy, plain and simple. And his presence had become as critical to my equilibrium as gravity or blood. So when he'd insisted on coming with me to Erron Zorn's house, I hadn't refused.

However, we'd opted to leave Giguhl behind at Madam Zenobia's Voodoo Apothecary. Some situations just demanded a distinct lack of Mischief demon. Besides, staying back gave my minion a chance to mend fences with his friend Brooks, a Changeling who had stormed out of New York a few days earlier after a nasty argument with Giguhl about his lifestyle choices.

To say I wasn't looking forward to our errand was the understatement of the millennium. Not only would I have to recount the shitty news of recent events in New York, but I also knew the favor I'd come to ask of Erron Zorn might get a door slammed in my face.

Adam squeezed my thigh, bringing my thoughts back to the present. "Whatever Erron says, try and keep your cool, okay?"

I nodded but didn't agree verbally. Even though Adam's sentiment was reasonable, I'd force Erron to go to Italy with us at gunpoint if I had to. Our mission was too critical to put up with squeamishness or attacks of conscience.

With each block's progress toward Erron's Garden District mansion, the more the memories of recent days weighed on my shoulders like a lead yoke. I picked up the moonstone amulet I wore around my neck. It had been given to me by my sister, Maisie, and advertised my position as the High Priestess of the Blood Moon. While the title was mostly symbolic, the amulet reminded me of better days when my twin was still alive. When lots of people were still alive, actually. I squeezed the round stone in my hand and closed my eyes, drawing on its strength.

The streetcar's wheels hissed against their tracks, signaling a stop. Frowning, I squinted out the windows, trying to see how many more until we reached First. But the trolley hadn't stopped at an intersection. Instead, it had squealed to a halt in the middle of the grassy median that held the tracks. I looked around to check if any of the other passengers had pulled the emergency stop cord.

The birthmark on my left shoulder suddenly itched and

burned, like a warning. That's when I realized all the other passengers were unnaturally still. Two old ladies near the front leaned toward each other with their mouths open. One had a hand raised in midair to make a point, but it didn't move.

My gaze swiveled toward Adam. His head was bowed like a man at prayer. His hand was still on my thigh, but he wasn't moving either.

I shook his shoulder. "Adam?" I whispered.

Nothing.

I waved a hand under his face.

Nothing.

"Shit." I turned and looked at the other passengers—the middle-aged dude with his much-younger mistress, the gangly teen with headphones glued to his ears, even the streetcar operator—everyone, frozen. A quick glance outside the windows revealed that every car and body on the street had gone still as well. It was as if someone had hit a universal pause button.

So why was I still mobile?

The ominous quiet roared in my ears. My heart beat like a spastic metronome. I rose slowly, looking for any sign of life. Panic rose in my throat like a fist.

Whatever was happening was bad. Really, really bad. I had no idea what was going on, but I knew I needed to get out of the trolley and into the open. If an attack was coming—and I was pretty sure one was—I didn't want to be trapped in the trolley.

But before I could make good on that plan, the doors opened with an ominous *click-clack*. A foot clad in a leather sandal appeared on the bottom step, followed by a male hand and the edge of a white sleeve. I reached back for the gun in my waistband. If this bastard thought I was easy prey, he was about to get a nasty surprise.

A mass of gray hair appeared next, on top of a face bearing a thick, white beard. With the help of a long staff, the intruder hefted himself up the rest of the steps. Finally, he turned toward me and smiled.

I frowned back and raised my gun. "Who the fuck are you?"

The old male sighed and waved a careless hand. My gun flew from my grasp and skittered down the aisle to land at his sandaled feet. "Your mundane weapons are useless here, Mixed-Blood." His voice was deep and strong, but also weary like he had little patience for my resistance. "You mortal realm beings are so lazy. Not to mention rude."

Instead of answering, I gathered my powers up into my solar plexus.

"Ah, ah, ah," he said. "You could try it but I'm afraid you won't like the results." He waved his staff menacingly. "Besides, is that any way to treat someone who's helped you?"

I crossed my arms, annoyed. "When have you helped me?"

Instead of answering, his face shifted and swirled until it morphed into the muzzle of a black dog. Seeing the familiar canine visage, I relaxed a fraction. "Well, shit, Asclepius, why didn't you just tell me it was you to begin with?" I waved a hand in a circle to indicate the frozen tableau around us. "And why all the drama? You could have just appeared in my dreams or whatever."

"Where's the fun in that? Besides, it's been too long since I visited the mortal realm."

"So what do you want?"

"Don't play coy." His friendly expression hardened into something more menacing. "You know why I'm here."

My stomach sank. "You've come to collect the favor I owe you."

"Correction: I've come to collect the *favors*, plural." He held up two fingers.

Shit, that's right. I'd made two blood sacrifices to the god of healing in exchange for his help. Once when Rhea and I performed a dream incubation healing rite on my twin, Maisie, to help her regain her gift of prophecy, and the second when I went into the Liminal to save her from Cain.

Or tried to, anyway.

"Is there any way this can wait? I kind of have a lot on my plate right now."

"No, it cannot wait. Your promise was to do my bidding at a time of my choosing. There are no rain checks."

"Yeah, but—"

He stabbed the tip of his staff into the floor. "I am well aware of your...issues. You're just going to have to figure out how to make it work. However, I do think you'll find my errands dovetail nicely with your own mission of vengeance."

My eyebrows slammed down. "How do you know about that?"

He shrugged. "Being a god has its privileges." As far as explanations went, it was actually pretty good. After all, deities knew all sorts of things. But hearing that my quest to kill Cain had become supernatural gossip worried me.

"Okay, what are these errands, exactly?"

"Actually it was quite fortuitous that it was you who owes me. Your former profession makes you the perfect tool for my needs."

In a former life that felt decades ago instead of mere months, I had been an assassin for the leaders of the vampire race. So, it didn't take a genius to guess he wanted me to kill someone. No sense telling him I was out of the killing business. Especially since we'd both know it was a lie. "Who?"

"A vampire, she goes by the name Nyx. No last name."

"Never heard of her."

"I'm not surprised. She was last seen in Italy..." He let the word hang there like a juicy pint of blood on the end of a stick. I kept my expression impassive, but he saw right through it. "Which, I understand, is exactly where you're headed."

"Why do you want her dead?"

Asclepius pursed his lips and shot me an offended glare. "Normally I would smite you for your impertinence, but since this is our first deal together, I'll overlook it." He paused as if collecting his thoughts. "Like you, Nyx made a blood offering in exchange for my aid. But she isn't as smart as you because she squelched on her promise."

I had to admire the way he managed to weave a threat into his explanation. "Why can't you just strike her down with a bolt of lightning or something?"

He tilted his head and shot me a pitying look. "I am a god of healing, Sabina. I cannot directly cause harm or death to anyone."

I supposed that made some sort of sense, but clearly his moral code didn't prevent him from extorting others to do his dirty work.

I pursed my lips and thought it over. "What's the second favor?"

"Nyx's request was for an item of power. A magical vest that protects the wearer from all weapons—magical and mundane. After you kill her, I want you to bring it to me."

"Um, not to split hairs or anything, but why would she want a vest to protect her from harm? As a vampire, she'd already be immune to most weapons."

"She had her reasons."

"What does she look like?"

"She's a redhead."

I rolled my eyes. "You just described one hundred percent of the vampire population." Because the race is descended from Cain, the biblical dude who was marked by the mortal deity with a shock of red hair, all vampires were gingers, too. "Are we talking deep auburn or strawberry blond?"

Asclepius pursed his lips and did a little wishy-washy head shake. "In between. More like cherry red."

I nodded. That meant I would be dealing with a youngish vamp, maybe a century or so old. Good, she would be easier to kill. "Any other distinguishing characteristics?"

"She's a hottie."

Again, this described most of the race. Because of their predatory advantages, vampires were usually incredibly attractive, which lowered the inhibitions of their mortal prey.

At my dubious look, Asclepius sighed. "I know what you're thinking, but this vamp is gorgeous. If I didn't want her dead, I'd try to fuck her myself."

I grimaced and decided to change the subject before I lost my patience completely. "Can you at least give me more specifics about where to find her? Italy isn't exactly small."

His eyes shifted left. "No."

"Why not?"

"You dare question a god?" he thundered.

I raised an eyebrow, sensing he was holding out on me.

He resisted my knowing glare for a few moments before he relented. "Fine. A cloaking ward was embedded in the chain mail so that she cannot be found by magical means."

I laughed before I could help myself. "Wait, so you gave her an item that prevented you from finding her and then got pissed when she didn't pay up? Way to screw yourself, dude."

"Enough!" He took a menacing step forward.

I sobered instantly. "I apologize." Time to get the conversation back to the big picture. "But if the vest protects her from all weapons, how exactly am I supposed to kill her?"

The god shrugged. "Not my concern."

I bit my tongue to trap the angry curse that begged to be spoken. "How much time do I have to find her?" I said instead.

"Sabina, time is a fluid thing." He raised his hands dismissively.

I supposed when you're an ancient god, that might be true, but I lived in the mortal realm, where time was decidedly inflexible. I didn't want to leave this detail open to interpretation so he could use it against me later.

"I'm gonna need something more specific."

He sighed. "Fine. I'll check in on you in a few days. By that time, I expect to hear you've put serious effort toward the task."

In other words, I couldn't just conveniently forget to track down this Nyx while I focused on my real goals. "Understood. I just ask that you don't expect immediate success. Finding her alone could take several days."

"I accept these terms." He nodded and *thunked* his staff on the floor three times. I got the impression this was some sort of supernatural handshake. "So it is done. Gods speed, Sabina Kane."

I expected the god to vanish in an intimidating display of fireworks; instead he simply opened the doors and exited like any mundane passenger. Only after he reached the sidewalk did he wave his staff and disappear. The instant he did, the world exploded into a kaleidoscope of movement, color, and sound. The trolley jerked into motion with a screech. The sudden movement knocked Adam forward off the bench, where he landed at my feet. He looked up at me with a sober expression.

"What the hell just happened?"

I sighed and held out a hand to help him up. "I'll tell you in a sec. I need to get something first."

While the mancy dusted himself off, I wound my way through the disoriented passengers to retrieve my gun from the floor. The old biddies nearby gasped when they saw the weapon. Luckily, the trolley was already slowing again as it approached the stop at First. I tucked the gun into my waistband and pushed Adam toward the door.

"Red?" he said, shooting me a tense glance over his shoulder.

I leaned in so no one else could hear. "Asclepius just threw a colossal wrench in our plans."

The doors finally opened. Adam hopped into the street, turned to help me down, and without missing a beat said, "Of course he did."

We headed up First into the heart of the Garden District. Rain dropped like tears from the drooping boughs of the stately oaks. Golden lights winked at us from a few windows set high in the mansion walls, but the late hour meant we had the night mostly to ourselves.

As we walked, I filled the mancy in on the god's request. When I finished, he was surprisingly calm. "We'll be in Italy anyway, so I don't see that it will distract too much from our original mission," he said in a reasonable tone. "Besides, assuming we even find this Nyx, it wouldn't hurt to have a healing god on our side when shit goes down with Cain."

"You're probably right, but it's a complication we don't need."

Adam put his arm around my shoulder and leaned into me. "Oh, what's one more?" His tone was dry, teasing. I shot him a glare. "Listen, he said he just expects you to make an effort, right?"

I nodded.

"So we make a couple of inquiries when we get to Rome. As long as you show a good-faith effort, he can't be pissed."

Erron's home was on the corner of Prytania and First. We'd visited the house a couple of times during our last trip to New Orleans, and it hadn't changed much. Same Greek Revival architecture. Same stately columns and deep porch. Same wrought-iron fence standing guard at the sidewalk.

I paused at the gate, my sweaty palm slicking against the cold metal. My promise to find this Nyx chick would be worth nothing if I couldn't convince Erron to help us in Rome. If he refused, we'd have no hope of tracking down the mysterious mage who went by the name "Abel" and knew more about Cain than any living being on the planet.

"Here we go," I said. "Remind me again not to use force."

Adam smiled. "You'll do fine. Erron's a reasonable guy."

I shot Adam an ironic look. *Reasonable* wasn't the first word that came to mind when I thought of Erron Zorn. The first time we'd met the lead singer of Necrospank 5000, he was hosting a midget orgy in his living room. "Reasonable," I said. "Sure."

Adam nudged me. "Just get it over with. Like pulling off a bandage."

Taking a deep breath, I pushed open the gate. It creaked in protest, as if warning me to turn back. If I'd had the choice, I'd have done just that. But I didn't have that luxury.

The minute Cain killed my sister, he'd cemented both our fates. I just hoped that this time, fate would be in my corner. But if it wasn't, I prayed that I at least would be able to kill the bastard before I joined my sister in Irkalla.

As we got closer to the house, the muted strains of piano music reached my ears. At first I couldn't place the melody. Not until I climbed the front steps and stood directly outside the front door.

Beethoven's "Moonlight Sonata" curled under the threshold and grabbed me by the throat. As beautiful as the song was, each mournful note felt like a punch in the gut. I glanced at Adam, whose face was cast in the porch's shadows.

"Well," he said, "at least his taste in music has improved."

I tried to smile, but my mouth tightened into a grimace instead. "I was hoping to find him in a good mood, but now I'm not so sure."

The last time I'd spoken to Erron, he'd been lecturing me about optimism. Telling me that Cain was a nonissue and I could relax my guard. As far as famous parting words went, those ranked right up there with "Hey, y'all, watch this."

I paused, wondering if I should wait. Go sit on his front steps until the song was over, or better yet come back the next night. But part of me knew I was looking for an excuse to escape the music. The melodic reminder of the things I wanted to forget.

Adam nudged me with his elbow. "Clock's ticking, Red."

My hand pounded on the door before I was aware of instructing it to do so. In the house, a discordant note signaled the end of the song. I stood waiting, my heart thudding in my chest. Would he answer? Or was he praying the intruder at his door would just go away?

I pounded again, calling out, "Erron! It's Sabina and Adam."

The door flew open. No one stood on the other side, which meant Erron had used magic to open it. Figuring this was as close to a "come in" as we'd get, I stepped into the foyer. The entire house was dark, but I could feel the beating of another heart somewhere inside. Erron's heart. The slow, methodical beat should have reassured me, but I was too on edge to relax.

"Erron?" I whispered. The dark made calling out seem sacrilegious.

"Here." The voice had come from the living area, where I remembered seeing a piano on my last visit. The darkness wasn't a challenge for my vampiric sight, but something about the whole scene had my instincts on red alert.

I exchanged a wary look with Adam and withdrew the gun from my waistband. My palms were clammy and my pulse thumped in my ears. Taking careful steps, I proceeded to the archway between us and the living room. I plastered my back to the wall, and Adam took a similar posture across the way. We went still, waiting, listening.

Nothing.

"Are you alone?" I finally said in a low tone.

A light flared to life in the other room. A cynical laugh reached me. "Always."

I frowned and chanced a peek around the corner. Sure enough, Erron slumped on the bench in front of his Steinway. His back was to us, but the bend of his shoulders and the half-empty bottle of amber liquor told me he wasn't in trouble or afraid. Erron Zorn, famous musician and Recreant mage, was dead drunk.

We entered the room slowly, scanning the periphery for signs of another occupant, just in case. But sure enough, Erron was alone. I relaxed my shoulders and lowered the gun. I didn't holster it, though, didn't trust the silence or the mood enough to relax completely.

Adam cleared his throat. "Didn't anyone ever tell you it's not healthy to drink alone?"

As an Adherent mage, Adam had always been a little tense around Erron. The rocker's refusal to follow the Hekate Council's laws made him a bit of a loose cannon in Adam's eyes. Still, the two men also had a sort of fragile mutual respect thing going—the type that naturally builds when you've fought side by side.

Erron turned slowly on the bench to look at us. The last time I'd seen him, he'd been sweaty and exhausted after a show at the Jupiter Ballroom in Manhattan. But that didn't compare to the haggard specter sitting in front of me.

His black hair was longer than when I'd last seen him, and the way it drooped limply around his face indicated he had shunned his normal regimen of styling products. Dark circles shadowed the skin under his gray eyes. Instead of the Johnny Cash wardrobe he usually favored, he wore a ratty T-shirt advertising a tour he'd done in Asia five years earlier and a pair of frayed jeans.

"Where's Ziggy?" I asked, referring to the mage's best friend and drummer.

Erron shrugged and played three discordant notes on the keyboard. "He quit the band. He and my stylist ran off to a private beach in the Caribbean."

I frowned at him. "Wait, Ziggy ran off with Goldie?"

Goldie Schwartz, in addition to being Erron's stylist, was also a sassy midget with a predilection for kinky sex.

His nod was morose. "I guess they fell in love on tour. Zig said they're talking about a Vegas wedding."

"But why did he quit the band?" Adam asked.

"He said I'd lost my edge." Erron laughed bitterly. "That having mortals in the band was ruining our original vision. I told him things were safer with the mortals, but he wouldn't listen."

Adam and I exchanged a look. Years earlier, Cain had decided to try and recruit Erron into his secret cabal of dark races troublemakers. When the Recreant refused, Cain had punished him by hurting his mage bandmates.

While it was tempting to talk to Erron about his drama, we had more pressing matters to discuss. Ones that tied in with his reasons for insisting on a mostly human band now.

He lifted the liquor bottle and toasted us. "Anyway, I'm not drinking alone anymore, thanks to you two." He frowned like his brain was having trouble processing information. "Wait. Why are you here? I thought you were still in New York."

I went still. "Zen didn't call you?"

"No, why?" Erron looked me in the eye, his expression suddenly much more sober. "What happened?"

I motioned him to pass me the bottle. He handed it over with great reluctance, like I was stealing his security blanket. I took a long pull and savored the fire spreading down my throat and into my stomach. Adam shot me a look, but I ignored it. "You know the murders we discussed when you were in New York?" I didn't wait for him to answer. I needed to get this out as quickly as possible. "After you left, there were two more: Tanith and Orpheus were poisoned at the peace treaty signing. One second they were toasting to peace and the next"—I snapped—"toast."

"Particularly in Tanith's case," Adam added, referring to the way the vampire had exploded all over the unsigned treaty.

Erron grabbed the bottle back and took a bracing swig. "Who killed them?"

I hesitated. Putting the truth into words was harder than I expected. Luckily, Adam came to my rescue.

"Maisie."

Erron dropped the bottle like it burned him. Glass shattered and alcohol pooled on the wooden floor. "What?"

"Turns out when your friend Abel imprisoned Cain physically, it didn't occur to him that the bastard would be able to wreak havoc through his subconscious," Adam continued. "He was controlling Maisie through the Liminal."

Erron scrubbed his hand over his face like he was having trouble following. "What's the Liminal?"

This was my area of expertise and was far less painful to explain. "It's the plane between our existence and Irkalla. It's also where our subconscious goes when we sleep. By the time we figured out Cain was manipulating Maisie through her dreams, it was too late. His hold on her was too strong. He made her perform the ritual to free him." I swallowed the guilt lodged in my throat. "Then he...killed her."

Erron blanched. "Maisie's dead?"

I nodded because I couldn't speak. Adam's hand came up to rest on my back. Part of me wanted to resist the comfort because I worried it might make the dam burst open. But the other part of me was thankful I hadn't come alone to talk to the Recreant. Hell, I was relieved Adam was around, period—after all, Maisie had tried to kill him, too.

Erron ran a hand through his hair and went to retrieve more liquor. As he uncapped the bottle, his hand shook. "So Cain's free and you came here hoping I'd help you find him?"

"Yes," Adam said. "We figure Abel is the best place to start. And since you're the only one we know who's actually talked to the guy…" Adam trailed off with a shrug.

"If Cain's free from Abel's spell, it'll be a miracle if he's still alive."

I raised my chin with a bravado I barely felt. "Just so happens we're in the market for one of those right now." I refused to believe Abel was dead. It simply was not an option.

"That's good because you're going to need seven kinds of miracles to defeat Cain and survive. He can't be killed, remember?"

After he had marked Cain with red hair for the sin of killing his brother—the original Abel—the mortal god, Elohim, declared that anyone who killed Cain would reap the punishment sevenfold. Therefore, killing Cain was a death sentence for you and all your loved ones.

When Adam and I didn't respond, Erron started pacing and continued. "I know you're hurting right now. And I know you think revenge is the only thing that will stop the pain. But as your friend, I'm asking you not to pursue this."

I jerked as if he'd struck me. "How can you say that? You know I can't just walk away."

"Sabina"—he jabbed a finger toward me—"if you go to Italy, you will lose and Cain will win. Period." He crossed his arms. "You want my advice? Run and keep running until you find a remote cave far from civilization. Take the Adherent and your demon with you, too, because he'll go after them next. It's the only way you'll all survive."

"I'd rather die than run."

"Brave words are easy when you're safe. Have you considered that Cain's luring you into a trap?"

"I know he is. Just before he killed Maisie, he told me he

wants me to use my Chthonic magic to help him access Irkalla. I think he's planning on kidnapping Lilith."

In addition to being the man who invented murder, Cain was also the psycho ex-boyfriend of the Great Mother. They'd created the vampire race together before Lilith kicked him to the curb to marry the demon Asmodeus and become the Queen of Irkalla. Cain was convinced he and Lilith belonged together, and most of his plots revolved around getting her back. But according to the prophecies of the *Praescarium Lilitu*, if any of the dark races gained power over the other races, Lilith would return to the mortal realm and kill us all. Every werewolf, faery, vampire, and mage would die. Cain's obsession would have been sad and desperate if succeeding didn't mean the destruction of all the dark races.

"Can you do that?" Erron asked. "Access Irkalla?"

I shrugged. "Rhea seems to think it's possible." Rhea was Adam's aunt and the interim leader of the mage race. She'd also been my magical mentor.

"And you're still planning on going after him? That's just what he wants!"

"Which is why we need to find Abel," Adam pointed out. "You said yourself he knows Cain better than anyone. He figured out how to trap the bastard once. Maybe he can help us find a new way to stop Cain before he destroys us all."

"What if Abel is dead? What then?"

I shrugged. "Then I'll try something else. But I'm going to Italy with or without your help. I just thought you..." I trailed off, letting the words float there like chum in water.

As expected, Erron attacked the bait like a hungry shark. "You just thought I'd what?"

"I just thought you of all beings would want to help stop Cain once and for all. This is your chance to make him pay for what he did to Ziggy and your old band."

Ziggy had been deafened after a vicious attack by Cain several years earlier. But the drummer had gotten off easy. He'd lost only his hearing; the rest of Erron's bandmates lost their lives.

Air escaped the Recreant's lungs in a rush. "You're playing dirty."

"I don't have the luxury of playing this clean, Erron. Now, are you going to help us find Abel or are you going to bury your face in a bottle of whisky until it's time to kiss your ass good-bye?"

Erron took a deep breath, as if bracing himself for the inevitable. "All right. I'll help you find Abel. That's all I'm willing to promise right now."

I nodded. "Fair enough."

He stood slowly, like an old man instead of a powerful magical being. "You want to head out tonight, I assume?"

"I have some business to take care of first. We'll leave tomorrow. What's the time difference between New Orleans and Italy?"

He pursed his lips. "Seven hours?"

Adam nodded. "We'll want to get there as close to dusk as possible so we can hit the ground running. Meet us at Zen's by ten and we'll head out."

Erron looked me in the eye. "Are you ready for this?" By that, he didn't mean the interspatial travel to Rome. He meant facing the tough choices I'd need to make to kill an unkillable foe. He meant, was I ready to sell my soul to get revenge?

My jaw clenched. "No, but I'm doing it anyway."

That seemed to satisfy him. He raised the new bottle. "To justice, then."

I grabbed the liquor and took a long, searing swallow. As heat spread down to my stomach, fortifying my resolve, I toasted him. "No, Erron, to revenge."

By the time Adam and I made it back to the French Quarter, it was close to midnight. All the bars and restaurants in the area were bustling with people. Mardi Gras was still a couple of weeks away, but the early parties filled the streets with revelers.

However, despite the festive atmosphere and bustling streets, Lagniappe's doors were locked and every light extinguished. A weathered sign on the window advertised the bar's infamous Gender Bender Drag Night, which happened every Wednesday. It was Thursday, but the place still should have been packed. Or rather, it would have been if the bar's owner weren't stuck in New York.

Lagniappe belonged to our werewolf friend Mackenzie Romulus. Last time I'd seen Mac, she was being forced to mate to a werewolf male who'd been chosen for her by her uncle, the Alpha of New York. The entire situation was sad and not a little bit infuriating, but when I'd last spoken to her, she was resigned to carry out her uncle's will.

"I assumed Mac would have left someone in charge when she left for New York," Adam said. He had his hands cupped against the glass, peering inside for some sign of life.

"She probably thought she and Georgia would be back in a few days."

Georgia was Mac's vampire ex-girlfriend. The one who got royally screwed when Mac proved too weak to stand up to her pack. The last time I'd seen Georgia, she'd been pretty pissed at me. I knew she didn't really blame me for what happened between her and Mac, but I certainly hadn't helped matters when I'd publicly challenged Mac's Alpha for being such a stubborn ass. The confrontation had resulted in Michael Romulus stepping up the date of Mac's mating ceremony. After she'd told me off, Georgia had returned to New Orleans to lick her wounds.

Adam sighed and pulled away from the window. "You want to go back to Zen's and see if she knows where we can find Georgia?"

I nodded. "I suppose I was being overly optimistic thinking she'd would be here."

Adam and I headed toward the street. But just before I stepped off the curb, I glanced back at the building. A light from one of the upper stories caught my eye.

"Hold on," I said, pointing. "Isn't that Mac's apartment?"

Adam counted up and over, his lips pursed. "I think so."

I shot him a speculative glance. "Surely Georgia's not that masochistic."

Adam shrugged. "She's been back in New Orleans for only a few days. Maybe she hasn't had time to find a new place."

I blew out a breath. "Okay, you'd better stay out here."

Adam frowned. "Why?"

"I have a feeling that whatever state of mind she's in will only get worse when she sees this letter." I held up the envelope Mac had given me. She had made me promise to deliver it to Georgia personally. "Probably she'd appreciate not having an audience."

"Gotcha." He placed a heavy hand on my shoulder. "Just try to be sensitive, okay?"

I shot him an offended glance. "What's that supposed to mean?"

"No offense, Red, but you're not exactly comfortable around vulnerability. You tend to get a tad ... snappish."

I pursed my lips and considered arguing. However, he had a decent point. "Maybe we should have brought Giguhl along after all. He's much better at this kind of stuff."

Adam squeezed my shoulder. "You'll do fine." I wasn't sure which of us he was trying to reassure. Regardless, I took a deep breath and braced myself to face the broken-hearted vampire.

"If she tries to cry on my shoulder, I'm out of there."

His lips quirked. "Don't worry. After the fight you guys had, she's more likely to punch you."

Now that I could definitely handle. Fists were always preferable to tears, in my book.

I left Adam at the sidewalk and beelined for the steel door on the side of the building. In addition to the apartment she'd shared with Georgia, Mac also rented rooms to a few drag queens employed by the club. If I was wrong and Georgia wasn't up there, I'd at least have the chance to ask some of the other tenants if they'd seen her.

As I climbed the stairs to the correct floor, I tried to figure out what I'd say to the vampire. But how exactly does one offer condolences in that kind of situation? "Sorry your werewolf lover was forced to marry a dude against her will" didn't sound quite right.

I shook my head. Honestly, there were no words that

could erase Georgia's heartache. The envelope crinkled inside my pocket. I hoped that whatever she'd written there would help Georgia move on.

When I reached the top of the stairs, the mournful strains of Joni Mitchell spilled out into the hallway from beneath the red door of Mac's apartment. Guess I'd found the right place after all.

I blew out a breath, hoping to dispel the nerves jumping around in my gut. "Here goes nothing." I rapped a knuckle on the door.

"Go away!" The voice rose over Joni's melancholy singing.

I knocked again, hoping persistence would piss Georgia off enough to open the door. I didn't want to tell her it was me in case she was still holding a grudge.

"I said"—the door flew open—"fuck off!" Georgia's fangs flashed with threat but her eyes were bloodshot from recent tears. Her red hair hung limply around her pale face, hinting that she hadn't bathed in days.

"Hi," I said lamely.

Georgia's posture relaxed a fraction but her fangs didn't recede. "You." Funny how one little word, three little letters, can sound so hateful.

"Georgia, I know you're still mad, but I—"

The door slammed in my face with a loud crash.

I sighed and pounded again. "I need to talk to you."

"Go away!"

Pound, pound. "Open the door. Please."

"Haven't you done enough already?" she ranted. "Now you have to come here and bother me? I just want to be left alone!"

Something broke inside me. I didn't have time for this shit. I didn't have time to play intermediary for the lovelorn when my own life was so fucked up. Didn't deserve to be yelled at when I was nursing my own heartache. I'd promised Mac I'd deliver her message and that's just what I'd do.

I removed the envelope from my coat pocket. Held it up under the light so Georgia could see it through the peephole. "I have a message for you."

She laughed bitterly. "Oh, I'm sure."

"It's from Mac."

Silence.

"You want to read it? Fine. You want to burn it? That's fine, too. I'm just the messenger. Do what you want." I wedged the envelope into the doorjamb. "I'm leaving for Italy tomorrow morning. If you want to talk about this, you'll have to find me before then."

She snorted. "Not likely."

No doubt she thought my comment was a casual one. But it wasn't. The truth was if Georgia didn't come find me before I left, chances were good she'd never see me again.

I put my hand on the door. "Have a good life, Georgia."

With that, I turned and walked away. The silence behind me weighed on my back. I could practically feel her arguing with herself through the door. I don't know if those locks clicked open before I made it out of the building, but Georgia didn't run after me. Which, I decided as I made my way back outside to Adam, was probably a good thing. I'd always sucked at good-byes.

When Adam and I returned to Zen's shop, everyone was gathered in the sitting room on the second floor. Zen and Brooks had closed the shop for the evening and convened over steaming mugs of chicory coffee doctored up with a little whisky.

"How'd it go?" Giguhl jumped up like a tightly wound spring. With his seven-foot-tall frame, black horns, and green-scaled skin, he should have been intimidating to most beings. But the too-short sweatpants and concerned expression on his face ruined the effect.

"Erron's in," I said.

The demon frowned. "Why do I sense there's a but?"

I dropped into a chair and smiled at Zen when she brought me a mug. "Well, first, he's super reluctant. Said we'd be better off hiding in a remote cave."

Giguhl sniffed. "Please. We're not cowards."

I smiled at my best friend.

"Besides, between the no porn and dealing with your two whiny asses, I'd eat you both within a week," he continued.

"But you'd regret it," Brooks said. "Sabina alone would give you heartburn for a decade."

"It's true." Giguhl nodded.

Brooks's lips formed into a flirty pucker. "Now Adam, on the other hand, would be a delicious snack."

"I'm not sure whether to feel flattered or afraid," Adam responded.

Brooks winked at the mancy. "Both."

The Changeling caught my eye and winked. I smiled back. "I have to say, it's good to have you back, Brooks. You seem...like yourself again."

By that I wasn't just referring to the fact that he hadn't dressed in a wig and sequined gown. Although it was nice to see him in jeans and black-framed hipster glasses and with a bald head again, I was referring to his flirty, fun personality, which had disappeared a few months earlier after a violent beating had robbed him of his confidence.

He smiled sheepishly. "Thanks, Sabina. Sorry if I was a little cranky in New York."

When he'd moved to the Big Apple to launch his singing career, Brooks had adopted his female drag persona full-time, going so far as insisting we call "her" Pussy Willow. But he'd taken the diva routine a bit too far. It'd taken everything in me not to drop-kick the drama queen into the Hudson.

"A little?" Giguhl said. "Bitch, please. You turned into Joan Crawford with PMS there for a while."

The Changeling shot the demon a mock-serious scowl. "Anyway"—he performed an impressive neck swivel—"Zen helped me realize that I was hiding my pain behind all the makeup and fabulous accessories. She encouraged me to let my Brooks flag fly." He executed a Z-shaped snap through the air.

"And by that he means, I threatened to kick his ass to the curb if he didn't stop throwing diva fits in my store."

Brooks pursed him lips. "That too."

"Either way," Giguhl said, "Sabina's right. We all missed you."

"I missed you, too, Gigi," Brooks said quietly.

It was good to see the demon and the faery had made amends. Back in New York, Giguhl had grown as tired of Pussy Willow's attitude as the rest of us and had called her on it, which resulted in a nasty argument. But it looked like they'd dealt with their issues and were back to being BFFs.

"When do you head to Rome?" Zen asked me.

"Tomorrow morning."

"Good idea." She nodded approvingly. "Give you guys a chance to catch up on your rest. Sounds like you'll need it. In the meantime, I'm going to whip up some amulets and potions for you guys to take with you."

"Thanks, Zen," I said.

Brooks rose. "Giguhl and I will get started on getting the ingredients together."

The demon shot the fae a look. "We will?"

Brooks nodded in the exaggerated way of someone with mischief on their minds. Giguhl's eyes widened. "We will!"

The pair ran off without another word. Adam, Zen, and I exchanged worried glances. "How much trouble can they get into, really?" Zen said, sounding unsure.

I sighed. "We'll go check on them on our way up." I leaned back. "In the meantime, I need you to promise me something."

Zen's head tilted. "Sure, anything."

"Can you check on Georgia? I tried to talk to her tonight but she wouldn't even open her door."

Zen sighed and leaned back. "Yes, she's been avoiding all of us."

Adam leaned forward. "Even Brooks?"

The voodoo priestess nodded. "Yeah. The minute they got back to New Orleans, she just kind of retreated into herself. Living in that apartment probably isn't helping matters since she's surrounded by memories of Mac."

"I went to give her a message Mac asked me to deliver. I'm not sure if it will help or make things worse."

Zen nodded. "I'll check on her. The sooner she accepts that Mac isn't coming back, the easier it will be for her to move on."

My stomach cramped. I didn't want to argue with Zen, but I wasn't sure she was right. If Adam had been taken from me like that, it would take a hell of a lot more than a few weeks to get over it. Heartbreak takes on a whole new dimension when you're immortal. But I couldn't expect Zen—a human—to understand that. "Yes, well, I appreciate it."

Adam clapped his hands on his thighs. "On that note, I'm exhausted."

I nodded. "Me too. Getting up in the morning is going to be harsh."

Unlike full-blooded vampires, I could actually be in the sun without dying, but the UV rays depleted my energy quickly. That meant we'd have to move fast in the morning to get out of town and into Italy's later time zone before the sun sapped my strength.

"Check on Brooks and Giguhl on your way up, please. I need to do a quick thing here." She motioned to the altar on the other side of the room. As usual, it was covered with an assortment of liquor bottles, old bones, scraps of cloth, and old keys—offerings to the Catholic saints and voodoo gods she worshiped. She didn't say as much, but I assumed she wanted to hang back to make an offering to them so they'd watch over us.

I nodded. "Okay. Thanks, Zen."

"Sleep well, my friends." She smiled and held my gaze. "You're going to need it."

After we'd made our way into the hall, Adam took my hand and squeezed. I forced a wan smile at him. It's not that I didn't enjoy his touch. I just had so much on my mind, I felt like I was going a little crazy.

"Hey," he said. "What's going on in that head of yours?"

I shook my head, but I knew he wouldn't let me get away without an explanation. "Honestly? Ever since I left Georgia's door, I've thinking about our fight—fights—in New York. How close we were to…" I paused, unable to put into words how afraid I'd been of losing him. Before Adam and I were officially together, I'd been on a sort of self-sabotage kick that included sleeping with an ex-boyfriend. When the truth finally came out, Adam was more hurt by the betrayal of keeping the secret than the act itself. And I'd reacted by accusing him of not being able to love all of me—vampire nature and all. In short, it was a total painful clusterfuck.

"I don't ever want to go through a fight like that again," I said.

He blew out a breath and pulled me in for a hug. "Oh that," he said.

I looked up. "What did you think I was going to say?"

He shot me a sidelong look. I tensed. Begged him with my eyes not to bring up my sister. I just…couldn't. Not yet. That particular wound was too fresh and raw. He opened his mouth but thought better of whatever he was going to say. "Anyway," he said finally, "I don't want to go through that again either. I think I did some permanent damage to my liver."

I pulled back. "Really? You too?" I asked, thinking of the night Giguhl and I had drowned our sorrows in a gallon of ice cream and a bottle of tequila.

"When I thought I'd lost you, I was a wreck. That night Mac got mated and we had our huge fight?" I nodded, remembering. "I killed two bottles of whisky. Luckily, I'd locked myself in the room or gods only knew what I'd have done."

I frowned at him. I had no idea he'd been that bad off. Although, given my own pain, I guess I should have known he'd have been hurting, too. I wrapped my arms around him and squeezed. "I was terrified I'd lost you."

"Me too," he whispered. "But we're together now."

I kept my face on his chest, not able to look him in the eye. "But what if—"

"Shhh," he said. "Look, we've got issues. We both know that. And guaranteed we'll fight again. But all we can do is make sure we're honest with each other from here out." He pulled back and made me look up at him. "Right?"

I swallowed. It had been my own lack of honesty that had forced our issues to the surface. But I'd learned my lesson in spades. "Right."

"Good." He planted a quick kiss on my lips. "You know what?"

I smiled up into his handsome face. "What?"

"There is a silver lining to fighting every now and then."

"Oh yeah? What's that?"

He waggled his eyebrows suggestively. "Makeup sex."

I pursed my lips like I was debating the merits of him claim. "Speaking of, we never—"

Crash!

Adam ignored the sound and pulled me closer. "You were saying?"

"I was saying that we never—"

Bang, bang, bang!

Adam put his forehead against mine and closed his eyes. "I don't suppose we can just ignore that?"

I laughed and patted his cheek. "Right, because how much trouble can a Mischief demon and a Changeling drag queen get into?"

"Shit," he breathed. "All right, but remember what you were about to say because I'm planning on having a very long, slow, deep discussion about it later."

"Ouch!" The high-pitched yelp was followed by the kind of shushing sound that accompanied covert shenanigans.

"It's a deal," I said to Adam. "Now let's go make sure those two aren't about to blow up the joint."

A few moments later, we pushed open the door to Zen's workroom. The demon and the Changeling had their heads together like conspirators. When we walked in they both shot up and their expressions instantly turned guilty.

Adam crossed his arms. "What's going on?"

"Nothing," Brooks squeaked.

I narrowed my eyes at the seven-foot-tall demon, who would not look at me. "Giguhl?"

He pursed his lips and shook his head.

"Don't make me make it a command," I warned. Since the demon was my minion, I could force him to tell me anything or do anything if I made it a direct order. But I tried not to abuse that power since he was also my friend.

The demon's massive shoulders slumped and he shot an apologetic look at Brooks. "We're making a voodoo doll of Cain."

"What?" Adam asked. He shot toward the table to inspect their work. "How far are you into the ritual?" he demanded, all business.

"We were putting finishing touches on his ensemble." As he spoke, Brooks used glue to attach rhinestones to Cain's jacket. They'd also hot-glued red yarn to the doll's head and used two green sequins for the eyes. Apparently, the Changeling believed the mastermind behind all our suffering looked a lot like vampire Elvis, the later years.

Zen walked in and froze when she saw the guilty expressions. "What's going on?" Her tone was part suspicious and part terrified of finding out what had us all tense.

"Um," Brooks said, cringing, "Giguhl and I were sort of *makingavoodoodoll.*"

Zen looked at him with laserlike intensity. "Holy Loa, what in the world were you thinking, child? Please tell me you haven't used the goofer dust yet."

Giguhl nudged a small vial with his claw. "You mean this?"

Brooks groaned in a way that told me he'd been hoping to hide that part from Zen.

"We haven't used it yet," he rushed to add.

Zen rounded on her assistant. "You know I don't allow red magic on my property. Besides, you're not fully trained in the voodoo arts."

The fae crossed his arms. "I've helped you make dolls lots of times. Besides, it's not really red magic."

"Well, it sure as hell ain't white magic." She narrowed her eyes at him. "Evil intentions aren't something you do for the heck of it. You know that. The Law of Three won't listen to excuses. I don't want that kind of karma."

"Don't worry," Giguhl said. "Brooks said he figured out how to avoid the Law of Three altogether."

Zen frowned and pulled back to get a good look at her assistant. "How?"

Brooks took a deep breath and prepared to make his

case. "I'm doing a banishment and equalizer spell," he began. "I figured if we ask Ogun to intercede on our behalf, then the Law of Three wouldn't apply."

I held up a hand. "Can someone translate that for the voodoo challenged?"

Zen sighed. "It's a spell that asks the holy one to protect you and also punish one who's done you wrong. The Law of Three dictates that whatever magical energy you put out into the universe will return threefold. Thus, if you curse someone, you're inviting three times bad karma to your door. But in this case, Brooks is invoking the warrior god Ogun to do the dirty work so he won't experience any bad karma after."

"And what's gopher dust, exactly?" I asked.

"Goofer dust, Sabina," Adam corrected.

Ever since our brief stint in New Orleans, Adam had started a casual study of basic voodoo in his spare time. His interest was merely academic, though. To a mage with inherent magic, the human practices were merely a curiosity.

I nodded impatiently. "Okay, what's goofer dust?"

"It's used in spells meant to cause suffering. There's lots of stuff in it, but the two main ingredients are snake skin and graveyard dirt."

"Sounds like a Chthonic spell," I said, referring to my own magical specialty.

In mage terms, Chthonic magic dealt with primordial powers like sex and death. Powers that were strongest in deathy places, like graveyards. In addition, snakes were powerful Chthonic symbols.

"Similar." Zen nodded. "Brooks is basically asking a god to use death magic on Cain."

"Awesome, right?" Giguhl said.

I sighed. "Guys, I appreciate your support, but Cain is my problem."

Giguhl pursed his lips. "Correction: Cain is *our* problem. All of us."

I grimaced. He was right, of course. Especially since, as my minion, he kind of had to go to Italy since that's where I was headed.

"If we do this spell, you guys won't need to go anywhere," Brooks said. "You can stay here, where it's safe."

I exchanged a look with Adam. While the demon's and the faery's hearts were in the right place, their methods could spell disaster for all of us. "But if the spell backfires, it would put all of us in danger," I said.

"What do you mean?" Zen said.

"Whoever kills Cain will reap the punishment sevenfold," Adam explained. "That means if Brooks's plan to ask Ogun to take the heat for the death doesn't work, he and six of his nearest and dearest will die, which I assume includes you, Zen, as well as this guy." He jerked a thumb toward Giguhl.

"But Ogun will absorb the karmic fallout," Brooks said. "Right, Zen?"

The voodooienne chewed her bottom lip, obviously weighing her words. "I'm not sure Brooks has enough experience to control Ogun's powers to ensure the spell will work...but I do."

Brooks gasped. "You'll do it?"

Zen shrugged. "Even though I don't normally approve of this sort of magic, some situations require some moral flexibility. If asking Ogun to intercede will protect you guys, I'll do it."

I held up my hands to stall Brooks's victory dance and spoke to Zen. "Trust me, the price you'll have to pay to the god to do this for you will be steeper than you're willing to pay. I speak from experience." I couldn't imagine what a war god would demand in exchange for killing Cain, but I had a feeling it would be a hundred times worse than Asclepius's demands.

Zen went still at my comment and Giguhl's eyes narrowed, like he was about to demand an explanation. I rushed ahead to avoid muddying the conversation with a rehash of the Asclepius situation.

"Look, guys, we appreciate why you're trying to do this. Really. But it's not going to fix anything. We have a plan and we're going to manage the risk as much as possible."

"She's right," Adam said. "If we thought magic would solve this problem, we would have already tried it. Trust me."

Giguhl sighed. "They might be right, Brooks."

"Wait a second," the Changeling said. "The rule about killing Cain applies to you, too, right? So we could all die anyway."

I hesitated. "Yeah."

"But that's why we're going to Italy," Adam jumped in to explain. "According to Erron, there's a mage there who knows Cain better than anyone. We're hoping Abel can help us find a way to stop him without any of us dying."

Brooks's shoulders slumped. "Well, shit."

Giguhl shot his friend a disappointed frown. "Sorry, dude. We tried."

Brooks picked up the gaudy doll and looked it over. "I just hate for this to go to waste. It's some of my best work." He fingered the sequins longingly.

Zen patted the faery on the shoulder. "Actually, we might be able to use it after all."

Brooks and Giguhl perked up. "Really?" they said in unison.

She nodded. "Anybody in the mood to craft a good vexing spell?"

Brooks rubbed his hands together. "Now you're talking."

"And while we're at it, we'll whip up some protection amulets for the three of you."

"Hold on," I asked in a wary tone. "What exactly does a vexing spell do?" I trusted Zen, but I didn't want to take any chances on complicating our situation any more than it already was.

"The one I have in mind causes a severe case of anal itching." While Adam and I blinked in shock, she turned and smirked at Giguhl and Brooks. "You in?"

The demon and the faery faced each other with wicked grins before turning back to Zen and announcing in unison, "Abso-fucking-lutely!"

4

*A*fter we escaped the voodoo party, Adam and I closed ourselves in the attic apartment. He locked the door behind us with a decisive flick of his wrist. Judging from the heat the mancy was shooting at me, sleep was the last thing on his mind.

"So"—he began sidling toward me—"you were saying something about makeup sex?"

I laughed out loud. Leave it to a male to skip a postmortem about aborted voodoo rituals and the impending suicide mission everyone thought we were about to undertake when sex was on the line. Although, now that I thought about it, with everything going on maybe it was the perfect excuse to grab the time we had by the reins and ride it for all it was worth.

I crooked my finger at him. "Come closer and I'll tell you."

Two hours later, I fell onto the mattress. Sweat soaked my skin and my muscles felt like gelatin.

"Am I forgiven?" Adam said, nipping at my shoulder.

Lethargy pulled at me. The physical exertion of our lovemaking combined with the emotional stress of the last few days left me feeling hollow and dried out. Sex with Adam had ignited my bloodlust and my fangs throbbed hotly against my gums. I needed blood more than I needed air, but I'd be damned if I let Adam know that. I didn't want to ruin our postmakeup-sex bliss with a reminder of why we'd fought in the first place.

So, when I smiled at my mage, I did so with a closed mouth. And when I spoke, I turned my head slightly, so he wouldn't catch the telltale flash of fang. "If this is what happens after we fight, I might have to piss you off more often."

Gentle fingers grasped my chin and turned my face toward him. I clamped my lips closed, but he ran a gentle thumb across them. No way he missed the telling bumps. "You need blood."

My tongue felt like sandpaper in my mouth. My stomach cramped. I considered lying, but what was the use? "You're not wrong," I said carefully.

Adam leaned down and placed a kiss on my parched lips. He leaned back a fraction to look in my eyes. I could feel the indecision coming off him in hot waves. Before he could say anything, I decided to let him off the hook. "Don't worry about it. I'll just hit the butcher shop tomorrow or something. I'll be fine."

He tilted his head and gave me a dubious scowl. "Liar."

I sighed. "Adam, it's fine. Really. I don't expect you to get over your issues about being my blood source this fast. I know it's not easy for you." As I raised a hand to cup his cheek, his eyes flicked to my fingers, where a consistent tremor gave away my lie.

"Red, I'm not saying that I'm looking to be your convenient blood dispenser, but I'd be a real bastard to deny you when you're so clearly in need. Let me help you."

My fangs sprang fully from my gums and my core spasmed with an aftershock. Still, I considered refusing. The last time I'd fed from Adam, we'd had that huge fight and our relationship barely survived it. But his expression was so open, so earnest. He was offering himself despite his misgivings. It felt...well, not right, exactly, but like progress.

"You're sure?" I rasped.

He nodded. "I'm sure about you. About us. I trust you and I love you. Let me help."

My eyes stung. A small, petty voice deep inside told me I didn't deserve him. Another voice, this one louder, told that one to shut the hell up. This is what couples did, after all—helped each other. Healed each other's wounds.

Besides, his sweet blood called to me.

"Okay." I swallowed nervously, my throat clicking. "I promise I'll only take what I need."

He looked me in the eye and said, "I trust you."

He didn't lie back submissively. Instead, he kissed me once, twice, before leaning over and offering me his neck. Lifting my head was a challenge, but my fangs popped out, making up the distance. I didn't want to hurt him more than necessary, so I kissed his neck. Licked it to prepare for the sting. He moaned softy—whether he enjoyed the sensation or was simply anxious for me to begin, I didn't know. Regardless, I finally scraped over the spot, a little scratch to warn him. And then, quickly, I thrust into his vein.

His whole body tensed. Blood hit my tongue with the flavor of cloves and honey.

Adam's throat muscles worked, pumping the blood into my mouth even faster. I swallowed greedily. The blood soothed my stinging throat and eased the pounding in my head. But I wasn't content to just take from him.

My palm found his sex. I stroked him in time with my swallows. He groaned and his hand found my hair, pressing my face harder to his throat.

It didn't take long until his body stiffened. I hadn't taken more than a pint, but it was enough. He sucked air through his teeth and bucked his hips. I gave one last hard pull on his vein. Wetness covered my hand. Blood surged into my mouth.

He went limp and I let my fangs slowly slide from his skin. My arms curled around his back, holding him to my breast.

Adam's blood sizzled through my veins, like a shot of adrenaline. My cells knit themselves back together and my thoughts became clear and sharp.

The mancy shifted and lifted his head from my chest. I tensed for his reaction. Would he regret letting me feed from him? But when he looked at me, a lazy smile lifted the corner of his lips. "Well, now ..."

I licked my lips to capture every drop before kissing him. His tongue delved in farther. If the taste of his own blood bothered him, he didn't show it. When he finally pulled away, we both let out long, contented breaths.

"Thank you," I whispered. "I love you."

"I love you, too. All of you."

A surge of warmth flooded my chest and mixed his blood in my veins. The cocktail was potent and made me want him all over again, but I knew that even though I felt strong, Adam needed time to recover from the minor blood loss. So instead of attacking him, I pulled him closer.

He nestled between my breasts with a contented sigh. "See there, things are already looking up."

"What do you mean?"

"You told Erron we were in the market for some miracles, right?"

I nodded slowly, not following his logic.

Adam wove his fingers with mine and kissed my knuckles. "The fact we're still together after everything is miracle number one."

I huffed out a laugh. When he said "everything," he was referring to some pretty weighty shit: Me sleeping with another male and lying about it, Adam pressuring me to leave my vampire side behind and embrace mage life fully, and the father of the vampire race using my sister to try killing Adam for the crime of loving me. So, yeah, I guess he was right. If we could make this work despite all the odds stacked against us and our own emotional bullshit to contend with, I suppose we did count as a miracle.

"Okay, then, one miracle down." I blew out a breath and rolled into Adam's warm chest. "Let's just hope the gods are feeling generous because we're gonna need several more if we're going to defeat Cain."

Adam ran a thumb down my cheek. "If they're not, we'll just have to make some miracles of our own."

The sun burned like a demon in the eastern sky. Its evil rays came through the shop's windows like laser beams. After the infusion of Adam's blood the night before, I felt pretty freaking fantastic, but I didn't want to waste his blood fighting the UV damage. So I wore dark sunglasses, jeans, boots, and my leather jacket.

It was two minutes until ten. I sat on the counter chugging coffee while Zen and Brooks made final touches on the amulets and Giguhl and Adam double-checked supplies. I blew across the top of my cup and tried to not look concerned that Erron had yet to show.

"Red, you're not fooling anyone."

I looked up at the demon. "What?"

"Please, if you keep glaring at that door, you're going to burn a hole through it."

My shoulders slumped. "Are you telling me I'm the only one who is worried Erron might skip out on us?"

"Yes," Adam said. "He still has a couple of minutes."

"We said we were leaving at ten. He should have already been here."

"There are any number of possible explanations for his lateness."

"Right, like he skipped town—"

The front door burst open, causing the bell overhead to ring frantically. A dark figure rushed in with the bright sun at its back.

I slowly set the mug down and rose. "Erron?"

The being had some sort of tarp draped over its body and wore a ski mask with sunglasses over the eyeholes. Leather gloves hid the skin of its hands. Everyone in the room tensed.

"Well don't just stand there," a muffled female voice yelled. "Close the blinds!"

I jerked in surprise. "Georgia?"

"Not for long if you don't make it dark in here!"

I nodded at the others. "Do it!"

Giguhl, Brooks, Zen, and Adam rushed to close the wooden blinds and pull down the shade that covered the window on the door. Finally, the room was dark enough to be safe for the vampire. She pulled the ski mask off with a gasp. "Good gods, that sucked."

"What the hell are you doing traipsing around in the daylight like a damned fool?" Brooks demanded.

Georgia threw the tarp to the ground and pointed an accusing finger at me. "I need to give Sabina a piece of my mind!"

I crossed my arms and sighed. "Here we go. What'd I do now?"

She waved the envelope I'd left on her door around like a smoking gun. "If this is some sort of sick joke, I really don't appreciate it."

I tilted my head and frowned at her. "What? I told you, Mac asked me to bring it to you. You're welcome, by the way."

"Bullshit! Mac would never be this cruel. It has to be a fake."

"Georgia, I know you're hurting," Adam said. "But think about what you're saying. Why would Sabina come all the way to New Orleans to deliver a fake letter from Mac?"

The vampire deflated a fraction and her eyes swiveled to take in all of us. Brooks and Zen were watching her with looks bordering on pity. Adam and Giguhl were puffed up, ready to defend me. And me? I watched her with my hands on my hips. We were burning daylight, Erron had yet to show, and we needed to get to Italy ASAP so we'd have the whole night there to make headway in finding Cain.

"Look, Georgia, I don't know what to tell you. Mac asked me to give you that. I had no idea what was in it. I'm sorry if it upset you—"

"Upset me?" she yelled. "I'm not upset. I'm pissed! How dare she do this?"

I frowned, curious despite my best intentions to stay out of the middle. "What'd she do?"

Georgia was red-faced and sputtering now. She held up the letter. Adam came forward and grabbed it. His eyes scanned the stack of pages for a few moments before widening in shock. "Mac signed the building and the license for Lagniappe over to her."

I frowned at the vampiress. "Let me get this straight. You're pissed that Mac ensured you had an income and a place to live? How dare she?" I said with exaggerated indignation.

Georgia threw up her arms. "How am I supposed to hate her now?"

My mouth fell open. "Ah."

"Ah?" Adam asked. "I don't follow that logic at all."

But I did. People always say anger is the strongest emotion. They're wrong. Anger is the easiest emotion, the least complex. When other feelings are too difficult to bear, you can wrap anger around you like insulation. Like a shield to deflect more complicated and hurtful emotions—like sadness and fear.

I sighed and stepped toward Georgia. "She loved you in her own way, Georgia. It wasn't the love you needed, but it *was* love. This is her way of proving that."

"Fuck that," she said. "I'm putting the building on the market ASAP."

"Like hell you will," Brooks said. His hands were on his hips and his head was swiveling with attitude. "You can't put all those proud queens out on the street!" he said, referring to the drag queen corps who lived and worked in that building. Since Brooks was also employed by the club, he had a personal stake in Georgia accepting Mac's gift.

"Besides, where are you going to go, baby girl?" Zen said, in full maternal mode. "That building is your home, too."

Georgia's lip trembled. "I don't know! It's just too hard."

"So give yourself some time. A month, three. Whatever," Zen said.

Brooks added, "Yeah, girl, don't throw away this gift just because it's easier than working through your shit."

Georgia wrapped her arms around herself protectively. Her expression was abashed, like she finally realized she'd been making a scene. "I'm sorry. I just…it was a shock."

Giguhl put his arm around the vampire. "Don't worry. Love makes fools of everyone."

The vampire blinked at the unexpected depth of the demon's statement. "I guess you're right. I just wish it didn't hurt so much."

"Trust me, it passes."

"You sound like you speak from experience."

The demon looked into the middle distance. "Even us badass demons aren't immune to heartbreak, Georgia."

I rolled my eyes. It's not that I didn't feel for Georgia or that I didn't remember how hurt Giguhl had been when his demon girlfriend dumped him, but with each passing minute I was growing more and more aware of Erron's absence.

"Look," I said, "I know this has been rough on you. But Zen's right—give yourself some time."

"I guess you're right. Thanks, guys." Georgia sighed. Then she looked around and noticed the supplies and baggage littering the story. "What are you guys doing?"

"We're going to Italy!" Giguhl said excitedly.

"Sabina mentioned you were leaving. Vacation?"

"Hardly. We need to see a mage about murdering the father of the Lilim," Adam said, using the ancient term for the vampire race.

Georgia's mouth fell open. "Cain? Jesus. What the hell happened after I left New York?"

"Well," Giguhl began, looking ready to settle in for a long gossip session. While he filled Georgia in, I pulled Adam aside.

"Should we call him?" I whispered.

Adam glanced at the clock. It was five after ten. He sighed. "Probably."

I nodded and went to the desk to pick up the phone. While I dialed, Giguhl wrapped up his summary.

Georgia looked devastated. "I can't believe they're all dead. Oh gods, that must have been horrible. Here I am bitching about my broken heart and you guys are dealing with worse losses."

She looked so abashed, I paused my dialing and looked up. "Georgia, it's okay," I sighed. "Loss is loss, right?"

She nodded. "I guess so. I just can't believe you guys are going to try to kill Cain."

"We're not even sure we can kill him," Adam said. "But hopefully we can at least find a way to prevent him from causing more trouble."

I bit my tongue and looked down to finish dialing. Adam might believe that killing Cain was the worst-case scenario, but for me it was the only one. Allowing Cain to live after he'd killed so many people I care about was not an option.

While Adam and the others discussed the plans for Italy, I focused on willing Erron to pick up his phone. It rang once, twice.

Click.

"You've reach Erron Zorn. Leave a message." *Beep!*

"Erron, it's Sabina. Get your ass to Zen's now!" I slammed the phone down. "Shit!"

Adam looked up. "What's wrong?"

"Voice mail."

"Should we go over there?" Giguhl asked.

While I considered the options, Adam went to the front and peeked out the window, like he expected to see Erron strolling along the sidewalk. "I'll be damned," the mancy breathed. With his free hand, he waved me over. "Sabina, you've got to come see this."

"What?" I demanded, moving around the desk to go join him.

I stepped up to the blinds and looked out. Sure enough, Erron Zorn was pacing back and forth in front of the store. His lips moved rapidly like he was arguing with himself. I let out a frustrated sigh. With my fist, I pounded on the window.

Erron's head jerked up. When he saw me scowling at

him through the window, his shoulders dropped. I mouthed, *Get your ass in here*. He shot me a scowl but slowly made his way toward the front door.

"Georgia, back up, he's coming in," Adam warned.

The vampire immediately moved toward the far end of the store to avoid the pool of sunlight that burst in when Erron entered.

"You knew we were leaving at ten," I said, crossing my arms. "What gives?"

He looked better than he had the night before, in that he was sober, but the scowl on his face said someone had woken up on the wrong side of the bed that morning.

"For the record," he said, "I tried Abel's cell last night after you left. He didn't answer."

"Good morning to you, too, sunshine," Adam said.

"So?" I said.

"So, I called him five times this morning, too. Voice mail, every time."

"Hey, Erron!" Giguhl called, rushing across the shop to high-five the Recreant. Erron lifted his hand halfheartedly to receive the demon's claw, but his eyes were on me.

"Well?" he said.

"Well, what?"

Erron raised his hands. "Doesn't it worry you that the mage you're seeking isn't answering his phone?"

Despite the fact I shared Erron's concerns about the status of Abel's existence, I wasn't about to indulge in hand wringing. "There's only one way to find out for sure, which we can finally do now that you've graced us with your presence."

Erron raised his eyebrows. "You sure you want to do this?"

I sighed. "I believe we've already covered this."

"I know, just want to be sure you know there's no shame in backing out."

I looked him directly in the eye. "Yes, there is. But no one's stopping you from running if that's what this is really about."

"How would you find Abel then?"

"We'll manage. Between Adam, Giguhl, and me, we've made it through all sorts of impossible situations. Granted, this is the most impossible, but still. There's too much riding on this for any of us to lack commitment. I don't blame you for being scared, but I don't have that luxury. So if you want to walk away, say so now."

He fell silent, his gaze locked with mine. "You sure know how to put a man's balls in a vise, Mixed-Blood."

I smirked. "This isn't about your balls."

"Bullshit." He blew out a breath. "All right. I'm in."

"Yes!" Giguhl said, pumping a fist in the air.

I smiled at the Recreant. "Grab whatever supplies you need."

He hefted his backpack and the guitar case in his right hand. "This is all I need."

I didn't comment that his light load clearly indicated he wasn't planning on an extended visit in Italy. But I'd take whatever help he was willing to give as long as he was willing to give it. "Okay, then, help Adam and Giguhl load the rest of the stuff. We head out in five."

He nodded and turned to talk to Adam. While they discussed logistics, Zen waved me over to the counter. A few amulets lay on a black cloth she'd spread out. "Okay," she said. "I'll make this quick. This"—she picked up the first item, a small bag that smelled like gym socks—"this is a vexing gris-gris. Throw it at an enemy and they'll be so busy scratching you can make a quick getaway."

"How long does the spell last?"

"Not long. A few minutes. But it's long enough to give yourself a head start."

"Got it," I said with a nod. I tucked the gris-gris into my jacket pocket. "What's next?"

"This is a gris-gris of protection for travelers." She held up a black bag tied with a small metal charm and an evil eye protection bead. I sniffed the bag and was surprised to smell the pleasing scents of rosemary and sage. "That's a St. Christopher medal," she explained, touching the charm. "He's the patron saint of travelers."

I grimaced. As much as I appreciated the effort, I didn't put much stock in any spell that invoked mortal saints. Smacked too much of superstition to me to be useful.

"Now, don't give me that look, Mixed-Blood. My saints and the Loa are every bit as real and powerful as your deities." She shoved the bag into my hand. "Go on, now."

"Thanks, Zen," I said. The black gris-gris went in my other pocket.

"Finally, there's this." She picked up an amulet hanging from a long leather cord. The amulet consisted of four stones wrapped into a bunch with coils of copper wire. I looked up at her for an explanation of the components. "The brown stone that feels like marble is actually lignum vitae, also called Tree of Life wood. It's incredibly protective and healing. The red stone is garnet. Well known for helping increase strength and endurance and its wonderful balancing powers. Of course, it's also associated with blood, which I thought you'd like." She shot me a conspiratorial smile. "And finally, there are two pieces of lodestone. One to attract luck and the other to ward off evil."

I took the amulet with a gentle touch. "It's beautiful, Zen. Thanks."

Her lips formed into a stern line. "The best way to thank me is to make sure you wear it." Her voice was gruff with emotion.

I slipped the necklace over my head. The stone clinked against the moonstone pendant Maisie had given me. "Done," I said. "I promise I won't take it off."

Zen nodded curtly. "You watch your ass, Sabina." With that heartfelt sentiment, she grabbed me and hugged me hard and quick. Then she turned away abruptly, leaving me with my mouth hanging open. Zen and I had never been hugging friends. Hell, we'd barely even been friends much of the time we'd known each other. But I respected the hell out of her and I was thankful she was on my side.

Zen moved away then to say her good-byes to Giguhl and Adam. Behind me, Georgia called my name. I turned and was surprised to see a determined expression on her face. "What's up?"

She raised her chin. "I want to go with you."

I paused. To reject her outright when she was still clearly so bitter wouldn't end well. I chose my words carefully. "Georgia, I—"

She held up a hand. "I'm strong and I'm fast, so I will be an asset if you get into any scrapes."

I nodded. "That's true." And it was. Having another vampire on the team would be helpful, but her emotional state could end up making her a liability. "But I'm afraid it's just not possible. Besides, you need to stay here and figure out what you're going to do about Lagniappe."

"I don't care about that. I just need…I need to get away from here."

I approached her and put a hand on her shoulder. "Running from your problems won't make them disappear. Besides, battling a psychotic murderer isn't exactly the best path toward mental peace, you know?" Her face fell and I worried she might cry, so I rushed ahead. "But I promise that if things get too hairy, I'll call you in from the bench, okay?"

She pursed her lips and thought things over. "I really wanted to help you."

An idea occurred to me, a way she could help me without getting involved directly. "Actually, there is something you can do for me."

Her eyebrows rose. "Anything."

"Have you ever heard of a vampire named Nyx?"

Georgia frowned. "I don't think so, why?"

I forced a casual shrug. "A friend asked me to look her up," I lied. I hadn't really expected Georgia to know Nyx, but I figured this way I could at least tell Asclepius I'd asked around. "Do you think you could ask your friends if they've heard of her? She was last seen in Italy, but I figure maybe someone here has run into her over the decades."

"I could ask around. I have some old friends in Europe, too. I'll make some inquiries and let you know if I find anything."

I smiled genuinely. "That would be great." I felt better that I'd figured out a way to let her help without risking her life. Even if I didn't expect her research to turn up much, I could at least tell Asclepius I'd made an effort when he showed up demanding answers.

"I'm sorry I freaked out on you earlier," Georgia said suddenly. "I know you have a lot of your own shit to deal with right now."

"Don't worry about it. You didn't know. But I'm glad you came by before we left."

She looked up, her expression unsure. "Really? Even after I yelled at you?"

I shrugged. "I consider it penance for sticking my nose into the situation to begin with."

Georgia waved her hand. "I know you were just trying to help."

"Red?" Adam said, his tone quiet but weighted. "We need to head out."

I turned back to Georgia. "Look, I don't know when I'll see you again, so I'm going to give you some unsolicited advice."

The corner of her mouth twitched. "Shoot."

"Don't avoid the pain. The sooner you face it, the sooner you'll come through on the other side."

Her face fell. "It hurts too much, Sabina."

I put my arms around her for a hug. "It'll keep hurting forever unless you deal with it. You've got too much living ahead of you to let a little heartache turn you bitter."

"Thanks." She sighed and hugged me back. "For everything."

I pulled back and smiled at my friend. "You're welcome. And let me know if you turn anything up about Nyx."

While Georgia moved on to say good-bye to Adam, I checked my gun and the knives I had stashed in my boots. Out of the corner of my eye, I noticed Giguhl and Brooks hugging as well. The Changeling was sobbing openly while the demon tried to comfort him. Adam and I had often speculated about their relationship, but Giguhl swore he and Brooks were platonic and I believed him. Brooks had come into Giguhl's life on the heels of a bad breakup with a Vanity demon. My theory was the demon's friendship with the faery had filled a hole left by that vindictive bitch and for that I was grateful. There's nothing more pathetic than a heartbroken demon.

Dismissing the tearful good-bye, I focused on Erron again, who was loitering nearby. "You ready?"

Erron crossed his arms and eyed me. "You know what? I think I am. I know I had reservations, but I want Cain to pay for what he did to my friends as bad as you do. That bastard needs to bleed."

I held up a hand to high-five the Recreant. "Now we're talking."

Adam and Giguhl had finished their good-byes and came to join us. I turned to the males so that we all formed a small circle. "All right, let's take this fight to Cain."

"Next stop, Rome!" Giguhl called excitedly.

The magic rose and the vortex opened. Over Adam's shoulder, I got one last look at the anxious expressions on Zen's, Georgia's, and Brooks's faces. Despite the bravado, we all knew this might be the last time we saw each other.

"Watch each other's backs," Georgia called.

"Be careful, bitches!" Brooks yelled.

Zen crossed herself. "Holy Loa, blessed saints and gods protect you."

A split second later, we disappeared.

6

Red-tiled roofs and church steeples glowed in the rosy aura of the setting sun. The waning moon hung low in the east along with the first hint of stars. In the distance, St. Peter's Basilica lorded over the skyline like an authoritarian father. The air smelled of exhaust and rosemary and ancient secrets. And everywhere, Italy's poetic mother tongue floated through the cool evening breeze like a song.

Erron led us down narrow cobbled streets to a discreet wooden door set back into a stone building. A small, hand-painted sign advertised the name of the establishment: Bar Sinister.

We'd headed straight here the instant we arrived in Rome. Luckily, the bar was only a few blocks from the park where we'd manifested, so we didn't have to risk our lives in one of the stunt-driving taxis.

Adam and Erron led the way, while I carried the canvas bag containing Giguhl in his hairless cat form. Not for the first time, I was thankful the demon could switch into the more portable and less-conspicuous body. I just wished he'd quit bitching.

"But I want to see Rome," he complained from inside the bag.

"G, we're not here for sightseeing."

"Can I at least ride on your shoulder?"

"No. And keep your head down. They may not allow pets in this place and I don't want to get kicked out because someone sees you."

He grumbled but hunkered down in the bag. For all his bellyaching, Giguhl knew I was in no mood to deal with his complaints. He'd been there with me when Maisie died, so he knew how much this mission meant to me—to all of us. But since I was so grateful he let the matter drop, I made a mental note to let him ride on my shoulder when we finished our meeting at the bar.

Erron opened the door, unleashing the scents of hops and barley mixed with the overpowering aroma of unfiltered cigarette smoke. Laughter and music stumbled into the street, like drunks on a bender.

Erron went right in, leaving Adam and me to follow. Despite being located in the center of Rome, the majority of voices I heard in the place spoke English with British accents rather than Italian.

When I caught up with Erron, I yanked on his jacket. He stopped and looked at me with raised eyebrows. "What is this place, exactly?"

Erron frowned like I asked a stupid question. "A bar?"

"No," I said, huffing out an annoyed breath. "Why does everyone in here look like an extra from *Benny Hill*?"

"The owner's a Brit—from Liverpool, I believe. Lots of expat mages use the joint as a gathering place."

I shot Adam an anxious glance. He shrugged. "Hey, at least we don't have to worry about language barriers." Then he nudged me to follow the Recreant farther into the pub.

Erron sidled up to the bar and flagged down the barkeep. The guy had the physique of a potato. His ruddy cheeks and jovial expression did little to endear me to him. I was in no mood to trust anyone.

"What'll it be, mates?"

"Three Boddingtons," Erron said, as if we were in Manchester instead of Rome.

The bartender toddled off to fill the order. Adam pulled up next to Erron. "I thought we were here to find Abel, not tie one on."

"We are. But there's a certain way these things are done."

"Do you think it could be done a little quicker?" I said.

"Sabina, this is Italy. Nothing happens quickly."

"I thought you said these guys are Brits," I grumbled.

"True but *la dolce vita* tends to soften even the most type A personality into complacence. You'll see."

I gritted my teeth and resisted the urge to remind Erron that we weren't in Italy on holiday. The mage might be a lot of things, but I'd spent enough time with him to understand that his laissez-faire attitude was mostly an act. He understood the gravity of the situation more than most. After all, he'd suffered his share of losses at Cain's hands, too.

He pointed to the bartender. "His name's Richard Green. Dicky to his friends. Last time I was in town, he put me in touch with Abel. Be patient and he may just do it again."

Three beers with thick, foamy heads appeared on the bar. Dicky leaned against the wood and told us the total for the drinks. Erron handed him an unnecessarily large bill.

"I'll just be getting you change, then," the bartender said, turning away.

"Keep it," Erron said, taking a casual sip from the pint.

"That's mighty kind of you," Dicky said. Instead of walking away, he leaned his elbows on the bar, ready to chat now. "You're Yanks, are ye?"

"Visiting from New Orleans," Erron said.

"Ah, well. Is this your first time in Italy, then?"

I covered my sigh with a hefty swig of beer. Obviously, our British friend had seen the large tip as an invitation to pry.

"I've been several times. In fact, I paid your fine bar a visit a few months back, Mr. Green."

"Haven't seen your mates before." The bartender's eyes, too shrewd for a man who looked like he bathed in whisky, gave Adam and me once-overs. "We don't get a lot of new visitors in Bar Sinister." Something about the way he said it made me think that "new visitors" was code for something else.

"We're actually here looking for an old friend," Erron continued. "The same one I was looking for last time."

Since the mages seemed intent on having a nice long chat, I decided to shuck my jacket. The stuffy bar combined with the hot air blowing between the males made the place stifling.

Dicky pursed his lips. "What's this bloke's name?"

"Abel."

The instant the word fell from Erron's lips, the entire atmosphere in the bar changed. Nothing overt. No one rose to confront us or anything. More like a tightening of the air. A slight lowering of volume. Awareness. Yes, that's what it was. Everyone suddenly seemed very aware of us.

The bartender hunched down and leaned toward us. "Only Abel I ever heard of was that poor bastard got killed by his brother in the mortals' mythology."

Erron's smile tightened. "Really?"

"In fact, I think maybe you're in the wrong place altogether."

"And what might be the right place?"

"I wouldn't be knowin' that." Dicky's lips tightened and his eyes were now as serious as life and death.

"This is a waste of time. This guy doesn't know anything." My aggressive tone earned me a sharp glance from the Recreant.

"If you'll be excusing me, I've got thirsty customers," the Brit said. "And I'll be asking you to leave once you finish your pints."

My mouth fell open at the dismissal. Erron kicked my ankle. I rounded on him but he shook his head with an expression that threatened pain if I caused a scene. "Let's go."

I slammed my pint on the bar and grabbed my jacket off the barstool. Erron had already turned to go, trusting I'd follow like a good girl. Part of me longed to stay and show these assholes who they were dealing with. But I could feel their eyes on me. Could feel the magic hanging heavy in the air. Powers gathering, waiting for me to try something. These chaps might look like barflies, but there was serious magic in that room. Erron, Adam, and I could have probably handled ourselves well enough to survive the brawl— especially if I let Giguhl come out to play—but to what end? We'd still be leaving without the information we needed.

So with my pride dragging behind me like a piece of toilet paper stuck to my shoe, I stalked toward the door.

"Oy!"

I kept going, figuring whoever had called out was trying to get someone else's attention.

"Oy! Mixed-Blood! Hold up!"

I turned slowly, my eyes narrow and my fists ready to

defend. The bartender rushed around the other end of the bar. He waddled toward me, his expression inscrutable but his movements anxious.

"What?" I snapped. Behind me, I felt Adam's presence looming like a threat should the mage step out of line.

"What's this, then?" he demanded when he reached me.

"What's what?" I'd run out of patience. If he wanted to talk, he'd have to work for it.

He lifted a hand. My arm shot out to stop what I thought was a strike. He paused and pulled back. "Relax, bird. I was just pointing to your back."

I frowned. "What about it?"

He frowned as if I was being purposefully obtuse. "What's your name?"

Jesus, this guy and his twenty questions. "I'm Sabina Kane, who the fuck are you?"

"Sabina Kane," the bartender repeated with a smile. A genuine one this time. "Well, well. This changes things, then, doesn't it?"

"Listen, Mr. Belvedere, I'm tired and my patience ran out about a week ago. You got something to say to me, then say it."

"I think you and your friends need to come back to my office."

Adam stepped forward. "Two seconds ago you kicked us out of your bar. Why the change?"

"You know what? I don't give a shit," I said. "Let's go."

"Sabina…," Erron warned.

Dicky ignored the Recreant and cocked an eyebrow at me. "You got a mouth, don't ya?"

"So I've been told," I retorted. "Come on, Adam."

"I got a message for you."

I plastered on my poker face. "Bullshit."

"Don't be like that. Can't blame a bloke for being careful. These are dangerous times we live in. Can't trust just anyone who walks in off the street."

I crossed my arms. "So why do you suddenly trust us now?"

The corner of Dicky's mouth lifted. "Because Abel told me a female bearing two eight-point stars on her back would come looking for him."

Cold sweat bloomed on my skin along with fear in the pit of my stomach. "How in the hell would he know that?"

I'd always had the star mark on my right shoulder, but the one on my left? That one I'd earned only a few days earlier. Somehow, when my sister had died, her birthmark had transferred to my left shoulder. Probably there was some mystical significance to the transfer, but it hadn't yet revealed itself. Until that happened, I used it as a talisman— a symbol that my sister, though dead, was still with me in spirit. She had my back now.

"I'm sure I don't know." He shrugged. "Regardless, he said you'd go by one of two names."

I frowned. "What was the other name?"

"Maisie Graecus."

My skin crawled like someone had just played hopscotch across my grave. Hearing my twin's name thrown about so casually made my stomach lurch. But hearing that Abel was expecting one of us to come find him made the hair on the back of my neck prickle. Neither Maisie nor I had ever met Abel.

Giguhl's head popped up from the bag. "What the fuck?"

Dicky's eyes narrowed at the cat. "You're lucky Abel's a friend, girl, or I'd kick your ass out again for bringing a demon into my bar."

I let that pass and squared off with the male. "So what's this message?"

He shook his head. "Not here." He waved us back toward the hallway. "It's not safe."

"You know what else isn't safe?" I said, my tone dripping menace. "Jerking me around. I'm not going anywhere with you until you tell me who Abel really is." Something told me that if Abel knew that much about me, I'd better find out his real identity sooner rather than later.

He crossed his arms and chuckled. "Now who's jerking who around?"

"What do you mean?" Adam said. "It's a fair question. If Abel really left a message for Sabina, then you obviously know his real identity."

The bartender raised a brow. "That's the rub, see. Because when Abel told me the names of the females who might show up with the twin birthmarks, he also said another interesting fact. One that leads me to believe you're lying about not knowing who he really is."

I raised my hands in an inpatient gesture. "Well?"

"After he told me the names of the female who'd come looking for him, he said I should treat the one who showed with respect because"—he leaned in to whisper—"she's his daughter."

The floor fell out from underneath me.

"What do you mean?" Adam demanded. "Are you saying Abel is Tristan Graecus?"

"Well fuck me sideways," Giguhl said. "The dude we're looking for is your dead dad?"

A hush fell over the bar. Dozens of gazes burned into us. A few mages even rose like they were expecting a fight—or looking for one.

"I think we'd better take this conversation someplace

more private," Adam said. He came up behind me and put a steadying hand on my shoulder. Good thing, too. I was either going to hurl or fall down. Or both.

"I already told ya that," Dicky said, looking annoyed. "Come along, then."

As the bartender led us back to his office, shock completely robbed me of the ability to speak or think clearly. I had that feeling you get when you pray that you're in the midst of a particularly fucked up nightmare. But something told me no amount of pinching would make this moment less real. Tristan Graecus was alive?

What. The. Fuck?

The office was little more than a cramped storage room with a paper-strewn table, kegs of beer, and nothing but crates to use as seats. Good thing I liked Erron and loved Adam because I was basically wedged in between them. I held the bag containing Giguhl close to my chest, partially out of concern for space and partially because I felt the need to hang on tight to something I could trust.

"There now," the bartender said with a relieved sigh. "Now we can speak openly. We'll begin with introductions. The name's Richard Green, but you can call me Dicky seeing as how you're Tristan's daughter and all."

"You know Erron and Sabina," Adam snapped. "I'm Adam and the demon's name is Giguhl. And you can start by telling us how the hell you know so much about Tristan Graecus."

He obviously still hadn't forgiven this guy for his earlier treatment. I liked to imagine his indignation was for my benefit, but I knew the bombshell about Tristan Graecus had to be affecting him pretty badly, too. After all, he'd grown up believing my father was a revered martyr to all of magekind.

"I'm the unofficial leader of the expat mages in Rome. It's my business to know lots of people."

"Who is the official leader?" Adam asked.

"There aren't many native mages in the Eternal City. Most left when things started getting hairy—or hairier, I guess—with the vamps a few months ago."

That made sense. Mages and vamps had always been sworn enemies, but it wasn't until last October that the hostilities had coalesced into an actual threat of war. Even though I knew all this, hearing the tensions had also affected mages and vamps abroad surprised me. I'd never given much thought to how the actions of the American dark races might influence the actions of those abroad. But it made sense, I guess, since although the centers of power for the races existed in the States, their reach extended worldwide. And since Rome had always been vampire territory, it wasn't a surprise the mages had fled.

"You said Abel is Sabina's father?" Erron prompted.

Dicky's face tightened with suspicion. "Yeah. I'm going to need some proof that you're really Sabina."

My mouth fell open. "You need proof? Fuck you. You need to prove to me that you're telling the truth. How do I know you don't work for Cain?"

Dicky threw back his head and laughed. "Sure, a mage working for the father of the bloodsuckers. Are ya drunk, girl? You came here looking for me. What I want to know is why you're looking for Abel if you didn't know he was your father?"

I took a deep breath to quell the cocktail of annoyance and panic stewing in my gut. "Assuming Abel really is Tristan Graecus—"

"He is."

I rolled my eyes. "I was told my entire life that my father was dead, that he died before I was born, in fact. So you'll forgive me for being a tad suspicious when you suddenly claim that he's not only alive but also the world's foremost expert on all things Cain."

Dicky raised his hands. "I don't know what to tell you. I have been friends with Abel for going on a decade now, but he told me his real name only a fortnight ago when he delivered the message. Said it was important I know his real identity in case something happened to him and one of his kin came looking for him." Dicky sighed and shook his head. "And now he's disappeared, so there's no way to ask him to sort this out."

I frowned. "Disappeared? When?"

"Three nights ago," Dicky said. "He was supposed to come by the bar that night but never showed."

I closed my eyes and willed the fist in my throat to disappear. Three nights earlier, the night Cain murdered Maisie, he'd figured out how to break the spell that kept him in a coma. According to Erron, Abel had captured Cain a decade earlier and placed him in a state of suspended animation. The fact no one had heard from Abel since told me Cain's first item of business after gaining his freedom was to punish his captor.

Giguhl piped up. "Maybe Abel escaped before Cain could kill him."

Dicky pursed his lips. "If he did, why hasn't he contacted me for help?"

"He could be hiding out. After all, if he's alive, he'd be high on Cain's To-Kill list, right?" Adam said. "Any idea where he'd go if he did escape?"

"I was hoping you might know," Dicky said, looking directly at me.

I scrubbed a hand over my face. "None of this makes any sense."

"You mentioned a message?" Erron prompted.

The Brit went over to a set of shelves that held supplies. He moved a few bottles around in what seemed to be a pattern or code and then suddenly the shelves popped away from the wall. He pushed the whole thing aside, revealing a secret room. "Follow me."

Adam and I exchanged tense looks. Erron, however, didn't seem fazed by Dicky's behavior and followed him into the room. I was tired of the mysterious bullshit, but I knew if I wanted answers, I'd have to follow him, too. And, holy shit, did I want answers.

The room had a recessed floor that required a couple of steps down. "What is this place?" I asked, ducking under the low stone arch to descend the stairs. The air here had the musty heaviness of age and the temperature seemed to drop about ten degrees.

"Originally it was a tomb, left by the Etruscans. But since then, the various proprietors have used it for different purposes. The cheese maker who owned this building before I opened the bar used it as an aging cellar for his pecorino."

"Really?" Giguhl exclaimed. "I don't suppose you got any more of that cheese lying around?"

I shot the demon a glare.

"What?" he said defensively. "It smells fucking delicious in here."

Actually, it smelled like feet and wet stone. I rolled my eyes at the demon and shot Dicky an apologetic look. "What do you use it for?"

He snapped his fingers and the room was suddenly bathed in the warm glow of hundreds of candles set into niches in the walls. Niches that used to house cheese wheels and bodies. Now, the shelves without candles stored antique bottles filled with herbs and mysterious liquids. "This is my spell room," he said. "The bar is a front for my magic solutions business."

"Magic solutions?"

He nodded. "Sure. Italians love homemade remedies. Took a while for word to spread that a Brit had some skill in potions but now I supply all sorts of elixirs to little old ladies and lovesick boys."

As he spoke, he bent down and pulled an old leather-bound book from one of the shelves. I had assumed it was his magical grimoire, a book mages used to record their spells, so I was surprised when he opened it to reveal the book was hollow. The interior was lined in wood—cedar, judging from the scent that tickled my nose. Lying inside was a black velvet bag.

Dicky held the box out to me. "Take it."

I frowned, wondering why he didn't just hand the bag to me. It made my sense of self-preservation prickle. What did we know about this guy, anyway? For all I knew, he could work for Cain and this could be a trap.

I guess Dicky noticed the indecision on my face because he quickly explained. "Your father warded the bag. Didn't want anyone to see it but you, I guess."

Adam grabbed my arm. "Wait a second." Turning to Dicky, he said, "There's no ward on earth that is undone just by a certain person touching it. There's usually some sort of magical key."

The Brit smiled. "Righto. Only someone from Tristan's lineage can open it. She's going to have to prick her finger first and let the blood drop on the bag."

I sighed deeply. Blood was serious. I was already up to my ass in debt to a god over blood sacrifices. "No way, dude."

Even Erron, who until this point had remained quiet and unruffled, looked concerned. "What kind of trick are you trying to pull?"

"No trick." Dicky shrugged. "Tristan wanted to be sure no one could see this except his own flesh and blood." He nodded in my direction. "This was the best way to ensure that."

"I think we're going to need to see some proof this is really from Tristan," Adam said.

Dicky's smile fell. He stepped forward. "Are you sayin' I'm lying?"

Adam didn't hesitate. "Yes."

Giguhl nodded his bald head vigorously.

The Brit blustered for a few moments. "I didn't ask for this, you know. Just doing a favor for a friend."

"Look, dude," I said. "You said it yourself—these are dangerous times. We'd be idiots not to ask."

"I'm tempted to kick you out again," he grumbled. "But I suppose you have a point."

His lips pursed in annoyance. "Look at the bag." He held up the false book for us to gather around it. Sure enough, there was a symbol embossed into the velvet.

Silence followed. I frowned at him. "What the hell is that?" The symbol depicted a sword and chalice. I'd never seen it before, but generally anything involving a mysterious symbol spelled trouble.

Dicky frowned. "What do you mean? It's the symbol of Abel. All his allies know about it." His eyes widened. "You really have no idea what you're doing, do ye?"

I threw my hands up. "No shit."

"Wait a second," Erron said. "He's right. Abel was wearing an amulet with that symbol when I met him."

"Anyone could have placed Abel's symbol on that bag," Adam said, crossing his arms.

"Janus, Minerva, and Jupiter," the Brit exclaimed. "I don't know what else you want from me." He jiggled the box at me. "There's only one way to find out if I'm telling the truth."

I looked up, not at Adam whose opinion I had a pretty good grasp on, but at Erron. He had far more experience with both Dicky and Abel and thus had the most informed opinion of the three of us. "Do it," he said, his expression grave.

Finally, annoyed and ready to just get some freaking answers already, I handed Giguhl to Adam and pricked my finger with my fang. I massaged the tip until a bright red drop formed. "Here goes nothing." I blew out a lungful of air and slowly moved my hand to hover over the bag.

Everyone held their breath. The blood fell in slow motion. The instant it made contact with the velvet, a bright blue flame flared. In the blink of an eye, the bag disappeared and revealed a small, yellowed scroll. I couldn't tell if it was yellowed from age or the effects of the flames, but either way the paper had seen better days.

No one moved. Then I realized they were all waiting for me to do something. With a trembling hand, I reached for the message. When my fingers made contact, a tingle spread up through my digits and through my wrist and up my arm. The mark on my left shoulder—Maisie's mark— tingled. It wasn't an unpleasant sensation but it felt meaningful. I stilled, waiting for some sort of magical fallout, but…nothing.

"Open it," Giguhl urged.

I looked up quickly. Erron, Adam, and the cat were leaning toward the box, their eyes lit up like treasure hunters on the trail of pirate gold. My heart thudded against my rib cage. My palms were sweaty but my skin cold.

Finally unable to stand the suspense any longer, I grabbed the parchment and unrolled it. Holding it close to my chest, I peeked down. A single word written in bold calligraphic strokes stood out starkly against the yellowed paper.

Pasquino.

Almost as an afterthought, someone had written in hasty scrawl at the bottom, "Trust no one."

I frowned and flipped the sheet over, wondering if I'd missed something. I held it up to the light in case Abel had used invisible ink or something, but no other clues appeared.

"What's it say?" Dicky tried to move closer, but I held it out of reach.

"I'm not sure." That wasn't a lie. But I also wasn't eager to share this one meager clue with him, either. Abel had gone to great lengths to magically guard this word from any eyes that were not mine or my sister's. So even though I didn't know what the hell it meant, I wasn't about to share the single word with anyone I didn't trust implicitly.

Pasquino.

Adam caught my eye and raised his brows. I shook my head slightly. We'd discuss it later. In the meantime, I needed some answers from the expat. "When did he give this to you?"

He frowned and pursed his lips, thinking back. "I told ya, two weeks ago."

"What?" I said, my voice rising in shock. "That's impossible."

"Why?" Erron asked.

"Tristan told Dicky that one of his daughters would show up with two birthmarks." Adam jerked a thumb toward my back. "She got the second one only forty-eight hours ago. How in the hell would he know that was coming?"

Giguhl shrugged. "Maybe he's got prophetic skills? After all, Maisie was an Oracle. She could have gotten the skills from him."

I shook my head. "Nope. Maisie got those skills from Tristan's mother, Ameritat. She was the Oracle before Maisie. Plus, Rhea told me explicitly that Tristan was a Chthonic mage like me."

Adam blew out a breath. "Look, the only one who can answer your questions now is Tristan Graecus. We need to follow that clue and find him."

"That's what worries me. This secretive shit he's pulling right now? The fact he's hidden his existence for more than fifty years? Reminds me of some of the Caste of Nod's tricks."

Adam put his hand on my arm. "I know it's suspicious but think about what you're saying. According to Erron, Abel—or Tristan, rather—is the one who imprisoned Cain. If Dicky's telling the truth and Abel is your dad, then I think it's safe to assume he's on our side."

I shook my head. "I think it's dangerous to assume anything."

"That may be a nonissue," Erron said. "After all, we're not even sure he's still alive."

A hush fell over the room as this sank in. Other than putting a major crimp in my plans, I wasn't sure exactly how to feel about the possibility that the father I thought was dead was . . . dead again.

"This is all making my head hurt," I said.

"Word," said the cat.

"What do you want to do, Sabina?" Adam asked.

"I want to get the hell out of here. The longer we're in public, the better the chance Cain will discover we're here and set a trap. Let's get to the hotel and then we can figure out our next step."

Adam nodded resolutely. "Let's go."

Erron turned to the Brit. "Thanks for your help, Dicky."

He waved away the thanks. "Abel was a difficult man to be friends with, but he did me favors more than once. This was the least I could do for his daughter." The word "daughter" made my eye twitch. But Dicky wasn't done. "If you find him, tell him we're square."

"If we find him, we'll tell him," Adam said.

After I punch him for putting me through this bullshit, I silently amended.

$\mathcal{W}$e made it back to the street and walked in silence for about two minutes before Giguhl broke the tension.

"So," the cat said with exaggerated slowness, "your dad's alive." He sat on my shoulder and his hot cat breath added insult to the injury of his words.

"Not now, G," I snapped.

"Sabina, we're going to have to talk about it," Adam said.

"I know that," I said, picking up my pace. "Eventually. But first I need everyone to lay off so I can wrap my head around what the hell just happened."

Adam put his arm around my shoulders and kissed the top of my head. "Okay."

"How about you tell us what was on that paper instead?" Erron said.

With a sigh, I switched from avoidance mode into business mode. "Okay," I said, waving them in closer. We were huddled on a street corner. "Pasquino."

Adam pulled back with a frown. "That's it?"

I nodded. "That one word and a note not to trust anyone." I glanced at Erron. "Any idea what it means?"

"No clue," he said. "Could be anything, really."

"Maybe we should have asked Dicky," Adam said.

"No offense, but I don't entirely trust that guy," I said.

Erron waved away my apologetic tone. "Me neither. You were smart to keep it to yourself."

"Wait a second," Adam said. "If you didn't trust him, why take us there?"

"Because besides the cell number no one's answering, Dicky was my only point of contact for Abel and his team. Anyway, he can't be all bad if Sabina's d—" He cut himself off when I shot him a warning glare. "I mean, Tristan trusted him to keep this message."

"Apparently Tristan's trust was conditional, too," Giguhl said. "Otherwise, why ward it so heavily?"

"Good point," Erron said. "So it looks like we're on our own to find out what this Pasquino is."

Adam smirked. "That would have worried me more before the Internet age."

I nodded and kept walking. In my mind, I worried over that one word and what it could possibly mean. "Pasquino," I said, testing the word. "Could be a person."

"Or a city or a restaurant or a street," Adam continued, talking it out.

"Gods, why all the cloak-and-dagger bullshit?" I asked.

"Who knows?" Giguhl said with a feline shrug.

"It's probably more productive to try to figure out the 'what' instead of the 'why' at this point," Adam said.

By then, we'd reached the hotel where Erron had made reservations before we left New Orleans. "Here we are," the Recreant said with a grand gesture. "Hotel Caligula!"

I looked up and my mouth fell open. The building rose ten floors and looked like a palace. "Jesus, Erron. Does the phrase 'low profile' mean anything to you?"

"What?" He shrugged. "This is where I stay in Rome when I'm on tour. The location can't be beat since we're in the center of the city. Plus, the suites are big enough for all of us and the security's tight."

I made a mental note not to trust a famous rock star with the sleeping arrangements again. "Rhea's going to shit a brick when she sees the expense report," Adam said.

"I, for one, say we deserve a little luxury," Giguhl said.

"Of course you do," I said, my tone arid. To Erron, I said, "I was hoping for a small apartment or something that we could easily ward against attack."

Erron waved a hand. "No problem. I've reserved the penthouse so we can ward the entire floor."

Twenty minutes later, our enthusiastic bellhop showed us into the largest suite I'd ever seen. The place was larger than the apartment I shared with Adam at Prytania Place in New York.

"Well," Adam said, setting down my backpack, "it's certainly . . . stark."

The décor must have been planned by a dominatrix with a fetish for modern art. Everything in the place was black and white, from the parquet floors to the black leather sofa to the ebony statues of women's torsos.

"Awesome, right?" Erron exclaimed, shoving a few euros in the bellhop's hand. After he shut the door and locked it, he turned to give us a rundown. "Two large bedrooms—a master with a king-sized bed and a smaller one with two queens—a full kitchen, a wet bar, and a roof-top terrace with a garden."

"Nice!" Giguhl said. "I call the biggest bedroom."

I shot the demon a look. "Dream on. You and Erron will take the one with two beds. Also, I feel I need to remind you we're not here on vacation. The hotel's nice but we won't be around long enough to pretend we're in an episode of *Lifestyles of the Rich and Hairless*."

"Party pooper," the cat grumbled. "I'm gonna go check out the garden." With that, he swung around and sashayed toward the spiral staircase leading to the roof.

Erron clapped his hands. "Let's order some room service and get down to business."

Thirty minutes later, we all gathered around the table to eat. For a little while the only sounds in the room were the occasional clink of a fork against porcelain and Giguhl's exaggerated slurping.

"Dude," I said. "Didn't anyone ever teach you to use a spoon when you eat pasta?"

The demon looked up at me. His black lips were glossy from butter. "Um, hello? They don't exactly stress table manners in Irkalla, Sabina."

"Obviously."

In all honesty, it's not like this was the first time I'd witnessed the demon's abysmal eating habits. They'd never really bothered me before because, as he pointed out, you can't exactly expect a demon to care much about etiquette. But for some reason it grated on me that night. I grabbed my glass of wine and took a long gulp. Probably it was just stress talking. Nothing a little liquid Valium couldn't fix.

"Giguhl," Adam said, changing the subject. "You find anything interesting on the terrace?"

The demon shrugged. He was in his demon body now and wore a plush terry-cloth robe with the name of the hotel embroidered on the lapel. "The view's pretty awesome. I saw that big old dome for that temple the mortals worship at."

"The Vatican?" Adam said.

"Is that the place where the guy with the pointy hat lives?"

"You mean the Pope? Yes."

"Yeah, that. Anyway, there's a kick-ass hot tub and an herb garden."

"Adam, we should check out the garden after dinner to see if there's anything useful in there," I said.

Erron, who'd been pretty quiet, spoke up then. "I didn't know you did herb magic."

Adam shrugged. "I don't, really. But my aunt Rhea taught me a few things. Sabina actually knows more about them than me."

I looked up from my wine. "I doubt that."

Adam didn't comment on my denial. "Anyway, we'll check it out. Wouldn't hurt to have some backups for Zen's amulets."

I fingered the one she gave me before we left and smiled. It'd been good to see both Zen and Brooks before we left. Although, to be honest, considering the gravity of our mission, it was as much a good-bye as a quick hello.

Giguhl set down his fork suddenly and scooted his chair back. "Oh! Speaking of amulets," he said. He walked over to the small bag he'd brought with him. "I almost forgot. Rhea gave me this before we left New York. Things were so hectic in New Orleans, I almost forgot to give it to you."

He removed something from the bag and clasped it in his large claw. I couldn't tell what it was beyond the brief flash of gold. Frowning, I held out my hand to receive the mystery object. "What's this?"

The instant the warm metal touched my hand, a zing of magic zipped up my arm. But I was too busy dealing with the emotional pain of seeing the amulet that I didn't register the brief flare of physical pain. The moonstone in the center of the gold setting winked at me like some sort of cosmic joke. "Why did she give you this?" I choked the words out over the pain tightening my throat.

Adam craned his neck to see what the demon had given me. When he recognized the necklace, he hissed out a breath.

Giguhl patted me on the shoulder. "Rhea thought you might want it. You know, for strength."

I'm sure Rhea's heart was in the right place when she'd taken this necklace off my sister's corpse, but it was having the opposite effect. My hand started to tremble.

"What is it?" Erron asked, clueless.

"It belonged to Maisie," Giguhl said. "It's the amulet that identified her as the High Priestess of the Chaste Moon. Sabina's got one just like it." I normally wore my amulet inside my shirt, so at that moment only the one Zen had given me was visible.

Adam scooted closer and put an arm around me. "You okay?" he whispered.

I looked up at him. The tears stinging my eyes made him blurry. I didn't know what to say. Was I okay? How could I be? My twin was dead and my fucking father was alive.

Instead of answering, I groped with my free hand for my wine.

"Speaking of Maisie," Erron said, oblivious to my impending breakdown. "You never told me exactly what happened with her."

My hand stilled with the wine halfway to my mouth. When I'd approached Erron in New Orleans to ask for his help, I'd kept the details pretty vague on Maisie's death. I feared if I'd told him everything, I wouldn't get through the request without tears. She'd died four nights earlier and the extra ninety-six hours hadn't done much to ease the pain.

Luckily, Adam sensed my chaotic emotions and said, "I'll tell you later."

I appreciated him sparing my feelings, but the damage was

already done. The legs of my chair screeched against the marble floor. All the males froze and stared at me with concern. "Excuse me," I whispered, and rushed out of the room.

I didn't stop until the bedroom door was closed firmly behind me. I slid down the panel until I was crouched on the floor with Maisie's necklace clutched between my trembling hands. The rumble of low male voices reached me beneath the door. I couldn't make out the words, but I could imagine Giguhl and Adam filling Erron in on what had gone down the night Maisie died.

My own memories forced me back to that night, too. After we'd figured out Maisie was responsible for four murders under Cain's influence, I'd entered the dream realm to try and free my twin's subconscious from Cain. Unfortunately, his hold was too strong. Just after he forced Maisie to break the binding spell, Cain slit her throat. She bled out in my arms.

I lifted the necklace to the light. It spun in blurry, hypnotic circles. The Hekatian symbols engraved in the gold caught my eye. In my mind, I translated the words: *For she is the torchbearer, this daughter of Hekate, she will light the way.*

I snorted and closed my eyes. Maisie wouldn't light the way for anyone. Not anymore. Not since Cain had snuffed out her flame.

I bit my lip to hold back the sobs I'd stored up. Things had been so hectic since we left New York that I hadn't really had time to mourn my sister's death properly. In all honesty, I hadn't wanted to. Not because I didn't miss her. Not because I didn't think she deserved to be mourned. But because I worried that if I unbridled my grief, it would consume me. Far better to just be angry about it and use that anger to fuel my resolve. Anger made me a better fighter. Crying just made me weak. Then I remembered what I'd told Georgia about the only way to get over pain is to face it head-on.

Maybe it was time to take a dose of my own bitter medicine. I allowed the tears to fall. Fat, hot drops rolled down my cheeks. Sobs made my throat ache and my stomach cramp. I gripped the amulet until the metal cut into the skin. But that pain paled in comparison to the deep ache of Maisie's loss. The void she left behind haunted me like a phantom limb.

"Maisie," I whispered brokenly. "Gods, I'm so sorry."

My left shoulder warmed. It wasn't the warning sting I'd felt right before Asclepius arrived, but almost like a comforting hand's weight. Maybe it was just some trick of my mind born from a longing for connection. As much as I liked to believe my sister was communicating with me from the grave, I knew better than to indulge in the fantasy.

Maisie was dead. Period. And mixed with the pain of loss was an all-consuming guilt. Because no matter what anyone said, I felt responsible for what had happened to my sister. If only I'd seen the signs earlier. If only I'd intervened faster. If only I'd killed Cain before he'd killed her.

The irrational side of me whispered that it didn't matter that killing Cain would have doomed us all. Given Cain's murderous track record, I wasn't so sure any of us would survive, anyway. It was only a matter of time before he killed again. And now that he knew how to hurt me, he'd go after each person I loved until I gave him what he wanted.

To make things worse, I'd just found out that in order to get to Cain, I'd first have to get through my father. Gods, how fucked up was that? The very idea of meeting the man who was responsible for my birth and the subsequent punishments I'd faced for carrying his blood in my veins made me nauseous. I had no interest in knowing that bastard. But if I wanted to save everyone, I'd eventually have to deal with dear old dad so I could finally ask the questions that needed to be asked.

I was dreaming again.

I hadn't had much sleep in the last three nights, so the fact that I was able to rest long enough to enter the REM state should have been a positive thing. But my subconscious had ulterior motives.

Maisie stood in the Sacred Grove at the mage estate in Sleepy Hollow. She wore the ceremonial chiton that identified her as the Hekatian Oracle, and she stood in front of the old stone altar in the center of the clearing. For some reason, a peacock in full display was strutting around in the background. I ignored the bird and focused on my sister.

"Maisie?" I whispered. She looked so…alive. So vibrant and healthy. So unlike the gaunt specter who haunted my waking hours in the months before she was murdered.

When I arrived, my sister smiled widely and raised her arms to greet me. I ran to her, wanting to believe her death had been the nightmare and this dream was reality. Soon, her arms were around me and I breathed in her copper and sandalwood scent. Felt her warmth and heard her pulse.

"I thought you were dead." The words squeezed out of my tight throat in an agonized whisper.

She ignored that and pulled back to look me in the eye. "There's no time for that. I've had a vision."

My stomach tightened. From the sound of her voice, this prophecy wasn't going to be positive. Not that they ever were anymore. "Tell me."

She stepped back and took a deep breath. I crossed my arms to brace myself for the news. "The Great Goddess Hekate has blessed me with a vision. I have painted the symbols and am ready to deliver my interpretation."

In her role as Oracle, Maisie had prophetic dreams and then took those images and painted them to interpret the message the gods were sending her.

I nodded to encourage her to continue, but the scene shifted. Suddenly, hundreds of other beings filled the space. In fact, the area looked almost exactly as it had the night of the botched peace treaty signing in New York.

Over to the side, a black dog entered the clearing. I instantly recognized the animal as Asclepius. He didn't approach me, though, just hung off to the side, watching the proceedings.

On a raised dais behind Maisie, High Councilman Orpheus, Despina Tanith Severinus, and Queen Maeve watched over the proceedings like judges. Behind me, mages, vampires, faeries, werewolves, and a smattering of demons waited to hear my sister's verdict. I frowned. Why did I suddenly feel like I was on trial?

Maisie didn't seem bothered by the sudden appearance of so many observers. She raised her arms and called out in a loud, clear voice, "I will be murdered."

Gasps filled the clearing. I frowned, confused. Time tangled in on itself.

"I know the identity of my killer," Maisie continued in a dire voice. She paused dramatically. In real life, Maisie had been murdered by Cain. But I suddenly had a very bad feeling that his name was not the one on her lips. "Sabina Kane!"

"No!" I yelled. "It was Cain!"

But my denials were lost among the outraged shouts of the dark race leaders and the angry boos and growls from the crowd. Suddenly, the mass of beings swarmed me. Rough hands pulled my clothes, my hair. Sharp nails scratched my face. Someone punched me in the gut. There were too many of them, so all I could do was cover my head with my arms and scream impotent pleas for mercy.

Over the cacophony, Maisie's voice rang out loud and clear. "How could you do it, sister? How could you kill me?"

"It wasn't me!" I screamed.

My attackers knocked me to the ground. I blinked through the blood running in my eyes and saw a feminine figure standing over me. At first, I thought it was Maisie come to do me in. But Maisie didn't have midnight-black hair. Plus, the instant the female appeared, all of my attackers backed away and bowed like they were in the presence of royalty—or a goddess.

"Lilith?" I whispered.

The Great Mother's lush red lips spread into a seductive smile. "Finally, you're mine."

She pulled back her lips, revealing black metal fangs.

Time slowed. Lilith launched at me, her fangs aimed at my jugular. In a flash, my entire life passed through my mind's eye. All the beings I'd killed. Everyone I'd hurt and betrayed. Every mistake I'd ever made, every lie.

I wanted to close my eyes but couldn't. A scream ripped from my chest an instant before the fangs broke my—

I woke with a start, sitting straight up in bed. My heart

galloped in my chest. Cold sweat glued my clothes to trembling limbs.

Beside me, Adam turned over restlessly. I wiped my brow and glanced toward the window. Dim light shone through the black curtains. Judging from the weakening pressure on my solar plexus, it was close to dusk.

Since going back to sleep meant the possibility of more fucked up dreams, I carefully crawled out of bed and padded to the bathroom. Inside, I closed the door behind me and clicked on the overhead light.

The woman staring back at me from the mirror looked haunted—or hunted.

I splashed cold water on my face. It woke me up like a slap in the face. "Keep it together, Sabina," I said to my reflection. The dream about Maisie had been just that—a dream.

While it was understandable that my subconscious needed to sort through the guilt I felt about Maisie's death, I wasn't about to tempt fate and go back to sleep. With my luck, Asclepius would show up again and remind me about my promise. No doubt that's why he'd been eavesdropping in my dream in the first place. The thought of him analyzing the contents of my subconscious made me want to rinse my mind out with soap.

It looked like sleeping had become almost as dangerous as being awake.

I grabbed a quick shower and dressed before heading out to the living area. When I tiptoed through the room, Adam was still asleep. I decided not to wake him. Just like me, he'd had little sleep since we'd left New York.

The night Maisie died, she'd still been under Cain's influence and kidnapped Adam. She's strung him up and whipped him until he'd passed out from blood loss and pain. However, the physical wounds he'd suffered were nothing compared to the emotional ones. I'd lost my sister, but Adam had lost his best friend. A best friend who'd tried to murder him not once, but twice.

So, yeah, I figured he needed the rest.

I walked out into the living room of the apartment and found Erron and Giguhl sitting in front of the suite's laptop.

"Hey," I said, surprised to see them up. "I didn't expect anyone else would be up yet."

Until I'd spoken, neither had noticed me, but now Giguhl looked up from the screen and blinked. "Oh, hey, Red. We've been up for hours, actually."

I frowned. "What? Why?"

Erron looked up finally. "I got up first because the demon snores like an asthmatic wildebeest."

Giguhl nudged the mage with his elbow. "Please, it's not that bad."

"You're right." Erron shuddered. "But the dry humping was fucking terrifying."

I raised an accusing brow at the demon. Giguhl's randy nocturnal activities were well documented. Several months earlier, in fact, he'd tried to sleep-sex Adam.

"Don't flatter yourself. I was dreaming about having a three-way with a hot demoness and a nymph," the demon said with an eye roll. But judging from his defensive tone, he'd been dreaming of something—or someone— embarrassing. "Anyway, I woke up not long after because I'm still stuck on New York time. We both figured since we were already awake we might as well get a head start on tracking down Dicky's clue."

The scent of coffee beckoned me toward the kitchen. I yawned and headed toward lifesaving caffeine as I spoke. "Oh yeah? Find anything good?"

Giguhl leaned back and put his claws behind his head. "Oh yes. Turns out Pasquino is pretty famous around Rome."

I stopped pouring coffee and looked at them over the bar separating the living room from the kitchen. "Wait, it's a person?"

The demon and the Recreant shared a grin. "No, actually," Erron said. "It's a statue."

They waved me over to the laptop for explanation. A website on Roman tourist sites popped on-screen. The site showed a picture of a timeworn statue without arms or a head. "Pasquino is one of Rome's famous talking statues."

"*Talking* statues?"

"They don't literally talk," the demon explained. "But apparently there's an old tradition of people using these statues to post poems criticizing the government, and they're all signed as if the statue wrote it."

"Hmm," I said, going in closer. According to the site, Pasquino was the original statue used for the purpose. "Where is it?"

"It's near the Piazza Navona," Erron explained. He clicked on a map link, pulling up a layout of the area in question. "It's like a fifteen-minute walk from here, actually."

"Well, that's something," I said.

"Assuming we're right and this is the correct Pasquino," Erron said. "We're thinking your father probably left a clue on the statue for you. So all we have to do is go check it out and find the right one."

At that moment, Adam appeared in the doorway. "Evening," he said. He wore nothing but boxers, sleep-mussed hair, and a yawn. He looked so adorable I almost forgot about the statue as my mind filled with images of me inviting him back to bed for some sleep-sexing of our own.

"Hey, mancy!" Giguhl called, interrupting my naughty thoughts. "Erron and I found out what the clue means."

Adam perked up. "Oh?"

While Giguhl and the Recreant talked over each other in their rush to explain their findings, I got up for more coffee. While I poured, I thought about whether to talk to the guys about Asclepius's appearance in my dream. Probably not a coincidence he showed up on my first night in Italy. He'd promised not to demand results for a few days, but I assumed more of these subtle reminders would follow until he confronted me directly. Since I didn't really expect Georgia's inquiries to lead anywhere, I probably needed to do some asking around of my own while we were out, which meant letting the dudes know what was what.

By the time I returned with mugs, Adam had seen the evidence on the laptop and was checking out a map of the section of the city where the statue lived. "Okay, so we'll head out in a few to look this statue over. Sound good, Red?"

I handed him a cup and nodded. "Yeah, but before we do, I have another item to add to our to-do list."

Giguhl frowned. "Already? How much trouble could you get into in the kitchen?"

I grimaced at his lame joke. "Asclepius showed up in my dream last night."

Adam stilled, looking wary. Giguhl, too, had gone on red alert. Both of them were well aware of the bargain I'd made with the god. But Erron simply frowned. "Who's that?"

"He's a god of healing. I made a couple of sacrifices to him in the process of trying to help Maisie," I explained. "Anyway, he wants me to kill this vampire chick who's supposedly here in Italy."

"What happened in the dream?" Giguhl asked.

"He didn't say anything, so I assume it was just a reminder that he was watching me."

"Sabina, please tell me you're taking this seriously," Erron said, his tone sober. "You can't dick around with the gods."

"I know," I said defensively. "He knows I have more pressing matters right now. I should have a few days to make progress with Tristan before Asclepius gets his panties in a twist."

Erron blew out a breath. "Seriously. The last thing we need is a pissed-off god smiting you before we catch Cain."

"Anyway, I just wanted to let you know. The vamp's name is Nyx. I figure if we don't run into any local vamps, we can go ask Dicky if he's heard of her."

Adam nodded resolutely. "Sounds like a plan. In the meantime, let's pray this statue offers up something useful."

We decided to walk to the statue instead of flashing over. Pasquino wasn't too far from the hotel and we didn't want to just magically appear in the middle of what might be a crowded square.

It was a beautiful, clear night in Rome. The cloudless night made the air crisp and chilly. Giguhl had balked about being back in the canvas tote, but I told him it was either that or he had to don a sweater and booties. His thin kitty skin couldn't handle low temperatures, nor, I reminded him, could his bald testicles. That shut him right up.

As we walked, we chatted about the possibility that this statue thing would pan out.

"What else do we have to go on?" Erron asked reasonably.

"It's true. Still, I wish I knew why Tristan was being so cagey about all this," Adam said.

"He's probably just being cautious," Erron said. "He's in as much, if not more, danger as us right now."

"If he's even alive," I said in a hushed tone.

Adam shot me a look. "Let's not admit defeat before we have reason to."

"I know. It's just... we have to be prepared for anything."

We all fell silent as we pondered what that "anything" might be. Gods knew that statement was inviting trouble. The universe had a way of throwing complications the size of buses into our plans.

We'd turned right down a darkened street when foreboding hissed its cold breath down my neck. At the same instant, my left shoulder blade flared with a burning sensation. I held out a hand to stop the males.

Adam looked at me. "What's wrong?"

"Trouble." No sooner had the word left my mouth than a dozen vampires emerged from the shadows. Judging from the flashing fangs and feral expressions, this wasn't a Roman welcome committee.

I dropped the bag and fell back into my fighting stance. The gun in my hand appeared as if summoned, but in reality I'd drawn it on instinct. After months of not shooting anyone, it's amazing how quickly the automatic draw had come back to me. Erron swung his arms together, gathering his power into a tight ball of energy. Adam chanted under his breath, calling up his own powers. Giguhl crouched at my feet waiting for permission to shift.

As we stood our ground, my stomach dipped and adrenaline surged through my veins. The band of vampires moved first, advancing like a bloodthirsty phalanx.

I was just about to give the order to attack when a loud male voice shouted, "*Basta!*"

The vamps stilled.

A male in a sleek Italian suit pushed through the pack. His deep red hair was slicked back and his skin was as pale as alabaster, telling me this one was older than the rest. He spread his arms to indicate he held no weapons. *"Buona notte, Signorina Kane. Si prega di perdonare I miei amici."*

"No parlo Italiano, asshole." I kept the gun trained on his forehead.

He nodded. "Forgive my friends, Miss Kane. We mean you no harm."

I snorted. "I'm not sure how you do things in Italy, but where I come from, we don't flash fangs at people we want to be friends with."

"I apologize for their...aggressive greeting. Now, you will come with us, yes?"

I laughed. "Not fucking likely."

"Please don't make this more difficult than is necessary."

"You made it difficult when you showed up with the twelve angry apostles," Adam observed in an acidic tone.

The vampire dipped his head to acknowledge our concern. "We were informed that you might have some...reservations about accompanying us."

I cocked the gun. "Your source was correct."

"Who sent you?" Erron said. The bolt of magic glowed ominously between his cupped palms.

"A mutual friend."

"You're gonna have to start being a little more specific if you don't want this gun to start barking," I warned.

Italian Suit's eyebrows slammed down like he had trouble following my English. But he must have gotten the gist. "It is too dangerous to say her name on the streets during these troubled times. However, I can tell you that my mistress, Donna Chiara Rossi, is playing host to an esteemed vampire of your acquaintance." He paused for dramatic effect. "Very esteemed."

I tried to figure out who he could be referring to. All of the esteemed vampires I'd known were now dead—Lavinia, Tanith...Oh shit! "Wait, do you mean Per—"

The Italian cut off the name I was about to say with a tsking sound. "I believe we understand each other."

"Hold on." I held up a finger and dragged Adam away for a confab. Erron was close enough to hear us but kept his magic trained on the vamps. "I think we should go with them."

His eyebrows brushed his hairline. "What? Two seconds ago you were ready to cause an international incident."

I leaned in closer, my volume barely above a whisper. "Persephone sent them."

His eyes widened as the implications hit him. Persephone had disappeared four nights earlier from the mage compound near Sleepy Hollow. As the last surviving Domina, she was now the sole leader of the vampire race. However, since she earned that title because the last leader, Tanith Severinus, exploded all over the unsigned peace treaty, she obviously had a few reservations about taking over.

"The plot thickens," Adam said. "What's our play?"

"Do you trust me?" I asked.

A crease formed between his brows. "Yes, but—"

I held up a hand. "No buts. Just follow my lead and do what I say." When he didn't continue to argue, I turned back to the Italian vampire contingent. "Okay, we'll go with you. But the first sign of aggression and I'll reduce the Roman vampire population by thirteen. Got it?"

"The mages are not invited. This is vampire business."

I didn't bother pointing out to him that I was half mage.

Having grown up in the vampire community myself, I understood how insular the politics could be. Arguing in favor of Adam and Erron's presence at the meeting was a waste of breath. Besides, I had a chore for the mages now, anyway.

"Fine, but I need to bring my cat with me."

He eyed Giguhl, who fell back on his haunches to lick his undercarriage. Obviously dismissing the feline as a nonthreat, the vampire nodded. "That is agreeable to me."

I turned to Erron and Adam. "Go on ahead to the statue and see what you can find. When you get back to the hotel, call Rhea and let her know we found her," I said, referring to Persephone.

Adam opened his mouth to argue, but my dead-serious expression must have dissuaded him. "How long should I wait until I start worrying?"

I glanced at the Italian, who was tapping his black Gucci loafer on the damp cobblestones. "If there's trouble, I'll just introduce them to our horny green friend." I nodded toward the cat. Between Giguhl and me, we'd be able to escape just about any trouble the vampires could conjure up.

"Got it." With that, Adam planted a fast, hard kiss on my lips. In the next instant, before the warmth of his touch cooled, he and Erron flashed away.

Normally when someone flashes out through interspatial travel, there isn't much to see. But Adam and Erron, gods bless them, made quite a show of smoke and sparks.

The fireworks seemed to unsettle the vampires. Good.

I turned back to my hosts and raised my hands. "Lead the way."

I almost changed my mind when I saw the mode of transport the Italian vamp, who'd introduced himself as Damiano, led us toward.

"You've got to be fucking kidding me."

Damiano frowned. "*Scusi?*"

I pointed. "You don't seriously expect me to ride on a Vespa?"

He pursed his lips. "But of course."

All around us, the twelve vamp apostles were climbing atop their own scooters. Sans helmets, naturally. Because that would be ridiculous.

Thus far, Giguhl had remained silent, lest he give away his demonic identity. But once he got a load of our ride, he climbed up my shoulder to hiss in my ear, "Douchemobiles?"

I shrugged and covered the cat's commentary by giving him a pet between the ears. But he was totally right. The flames on the sides of the bikes did seem a tad overkill.

"Please," Damiano said. He climbed on the Vespa and indicated I should get on behind him.

Back in Los Angeles, I'd been the proud owner of a

cherry-condition Ducati. After experiencing the thrill of one hundred and eighty horses galloping between my thighs, the mere idea of riding on this child's toy nicked at my ego. I probably could have jogged alongside the entire way to Chiara's and not get winded.

But under the weight of thirteen expectant stares and the promise of getting to the bottom of Persephone's disappearance forced me to harness my pride.

Cradling Giguhl to my chest, I swung a leg over the low back of the scooter. I refused to wrap my arms around Damiano, however. He simply shrugged and fired up the engine. Unlike the dead sexy roar of my Ducati's stampeding engine, this damned thing *whirred* to life like a cheap vibrator.

"How much horsepower does this thing have?"

Damiano pursed his lips, thinking it over. "She has eleven horses." He patted the buzzing engine proudly.

My mouth fell open, but before I could laugh or make a snarky comment, he took off. The acceleration barely jostled me. Giguhl looked up at me from my chest and rolled his eyes. No doubt we'd laugh about this later. In the meantime, I thanked the gods I didn't know anyone in Rome who might witness the indignity of me clutching a hairless cat on the back of a fucking Vespa.

As we wound our way through Rome's streets, Damiano chatted like we were on a Sunday drive. "So how are you enjoying your time in Roma thus far?"

I frowned at his back. "It's fine."

"Excellent. You should see the sites." He waved his hands around like steering was optional. "Experience the romance of the Eternal City." He kissed his fingertips.

"Yeah, I'll be sure to do that," I said, and didn't bother covering the eye roll since he couldn't see me anyway.

Apparently, this guy was completely unaware of the chaos facing all the dark races. Even though the drama was centered stateside, the assassination of the Despina was sure to have wide-ranging effects for all the vampire covens in the world.

As we drove, the other vampires would occasionally close in the ranks like a motorcade, but the narrow streets and insane traffic made anything other than single file impossible for most of the trip.

"Will you be in town long?"

I sighed and shot the guy a level glare. "How much farther?"

He stiffened. Whether this reaction was due to my rudeness or a translation issue, I didn't care. I just wanted to get there already and figure out what the hell Persephone was doing in Italy. "It is just there." He pointed to a building across the street and down a bit. The building he indicated was nothing short of a villa.

I'd expected the leader of Rome's vampires to have impressive security, but no dice. Not one gate, video camera, or guard with a machine gun. Chiara Rossi was either incredibly cocky or incredibly stupid. Possibly both.

Our lame biker gang turned left into an alley next to the building and pulled around back to a driveway of sorts. Above us, the building's rear rose up, all leaded windows and carved columns and huge balconies. Just beyond the driveway, a garden lay dormant in February's chill, but I imagined in the spring it would be like a little Eden in the city.

I jumped off the scooter before Damiano pulled to a complete stop. He and the other vamps got off their bikes more slowly. I stood there, waiting for them to lead me wherever I was supposed to go, but they all just stood there. I raised my brows. "Well?"

"The Donna is waiting for you through that gate in the courtyard."

"You're not coming in?"

Damiano shook his head. "No. It's time for us to hunt."

I nodded. Back in the day, I'd spent most of my nights hunting, too. Part of me longed to go with them. See what kind of sport the citizens of Rome offered. But then I reminded myself that I didn't have the luxury of wasting my predatory instincts on innocent humans. I had to save them up to hunt more cunning prey—Cain.

"All right," I said. "Thanks, I guess."

Damiano smiled. "*Prego, Signorina* Kane." He executed a little bow. "I hope we shall meet again."

"Uh-huh," I said. "Bye now."

"*Buone notte!*" several of the vampires called as they got back on their bikes. Some even waved enthusiastically, like they hadn't just tried to intimidate me thirty minutes earlier.

Giguhl and I waited until their taillights disappeared around the corner of the house. Once they were gone, the cat looked up at me. "That was the strangest thing I've ever seen."

I lowered my brows and pursed my lips at my hairless demon cat. "Stranger than demon fight club or dark races roller derby?"

The cat shrugged. "Okay, it's the strangest thing I've seen *tonight*."

I hefted his bulk higher. "The night's young. Give it time."

With that, I walked to the black iron gate set into the stone wall at the base of the building. Through the elaborate scrollwork, I could tell it led to a courtyard. I opened the gate, not sure what to expect, exactly. Before I stepped in, I set Giguhl down on the gravel. Kneeling down next to him, I whispered my instructions. "Stay close to me but say nothing."

The cat nodded once and streaked into the shadows to do a perimeter check. I rose and stepped inside, seeing that he'd have plenty of places to hide out. The central garden area had several intersecting paths that stretched to a colonnade around the perimeter. On the far end of the space, long steps led to a row of French doors. The windows cast a warm glow on the grass and plant-filled urns that dotted the paths.

Chiara Rossi stood in the center of the courtyard, still as a statue. The moonlight flashed against her cherry-red hair, which was pulled back into an elaborate updo. She wore a simple black wrap dress and black stiletto pumps, which seemed out of place in the timeworn villa. Both her formal posture and the opulent surroundings were supposed to remind me that I was outranked.

I raised my chin and held my ground. She might outrank me as a vampire, but in the broader dark races perspective, I was of both vampire and mage noble bloodlines. But rank meant next to nothing to me. All I cared about was if she could take me in a fight.

I took in her mile-high Louboutins.

Absolutely not.

No woman who knew the first thing about fighting would ever wear those ridiculous ankle-breakers.

I'd heard of Chiara before. I'd never interacted with the vampire leaders abroad, but I'd heard snippets of gossip about her. If I remembered correctly, Chiara hadn't earned her title through the usually bloody means. Instead, she'd benefited from old-fashioned nepotism. Namely, she was Persephone's cousin.

Now that I was here, standing before her, I couldn't

believe no one had thought to check here for the missing Domina. But, then, I guess we'd all assumed Persephone was still stateside. For her to escape New York and make it here to Rome so quickly told me that she had the escape plan in place long before Tanith's murder.

"Welcome to Roma, Miss Kane." Her words were accented with an Italian inflection but were spoken with the confidence of one used to conversing in English.

"Thanks."

"I was disappointed you did not call on me the instant you arrived in my city."

"I would have," I lied, "but I'm not here on vampire business."

"Regardless, you of all Lilim should be aware of the protocol."

"Forgive me, but I don't give a damn about vampire protocol. Not anymore."

She nodded and took a few steps forward. I stayed put, content to let her come to me. "Yes, I've heard you turned your back on your blood kin."

I laughed. "That's one perspective. The wrong one. Not that it matters." My so-called betrayal wasn't the reason I was *vampira non grata*. The Lilim wanted nothing to do with me since birth because of my tainted blood. The only reason I'd been allowed to live in the first place was that my maternal grandmother and Alpha Domina, Lavinia Kane, found me useful as an assassin.

"Regardless, you're here now." Chiara smiled but the emotion didn't reach her eyes. "What is your business in my city?"

I crossed my arms. "Look, can we cut the shit here? I know Persephone's here. Surely she filled you in on the events at the treaty signing."

"Yes, I am aware that Despina Tanith and High Councilman Orpheus were murdered."

That's when it hit me that Chiara and Persephone wouldn't be privy to what happened after Persephone ran off into the night just after the Despina died. But I really didn't want to get into the sordid details about my twin's guilt and subsequent death. Besides, I preferred to discuss this with Persephone. Time to change the subject. Since Chiara was Italy's most powerful vampire, I decided to see if she'd heard of the vamp Asclepius wanted me to kill.

"Do you know a vampire named Nyx?"

Chiara frowned at my mercurial change of topic. "Nyx? No."

"You sure? I heard she was in Italy."

"I am certain. No vampires enter Italia without my knowledge."

I raised my brows. Either Asclepius was wrong or Chiara's intel was seriously lacking. If I had to bet, I'd go double down on the latter.

"Is this Nyx why you have come to Roma?"

"It's one of the reasons," I said.

"And the other?"

I crossed my arms. "That I will only discuss with the Domina. That's why I was brought here, right? To speak with her."

She nodded reluctantly. "*Si*, my dear cousin would like a word with you."

I raised my brows. "I'm waiting."

Chiara snapped her fingers and a male vampire who'd been standing guard near the bushes rushed forward. The Donna spoke to him in a low tone before he ran off, presumably to retrieve Persephone. "She'll be with us shortly.

But first, I must ask you to refrain from upsetting her. She still suffers greatly."

I didn't bother mentioning that Persephone's problems didn't begin to compare to the ones I was facing. Before Tanith died, she'd had my grandmother killed so she could take control of the vampire race. In the process, she'd reduced Persephone to little more than a puppet. I found it hard to believe the last surviving Domina was too broken up about her tormentor dying. If I had to guess, Persephone's real worry was that her own days were numbered. Which, come to think of it, wasn't out of the realm of possibility at present.

"I'll try to be gentle," I said, my tone heavy with irony. After all, Persephone might have been considered the weakest Domina, but she was still an ancient vampire. Not one to trifle with in any arena.

A few moments later, a side door opened and Persephone swept out into the courtyard. Last time I'd seen her she'd been wearing dove gray, like a woman in mourning for her lost power. But now she wore a bright sapphire dress that played brilliantly against her deep auburn hair. The moonlight made her pale skin glow like a pearl. No doubt about it, Persephone was still the most beautiful female I'd ever seen.

Watching her stride toward us, I wondered if maybe I'd misjudged her all along. I'd always thought Tanith was the smart one and Lavinia was the strongest of the three Dominae. But now they were both dead and pretty Persephone had the entire dark races scrambling.

"Sabina." She tipped her head regally in greeting.

"Domina," I responded. While I'd lost my need to kowtow to the Dominae long ago, I'd always viewed Persephone with less contempt than her two partners. And since part of the reason I'd agreed to this meeting was the need to convince her to return to the States to take control of the vampire race, I figured I'd stack my bets and show her the respect she expected. However, I refused to bow to her. I wasn't that desperate for her favor.

"Thank you for agreeing to this meeting."

I didn't bother pointing out I didn't have much of a choice in the matter. "Of course. I was surprised to learn you were in Rome. Everyone thinks you're still stateside."

"I assume your cohorts are already in touch with Rhea and the Queen regarding my location."

Adam's aunt and Queen Maeve of the fae were trying to hold down the dark races in America until Persephone returned to take control of the vampires.

"You know you have to go back."

"Not necessarily," she said, looking thoughtful. "I have decided to renounce my right to rule the Lilim."

My stomach dipped. While I'd known this was a possibility all along, I'd hoped that she'd suck it up and do what was right in the end. "Domina, I'm sorry, but that's bullshit."

"Hey!" Chiara protested.

Persephone waved her cousin down. "I am quite decided on the matter."

"Well, that's just perfect," I said, my voice rising. "We were so close to finally achieving peace between the races and now you're going to just walk away and leave the vampire race without any sort of leadership?"

"Sabina, let's not be overly dramatic. The Undercouncil is perfectly capable of running things until a new candidate can be found."

I sighed. Yelling at her wasn't going to get us anywhere. "Look, I understand your misgivings. I'd be reluctant to take over, too, after my two predecessors were murdered. But times have changed."

Persephone raised a perfectly arched brow. "Have they? Have you found Tanith's murderer yet?"

"No, not yet. But we know who's responsible. That's why I'm here."

Her forehead crinkled. "Who?"

"Cain."

Her hand flew to her midsection. "Great Mother protect us. How is that possible?"

I quickly gave her an abbreviated version of Cain's plot to destroy any chance at peace, leaving out the part about him using Maisie as his weapon. "So the Hekate Council and the Queen sent me here to find him and make sure he's out of the equation."

"But how will you manage that? Cain can't be killed."

"Which is why I'm trying to locate the mage who calls himself Abel." I conveniently left out the part about Abel maybe being my father. No sense delving into that quagmire when things were complex enough as it was. "I'm hoping his knowledge of Cain will give me the key to stopping him."

"A mage named Abel?" Persephone said, frowning.

I realized the source of her confusion. "Not the same Abel as in the mortal mythology—the brother Cain killed. This mage I'm looking for apparently adopted the name when he decided to make Cain his enemy. Maybe he sees himself as the original Abel's avenger or something."

Which begged the question again of why my father hated Cain so badly. But that was an issue for another time and definitely not one to analyze with Persephone.

The Domina blew out a breath. "I wish you luck, but I'm afraid I don't share your optimism. This does nothing but confirm my decision to get out of dark race politics." She turned to Chiara. "Tell the servants to start packing up. We're leaving Rome."

My mouth fell open. "So that's it? You're going to just run away?"

Persephone speared me with a glare. "Sabina, I am two thousand years old. Do you think I reached this advanced age by being a coward?"

"No, Domina."

"I reached this age by being smart and choosing my battles. For whatever reason, Cain is determined to kill anyone who attempts to make peace a reality for the dark races. You said it yourself: The Queen and Rhea need me to bring the vampires back to the table. That means I am a threat to Cain's plans. I'd be a fool to return. Just as I'd be a fool to stay in this house when the man who wants me dead is loose in Rome."

As much as I hated to admit it, she made a good point. But I wasn't ready to surrender. "Who will rule the race, then?"

Persephone's lips spread into a calculating smile. "If you want peace so badly, why don't you volunteer? You're a descendant of a Domina."

A harsh laugh escaped my lips. "Don't be ridiculous. The vampires would never follow a mixed-blood." Not to mention, I didn't want to rule the vampires or any race.

"They would if they believed you were the only leader who could guarantee peace. Your blood may be mixed, but it's noble. Plus, your connection to the Hekate Council means you'd be able to negotiate favorable terms for all parties."

I shook my head so hard my brain rattled in my skull. "Impossible. There has to be someone else."

Some emotion flickered in her eyes, but it disappeared as soon as I saw it. "It is only impossible if you believe it to be. Regardless, it's no longer my business. Please give the Queen and Rhea my regards when you deliver my decision."

I crossed my arms and glared at her. "You can tell them yourself. I'm not your messenger."

"I don't believe for a moment you won't report our conversation. If the Queen and Rhea want to hear it from me, they'll have to find me first."

I raised a brow in challenge. "I found you."

"Oh, child," she laughed. "Please don't fool yourself. I found *you*."

She had me there. If Chiara's vampires hadn't approached me, I would have had no idea Persephone was in Rome.

"Now, if you'll excuse me, I have plans to make."

"This isn't over," I said.

"Yes," she said, "it is. Except, I have one parting bit of advice to offer you, if I may?"

I pursed my lips but nodded. This should be good.

"I watched you fight your whole life, Sabina. First for respect among the race that rejected you. Then against your grandmother. Now you're fighting for revenge against Cain. All this fighting and what has it gotten you?"

"What? I should be like you? Run when things get tough? Sorry, Persephone, but that's not my style."

"You must get your stubbornness from your mage blood."

I could be wrong, but I thought I detected a hint of respect in her voice.

"Damn straight, I do."

"I'm just saying maybe instead of trying to force the world to be as you want it to be, maybe you should stop and accept reality. Fighting isn't always the answer."

I snorted. That was rich coming from a Domina. "I fight because surrender is never an option. Not to you, not to Cain, and certainly not to fate."

Persephone's expression was unreadable, but I sensed her sadness and disappointment. "So be it. I just pray that while you're off fighting dragons, everyone else doesn't get burned." She pulled something from the pocket of her gown. A golden circlet of some sort. She held it out to me. "Take this."

I frowned and moved forward to take it. "What is it?" The metal was warm to the touch. It looked like a crown of sorts made of thick filigree work with a large lotus on the center.

"It belonged to Tanith. She had it made as a symbol of her new role as Despina. When she died, it came to me. You should make sure whoever takes over the race gets it."

I tried to hand it back to her. "But I don't—"

With that, Persephone, former Domina of the Lilim, shook her head and walked away, leaving me holding the crown.

10

*B*y the time Giguhl and I got into a cab to go back to our hotel, I was exhausted and frustrated. Our simple mission to find Abel had gotten complicated very quickly. First the Asclepius bullshit and now Persephone was being a pain in my ass. I just prayed Adam and Erron had some good news from their trek to visit Pasquino.

In the cab, Giguhl was quiet. Too quiet. After about ten minutes with no sarcasm, I started to get worried. "What's going on in that head of yours?"

He shook his head. "Nothing."

"Oh, come on," I said. "Surely you have something to say about what just happened."

The cat sighed. "Are you really going to take over the vampire race?"

I stilled. The driver couldn't hear us through the closed partition, but occasionally he'd eye me in the rearview. I kept my reaction to Giguhl's question subdued despite the fact that my cat just shocked the hell out of me. Luckily, the driver spent most of the drive talking at breakneck pace into a cell phone while simultaneously almost clipping several pedestrians and narrowly avoiding multi-car pileups.

I looked down at the cat with a dead-serious expression. "Of course I'm not going to lead the vamps. How can you even ask that?"

The cat shrugged. "It's not completely crazy."

"Yes, it is," I whisper-yelled. "It's one hundred percent batshit insane."

"I'm just saying. There's a certain poetic justice to it all."

"Giguhl, listen to me," I said, lowering my voice so he'd pay attention. "My only goal right now is to find Cain. Rhea, the Queen, and the Undercouncil will have to find someone else to lead the vamps."

"And if they don't? Find anyone else, I mean."

"Not my problem." I set my lips into a tight line and leaned back against the seat. Giguhl figured out this meant the subject was closed. I simply refused to even consider the idea anymore. It was too preposterous for words.

Erron was staring at the laptop when we walked in.

"Hey, guys." His gaze stayed on the screen. I scanned the room for signs of Adam but found none.

"Where's the mancy?"

Erron shrugged. "He's up on the terrace. Said he was calling his aunt."

I nodded and told Giguhl to go fetch Adam. Then I plopped into a club chair with a sigh. I wanted blood and a stiff drink, but first we needed to figure out what the hell to do about Persephone.

A couple seconds later, the cat and the mage ran down the spiral staircase to join us. Judging from the deep frown on Adam's face, he'd been impatient for my return and wasn't happy it took so long.

"Oh thank the gods you're back." He pulled me into a hard hug.

I waved a hand to dismiss his concerns for my safety. "I'm fine."

He eyed me for a moment as if he was looking for signs I was fudging the truth. "Please tell me you have good news."

I grimaced. "Afraid not. Persephone's officially refusing to return as leader of the Lilim."

"Shit," Adam said. "I just called Rhea with a preliminary report. She said once you got back, she'd want to conference in the Queen for a postmortem."

I sighed, but he was right. A meeting was long overdue. It had been a few nights since we'd spoken to the leaders, and they were no doubt anxious for a report. I just wished we had some positive news to give along with all the problems. But before we called them, I wanted to hear how the Pasquino mission went. "Please tell me the statue turned up something useful."

Adam raised a brow at Erron. "I hope so. We took pictures of every message on the statue, but I left to call Rhea before we had a chance to look them over on the computer." He glanced at Erron.

The Recreant waved us over to the laptop. "Most of the messages were in Italian, so I've been busy using translation software to translate them all while I waited for you to return."

"And?" I prodded.

The Recreant smiled. "And I think I've found something." He pulled up an image and zoomed in. The message was written in thick black marker in bold masculine script.

"It's laminated," I said. "Someone didn't want the elements ruining their message."

Erron nodded. "It stuck out for me because of this." He pointed to a word on the first line: "Hekate."

My pulse picked up pace as my eyes scanned the rest of the message for clues. "Shit, it's all in Italian."

Erron smirked. "Not anymore." He clicked the mouse a couple of times and an English translation popped up on the screen. "Anyone recognize this?"

Adam gasped softly. "It's the Hekatian Oracle prayer."

I frowned at him. "What?"

"Back in the day, when the Hekate Council didn't exist and the race was ruled by the Oracles, they began each reading of the prophecy with this prayer to the goddess."

I squinted at the screen and read the prayer quickly:

Hekate, Queen of the Night, Goddess of the Crossroad, Goddess of Magic and Protector of Spirits, we your humble servants implore you to guide your faithful Oracle to the true light of knowledge. Light Bringer, guide your servant's hands to do good deeds, guide her eyes to see the path, guide her tongue to speak the truth. Blessed is your name on our lips, blessed is your favor on our people, blessed is your power in our hearts. In your name, we give thee thanks.

"Huh," I said. "I've never heard that."

Adam shrugged. "These days it's used only by priestesses and Oracles. It was a particular favorite of—" He stopped short.

I realized he'd been about to say Maisie's name. She had been the only Oracle for the Hekate Council. And now there was none.

Giguhl, noticing the tension, cleared his throat. "So I guess it's a good bet that Tristan left this assuming you'd be familiar with it."

"I guess so. But it doesn't really tell us much, does it?"

"Not so fast. I just showed you the translation of the prayer. There's more." He pointed to a series of numbers under the prayer.

My eyes widened. "What is that?"

Erron smiled. "A phone number. Local, judging by the code."

"I assume it's a different one than Abel gave you last time you talked."

Erron nodded. My stomach dipped. "Did you call it?"

He shook his head. "I just figured it out before you arrived. Plus, I thought you'd want to do the honors."

My palms were suddenly sweaty. I quickly wiped them on my jeans. It was one thing to talk about finding my father. It was something else to face the prospect of chatting with him on the phone.

"Hold on," Adam said. "Dicky told us Tristan left that clue a couple weeks ago, right?"

"And?"

"And I just don't want you getting your hopes up in case the number doesn't work or no one answers."

"I think I can manage to not be destroyed if I get voice mail." I shook my head at him and dialed. I knew he didn't want me to be disappointed, but his patronizing tone put me on edge. Or maybe I was taking my nerves out on the mage. Either way, I hit the SEND button.

The phone rang once, twice, three times. My pulse hammered.

Click. Silence.

I frowned. "Hello?"

"*Prego*?" A male voice. Deep, unfamiliar.

"Tristan?" My voice shook a little.

A pause. "Depends. How did you get this number?"

"Pasquino gave it to me."

The creak of a chair and the rustle of fabric reached me through the receiver. I had his attention now. "Spanish Steps tomorrow, eight p.m."

"Oka—"

"Come alone." *Click*.

I pulled the phone away from my face and grimaced at it for a few moments. Finally, I hit the END button and turned to face the eager gazes of my three cohorts.

"Well?" Giguhl prompted.

"I'm meeting him tomorrow night."

"Where?" Adam asked.

"The Spanish Steps."

"Did he say anything else?" Erron asked.

I nodded, knowing this wouldn't go over well. "He said to come alone."

An explosion of raised, masculine voices.

"I'll be damned if I'm allowing you to go alone!" Adam yelled.

"Bullshit!" Giguhl shouted.

They then continued to rant, stomping around like Alpha males, ready to shout until I conceded.

I stood by with my arms crossed, waiting for them to settle down. Arguing at that point was a waste of breath. Meanwhile, Erron sat calmly by with his hands behind his head, watching the display with his lips curled into a smile.

Finally, Adam threw up his hands. "I can't believe you'd even consider going without us!"

He paused to take a deep breath; his face was red and a

vein throbbed on his neck. Next to him, Giguhl was all puffed up like an adder looking for a fight.

"Are you finished?" I said in a very calm, rational tone.

Two sets of narrowed eyes glared at me, but they both nodded.

"I never said I planned on going alone."

"But—" Giguhl started.

I shot him a look that shut him right up. "I simply said he wanted me to go alone. Jesus, guys, I'm not an idiot."

Adam's lips formed a shocked O and his cheeks got all hot and red. "Sorry, I just thought you'd—"

I waved away his apology. "With Cain out there"—I pointed toward the window to indicate the city beyond—"I'd have to be a fool to go anywhere without backup. So of course you're all going. We'll simply have to make sure he doesn't see any of you."

Erron sat forward. "I've been to the Spanish Steps. They're huge and always crawling with tourists. It should be no problem to blend."

"Okay," Adam said. "We definitely need to check in with Rhea and the Queen."

I nodded. "Get them on the horn."

I would have preferred talking to Rhea and Queen Maeve in person, but even magical beings are slaves to the vagaries of time and space. Namely, Rhea was in New York and Queen Maeve was in North Carolina. And sometimes despite our access to spells and different dimensions, the Internet was just more convenient than magic.

The four of us gathered around the large desk in the alcove. The laptop sat open on the surface and two windows were open on the screen. On the left Queen Maeve frowned at us from the conference room in her treetop palace in the Blue Ridge Mountains. Because her quadruple nature was nearing the end of its Crone cycle, she looked older than Methuselah. Her hair was so thin the pink of her scalp shined through the white strands. Her parchment skin was nearly translucent and was wrinkled like a sharpei's ass.

Rhea glared at the screen from the Hekate Council meeting room at the Crossroads estate near Sleepy Hollow. Her metallic-silver hair shone like tinsel and her green eyes flashed with annoyance. In deference to her newly elevated position as the head of the Hekate Council, she wore a white chiton. But her expression was pure schoolmarm—the same one she often wore when I screwed up during my magic lessons. "What part of 'we expect daily reports' did you not understand?"

I cringed. "Yeah, about that. Sorry—things have been a little crazy."

Rhea raised a brow. "Crazy good or crazy bad?"

I glanced at Adam for help. "Crazy…it could be worse?" he offered.

The Queen pointed at us. "Who is the mage lingering in the background there?"

"This is Erron Zorn, Your Benevolence," Adam said. "He volunteered to put us in touch with Abel's contact here."

The Queen nodded regally in Erron's direction. "Well it's good to hear some part of your mission was successful."

Rhea's expression was friendlier. "Thank you for your aid, Mr. Zorn. The Hekate Council is in your debt."

Behind me, Erron shifted uncomfortably and cleared his throat. "You're welcome."

As a Recreant, it had to be odd for him to be having a

discussion with the head of the Council that stripped him of his healing power when he dared challenge their authority. Of course, Rhea hadn't been in charge when that happened, but still.

"And the meeting with the contact?" the Queen prompted.

"It went well," I said. Not quite a lie, but not the whole truth either. I wanted to ease into dropping the bombshell. "We've managed to make contact with Abel and have a meeting set up for tomorrow night."

Rhea smiled. "Excellent. Great job, you guys."

"Err," Adam said, shifting in his seat, "thanks, but there's some new information about Abel you need to know."

"Oh?" the Queen said.

"Yeah," I said. "We found out his real identity."

She banged an impatient hand on the table. "Out with it, girl!"

"We haven't seen him in person, but we have good reason to believe that Abel is really..." Now that it was time to spill the beans, I couldn't do it. Saying it out loud to Rhea, who'd known my father since he was a child and witnessed the fallout when everyone believed he had died, felt weird. Luckily Adam stepped in before the tension could mount too much further.

"Turns out Abel is someone you already know. Or knew." Adam let out a breath. "Tristan Graecus."

Rhea's hand flew up to her mouth and a gasp escaped her. Queen Maeve simply blinked, the news far less shocking to her since she'd never met him and couldn't care less about my personal dramas. However, since Tristan had been the son of the leader of the mage race, she no doubt knew the history about his disappearance fifty-odd years earlier.

"Are you certain?" Maeve said in the wake of Rhea's shocked silence.

I shrugged. "Like I said, we haven't met with him yet. But our contact swore it to be truth. Also, I spoke to him on the phone earlier and he answered to the name Tristan."

"Oh gods, Sabina!" Rhea finally exclaimed. "Are you okay?"

I nodded. "I want answers and I really don't like this kind of surprise falling in my lap right now, but as far as I'm concerned, it changes nothing."

"Sabina, you're not serious." Rhea frowned. "This changes everything."

I crossed my arms and set my jaw. "No, it doesn't. I'm here to do a job. He has information I need to get the job done. I'm not interested in tearful reunions or heart-to-hearts or whatever."

Rhea sighed a martyred sigh. She knew my mulish expression and tone very well. "Just…be careful, okay? This is pretty big news."

Adam cleared his throat and leaned in toward the screen. "You didn't…uh…I mean, this was a shock for you, too, right?"

Rhea tilted her head. "What? Are you asking if I knew he was alive all this time?" She looked like he'd slapped her. "Of course not. Adam, how could you think that?"

Adam's cheeks went red. "Look, I'm sorry, but someone had to know he wasn't dead."

"What about Orpheus?" the Queen said. "Weren't he and Tristan good friends back in the day?"

She had a point. If anyone would have known about Tristan being alive, it would have been Rhea's predecessor, who'd run the mage race following Tristan's mother. He and my father were apparently both members of the Pythian Guards, a special-ops unit under the Hekate Council.

The mention of Orpheus's name made Rhea blanch. She

and the former High Councilman had been good friends—
and maybe more, according to my theory. The implication
that he'd hidden a secret this huge made Rhea's voice tremble with rage. "You all listen to me right now. Orpheus
would not have hidden this from us. He loved Maisie and
respected Sabina too much to hide something this huge."

"Unless he had a good reason for wanting us to continue
believing Tristan was dead," I said.

Rhea slashed a hand through the air. "Regardless, it
doesn't matter now. Orpheus is dead. I say you focus on
demanding answers from the one who is alive—Tristan."

I sighed deeply. "We'll leap off that bridge when we
come to it."

The Queen was ready to move on. "Is that all you have
to report?" Clearly Rhea hadn't had a chance to fill the
Queen in on the Persephone situation yet.

"No, actually," I said. "We had a bit of a surprise turn up.
You'll never guess who's in Rome." Maeve looked totally
uninterested in playing the guessing game. "Persephone."

That got her attention. "You're certain?" the Queen
snapped.

"Yes. I met with her tonight at the home of the Donna of
Italy, Chiara Rossi."

"When is she returning stateside?" Rhea asked.

"If it's up to her, never," I said. "She officially abdicated
her right to rule the Lilim to me."

The Queen muttered an unladylike curse. Then she
snapped at someone off camera. When she was finished,
she looked at us and said, "My people are getting Slade and
Alexis on the line."

"Good idea," Rhea said.

"Why?" I asked.

"There's some trouble in Los Angeles," Rhea explained.

"The Undercouncil has started losing control of the California vamps. Some turf wars have started now that word's spread the Despina's dead and Persephone is missing."

"Turf wars?" Giguhl asked. "That doesn't sound good."

The Queen nodded. "Some ambitious local vamps are making noises about staging a coup against the Undercouncil. We sent Alexis and Slade to Los Angeles to try to convince them to crack down."

Alexis Vega had been Tanith's personal guard before the Despina was killed, and Slade Corbin was the leader of New York's vampires. They'd been the ones originally charged with locating Persephone.

"Unless we can convince Persephone to get back and take control, things are only going to get worse," Rhea concluded.

I pulled Persephone's crown from the pocket of my jacket. "Well, I'm afraid she's pretty serious. She gave me this and said to hand it over to the next leader."

Now it was Rhea's turn to curse. Before she could elaborate, though, the screen flickered and a new window popped up. Alexis and Slade blinked blearily at the camera. Since they were in California, it was only just dusk and they'd probably just woken up.

"Well, well, it's a party," Slade said in a droll tone. "What's the occasion?"

Beside me, I felt Adam tense. Not surprising given my past intimate history with Slade.

"Hey, Slade!" Giguhl said. He'd always had a kind of hero worship thing going for Slade. "Vampinatrix," he said in a more sullen tone to Alexis.

"Guys, we've had a development in Rome," I said, getting down to business. "Persephone's here and she's refusing to return to take over the vamps."

"Shit!" Alexis snapped. "You need us to come drag her back?"

"Actually," Rhea said, "I think we need to approach this situation with a lighter touch. If we barge in and force her to return, we won't be doing the peace progress any favors."

"Besides," the Queen said, "nothing would stop her from leaving again. No, we need to convince her it's in her best interest to return."

I raised my hands. "How?"

Rhea sighed. "How did you leave it with her?"

"Not well, I'm afraid. I told her about Cain being a real threat here and she decided to leave the city. She wouldn't tell me where she planned on going."

"Has she left already?" the Queen asked, her tone urgent.

I shook my head. "No. She won't be able to rally her resources and get out of town before tomorrow dusk earliest."

"So go back over there and talk some sense into her!" Queen Maeve said.

"It's not that easy," Adam said. "It's almost dawn here. And tomorrow night we have our meeting with Tristan, which I think you'll agree is the priority."

The Queen sighed. "You're correct."

"Sabina and her crew need to focus on the Tristan situation," Rhea said. "Alexis and Slade, you need to get to Rome ASAP to take point with Persephone."

Adam stiffened next to me. Slade's eyes flicked toward me through the screen. I tried to keep my expression neutral, but my stomach sank with dread.

"Um, actually," Slade said, "if it's all the same to you, I'd prefer to stay in Los Angeles."

Alexis swiveled her head and stared at Slade with open-mouthed shock.

"Why?" the Queen snapped.

"Yeah, why?" Alexis demanded.

Slade shifted and switched into persuader mode. "Someone needs to stay and make sure the Undercouncil doesn't do anything stupid. Besides, Alexis knows the Domina the best. My presence might only put her on edge. Especially since she'd remember me as the assassin who screwed over the Dominae and went to work with the Hekate Council in New York."

As far as excuses went, they weren't half bad. But I knew it wasn't Slade's entire reason for bowing out. Slade and I had a somewhat…involved past. That past had caught up with me a few weeks earlier when Adam found out I'd lied about sleeping with Slade. Adam and I had worked through most of the issues that brought up, but I had been worried Slade's arrival in the middle of our mission would only complicate matters. Judging from his quick work at bowing out of the mission, it appeared Slade shared those concerns.

Rhea sighed. "Alexis, do you think you can handle Persephone alone?"

The vampire jerked her gaze away from Slade. Rhea's question put her in a difficult situation. If she said she couldn't handle it alone, she'd look weak. But I could tell she was pissed at Slade for bowing out.

"Hold on," she said. With a hand, she covered the computer's mic, but she forgot to minimize the camera. So we all watched her and Slade argue for a few minutes. Actually, from the looks of things, Alexis was doing all the yelling. Slade talked calmly and rationally, no doubt using his charm to get her to see reason. Finally, she let out a frustrated sigh and threw up her hands.

"Fine!" she shouted.

I frowned at the screen. Something told me their fight wasn't just about her not wanting to face Persephone alone. In fact, if I had to guess, Alexis was most pissed about having to face me alone. After all, there was no love lost between us after we'd each mistakenly accused the other of murder before we realized my sister was the culprit.

Rhea cleared her throat and shifted uncomfortably. "So does that mean, yes, you're fine handling Persephone alone?"

Alexis crossed her arms and sighed. "Yes, I can handle Persephone alone."

The sound of angry keyboard clicking came out of the laptop's speakers. "I'm checking flights, and the earliest I can get to Rome is five p.m. local time."

"Crap," Rhea said. "I forgot you guys can't travel magically."

"The sun's an issue, too," I said. "That's cutting it close. Sundown here is around five-thirty. By the time you reached Chiara's villa, Persephone will be gone."

Erron leaned between Adam and me. "Wait. How about I just flash there and bring her back?"

Slade squinted at the screen. "Sorry, but who are you?"

I sat up straighter, realizing I hadn't made the introductions. "Slade, Alexis, this is Erron Zorn. He's a mage friend from New Orleans."

"What's up?" Erron nodded a greeting.

Alexis crossed her arms. "Um, I'm not so sure about traveling magically."

"Ah, it'll be fine," Giguhl said. "You might hurl, but it sure beats taking the red eye."

"Whatever," Alexis said.

"Just tell me where you are and I can be there in a couple minutes," Erron said.

While Alexis filled Erron in on their location, I took a deep breath and glanced at Adam. His jaw was clenched and he stared at Slade through the screen like he wanted to throttle the dude. Looked like it was a good move on Slade's part to decline joining our little party.

"Now that the travel arrangements have been sorted out, I'll sign off," the Queen said. "But, Sabina?"

"Yes?"

"We expect another report tomorrow night after you meet with this Tristan. Also from Alexis on the Persephone situation."

"Right," I said.

"Yes, ma'am," Alexis added.

"And, Slade?" Rhea said. "Let us know if you make any headway with the Undercouncil."

"Will do." The vampire grinned into the camera, charming as ever.

"All right," Rhea continued. "I know this goes without saying, but everyone be careful out there. Cain's still waiting for you to let down your guard."

We all fell silent as this sunk in. I'd been so busy scrambling I'd almost forgotten that Cain could jump out from any dark shadow I passed.

"Let him try it," Alexis said, all bravado as usual.

"Oh," Giguhl said. "You can bet your sweet ass he will."

Alexis and Erron returned about an hour later. One second, Adam, Giguhl, and I were poring over a map of the Spanish Steps and the next they appeared in the living room.

Alexis wore her trademark black leather pants, a black bustier, and knee-high stiletto boots. Hardly proper attire for any situation, but especially not for the chilly Italian

February. But before we addressed that issue, there was the little matter of her green complexion to deal with.

"Bathroom," she barked.

Adam showed her to the bathroom. A few seconds later, the gut-clenching sounds of gagging echoed through the penthouse.

"Virgins," Giguhl muttered.

I shot him an annoyed look and went to Erron. "What took so long?" I demanded. They'd been gone almost an hour on an errand that should have taken five, ten minutes tops.

The mage dropped a paper bag onto the couch. "We made a pit stop to get some bagged blood. I figured you wouldn't want Alexis feeding off the tourists in the lobby."

I pulled back and relaxed my shoulder. "Oh. That was smart thinking. Thanks."

Erron nodded. "I'll just go put it in the fridge. She'll probably need some to help recover from the stress of the trip."

Alexis came out of the bathroom then. Her skin was paler than usual, but she wasn't green anymore. "I'd rather be stuck in the back of a plane with three squalling mortal babies than repeat that magic-travel shit again."

"Ah, c'mon," Giguhl said. "It's that bad?"

I shot him a look. "Please. You screamed like a girl your first time."

Giguhl's complexion took on a decidedly red cast. He adjusted his sweatpants carefully and avoided all our gazes. "That must have been the wind whistling in your ears."

"Whatever," Alexis said. "Anyway, I'm here. What now?"

I stifled a huge yawn. The horizon was already pink and yellow, indicating the sun's imminent arrival. "Now we sleep."

*   *   *

I'd like to say that after my declaration of bedtime, we'd all docilely turned in. However, an argument ensued until the sun's inevitable rise forced a decision. Which is how, at five p.m. the next evening, I woke with Alexis Vega's arm draped across my midsection. Her face was only a few inches from mine, so when she murmured Slade's name, I got a blast of vampire morning breath.

I pushed her until she rolled over and got out of bed with a disgusted sigh. I couldn't muster up too much indignation, though. At least I didn't have to sleep on the couch like Adam.

The night before, Alexis had refused to share a room with a demon and a mage. I couldn't really blame her. I wouldn't want to share a room with those two either. But for Alexis, the discomfort came from an inherent mistrust in all magical beings, which was bred into every full-blooded vampire from birth. Adam had tried to suggest Alexis take the couch instead, but I nixed that idea. With the bank of windows facing east, she would have been fried while she slept.

And that's how I ended up sharing a bed with Alexis and the mancy got the couch. He could have slept with Erron and Giguhl, but he flat-out refused to subject himself to Giguhl's randy nocturnal activities.

After I grabbed a quick shower, I rudely woke my bedmate and told her she had thirty minutes before it was time to head out. Then I left her and went to join the others. Erron sat on the couch plucking away on his guitar. I greeted him as I passed, but he seemed lost in the song, so I continued to the kitchen. Giguhl and Adam were at the table, drinking coffee.

I grabbed a mug and had just settled in when the demon leaned across the table like a conspirator.

"So...is it just me or did anyone else pick up some

major sexual tension between Alexis and Slade last night?" Giguhl said.

"Totally." I nodded. "Alexis said his name in her sleep last night, too. Not surprising really. They totally did the deed in New York before we left."

Adam's head jerked up. "Really?"

I shrugged. "Yeah."

"And you're not upset?"

I set down my coffee and looked him right in the eye. "Of course not."

He held my gaze for a moment. "Good."

I nodded. "Good."

Giguhl sighed and made a clucking sound with his tongue. "Jesus, you two are idiots."

"Hey!" Adam and I said in unison.

"I'm just sayin'."

The demon was saved from a cutting retort when my cell phone started jumping around on the table. I picked it up and didn't recognize the number. My heart picked up its pace. Was Tristan calling to cancel the meeting?

I clicked the button to answer. "Yes?"

"Sabina? It's Georgia."

Relief flooded through me. I'd totally forgotten I asked Georgia to check up on Nyx for me. "Hey, Georgia. What's up?"

"I might have turned up something for you about Nyx."

I sat up straighter. Adam and Giguhl watched me carefully, their expressions wary. "Okay, shoot."

"None of the vamps in New Orleans have heard of her, but when I tried some friends in the old country"—the old country in Georgia's case was France—"I got a couple of hits. Seems there was a vampire who came through Lyon about fifty years ago."

"That's a long time ago, Georgia." Too long ago to be of any help now.

"Yeah, I was surprised, too, but my friend said he remembered her because she was extraordinarily beautiful, even for a vamp. Do you think it's the same Nyx you're looking for?"

I pursed my lips. Hadn't Asclepius said the same thing, although in less gracious terms? "That jives with what I was told, too. Plus, Nyx isn't exactly a common name. Did your friend give you any other info?"

She sighed. "Unfortunately, no. He said she was only in town for a week or two. Said she seemed real nervous, like she was on the run."

I frowned. Asclepius hadn't mentioned when Nyx had asked him to make the vest, but I had the impression it happened more recently than half a century ago. Although, maybe the reasons she was on the run tied into her need for the vest in the first place. "Hmm, well, if it was the same Nyx, she obviously headed to Italy sometime after your friend saw her."

"I'm sorry, Sabina. I wish I could have turned up more. I even called an old friend in Florence, and she hadn't heard of Nyx, either. It's surprising because the vampire population in Europe is a lot smaller than in the States since the Dominae moved their power base to the New World."

"Well, I appreciate the effort."

"Does this mean you haven't made any progress on your end?"

"Not where Nyx is concerned. But honestly, it's probably fourth on my list of priorities right now."

"How goes the hunt for Cain?"

Alexis chose that moment to make her appearance. "Hey, Sabina? You got any of that bagged blood Erron scored?"

I covered the mouthpiece to answer her, but Giguhl jumped up.

"I'll grab it." While he went to the fridge, Alexis took the last spot at the table.

I uncovered the phone to rejoin the conversation with Georgia. "Sorry about that. We've made some progress with Cain, but some new complications have popped up."

"Who was that?" Georgia asked.

"That was Alexis, actually. You remember her from New York?"

"Yeah, I remember. She's the bitchy one who worked for Tanith, right?"

My lips twitched at her accurate description. "Yeah."

"Why is she there?"

I paused, weighing my answer. I'd told Georgia she couldn't help with the mission because we didn't need more bodies complicating things, but now I was about to tell her Alexis had joined the crew. "Queen Maeve and Rhea sent her to take point on a side errand they needed done." I could have explained about Persephone, but that would have taken more time than I had once Georgia started asking the inevitable questions. Plus, the answer I gave was close enough to the truth with the added bonus of assuaging Georgia's ego.

"Well, I hope you're all staying safe. Or as safe as is possible when you're tracking down a psycho."

I chuckled. "We're all okay. How are you doing?" I asked carefully.

"Better. I promoted Brooks to bar manager at Lagniappe."

"That's great, Georgia. He'll be a huge help."

She sighed. "It's only until I figure out what to do next."

"You don't have to make any final decisions yet. It's only been a few days."

"It's true. We've got Gender Bender night in a couple of days, so Brooks and the queens have been having dress rehearsals after hours." She yawned into the phone. "I've been so busy I haven't had time to think about Mac."

A couple of minutes later, I ended my call with Georgia. Before she hung up, she promised to keep trying to track down Nyx's trail. While I appreciated her optimism, I didn't expect she'd come up with anything useful. Whoever this Nyx really was she obviously hadn't wanted anyone keeping tabs on her over the years.

I leaned back in my chair and tossed the phone onto the table.

"No news?" Adam asked.

I shook my head. "Nothing useful."

"So," Alexis said, polishing off her bag of blood, "what time do we head out?"

I glanced at the windows. The gray hues of evening had descended over the city, but brilliant orange streaks still flashed on the horizon. "As soon as it's full dark."

Alexis took a second bag of blood from the refrigerator. "Where is Persephone staying?" She pierced the silicone with her fangs and started gulping. Adam watched her with a look of distaste. He might be more comfortable with the idea of me taking his own blood, but I guess watching Alexis gulp down cold type O neg wasn't the most appetizing sight.

I ignored him and wrote down the address on a pad. "I've been thinking, and I'd feel a lot better if Erron went with you."

"Why?" Alexis demanded.

"Because that way if there's trouble, he can flash you out."

She laughed, exposing her blood-tinged fangs. "Sabina, don't be ridiculous. I think I can handle myself."

"What if Cain decides to use you to get to Sabina?" Adam pointed out.

"I'll kill him." Alexis shrugged.

"Not possible. Remember?"

"Shit," Alexis said. "Okay, fine. I'll take the Recreant with me. But he better stay out of my way. This is vampire business."

"Trust me, he may look like a slacker," Adam said, "but I trust him to get my back when shit goes down."

Alexis glanced at me for confirmation. "It's true. He's a great wingman."

"That's good enough for me," Alexis said, surprising me. When we'd worked together in New York, she'd spent most of her time questioning my skills and accusing me of losing my edge. But I guess we'd made more progress than I thought.

"All right," Giguhl said, clapping his claws. "Who's ready to go meet Sabina's dad?"

Tourists swarmed across the Spanish Steps like hungry ants. In the piazza below the steps, the lights of the Fontana della Barcaccia glowed on the eager faces of those who tossed pennies into the blue waters hoping for a blessing from Poseidon.

The public location should have added a measure of safety, but I was anxious. I suppose some nerves were understandable given I was about to meet my father for the first time. But this wasn't your average family reunion. Especially when I expected Cain to swoop in like that creepy uncle no one ever wanted to invite.

Adam lounged on the steps. He'd purchased gelato from a cart in the square and nibbled at it while staring meditatively into the fountain. Despite his fairly convincing ruse, his shoulders were tense and his gaze alert. Meanwhile, Giguhl, in cat form, crouched in a tree on the balcony level below me, ready to get my back should the need arise.

I stood high above them in the upper piazza in front of the Trinità dei Monti church. I'd chosen the location because of the obelisk that rose at my back, preventing a rear attack. Plus, from this vantage point, I could see the entire steps, the plaza below, as well as the Keats-Shelley House on the left.

After standing in the cold until half past eight, I wondered if Tristan changed his mind. But just as I was about to call the mission, he arrived.

It wasn't that he stood out in the crowd. Quite the opposite. Among the hunched shoulders, heavy winter coats, and hats of the mortals at the base of the steps, he fit right in. In fact, he blended too well. Instead, it was the overpowering punch in my gut that warned me a real magical threat entered the vicinity. The power vibrated in my molars and made my hackles rise like tiny daggers.

I rose to my full height, raised my chin, and stayed put. If he was making me jump through hoops to get this meeting, he could come to me. He might know more about me than I did about him, but I'd be damned if his first impression of me had any hint of vulnerability.

He'd made it past Adam and had begun his ascent up the steps. As if compelled, the crowd between us parted. Time slowed. Wind picked up the edges of his black coat, which flew out around him like black wings. His pace was confident, unhurried as he climbed. Deliberate. A black hat cast shadows over his face, revealing only a strong jaw and lips set into a hard line.

Closer now. My pulse ratcheted up with each step he took. A wide circle of power surrounded him and reached me well before his body did. Several steps behind him, Adam kept pace with his movements. Far enough back not to raise alarm but close enough to intervene. A flash of gray in my peripheral told me Giguhl had taken position as well. I kept my gaze on Tristan and prayed they wouldn't jump the gun and spook him off.

Even if I wanted to look away, I couldn't. Whether he held me in his thrall through magical means or he was really that magnetic, I couldn't tell. Didn't matter because my eyes couldn't, wouldn't, leave him.

He made it to the top of the stairs and started my way. His chin tipped down, but I could feel his gaze like a spotlight. But then he stopped short. Utterly still and alert. There was no sense of him hesitating or doubting his next move. Instead, I felt more like I was being judged. Weighed and measured. I stayed still, not wanting to betray one hint of insecurity.

You'd better be worth all this fucking drama, I thought silently at him.

That hard mouth quirked, as if he'd read my mind. He moved forward, his pace determined. My knees locked and a cold chill passed over me that felt a lot like fear.

It's not every day a girl meets her father for the first time.

He pulled off his hat, revealing a head of thick black hair and piercing blue eyes.

I gasped. He looked exactly like the painting I'd seen of him in the library at the mage compound in New York.

It really was Tristan Graecus. My father was alive. Gods help me.

I opened my mouth to say...something, but a frigid wind rushed through the piazza. Tristan froze, lifted his chin, as if sniffing the air like a predator tensed for flight... or fight.

His head jerked toward me. "I told you to trust no one."

My first instinct was to get defensive and tell the guy off. What kind of idiot did he think I was to expect me to come here without backup? I put my hands on my hips. "I—"

Before I could say more, he grabbed my arm and pulled me toward the street. At first, I was too shocked to resist, but then my brain started working again. I dug my heels in. "Wait just a damned minute," I yelled.

He paused to shoot me an icy glare. "Cain is here," he hissed.

I jerked my gaze toward the piazza. It took only a second for my eyes to spot the fire-engine-red head at the base of the steps. Emerald-green eyes flashed with recognition. A snake smile spread across full lips.

Cain.

"Fuck!" My stomach dropped like it had been pitched from the top of St. Peter's Basilica.

"Giguhl!" I shouted. "Go help Adam."

The cat sped off down the steps, winding through people's legs. Adam, meanwhile, was running up, his gaze flicking between Cain and me.

"We've got to go!" Tristan urged, pulling me.

I jerked my arm from his grasp. "No! I'm not leaving my friends."

"You're who he wants."

While we argued, my eyes were on Cain's progress. He moved in an unhurried manner, like a man out for a stroll. But despite the languorous pace, his intent was clear. Cain was coming for me.

"My people are down there, too. They'll aid your friends."

As he spoke, I finally noticed a redhead, a male with a ponytail, break free from the crowd. Nearby, a willowy blonde wearing brown leggings and a green tunic wound her way toward Cain, too. The male had vampire written all over him, and the female was most likely fae.

Before they reached Cain, Adam came up behind the father of vampires and threw a small black bag at him. The bag bounced off of Cain's head and erupted into a small puff of black smoke. He whipped around to see who'd attacked him, but Adam had already disappeared.

I searched the crowd for signs of the mancy. He waved at me from ten steps below and mouthed, *Go!*

That was all the permission Tristan needed. He grabbed me again and we took off running like the hounds of hell were chomping at our feet. I was surprised he didn't just flash us out.

The last thing I saw before we exited the area was Cain dancing down the steps like a crazy man. His jerky movements told me that Zen's vexing spell was already working its magic. But it wouldn't last long.

"Where are we going?" I wasn't having trouble keeping up with Tristan's pace, but I needed answers.

"Safer ground. Faster!"

Like rats in a maze, we wound our way through the narrow Roman streets, dodging tourists and cars. Eventually, we burst out of the narrow streets and into the Piazza Barberini. The enormous Trevi Fountain loomed over the square. The lights from inside the water up-lit the faces of the stone gods, giving them an ominous appearance. Tristan ran straight through the piazza and turned onto Via Veneto.

Just past the piazza, he slowed and veered right to a small church. By this point, my legs burned from exertion and I was thankful for the respite. Tristan tossed a few euros at the outraged monk standing at the door as he pushed me through it.

"Where are we?" I whispered.

"The crypt of Santa Maria della Concezione," he said in a clipped tone.

The chapel itself was pretty standard, but below it was the creepiest tomb in Christendom. But I didn't know all that when I followed him in.

All I knew at that moment was that the instant I crossed the threshold into the crypt, every synapse in my body flared. The low-level vibration that usually hit me when I entered a cemetery exploded into a full-on shock, like I'd shoved my finger in a light socket. I stopped and placed a hand on the wall for support.

"Let's go," Tristan said, nudging me.

"Give me a second," I gritted out, my eyelids shut tight. I was incapable of moving while my body adjusted to the onslaught of energy. I swallowed and tried to get a hold of my galloping pulse.

"What's wrong with you?"

I opened my eyes to look at him. My vision was tinged black. "It's the crypt. The energy—"

Tristan shot me a confused look, like he didn't understand why the place would be affecting me. Which was odd since he was also a Chthonic. I could tell by the tightening of his jaw and the increased pulse of his power that the energy was affecting him, too. But before I could comment, I realized that my hand was not resting on a normal wall. The surface was both smooth and rough, like stone, but it most definitely was not stone.

Hollow eye sockets and a skeletal mouth grinned back at me. I jerked my hand away from the skull.

My breath caught in my chest. I scanned the room. Every surface in the small chamber was covered in bones. Thousands of skulls, femurs, and assorted other remains were laid out in a macabre mosaic. Full skeletons clad in brown monk's robes reclined in niches along the walls. "What the fuck?" I whispered.

"Come on," Tristan urged, grabbing my hand to pull me farther in.

The going was slow. Death tugged at me like a black

hole. We made it through a few more rooms—each filled with more bones than I could count—before stopping in the final chamber.

This place was clearly the altar room. Only instead of a pretty brocade altar cloth or golden chalices, the altar was decorated with browned bones and grinning skulls. The macabre decorator hadn't even spared the ceiling from the creepy décor. Up there, the bones formed a clock with hands made out of... well, actual hands. Over the altar there was a saying in Latin I couldn't translate, but I figured given the rest of the décor I probably didn't want to know.

Tristan rounded on me. His cheeks were ruddy and his chest heaved from exertion. "Now we can flash out."

"Wait!" I yelled, reaching toward him. He paused with his arms above his head. Suddenly, words escaped me. While I'd chased him, a million questions had filtered through my mind. But now, staring into the face of the man who was supposed to help me, I was overcome with doubts.

"Where are you taking me?"

"Out of the city. It's not safe here for you."

I shook my head. "No way. Not without Adam and Giguhl."

He made a disgusted sound. "My people will bring your little friends along."

I held up a hand. "No offense, but I don't know you or your people. We're not going anywhere with any of you until you give me some answers."

Under the brim of his hat, his mouth set into a grim line. "There is time for answers later. Now we need to get some-place safe."

I held up my hands to indicate the crypt. "We're safe right now. It's just you, me, and a bunch of dead monks."

"Fine." Tristan crossed his arms. The move made his

robes gape, revealing a silver amulet bearing the sword and chalice symbol that had been on the velvet bag at Dicky's. "What do you want to know?"

I scrambled to think of a good question, but so many words jockeyed for position on my tongue that I couldn't sort through the alphabet soup. Finally I settled with, "Shouldn't you be dead?"

He laughed, a hard, bitter sound. "Several beings certainly think so."

My confusion morphed into anger. It wasn't the most eloquent question ever, but I deserved a real answer. My hands and voice shook. "This isn't a joke. If you've been alive all this time, why haven't I met you before now?"

He shrugged. "It wasn't the time."

I raised my arms. "But now is? That's convenient."

"I'm sure it's a shock, Maisie—"

The name slammed into me like a shock from a live wire. "Sabina."

He froze. "What?"

I crossed my arms defensively. "I said, my name is Sabina."

He frowned. "Where's your twin?"

My mouth fell open. Guess dear old dad didn't know as much as he thought. "She's dead."

His face paled. "How is that possible?"

I raised a brow and pointed back toward the direction of the Spanish Steps. "How do you think? Cain killed her right after he forced her to release him from your spell."

Tristan swayed back like I'd struck him. "So that's how it happened."

I ignored his shock and forged ahead. "Speaking of, how did you survive that, anyway? I figured Cain would have killed you the instant he woke."

Tristan stared up at the ceiling. Either he was praying or looking for the answers among the skulls. In a distracted tone, he answered. "I wasn't there when he woke. He killed six of my people and razed our safe house to the ground."

I frowned. "If he killed your people, who are the ones back there?"

"I have a lot of people. Or I did, anyway," he said in an offhand tone. "Are you certain Maisie's dead?"

I stared at him. Was this guy for real? Who would joke about something like that. "Of course I'm sure."

"How did you get past Dicky, then? I gave him clear instructions to only give the message to the daughter with twin birthmarks."

I turned and pulled my shirt aside to show him my back. "You mean these?"

He made a noise that was a cross between a gasp and a prayer. "What? How did you get those?"

"Look, dude, I'm not sure why you're so upset, but it's a long story and I'm not—"

"You're not her," he interrupted. "This won't work."

I paused. Was he drunk or just crazy? "What won't work?" I asked slowly.

He stood straighter, like he'd made a decision. "Go back to America."

I couldn't have been more shocked if he'd struck me. "What? Why would I do that? We need to stop Cain."

He shook his head and his expression was filled with regret. "We can't."

I fell silent for a moment. He simply watched me. Finally I said, "Why not?"

"Because only the Chosen can kill Cain."

My stomach cramped at the mention of the C word, but I wasn't following him. "Yeah, and? I'm her."

"Sabina, I'm sorry but, no, you're not. Maisie was the Chosen."

"That's crazy. Maisie said I was the Chosen. She had a vision and everything." The irony of arguing that I was the Chosen when I'd spent so much time claiming I wanted nothing to do with that prophecy wasn't lost on me. But if this was the only way to convince Tristan to help me get revenge against Cain, I'd do it.

"She was wrong. Maisie was the Chosen. She was the only one who could kill Cain." His tone was totally lacking in hope. It made my skin go cold and my palms sweat.

"But surely there's something we can do—"

He slashed a hand through the air. "There's no we," he snapped. "If you stay in Italy, you'll just become another liability."

His words were like bullets, taking me out at the knees. Equilibrium fled and I groped behind me for purchase. My hand grasped a skull that broke free from the wall and crumbled in my hand.

"Leave Rome, Sabina," Tristan said, his tone quiet. "Good-bye."

With that, my father flashed out of the crypt of bones, leaving me behind like a dumped corpse.

Adam and Giguhl found me in the chamber five minutes later. I sat on the edge of a niche doing a bad impression of one of the drooping skeleton monks.

"Sabina?" Adam knelt in front of me and grabbed my hands. "Tell me."

"Get me out of here first."

Adam frowned but rose from his crouch and held out a hand to help me up. My fingers trembled in his palm. If he noticed it, he didn't say anything. Most likely, he sensed I was on the edge of losing it.

"Giguhl?" Adam said.

The cat crouched on the ground, looking up at the ceiling. "What does that say?"

Adam sighed and translated the Latin phrase over the altar. " 'What you are now, we once were; what we are now, you will be.' "

The cat turned toward us with wide eyes and shivered. "This place is freaking awesome!"

"We need to go," I said, my voice rising.

The panic I'd been holding back rushed up like bile. It mixed with the stench of death and the black energy vibrating around us until I felt like I was drowning.

Through the rising terror, one thought kept circling my head like a shark.

I am a failure.

"All right," Adam said. "Let's go. We'll sort all this out when we get back to the hotel."

He put his arm around me. For once, his sandalwood scent and warmth didn't reach me. I felt cold and hollow and detached. I just wanted to go sit in a dark room alone and never speak again. I wanted to vacate my head and never think again. I wanted to disappear.

When I didn't answer him, Adam exchanged a tense look with Giguhl. But neither spoke. They just circled around my mute form and flashed us out of the room where all my hope had died.

When we flashed back to the penthouse, I'd been hoping to find a quiet place to fall apart in private. But, as usual, fate didn't care about what I wanted.

Alexis bent over the sofa, her back to us. When we flashed in, she spun around, looking panicked. Adam gasped. Giguhl cursed. And I blinked at the blood coating her face, chest, and arms.

"What the hell?" Adam demanded.

With a grim expression, she stepped aside. Erron lay on the couch. Where his chest used to be, a mass of bloody wounds formed a gruesome bull's-eye.

Adam rushed forward. "Is he dead?" he demanded, kneeling next to Erron's unconscious form.

"Not yet," Alexis said. "I've slowed the bleeding, but I don't know what to do next."

"Sabina," Adam called.

I stayed where I was. Shock cushioned me from the reality of the scene. I was like a spectral observer to the drama, not a participant.

"Red! Now!" Adam shouted.

I jerked as the comforting veil of numbness fell away like shattered glass. Alexis looked at me with a worried expression. Giguhl wound through my legs, a comforting presence. A reminder that despite my own problems, bigger ones needed my attention. I cleared my throat and joined Adam at the couch.

"What happened?" I said in a clipped tone. Adrenaline surged and offered its own kind of comfort.

"We showed up at the address a few minutes after sundown. Persephone and Chiara were directing their people to load up their cars. When we approached, Persephone became combative. Said we needed to leave."

While she talked, I started counting gunshot wounds.

"I tried to talk to her calmly, but she wasn't listening. A few minutes later, a gang of vampires showed up on scooters. It was the weirdest thing."

By that point, I'd counted six wounds. "That was Damiano and his gang. They work for Chiara."

"We didn't get a chance for introductions because they attacked us," Alexis continued. "Luckily they were using mundane guns or I'd be toast. Unfortunately, Erron got the worst of it. He didn't even get a chance to use defensive magic when the first bullet hit him."

When I got to ten, I looked up at Adam. "Can you fix this?"

He shook his head, his face pale. Because Erron was a Recreant mage, his ability to heal himself had been stripped by the Hekate Council. Not that he was capable of any magic in his unconscious state.

"How'd you get out?" Giguhl asked.

"I shielded him. With me distracted, the vampires rounded up Persephone and Chiara and drove off."

"That's strange," Adam said. "Why would they attack

you guys? Persephone knows you. Surely she wouldn't think you were there to harm her?"

"Chiara's goons didn't know us, though. Maybe they saw us as a threat and decided Persephone needed defending."

I frowned up at him. "Wait. Are you saying Persephone didn't give the order to attack? Or Chiara?"

Alexis shook her head. "No. We were talking to both of the females when the other vampires arrived. They didn't speak to the Domina or the Donna. They just started shooting."

"We can puzzle that part out later," Adam said. "In the meantime, Sabina and I need to do a healing spell on Erron STAT or we'll lose him."

I looked up quickly. On some level, I knew the healing ritual was our only chance to save Erron. But on another other level, I was worried that I couldn't do it. Despite being grateful for the distraction from my own worries, my head still felt all out of whack. "Adam, I don't think—"

He put a hand on my arm and squeezed. "There's no time, Red. We've got to do this or we'll lose him."

I took a deep breath and nodded. "Let's hurry, then."

Alexis looked out of her depth. Not a surprise since, as a vampire, her own wounds had healed on their own. "What can I do?" she asked.

"Stay out of our way," I said. "And pray."

Giguhl carried Erron to the bedroom with the mancy and I following. "What do you need?" the demon asked once he set the Recreant on the bed.

I wracked my brain, trying to remember all the tools I'd need to re-create the healing spell I'd done with Rhea months earlier on Brooks after he'd been attacked by a secret cult. "See if you can find candles, preferably blue and purple. Then go to the roof and see if you can get me some sprigs of lavender and sage."

"Got it!" Giguhl ran off, his hooves pounding against the floors.

"I've got salt in my backpack," Adam said. He rushed over to grab the container of the special salt he always carried for drawing circles. It came from the Dead Sea and had been blessed by his aunt Rhea in a special invocation. Powerful stuff, which was good because we'd need all the help we could get.

He rushed over and set the container next to the bed. "Red?"

"Yeah?" I was busy stripping Erron's shirt off his bloodied chest.

"When was the last time you fed?"

I shook my head distractedly. "Back in New Orleans."

"You need to feed now or you won't have the strength to carry out the ritual."

I looked up at him then. "But if I feed from you, you'll be weak, too."

He held my eyes, but when he spoke, it was to call out to the living room. "Alexis?"

My stomach dropped. "No."

Alexis appeared at the door. "What's up?"

"You got any of that blood left over from this morning?"

"No, why?"

I shook my head urgently at Adam. I didn't exactly have time for an attack of conscience, yet it reared up like a beast. Adam was the only living being I'd fed from for months. While Alexis and I were in no danger of being attracted to each other, the act of taking blood from another vampire—male or female—was just too . . . intimate.

Besides, Alexis Vega was not someone I wanted to owe a debt.

"Sabina needs blood," Adam said.

"No," I said, shaking my head. "I'll be fine."

Just then, Giguhl ran through the door, brushing past a shocked Alexis. The demon juggled several candles, sprigs of herbs, and matches. He set everything down on the side of the bed before he clued into the tension in the room.

"Uh-oh. What happened?" he demanded.

"Adam just asked me to share my blood with Sabina." Alexis looked shell-shocked.

"Oh shit," Giguhl said, his goat eyes wide. "Can I watch?"

I crossed my arms. "No, because it's not going to happen."

"Sabina—" Adam started, but I slashed a hand through the air.

Giguhl scooted close. I looked up at him, an idea forming in my head. It was crazy but far preferable to the alternative.

I looked right into his goat-slit eyes. "Will you help me?"

He stood up straighter. I didn't have to explain what I was asking. He knew immediately. The room was silent as everyone waited to hear whether my minion would willingly give me his blood.

A broad smile stretched across his black lips. "Abso-fucking-lutely."

Alexis's breath whooshed out in a relieved rush. "Thank, Christ!" She disappeared through the door like a death-row inmate given a last-minute pardon.

"Okay, let's do this quickly."

Giguhl shifted excitedly from hoof to hoof. "Where do you want to bite me? Neck? Ooh, thigh?"

Maybe this wasn't such a hot idea after all. "Gross, G. How about your wrist?"

He held his arm out immediately. "Be gentle with me."

I licked my lips and nodded. Now that I was staring at his green-scaled wrist, it hit me how enormous this sacrifice was. Even though Giguhl wasn't a vampire, offering someone your blood freely demands an enormous amount of trust. I looked up. "Thanks, Giguhl."

He blushed. "Anytime, trampire."

Erron moaned from the bed. Time to get serious. In a fast movement, I slammed my fangs into Giguhl's wrist.

His blood hit my tongue like liquid fire. It seared a path down my throat and then sizzled through my veins. I moaned over his wrist, struggling against the onslaught of pain. I tried to pull away, but Giguhl's claw held my head to his arm. Then, as quickly as the pain began, it morphed into pure energy. I tasted brimstone on the back of my tongue and something spicy and dark, like turmeric. I swallowed once, twice more before Giguhl released me.

I pulled away with a gasp. My muscles bunched and strained for action. I felt like I could leap a tall building or fly right out the window and never hit the ground. "Holy hell!"

"Aww, yeah." The demon smiled a cocky smile. "My shit is delicious, right?"

I stretched my arms out and jumped up and down a few times to burn off some of the adrenaline. "I wouldn't say delicious exactly, but it's pretty fucking strong. I feel like I could swim across the ocean and still have energy left to build a house by hand."

Adam cleared his throat. "Or perhaps save your friend's life?"

I sobered then. "Right. Sorry. It's just...wow."

"Yes, yes. We all get it. Giguhl's blood is great. Can we get started, please?"

I shot Adam an annoyed look. If it had been up to him, I would have been sucking Alexis's bitter vein right then, so he had no reason to be jealous that Giguhl's blood was so powerful. I patted him on the arm. "Don't worry. I still prefer your blood."

He pursed his lips. "I'm so relieved."

Giguhl punched Adam in the arm. "Mancy, please, green is so not your color."

Adam grimaced and rubbed his bicep. "Shut it, demon boy."

Giguhl clicked his tongue. "Touchy, touchy."

I clapped my hands together, feeling better than I had in weeks. "All righty, then. Let's save us a life."

The candles were the only light in the room. Our breaths the only sounds. Adam clasped my hands over Erron's body. His warm hands slicked over my clammy palms. I winked at him with a confidence I didn't feel and started chanting.

"Goddess Hekate, Mother of Magic and Night Queen, raise your torch, that your light may illuminate the path toward healing. Open our vision and protect your humble servant so he may live to carry out your will."

We closed our eyes and focused our breathing.

With my third eye, I looked deep inside myself. Below the angry black power that coalesced in my diaphragm. Down to the deeper pool of more powerful energy. The powers of the moon. Hekate's power. I called up additional Chthonic forces through the floorboards. It pierced the soles of my bare feet and climbed my legs. Curled up my torso and into my chest. Melded with my inherent magic. Grew, swirled, danced up my throat.

Magic surged from me. Everything was tinted a bloody red, but my vision was sharper with black halos around the edges. Probably a result of the demon blood zinging through my veins. My skin tingled where it touched Adam's. His lids fluttered open. The pupils had overtaken his irises until his eyes looked like onyx marbles.

The instant our hands touched, a second wave of power slammed through my palms. I allowed the powers to equalize before I continued chanting.

"We unite to pour healing into this broken vessel. We unite to absorb his pain. We..." I nodded to Adam to pick up the chant. Soon his deep voice added a powerful bass.

"To pour healing into this broken vessel. We..."

The cone of power rising above our joined hands condensed and began to stream into Erron's body. His shoulders lifted from the bed as his body rose to receive the healing energy. At the same time, a second ribbon of energy—darker, thicker, and tinged smoky black—escaped Erron's ravaged body and split into two streams.

My stomach lurched against the pain we absorbed from the Recreant. Breathing deeply through my nose, I struggled to control the two opposing flows of energy. Cold sweat covered my skin.

I clenched my teeth against the strain of wielding such massive power. The bullets had forged a destructive trail, slashing intestines and embedding in bone and tissue. Healing those wounds took an enormous amount of energy that left me trembling.

Eventually, the bullets popped one by one from Erron's skin and rolled to the bedspread. The blood poured out thickly at first but soon slowed to trickles.

Adam's hands tightened on mine. Dark and light energy flowed through us, around us, between us. Until finally, a single clean stream of energy ran through us into Erron and back again, creating a circuit of healing.

I blew out a long, slow breath from deep in my belly. With it, I released the powers I'd called up from the goddess. As I did so, I said a silent prayer of thanks for her aid. I blinked and found my vision had returned to normal. Adam's gaze was green again and relieved. A ghost of a smile hovered on his lips.

"You did it."

"We did it." He squeezed my fingers one final time before releasing them. Then we both looked down at Erron.

It was hard to tell how many of his more superficial wounds had healed through the dried blood. However, his breathing had deepened and slowed, like a man enjoying a good night's sleep, instead of the shallow, rapid gasps of earlier.

Tears stung my eyes. Relief, not sadness. "I think he'll live," I whispered.

"Thank the gods," Giguhl said from the corner of the room.

I tilted my head and looked at my friend. "It's you who needs to be thanked. I couldn't have done it without you." I glanced at Adam, too. "Both of you."

Giguhl shot me a get-real look. "Bullshit. You're stronger than you admit to yourself. By the way, thank you for asking me to help. It means a lot."

"Of course. Erron's your friend, too."

"No, I meant"—the demon shook his head—"I meant it means a lot that you asked. You could have just commanded me to give you my blood."

The mood in the room shifted, creating a vacuum that sucked away all the easy banter and replaced it with something more sincere and, frankly, awkward.

"I'll just go tell Alexis how it went." Adam shot me a wink before he exited.

I was too busy avoiding Giguhl's eyes to smile back. "Oh...um...sure." I self-consciously wiped my hands on my jeans.

The demon cleared his throat and busied himself covering Erron with a blanket. Part of me was relieved he didn't pursue that conversational path any further. I'd never felt entirely comfortable with the idea that Giguhl was mine to command. I mean, sure, I didn't hesitate to boss him around when I needed him or when his infamous knack for causing trouble landed one or the both of us in hot water. But I tried not to abuse that power. However, despite my own misgivings, Giguhl rarely complained about being ordered around.

I hesitated. Was that true, though? I thought about all the times he'd bitched when I forced him to change into his cat form because I needed him in a convenient carrying size or when I needed someone tiny to do reconnaissance. I'd always blown that off as Giguhl just being snarky. But maybe I'd been ignoring his distress because it wasn't convenient to admit that it was unfair.

"Um, G?" I said. I cleared my throat.

He looked up. "Yeah?"

"I'm sorry if I ever made you feel like I don't take you seriously. You're...you're really important to me."

Giguhl stood up straighter, as if I'd finally managed to shock him. "Thanks." He nodded and moved toward the door, but just before he walked through it, he paused. "Sabina?"

I looked up. "Yeah?"

He paused. "You, um, have some blood on your chin."

With that, my red-faced best friend ducked through the door before either of us could embarrass ourselves further.

13

$\mathcal{E}$rron's vitals have stabilized," Alexis was saying to the computer screen. "We expect a full recovery once he wakes up."

We were in front of the laptop again, giving Rhea and the Queen an update. The only one missing was Erron, who was still sleeping, but he had a good excuse. Given the extent of the wounds and the complexity of the healing ritual, he'd be out for a good long time. However, last time we'd checked on him, his color was better and his pulse was strong and stable.

As for the meeting, we'd begun with a review of what happened with Persephone. I was grateful that Alexis handled that part because I was using the extra time to decide how to address my own news.

"Well, thank the gods Erron will be okay," Rhea said. "Sabina, I'm proud you used the healing ritual on your own." The last time I'd used it, Rhea had led the way, adding her own impressive powers to the spell.

"I couldn't have done it without Adam and Giguhl. I'm just glad we were here. If Erron had been alone..." I trailed off, not wanting to say what we were all thinking.

The Queen cleared her throat, signaling an abrupt subject change. "And what news of your meeting tonight, Sabina?"

I shifted uneasily in my seat. With all the craziness surrounding Erron's situation, I hadn't even had a chance to tell the others the full story of what happened.

"The good news—if you can call it that—is that we were right. Abel really is Tristan Graecus. I knew it the moment I saw him. He looks just like that painting in the library at Prytania Place, Rhea, except he's got some crow's-feet now."

Rhea's hand covered her mouth. "Praise the gods, he's still alive."

"Miracle number two," Adam said under his breath.

I ignored that because the next thing I had to report canceled out the miraculous bit. "The first bad news is that Cain showed up at the meeting." I looked at Adam to fill in his part of that tale.

"Luckily, between Tristan's people and Giguhl and me, we managed to hold him off."

"Tristan's people?" Rhea asked.

Giguhl nodded. "A vampire and a faery from what I could tell. We didn't speak to them, but we all kind of worked together to run him off. Once Cain ran away, they disappeared."

Rhea frowned. "Magically?"

Adam shook his head. "More like highly trained operatives."

"Any idea why Cain gave up so easily?" the Queen asked.

"Zen's vexing spell helped," Giguhl chimed in. "Remind me not to get on her bad side. That voodoo queen is dangerous!"

"It's true. The spell helped." Adam leaned forward on his elbows. "However, my theory is that his goal was intimidation instead of confrontation. Once Sabina and Tristan ran off, he gave up pretty quickly in his pursuit."

"Any idea how he knew about the meeting?" Rhea asked.

We all shook our heads. "No one outside this room on our end," Adam said. "I assume Tristan and his people didn't tell anyone, either. They were as shocked as we were to see him there."

"He's most likely got someone watching you."

I nodded. "I'd all but guarantee he does."

"So why hasn't he made a move and tried to get in here, then?" Alexis asked.

"Erron's and Adam's wards," I said. "No one's getting in here who they don't approve."

"Sabina, what happened after you and Tristan ran away?" Rhea asked.

I blew out a big breath. Moment of truth time. I felt their collective gazes and the weight of their expectations on my shoulders like anvils. So much was riding on my answer, and I was acutely aware how much I was about to disappoint them.

"That's the other bad news. When Tristan set up the meeting, he apparently thought he was going to meet Maisie."

Rhea made a distressed sound. "Why would he think that?"

I shrugged. "I guess he isn't as well informed about what's been going on as he thought. When I told him Maisie was dead, he got really upset."

"Understandable," Adam murmured. "She was his daughter."

I shot him a get-real look. "No, it wasn't that at all. He was upset because..." Here went nothing. "He seems to be under the impression that Maisie was the Chosen."

"What?" Rhea shouted.

Next to me, Adam jerked like he'd been shocked by a light socket.

I nodded and held up a hand. "It gets worse, I'm afraid. Not only was Maisie supposed to be the Chosen, but he also said the only person who could kill Cain was—"

"Let me guess," Giguhl said in a defeated tone. "The Chosen?"

I grimaced. "After he dropped that bombshell, he told me to leave Rome because I'd only be in his way."

Rhea crossed her arms. "Excuse me, but that's bullshit."

"Amen, sister," Giguhl said.

"My sentiments exactly," Adam said.

I appreciated their support, but it was misguided. "Guys, listen," I said, "I showed him the birthmarks. I even told him Maisie herself had a vision that I was the Chosen, but he wouldn't listen. Apparently he's got good reason to believe that when Maisie died, any chance of killing Cain died with her."

A hush fell over the meeting. I sat back in my chair, exhausted. Even Giguhl's potent blood in my veins couldn't dull the pain of letting everyone down.

The Queen spoke first. She'd been uncharacteristically quiet during my recounting of the event with my father, but now she had plenty to say. "In my opinion, we have two choices. Either we assume Tristan knows what he's talking about and trust that he has the resources to handle the situation. After all, he's got his own team and has proven he's capable of at least subduing Cain."

"And the other option?" Adam asked.

"We trust that Maisie, the *Oracle*, knew what she was talking about and that Tristan's intel is flawed. This scenario would, of course, require Sabina proving to her prodigal father that she is the Chosen." She smiled mischievously. "But, well, we all know how much Sabina hates confrontation."

"Please, like that reverse psychology bullshit is going to work." I rolled my eyes. "Maybe Tristan's right. Maybe we should head home and just circle the wagons."

The Queen raised a brow. "I'm surprised you're so quick to accept defeat."

I slammed my hands on the desk. "What do you want from me? He told me to leave Rome. He doesn't want my help."

Rhea raised a brow. "Since when do you ever listen when someone tells you no?"

I flopped back against the back of my chair and crossed my arms. "I don't even know where to find him."

"We found him once," Giguhl said.

"It's true," Adam said, shooting me an apologetic look.

"Sabina," Rhea said, "I want you to listen to me. I don't care what Tristan said. I believe in my bones, right down to the marrow, that you are the Chosen. But even if Tristan is right and you're not, there is no one else on this planet who I would trust to deal with Cain more than you and Adam and Giguhl. Forget the question about the Chosen and focus on the mission: Stop Cain."

I swallowed hard. She was right. I let my emotional reaction to Tristan's rejection muddy the waters. Renewed determination had me clenching my fists. "Okay, you're all right. Of course we won't give up."

"That's my girl," Adam said, rubbing my back.

Rhea winked at me. "I know you'll give 'im hell."

"Sure. Just have to find him first."

"In the meantime, I suggest you help Alexis locate Persephone."

"Is it really that important now?" Adam asked. "After all, she clearly doesn't want to return. And if we don't stop Cain, it won't matter who's in charge of the vampire race—or any race for that matter."

The Queen's cane banged against the floor. "Of course it matters."

Rhea grimaced. "She's right. There's been some… developments on the vampire front."

"Uh-oh," Giguhl said. "That doesn't sound good."

"While we were waiting on word from you about the meeting, we asked Slade to inform the Undercouncil about recent developments," the Queen said. "We figured if Persephone ultimately couldn't be convinced, we needed to prepare for next steps."

"Meaning, finding a suitable replacement?" Alexis asked.

Rhea and the Queen nodded.

"I don't understand," Adam said. "Doesn't the vampire government have some sort of succession rules in place in case something like this happens?"

Rhea shook her head. "It's confusing because once Tanith took over, she changed the system. Used to be there were three Dominae and if one of them died, the position would pass to the highest-ranking blood relative from the pool of Dominae offspring. But once Tanith made herself Despina, she became the sole leader. Since she didn't have any children, her new law was going to allow the vampires to vote on her successor in a general election."

This news shocked me. I'd never really bought Tanith's claims about wanting to form a more democratic vampire government. Guess I should have given her more credit. "That's surprising, but good, right?"

"It would have been positive"—Rhea grimaced—"if the Undercouncil had ever ratified the changes before she died. She fast-tracked being named Despina, but all the other legal amendments were delayed until after she could get the treaty signed. But of course that never happened."

My stomach clenched. "Wait," I said. "Are you saying that the lines of succession are still on the books?"

The Queen nodded and watched me carefully.

"Does Persephone have any children?" Adam asked, his voice rising.

"There were rumors of a daughter, but as far as I know, they were just gossip," Alexis said. "Sabina, do you know anything about that?"

All the blood left my face. "I heard the rumors, but as far as I knew, Lavinia forbade the other Domina from reproducing. She didn't want to chance one of them overthrowing her and sticking their own offspring in her place."

"She could do that?" Rhea frowned.

I tilted my head and raised a brow. "Please. This was Lavinia Kane we're talking about."

"Right," Rhea said with a sigh.

"So that means Lavinia was the only Domina with a bloodline to pull from?" Alexis asked, shooting me a speculative glance.

"As far as we know." Rhea shot me an apologetic look.

Giguhl put a claw on my shoulder. "Does this mean we have to call you Domina now?"

Adam watched me like one would watch a timer on a bundle of explosives. They all did. But I was too shocked to react at first. I froze to the spot, as if not moving might somehow make the moment not real.

"Sabina?" Adam whispered. "You okay?"

I didn't answer. On some level, one so deep that I wasn't

anywhere close to enjoying it, the irony of the situation was somewhat amusing. But the truth was, I was so busy scrambling to figure a way out of this that I didn't have the ability to find anything funny. It was too ridiculous to even contemplate.

Even if I wanted the position, which I absolutely did not, the mere idea that the vampire race would accept a half-breed as their leader wasn't funny at all—it was deadly. Especially since besides being a mixed-blood, I also used to make my living killing vampires who pissed off the Dominae. Vampires would be lining up to assassinate me if I was crazy enough to consider taking over the race.

"Okay," I said finally, "clearly I am not about to step up and claim my birthright. Which means our only option is to put the full-court press on Persephone until she agrees to return."

Adam had remained silent until that point. But the instant I confirmed I had no interest in pursuing taking over the vamps, he visibly relaxed. "Thank the gods."

My mouth fell open in shock. "I can't believe you thought I'd actually do it."

He shrugged. "Well, you were about to accept the role as vampire governor in New York."

Alexis made a sound with her throat that sounded suspiciously like "bitch."

Ugh. I'd forgotten about that. Tanith and Orpheus had ripped control of New York's vamps away from Slade and offered me the position. Alexis had wanted the job and had been furious when Tanith offered it to me instead. "Tanith was trying to force me into that role right before she was murdered. I told her I didn't want any part of it."

"Really?" Adam asked.

"Right," Alexis said, her tone dripping with sarcasm.

She'd been excused from the room before I'd given the Despina and Orpheus my answer.

I crossed my arms. "You can ask Giguhl. He was there."

Everyone looked at the demon for confirmation. "It's true." Giguhl laughed. "She told Tanith she'd rather kiss a snake than work for a Domina."

"Now, that I believe," Adam said. "I have to admit I was having trouble understanding why you'd willingly agree to work for a Domina again."

The irony was, it looked like instead of working for a Domina, I was about to become one myself if we didn't find Persephone.

"Don't worry about all that right now," Rhea said. "Focus on finding Persephone and getting in touch with Tristan. The rest will sort itself out."

But would it? Time had proven that the more faith I put into things working out, the worse the surprises.

A few minutes later, we got off the phone with the Queen and Rhea and got busy on our new plans. Adam offered to call Dicky to see if he'd heard from Tristan while I got on the horn to Damiano. The vampire had given me a small ivory business card before he'd driven off with his little gang. I figured our first step in making nice with Persephone was convincing her goons we didn't mean her any harm.

He answered on the fourth ring. "*Pronto?*"

"Damiano, it's Sabina."

Click.

I pulled the phone away to frown at it. As much as I wanted to believe we'd been accidentally disconnected, I was pretty sure the vampire had really hung up on me.

Highly annoyed now, I called back. This time the phone went to voice mail.

"Damiano, it's Sabina again. I apologize if my friends upset the Domina earlier. But I really need to speak with her. Please call me back. It's important."

Before I could report my failed call to the others, the phone vibrated in my hand. I glanced at the screen and realized it was the same number I'd just called.

"Yes?"

Silence.

"Damiano?"

"Hello, Sabina."

"Persephone?" Relief flooded my limbs. "Thanks goodness. Listen, I'm sorry if there was some confusion earlier. Alexis and Erron just—"

"Enough. I need you to listen to me." Something in her voice wasn't right. I gripped the phone tighter and prepared to receive whatever bad news she was about to share. "Earlier this evening, before your friends visited, Cain paid me a visit. He tried to convince me that you were going to assassinate me."

I gasped. "That's insane. I would never—"

"I know. But that's the reason Damiano attacked Alexis and the mage. I'd told him about Cain's threat and he assumed they worked for him."

"Oh," I said. "Have you heard from Cain again?"

A pause. "No, but it's only a matter of time," she said, talking quickly. "I saw what he did to Tanith, Sabina. He will kill me, too." Her voice rose with a hint of panic. Unusual for a vampire of her status and age. She really was scared and that set me on edge, too.

I blew out a breath. "Okay, I can help you but I need to know where you are."

"No. He could follow you here. If we're going to meet, it needs to be someplace public."

"What do you have in mind?" I glanced at Adam, who had hung up his phone and came to listen on my conversation. He shook his head to indicate that his call to Dicky hadn't netted any new information.

"Tomorrow night there is a carnevale festival in the Piazza del Popolo."

"You're not serious. That'll be a security nightmare."

"Fine. I will leave Rome tonight and you will never get your chance to change my mind."

I gritted my teeth. Gods save me from calculating leaders. "Are you saying there's a possibility I could change it?"

"There's only one way to find out. Tomorrow night, Piazza del Popolo. Nine o'clock."

Click.

I held the phone in my hand for a few seconds longer. I should have felt relieved it had been so easy to get another chance at Persephone. But it was precisely the ease with which it happened that had all my alarms flashing red.

She'd also lied. There was no way Cain could have stopped by to see her before he showed up at the Spanish Steps to spook me. But he could have sent his goons to—

"Holy shit," I breathed, putting it together.

Adam, Alexis, and Giguhl were surrounding me with tense expressions. I set down the phone and turned to give them the news. "Cain has Persephone."

"What!" they all yelled.

"She told you that?" Alexis said.

I shook my head. "No. She tried to tell me he came by tonight to threaten her. Said she was spooked and needed my help. She wants us all to meet her at the Piazza del Popolo tomorrow night."

"I don't get it," Giguhl said. "Why does that tell you Cain has her?"

Alexis crossed her arms and answered for me. "If Cain had visited and it scared her that bad, she would have already left town."

I nodded. "Exactly. But she was definitely spooked, which is why I think Cain manipulated Damiano and his gang into kidnapping Persephone under Alexis's nose. He's blackmailing her to get to me."

Adam frowned. "She's going to sacrifice you to save her life."

I shrugged. "Once a Domina, always a Domina."

Alexis blew out a breath. "So what's our play?"

Everyone looked at me. "Don't look so worried, guys," I said. "This works out perfectly."

Adam crossed his arms. "Red, how in the hell does walking into Cain's trap work on any level?"

"Because we're going to set a trap of our own." I smiled, feeling more hopeful than I had in weeks. Time to change up the game and start calling the shots for a change. "First we're going to capture Cain. And then we're going to blackmail Tristan Graecus into helping us kill him."

That night I dreamed we captured Cain and I was beating the ever-living shit out of him. Best dream I'd had in weeks.

Adam, Giguhl, and I were in the old Demon Fight Club ring in the basement of Slade's club in the Black Light District of New York City. I was straddling Cain's hips while my fists went to town on his face. A crowd circled us, screaming for me to end him.

Just behind me, Adam and Giguhl cheered me on. For some reason that only my subconscious could fathom, they wore outrageously short skirts and shook pom-poms like Dallas Cowboys cheerleaders.

The beauty of beating someone senseless in dreamland is there's no pesky knuckle swelling or broken bones. Just the delectable high, the tasty flavor of just desserts.

Cain spit out teeth like watermelon seeds. His right eye swelled, purple as a plum. The ripe, red strawberry that had been his nose gushed juicy blood. It coated my hands and splashed on my chest, my face. Delicious.

"Sabina, stop!" Adam called.

I looked back. Instead of the ridiculous cheerleading

uniforms, they were back in street clothes, which they accessorized with scowls.

"Don't hurt him." Adam came forward, his hands extended like he was going to pull me away. "We need him."

"Daughter." The word came out muffled and wet, pitiful and pleading.

I swiveled back around to look down and gasped. The male lying under me was no longer Cain. Instead, Tristan lay broken and hurting beneath me. Through the shattered teeth and bloody gums, he slurred, "Mercy."

I fell back onto the stained concrete floor, my mouth working in numb shock. Blood gurgled from his lips.

"Well, well, well," a taunting male voice said behind me. Asclepius stood with his arms crossed. Fucking gods and their bad timing.

My fingers were still cramped into fists. My stomach roiled and burned, like I'd swallowed an acid cocktail. But I rose as gracefully as I could, not wanting to kneel before the god.

Once I faced him eye-to-eye, I realized that while we were still in the fight ring, the crowd had disappeared. So had Adam and Giguhl. A bloodstain on the dirty concrete floor was all that was left of my father.

The god came forward and nudged at the pool of blood with the toe of his sandal. "Has anyone ever suggested that you check into some anger management classes?"

"What do you want?" I snapped. I wiped my forehead with the back of my hand and tried to get my heart rate back to normal.

Asclepius raised a brow. "Surely you haven't forgotten your promise so soon?"

I grimaced. Actually, yeah, I kind of had. But it's not like I could tell him that. "Of course not. Just don't have much to report yet."

"Sabina, I told you I expected you to make a concerted effort to uphold the terms of our bargain."

"And I told you I'd need some time."

"Ah, yes. The Cain situation. Any progress there?"

"Not that it's any of your business, but kind of."

Asclepius threw back his head and laughed. "In other words, you're no closer to stopping him than you were when we last spoke. Pitiful."

I rose slowly. "Look, dude, I've asked around and no one's heard of this Nyx. I'll keep trying, but you're going to have to lay off with the pressure."

"No, you look, girl. I am not some mortal you can boss around. I am a god and my will cannot be ignored."

I rolled my eyes. "Sure, sure."

Asclepius slammed his staff into the floor. The ground shook with the impact. "Do not test me!"

My heart rate picked up. But instead of showing him he'd intimidated me, I raised my chin. "I said I'd get to it. That's the best I can promise right now."

He thought for a moment, rubbing his thick, gray beard methodically. "All right, Sabina Kane. I will give you more time. However, when next we meet, I will expect concrete progress. I want that vest."

"I hear you loud and clear. Trust me, I want my debt to you cleared ASAP."

He nodded. "As do I. I'd wish you luck on finding Cain, but"—he shrugged—"I don't really care." Asclepius waggled his fingers. "Bye now."

The next evening, I called everyone together in the living room to discuss the plan.

"You want me to what now?" Giguhl said, his voice rising.

"It'll be just like that time we took Clovis to the Pit of Despair, remember?"

Erron raised a hand. "Can someone fill us in here?"

Alexis nodded that she'd appreciate a summary, too.

Adam, Giguhl, and I each took turns sharing the details of the Clovis Trakiya situation that happened six months earlier. Clovis was half vampire, half demon and all sorts of pain in my ass. The Dominae had sent me to infiltrate his cult of dark race brainwashees who claimed to want peace among all the races, but really Clovis was just trying to take over all the races.

When the inevitable showdown occurred at a vampire vineyard, I'd managed to trap Clovis in a circle and summoned Giguhl. The demon had dragged Clovis back to Irkalla. Last we'd heard, he was playing hide-the-hot-poker with a bunch of Lust demons in a nasty region of the underworld called the Pit of Despair.

My idea was basically to re-create that play but to have Giguhl trap Cain in the hotel instead of taking him to Irkalla. The demon would have to stay behind while we went to meet Persephone, but I could just summon him through my cell phone and send him and Cain back out before any witnesses realized what was going on. Easy peasy.

When we finished explaining, Erron snorted. "You really think it'll be that easy?"

"Well, why not?" Giguhl said. "Clovis wasn't exactly a pussy, seeing as how he's half vamp and half demon. Cain's smart but he's still a human. I'm in."

Alexis shrugged. "Why not? If it doesn't work, we can just beat the shit out of Cain and throw him into the trunk of a car."

Giguhl nodded. "I vote we do that anyway."

Erron scooted back from the table. His color was better

than it had been even before the attack, and he moved like a male in perfect health. We'd filled him in on how we healed him, but instead of being grateful he'd alternated between surly and silent.

"You're fooling yourselves," the Recreant said. "If it was that easy to be rid of him, don't you think someone else would have tried it before now?"

Giguhl raised a black, scraggly brow. "You got a better plan?"

"Yes. Don't go. He won't kill Persephone. She's the only ace he's got up his sleeve right now."

"The minute he thinks I don't care enough to save her, he'll kill her," I said. "Then he'll go after someone I really do care about."

"Let him try," Adam said, his jaw hard.

"Tough talk, Adherent," Erron taunted. "But if you recall, Orpheus and Tanith weren't exactly weaklings and he managed to kill them like that." He snapped his fingers and a flame sputtered up from the tips.

"In the past, Cain's always had the advantage, but this time we're the ones with surprise on our side. All we have to do is trap him."

"Oh, well, in that case." Erron's tone dripped with sarcasm. "We all saw how successfully that worked for Tristan. Or has everyone forgotten that's exactly how he managed to control and kill Maisie?"

My jaw hardened as I glared at him. "No, Erron. We haven't fucking forgotten."

Adam put a hand on my arm before the conversation could get out of hand.

"I'm sorry," the Recreant said. "But this is suicide mission. Gods, you guys, I almost *died* last night. I'm not willing to give Cain the chance to finish the job."

I threw up my hands. "What do you want us to do, then? Nothing?"

"Yes," Erron said, without a trace of irony. "Actually, scratch that. Listen to the advice your father gave you— run. Get as far away from Rome as you can. Warn everyone back in the States to watch their asses and then find a nice deserted island to hide out on for a few decades."

"That again?" I snorted. "You're insane."

"No, what's insane is thinking that you'll be able to defeat Cain. This whole ragtag team thing you got going here is charming and all, but this shit is as serious as it gets. Cain hasn't survived this long because he's dumb. You won't be able to trick him into letting his guard down. He'll keep coming for you until he gets what he wants."

"Which means your plan to run will only delay the inevitable," Adam said.

Erron raised an eyebrow. "Extra time will give you a chance to weigh your options and form a real plan. Not this half-assed quest that was doomed from the start. Besides, if being a coward means I get to live a few extra years, I'll always chose that option. You should, too."

"Bullshit!" I yelled. "That might be how you live your life, Recreant, but it sure as hell isn't how I live mine. Cain killed my sister. She died in my fucking arms, Erron. I couldn't live with myself if I ran away just to save my ass. At least this way I'll die on my own terms. Maisie never had that choice. Neither did your band when Cain killed them."

He flinched when I mentioned his own losses. "Right, we have a choice. What does it do for their memories to commit suicide?"

Adam raised his chin. "What does it do for their memories for us to run and hide when we have the ability to stand up and fight?"

Silence followed Adam's question. We didn't have time to beg him to stay and help the cause. The situation was dire enough without coercing allies. Everyone involved in this mission needed 100 percent commitment if we were going to win.

"I don't know what to tell you, Adherent," Erron said finally. "Maybe my decision isn't the brave one. But I'd rather be alive and a coward than a noble corpse."

Adam huffed out a breath. "Well, that's the difference between you and me, Recreant. You think you're free because you care about no one. But to me that's its own kind of prison. You want to go? Go. We appreciate your help and wish you the best, but we don't have time for long good-byes."

Erron held Adam's gaze. A muscle worked in his jaw, like he was considering whether to take the bait. But in the end, Erron stayed true to his convictions. "For what it's worth, I really hope you succeed. But if you don't, it's been an honor knowing all of you."

"Wait, you're just going to leave?" Alexis asked. "Like now?"

He nodded. "No sense drawing it out." He turned to Giguhl and held out his hand. "It's been nice knowing you."

Giguhl shook back but scowled the entire time.

Erron didn't offer his hand to Adam or me. Smart of him.

He turned to Alexis instead. "I'd be happy to transport you back to Los Angeles, if you want to cut out."

Alexis crossed her arms and shot the mage a superior look. "I'm with Sabina. Surrender isn't an option."

I shot her a grateful smile. Alexis might be prickly but she was no coward.

"I wish you luck, then," Erron said. "You're sure as hell going to need it."

With that, Erron gathered his powers and disappeared.

I blew out a breath and looked at Adam. "Well, that sucked."

"Forget him," Alexis said. "We'll be fine without him."

I nodded absently. It's not that I didn't understand Erron's point of view. He'd tangled with Cain before. More than anyone, he knew what we were up against. And it's not like he hadn't made his misgivings known from the beginning. I'd asked him to introduce us to his contact so we could find Abel. He'd fulfilled that promise when he took us to Dicky's.

I supposed I should have been grateful he'd stuck around as long as he had. And on some level, I understood how getting injured the night before would spook a being who didn't have the ability to heal himself. Instead, I felt disappointed and a little panicked. Now we'd be down one powerful mage, and we needed all the firepower we could get. But I didn't want Erron to hang around if he wasn't committed.

"Good riddance," Adam said.

I was surprised by his attitude, but I probably shouldn't have been. Adam was loyal to the Hekate Council, and Erron flaunted his rebellious Recreant status at every opportunity. We should have seen Erron's choice coming from the night we asked him for help.

"All right," Alexis said, "what's our play?"

"Erron's decision to leave changes nothing. We'll leave Giguhl here. That way I can summon him to me if we're right and this is a trap."

"Works for me," Giguhl said, and shrugged.

Adam nodded. "I'm going to call Rhea before we head out and let her know if she doesn't hear from us in two hours to circle the wagons."

"You think Cain will go after her anyway?"

"At this point, it's safest to assume no one is safe."

"Good point. Okay, let's do this." I rose to go grab the bag of weapons and amulets I'd packed the night before. In the other room, I heard chairs scrape and voices discuss logistics.

I checked my gun and stuck it into my rear waistband. The weight felt comforting, like slipping on a perfectly-broken-in pair of jeans.

I smelled Adam's sandalwood scent before he grabbed me. Before I knew what was happening, his lips found mine. The intensity of his kiss surprised me. But I surrendered to it, savoring the feel and taste of him. When he finally pulled back, I blinked a few times. "Wow, what was that for?"

He touched his forehead to mine and smiled. "For luck."

I held his gaze for a few moments. We both knew that kiss wasn't about luck. It was a just-in-case kiss. The kind you share with someone you love when you're not sure if it's the last one. I cupped his cheek with my palm and whispered, "For luck."

It just sounded so much better than good-bye.

15

Situated just east of the Tiber River, the Piazza del Popolo was a large oval, and the obelisk Persephone had mentioned stood in the center like a giant phallus. Hundreds of gyrating bodies danced around the monument like pagan worshippers. And, like something out of a Fellini hallucination, every damned one of them wore some sort of creepy mask.

Stag horns and curling tongues, long beaks, and evil eyes. Wine flowed, limbs gyrated, pelvises ground together. Rome's mortals, it seemed, were making the most of their last two weeks before the period of masochistic denial they called Lent.

The four of us stood on the perimeter of the plaza, watching the Technicolor swirl.

"Giguhl's going to be pissed he missed this," Adam observed.

"Oh gods," Alexis said. "Please tell me we don't have to wear those ridiculous things, too."

I shrugged. "When in Rome, right?" Don't get me wrong—I wasn't a big fan of dress-up, either. But the anonymity would come in handy if this all ended in gunplay or magical fireworks.

Adam flagged down a passing guy carrying a tall staff with several masks attached. He grabbed three and tossed the guy some euros. Unlike the animal-themed ones that caught my eye among the crowd, these were simpler white masks that left our mouths exposed. A few sequins and wilted feathers added splashes of color. We all dutifully donned our disguises and set off into the crowd.

"Okay," I said, "it's a quarter till nine. Let's break off and meet at the obelisk on the hour." When we'd formed this plan earlier, we'd decided that Alexis would go with me. If an attack happened, Adam could flash himself out, but Alexis didn't have magic in her arsenal and I did. I couldn't flash us to safety since my Chthonic magic always took me to the Liminal when I tried initiating interspatial travel, but I could immolate an attacker at twenty paces.

Adam took off to the left. The mancy shot me a weighted parting glance and allowed the crowd to swallow him.

"Cain will know I'd want to be here early," I said. "Stay alert."

Alexis shot me a wry smile. The effect was somewhat sinister combined with the mask. "Yes, ma'am."

The reminder was unnecessary and I knew it. Before Alexis had become Tanith's personal guard, she'd been an assassin just like me. She knew the drill.

I rolled my eyes at her sarcasm and nudged her with my hand. "Let's go, tough chick."

Now that we were in the thick of the crowd, I realized that my prediction of a security nightmare had been right on the nose. In addition to the disguises preventing us from recognizing enemies, it was difficult to hear anything. Besides the cacophony of cheering, a wall of sound blasted the area from the rock band on the stage in front of Rome's northern gate next to the piazza.

Working through the crowd was its own challenge. Some areas were little more than mosh pits where we had to dodge flying elbows and body slams. Alexis seemed to enjoy this part the most since it allowed her to punch mortals with abandon. I had to admit I didn't hate that part, either.

My knuckles stung from jabbing a big dude in his concrete jaw, but otherwise we got through the perimeter check without incident. Soon we switched direction toward the obelisk. About the same time, the band finished their set—thank the gods—and an emcee jumped onstage to rattle off some sort of announcement. He spoke in rapid Italian, naturally, so I wasn't sure what he was saying, but a ripple of excitement went through the crowd.

I spotted Adam standing next to one of the four stone lion fountains at the base of the obelisk. He waved to make sure I saw him. I nodded and turned toward Alexis, who had been bringing up the rear.

"There's Ad—" My words were swallowed by a sudden explosion. I ducked and covered my head. My heart pounded as I waited for the inevitable heat concussion. For the crowd to panic and stampede. Except the crowd didn't freak. Not even when the second explosion came, a third. I looked up and let out a part-relived, part-annoyed sigh.

The sky above the piazza sizzled with fireworks. All around, spectators craned their necks as they oohed and aahed over the impressive display. I shook my head and laughed at myself. The emcee must have been announcing that the show was about to begin.

Relieved and a little embarrassed by my brittle nerves, I turned to look for Alexis. The vampire had fallen behind as the crowd closed in to watch the show. Probably twelve beings separated us. I stood on my tiptoes and tried to flag her down. She saw me and I pointed toward the obelisk. *Adam*, I mouthed.

She nodded and started working her way toward me with an annoyed expression. I looked back over to where I'd seen Adam. He caught my gaze and raised his hands in a what's-the-holdup? gesture. I held up a finger. "Hold your horses, mancy," I grumbled.

I turned to check Alexis's progress and froze. Just behind her, a redhead in a devil's mask materialized out of the mass of people.

Panic, white hot and ice cold.

"Look out!" I shouted. Another explosion smothered my warning. "Fuck!" I shouted, and started hacking my way toward her. She'd stopped and was arguing with a woman who'd taken exception to Alexis shoving her aside. The devil was closer now, too close.

"Alexis!" I screamed.

She looked up and saw me. Her eyes narrowed into a confused expression.

Boom!

Alexis froze, her eyes wide. Her pale lips parted, emitting a thin trickle of blood.

Boom!

She swung around. A flash of metal in her hand.

Boom!

The devil and Alexis Vega both burst into flames.

"No!" I screamed. I started hacking my way through the crowd. A few spectators had noticed the pair combusting in their midst and were looking around in confusion. They clearly couldn't decide whether it was part of the show or something they should actually panic about.

Without thinking, I took off through the crowd. Alexis, gods protect her, had taken out her killer, but I knew better than to believe he'd been working alone. I needed to find his partners and show them what Chthonic mages did to enemies. As I prowled for other foes, I bowled over several pissed-off mortals, not caring if I was creating a scene.

"Sabina!" Adam's shout was faint, but it acted like a bucket of ice water on my fiery anger.

I slowed my pursuit. What the hell was I doing? If Cain was orchestrating this, he'd want nothing more than to separate me from my team. That's why they'd taken out Alexis. At the same moment, I saw a flash of red—a mask with black horns—running in the opposite direction. My muscles ached to pursue, but I fought the instinct. Instead, I watched as the crowd swallowed the devil. Fighting the urge to find and kill that prey wasn't easy. But it was necessary if I was going to win this battle.

I swiveled my body, intent on making my way back toward Adam. But when I did, I couldn't see him. The fireworks were picking up speed now and the constant barrage of explosions set every nerve in my body on overload.

Everywhere I looked, all I saw were masks. Strangers. Potential enemies. Any one of the bodies surrounding me could be Cain. Cold sweat broke out on my back. Time to abort this mission. I needed to find Adam and get us the fuck out of there.

I took a deep, calming breath and told my galloping heart to chill. Pulling the gun from my waistband, I held it down next to my side. The gun's heft and solidity calmed me. Centered me. I was not the prey here. I was the hunter.

I ripped off my mask to clear my vision and stalked through the crowd. Despite the noise and the confusion, I focused all my senses on seeking out my prey. Cain was there. I could feel it in my marrow. And I needed to find him before he found Adam. Because if he did, Cain would gain the upper hand and he knew it.

I headed back toward the obelisk since that's where I last saw Adam. On my way, I had to pass the burning embers that used to be Alexis. I sent a quick prayer to the Great Mother to accept the vampire into Irkalla. "Rest well, my friend," I said silently. "You earned it."

I stepped over the burned mass and continued on. The humans who'd witnessed Alexis's death cast occasional glances at the pile, but the brief panic had dissipated. That's the great thing about mortals. They're so determined to keep things normal that they rationalize all sorts of crazy shit. Including, it seemed, watching a vampire explode at their feet.

"Sabina," a voice whispered in my ear. I turned, trying to locate the source, but I was surrounded by mortals. I felt the hum of magic farther into the mass of people, but close by...nothing. No scent of dirty copper penny that would indicate a vampire, no lavender of the fae species, no mage sandalwood, or even the eau de wet dog that clung to were-wolves like body odor.

"Sabina." The whisper again. This time like a breeze against my ear. A chill ran down my spine. Dread mixed with anticipation. I forged ahead. Cain wanted me to turn and run scared into his trap. With my eyes scanning constantly, I pulled out my cell with my free hand.

"What's wrong?" Giguhl demanded by way of greeting.

"Get ready."

"Is everything okay? You sound pissed."

"No time. Just be ready to rock 'n' roll." My left shoulder burned like I'd pulled a muscle. I massaged the stiffness, but it didn't dissipate. If anything, it throbbed hotter.

"Always. Watch your ass, magepire."

"Always," I echoed. "Okay, I'm leaving the call connected but putting the phone in my pocket. Listen up for the signal."

I shoved the phone into my pocket, careful not to disconnect the call. I'd reached the obelisk now. Young children sat on the backs of the stone lions and splashed in the water that came from the statues' mouths.

And not ten feet from all the innocence stood the inventor of murder—Cain, aka Master Mahan, aka He Who Kills to Get Gain.

I stopped ten feet away. My features were passive but inside, my stomach roiled like it was filled with serpents. The last time I'd been this close to Cain, he was killing my twin.

Though not a large male, he seemed to take up the whole space. He was dressed in street clothes—jeans, a button-down, and loafers. But the modern clothes didn't reduce the magnetism, the wild, untamed energy coming off him. He had the kind of face sculptors dreamed of and the lithe body of a predator. High cheekbones, full lips, honeyed olive skin. His emerald-green eyes promised sin.

And by sin, I of course meant ritualized, sadistic murder.

"*Cara mia*," Cain drawled. He leaned back against the shaft of the obelisk. His arms were crossed, his posture relaxed. "Welcome to the party." He stepped down to my level, his movements predatory, like a jungle cat. He tipped his chin down like some sort of signal.

A dozen beings wearing red devil's masks emerged from the crowd and circled us. Their crushing presence closed in, blocking me and Cain from mortal eyes. The effect was...intimidating. But I stayed calm.

After all, I had a demon up my sleeve.

I could have sat there and exchanged clever banter with the deranged killer. But this wasn't some fucking movie and I wasn't about to miss my opportunity to take the upper hand. "Now, Gi—"

Pain exploded in my back. Like a steel fist punching through muscle and bone. The impact and the searing pain threw me to my knees. My gun skittered away, lost among a sea of feet. I choked on the bile and fear rising in my throat.

Ignoring the hot convulsions in my back, I pushed myself off the ground until my ass was resting on my heels. With great effort, I leveraged myself upright. I wanted to be looking directly into Cain's eyes when I said my next words. "Applewood stakes can't kill me."

Cain's seductive mouth spread into a lopsided grin. "It's not applewood."

"Then why—" I cut myself off. The loss of blood and the pain had addled my brains for a moment. I was wasting valuable time. It didn't matter what weapon he'd used. It was time to fire back with one of my own.

I screamed, "Now, Giguhl!"

Nothing happened.

Cain clucked his tongue. "Magic not working?"

I ignored him and tamped down the rise of panic. Scrambling, I pulled the phone from my pocket and yelled, "Giguhl get your ass here now!"

"Red?" Giguhl's muted shout came through the receiver.

"Sabina, darling, save your breath," Cain said. "Your demon friend's not coming."

I narrowed my eyes. "What did you do?"

Giguhl screamed now, demanding I talk to him, but I didn't have time to allay his fears. Especially when they were so well deserved. Something was really fucking wrong.

Cain pointed to my shoulder. "If you'd have let me explain before, I would have told you that stake in your back isn't applewood." He leaned forward and whispered like we were conspirators instead of enemies. "It's brass."

Gravity tripled, the force sucking every ounce of blood from my face. It weighed down my muscles with a sensation that felt a lot like defeat. With the brass embedded in my back, I couldn't use any sort of magic.

Cain came forward and took the phone from my limp grasp. "So sorry, Sabina's busy right now." A pause. "What's that? Well"—Cain laughed—"I look forward to seeing you attempt that. Good-bye now." He punched the END button and slipped the phone into his pocket.

The movement made the light dance off a polished brass cuff on his wrist. Looked like Mr. Immortal was worried about getting hit with another one of Zen's vexing spells. Unfortunately, the ones that remained were with Adam.

The air tightened and static rushed up my arms. Someone was gathering a massive amount of magical energy nearby. I looked around and finally spied Adam on the stage across the square. The fireworks highlighted the determination on his handsome face.

He was smart to position himself so far away. The range wasn't too great to prevent him from delivering potent spells, but it was far enough away that the vampires and werewolves among Cain's goons wouldn't be able to do anything but duck and cover when the spells came.

Cain had noticed Adam, too. "Get ready. Her lover"—he spat the word out like a curse—"is about to make a romantic but futile gesture."

Cain's tone was unconcerned. So carefree I knew right

then he had some more tricks up his sleeve. Namely, the three mages who stepped forward from the circle. I could feel their powers rising like a deep throbbing bass. Adam was an excellent fighter and a strong mage. But Cain had an irrational hatred for the mancy that would ensure his death was a priority in this exercise.

Not a fucking option. Time to cut a deal.

"Stop!" I yelled. "I'll go with you."

Cain laughed. "Yes, I know. You don't have a choice."

"No," I said, my tone desperate. "I'll go with you if you leave him alone."

Cain sighed. "Sabina, your weakness where the mage is concerned is pitiful. You're in no position to make demands."

The brass might have dampened my magic, but my vampire blood had already done quick work on the worst of my pain. "Oh, really?" I spun and clocked one of Cain's vampires in the face. While he reeled from the impact, I swiped his gun from his hand. I rounded on Cain. He looked mildly shocked but not exactly alarmed.

"The gun will do you no good, Lamashtu," he said, using the pet name he used for Lilith. For some reason, in his fucked up head, he got confused between the Great Mother and me.

Holding his gaze, I slowly lifted the gun to my temple. "Call them off or I pull the trigger,"

Cain's eyes narrowed at the cold steel in my voice.

Behind him, I saw Adam freeze on the stage. From his higher vantage point, he could see what was happening. His mouth opened wide as he yelled. That strong, powerful body was already in motion as he made to jump from the stage.

Cain watched me for a few tense heartbeats, as if trying to decide if I loved Adam enough to die for him. "You're bluffing."

Adam rematerialized on the far side of the obelisk, clearly planning on attacking, audience or no. Do or die time.

"Want to fucking bet?"

I cocked the hammer.

He paused and tilted his head. His eyes on me, he said to his goons, "It's time to change the location of our little soiree. Three of you stay behind and kill her lover."

"Yes, sir," said three of the goons, and broke off to go after Adam. The rest of Cain's men pressed in around Cain and me.

Overhead, the fireworks display was reaching its climax. I looked up at the kaleidoscope of color and heat. As I watched, the colors morphed and distorted, indicating that Cain's mages had opened the doorway that allowed mages to travel interspatially.

"Sabina!" Adam's tortured cry reached me.

"Say good-bye to your love, Sabina," Cain breathed into my ear. He pulled me close to his body, but I didn't fight him. My only goal was to get him as far away from Adam as possible. I knew once Cain and I disappeared, Adam wouldn't hang out to engage with the goons. He'd flash out and go find Giguhl so they could rescue me.

I looked up and met Adam's eyes over the heads of the crowd separating us. *Run!* I mouthed.

A split second later, the vortex sucked my body into the void.

16

I'd thought the aboveground Cities of the Dead in New Orleans were impressive, but the catacombs of Rome made those look like elaborate stage sets.

"Welcome to the Catacombs of Saint Domitilla," Cain said conversationally. Like he was leading a fucking tour group instead of a dark races death squad.

We had gained access to the underground tunnels through a sunken fourth-century basilica—another factoid Cain had shared. One of his people held a large flashlight since it was night and they didn't want to risk illuminating the lights installed for catacomb tours. Its beam flashed off high stone walls, tall columns, an altar, and artifacts along the walls of the church. Cain led us to an arched doorway that led down into the underground tunnels. The opening gaped like a mouth, ready to swallow us into the bowels of the underworld.

Even before we entered the catacombs proper, I could feel the tug of death magic on my diaphragm. Whispers echoed from the dark portal, inviting me to listen to their stories. The back of my neck prickled and a fine sheen of sweat coated my chest, despite the clammy air.

Unlike the crypt Tristan led me to a couple nights earlier, with its intricate designs made from skeletons, these catacombs were virtually bone-free. Despite the lack of remains, the death energy hit me with the force of a sledgehammer.

I swayed into the vampire that held my right arm. "Give me a minute," I gritted out through clenched teeth.

I concentrated on breathing slowly through my nose to slow my galloping pulse. The pressure of the energy came at me from all sides, and my Chthonic powers struggled to absorb the force in my solar plexus. The effect was something like going hundreds of feet below the sea very quickly. It took my body time to adjust to equalize the opposing forces. Because of the brass spike in my back, I couldn't use the magic, but it wouldn't hurt to stockpile some of the energy in case an opportunity presented itself.

The vampire grew impatient and shoved me forward. "Keep walking, bitch."

Cain swung around and backhanded the male. "Show some respect!"

I shied back from the wild expression on Cain's face. Angry I could handle, but crazy was unpredictable and far more dangerous than rage.

"I . . . I'm sorry, Master Mahan," the vampire simpered, using the name Cain's cult, the Caste of Nod, used for him. "I assumed since she was a prisoner—"

"Sabina is not a prisoner. She is a guest. You will treat her as such."

"Yes, master."

I kept my mouth shut. It wasn't the right time to point out that people usually didn't stab their guests in the back and then force them into creepy catacombs.

Speaking of being stabbed, the wound around the brass stake felt hot and achy. Most likely, my vampire blood was knitting the skin around the blade in a futile effort to heal the wound.

As we'd walked through the tunnels, I'd tried to use my free hand to reach the spike, but I couldn't do it without some serious contortion. Since I couldn't remove the brass, I decided to fill up on intel. "Hey, Cain?"

He'd started walking again and didn't turn to look at me when he replied. "Yes?"

"How far is this place?"

"Not far now, my dove."

I gritted my teeth against the endearment. "I'm surprised all this is down here."

He paused and looked over his shoulder. I tried to keep my expression innocent and interested. It must have worked because he started waxing poetic about the macabre setting.

"Yes, it's remarkable, isn't it?" He fingered a chipped fresco set between two niches. "There are hundreds of kilometers of catacombs all over the Roman countryside. Did you know that?"

I shook my head. "That's amazing." It was, but not because I was interested in ancient history. I wanted to know about escape routes. "How long are the ones we're in?"

Cain pursed his lips. "I believe these are seventeen kilometers, spread out over four levels. More than one hundred fifty thousand mortals were buried here." He took a deep inhale of the dank air. "Can you smell it? All the death. It's invigorating."

"I'll say." Cain had made a colossal mistake choosing this place as the spot for our confrontation. Chthonic magic is basically earth and death magic, so, once unleashed, my powers would thrive in this playground. That was, if I could get the fucking spike out first.

The long walk gave me time to adjust to the onslaught of powers. It also gave me some time to get used to the claustrophobic layout, with its low ceilings and narrow passages lined with niches carved in rock.

The farther we got, the quieter Cain and his acolytes grew. The quieter they got, the wetter my palms grew.

It was one thing to distract myself with fantasies of escape, but deep down I knew I couldn't defeat them on my own. Cain had planned this too well. He'd beaten me at my own game and now he'd make good on his promises. The chance of the cavalry finding me was a joke. With the brass in my back, they couldn't track any sort of magical trail. It'd take more than one of Adam's miracles to make this turn out all right.

My heart thudded in my ears. The energy I'd absorbed earlier writhed in my midsection, eager to be unleashed. But the more it built, the shakier I felt. There was only so much power I could stockpile before it overpowered me.

Eventually, Cain led our procession to a chamber at the end of a corridor. The room appeared to be an ancient chapel once used by those who dug the catacombs. Time hadn't been kind to the structural elements. The stone altar was pitted and large chunks were missing.

In the small, dark space, Cain's brilliant red hair flashed like a siren. But it was the other redheads waiting for us that made cold sweat cover my chest.

Behind the altar, in a niche, Persephone was bound and gagged, her body folded painfully into the tight space. Damiano stood next to her stone prison.

"Master! I am so relieved by your triumphant return."

"Silence," Cain said, his voice low and menacing.

Damiano's eyes flicked back to the Domina nervously, but his shoulders slumped in submission to Cain.

I wanted to interrogate Damiano, find out why he'd turned against Persephone and Chiara.

Wait a second, I thought. "Where's Chiara?"

Cain smiled. "She proved . . . superfluous."

I closed my eyes and crunched my face together to hold in the impotent rage. *Keep it together*, I thought. *Stay calm and you might just survive.*

When I opened them again, I looked at Persephone. Her eyes were open and her gaze was pitiful. Full of regret that arrived about twenty-four hours too late. "I hope you're happy with yourself."

She looked down at the dirt floor.

"Look at me," I demanded. She looked up again, her gaze hardened. "If he succeeds, you are to blame."

Cain tilted his head and smiled at me. "Your audacity is charming, dearest. There is no *if*—I will succeed."

"What's your plan?"

Cain raised a carmine brow. "You know what I want."

"This again?" I taunted. "No means no, Cain. I won't take you to Irkalla so you can beg Lilith to take you back." I was dragging this out, taunting him. Maybe if I shook his composure he'd be easier to outsmart. I leaned forward. "If you ask me, this whole psycho-ex-boyfriend thing is coming off as kind of creepy and desperate."

His lips twitched, like he was enjoying a private joke. "Perhaps I can change your mind." He jerked his chin at Damiano. "Bring her."

The vampire hesitated, but a threatening look from Cain had him hustling toward the niche and Persephone. He dragged the trussed Domina out like a sack of flour. She hit the ground with a groan.

"*Scusi*, Domina," Damiano whispered.

Cain cleared his throat menacingly. Damiano shot him a

guilty look; then he jerked Persephone to her feet. She glared at him with eyes fairly glowing with hatred.

The ancient human approached the ancient vampire. Most humans would be idiots to get so close to a vampire, much less one who was older than most civilizations. But Cain was the oldest being alive and had the added benefit of being de facto immortal thanks to a major loophole from the mortal deity.

He ran a thumb down her cheek and whispered, "You were wonderful last night."

A shudder wracked Persephone's body, but her chin came up. He may have violated her body, but he hadn't taken her spirit.

I, on the other hand, wanted to vomit. I'd had my share of anger toward the Dominae over the years, but no one deserved that kind of violation.

"Sabina, are you prepared to take me to Irkalla?" Cain asked, his hand stroking up and down the ivory of Persephone's arm. Even in the dim light, I could see the way her skin crawled at his touch.

I looked up and put every ounce of hatred I had for him in my glare. "You are an abomination." I spit at his feet. "I curse the mortal deity who protects you."

"Your stalling tactics have grown tiresome," Cain said wearily. "I see we're going to have to do this the hard way."

One instant his posture was loose and casual; the next he struck like a snake. A flash of silver slashed through the air, followed by a spray of red. Persephone's mouth worked open and closed like a carp's. The whites of her eyes overwhelmed her face. Air whistled through the gash on her throat. And the blood. So much blood. Her trembling hands rose to staunch the flow.

Her knees gave out and she sank to the packed earthen

floor. Left as she was, her vampire cells should have begun to knit themselves back together.

But Cain had other plans. He retrieved a syringe from his pocket. Held it up to the torchlight. Golden liquid inside flashed in the meager light. He stuck out his tongue and caught the spray. "Mmm," he said, smacking his lips. "Sweet."

Before I could recover from my shock and intervene, he stabbed the needle into Persephone's throat. Punching the plunger, he injected the vampire with a dose of the forbidden fruit.

"No!" I yelled. I ran to Persephone. Knelt down next to her with my ear close to her lips so she wouldn't have to struggle.

Blood gurgled from the Domina's blue lips. I grabbed her icy hand, trying to lend comfort. Persephone's advanced age drew out the process of death as her ancient blood struggled in vain to repair the damage.

The catacombs were silent, as if even the ghosts in this place held their breaths to witness such an important death.

"Sabina," she wheezed. The light in her eyes was dimming. "Find—" Wheeze, choke. "Find my Nicolette."

I frowned down at her. "Who is—"

A loud, sudden gasp and Persephone reared up from the ground. She tensed and emitted a death rattle. Then Persephone Delacroix, Domina of the Lilim, collapsed onto the packed earth. As she fell, her soul escaped and the resulting friction caused her body to ignite.

I fell and scrambled back to escape the heat. "Oh my gods," I whispered in horror.

All of the Dominae were dead. Which meant if I survived Cain's plans, I'd be next in line. It was almost enough to make me wish he'd succeed. The very idea of continuing Lavinia Kane's bloody legacy made me want to hurl.

But not more than being within arm's length of Cain did.

"Well now," Cain said. "Shall we begin?"

I rounded on him and shouted, "You fucking idiot. I don't even know how to access Irkalla through the Liminal!"

Cain pursed his lips. "You better hope for your lover's sake you're a fast learner. Because if you fail, I will find him and kill him while you watch."

I clenched my jaw to hide the terror his threat invoked. "How in the hell am I supposed to get you to Irkalla with this godsdamned blade in my back?" I jerked a thumb over my shoulder.

"Sabina, your bravado is breathtaking. It's really too bad you're determined for us to be enemies. We would make fierce and beautiful children together."

I reared back, but the beings behind me shoved my body forward. I fell toward Cain, who caught me and wrapped his arms around me. His touch made my stomach turn. "Don't touch me!" I yelled, straining away from him.

He clucked his tongue. "Relax. How will you get me to Irkalla if you're so tense?"

This fucking guy was a lunatic. How the hell was I supposed to relax?

"Besides, you will have to touch me to take me with you to the Liminal."

I swallowed the bile rising in my throat. "The blade?" I prompted. When he shot me a suspicious look, I tried not to punch him in the face. "If you want me to do magic, you're gonna have to get rid of the brass."

He kept his eyes on mine but nodded to the vampire behind me. A strong hand gripped my shoulder for leverage. I sucked a breath in through my nose and braced myself for the inevitable pain. The vampire was not swift or gentle. He twisted the blade roughly to reopen the wound. My skin ripped and wetness dripped down my back. Cold sweat coated my trembling skin. Finally, he slowly pulled the blade free, inch by agonizing inch.

I swallowed the pain and flicked my gaze to Cain's wrist. "Your brass too."

Holding my gaze, he removed the cuff and let it drop to the ground. Then he slowly unbuttoned his shirt. I opened my mouth to ask him why he was undressing, but then I saw the brass breastplate his shirt had hidden. For someone who used magical beings as his personal weapons, he was sure worried about becoming a target himself.

He dropped the plate to the dirt. Raised his arms and stretched, flexing his pecs and biceps. "There now." Cain smiled as if he expected me to swoon over his muscled torso. I barely managed to suppress my gag reflex.

Once his goons collected the brass items and had scooted back a safe distance, Cain held out his arms. "Shall we?"

He clearly wanted me to plaster myself against him. Instead, I used the tips of my fingers to touch his wrist.

I closed my eyes and prayed. *Hekate, Torch Bearer, light my way. Great Mother, Lilith, protect me and give me strength for what is to come. Also? Brace yourself. An enemy is at your gate.*

I breathed out slowly and rooted my feet in the dirt. All the power I'd absorbed in the catacombs sprang to life and coiled around my solar plexus. It crawled through my arms like thorny vines. My fingertips sizzled and my head pulsed with energy.

An explosion ripped through the tunnels.

One second I was preparing to transport us to the Liminal—where I planned to lose Cain and run like hell— and the next my body slammed into the hard stone altar. In my shock, I lost control of all the power I'd gathered. It rushed from me like a hot stinging wind and flew through the catacombs.

I blinked, trying to figure out what the hell had just happened, but the dust cloud and searing heat prevented clear vision. Shouts and the sounds of fighting pounded my ears. I tried to get my feet under me, but a strong hand grabbed my ankle. Cain.

He might be a sadist with a violent streak a mile wide, but in the end, his human strength was no match for an adrenaline-fueled magepire. I kicked off his clinging hand and ran into the veil of dust.

My only goal then was to get as far from Cain as possible. As I ran, I saw bodies moving through the smoke. The sounds of combat echoed through the chamber. I kept going until my body slammed into someone. My hands flew up immediately to ward off a blow. The smoke cleared between us and I saw a stoic but familiar male face.

Tristan Graecus.

"What the hell are you doing here?" I yelled.

He grabbed my arm. "Saving your ass!" My father wore a black trench coat and jeans with Doc Martens boots. Quite a change from the medieval monk thing he had going on a few nights earlier.

"We have to go!" he yelled, struggling to hang on to me.

A werewolf appeared from the smoke and took a swipe at me. Out of nowhere, a flash of green streaked past me and attacked the were. Relief flooded through me as I watched Giguhl make quick work of the humanoid werewolf. If it had been a full moon, the victory would not have been so easy.

A female vampire rushed toward us. Her cherry hair was cut into a sleek bob, but her outfit was pure commando.

The drab color and streaks of dirt were harsh counterpoints to the beauty of her delicate features. "T, we need to move!"

"Who the hell are you?" I demanded.

"She's with me," Tristan yelled over the din.

"Sabina!" Adam's shout reached me. I turned to see him battling his way through the weres to get to us. I had never been happier to see the mancy. I threw myself at him. His arms wrapped around me automatically.

"Thank the gods we got here in time," he said into my hair.

"How did you find me?"

"Lazarus, we've got to go!" Tristan yelled.

Adam nodded at my father. To me, he said, "I'll explain later." He kissed my forehead. "Promise."

I nodded. Now wasn't the time for talk. We needed to get the hell out of Dodge.

Tristan and the vampire started hacking through Cain's thugs. Instead of arguing, I grabbed the gun Adam offered and took off. At my nod, Giguhl fell in behind us.

"Sabina!" Cain's voice carried over the clash of weapons, the low growls of the weres, and the battle cries. The sound raised the hairs on the back of my neck. Wanting to get out of there suddenly became needing to get out. If I hesitated, I knew in my gut that Cain's punishment would be swift and severe.

"Please tell me you know a way out of here," I shouted to my father.

The vamp raised her free hand. "That way."

A male vampire with a silver sword and female fae with a quiver and bow flanked us. I blinked, realizing they were the same pair I'd seen at the Spanish Steps.

Even with the armed escort, I didn't let my guard down.

Until we were clear of the catacombs and far away from Cain, I wouldn't ever relax.

"SABINA!" Cain's scream shook the walls.

Tristan turned. "Horus, Calyx, fall back and hold them off until we're clear. Then run like hell." The pair nodded and turned out from our phalanx. Behind us, the sounds of fighting renewed. "Hurry!" my father urged the rest of us.

Running. After all those years as a predator, I'd now been reduced to prey. My thighs burned with exertion and my heart pumped blood like a piston. Our pounding footsteps and the harsh rasps of our breaths echoed off the tunnel walls.

The sounds of battle became muted as we wound our way through countless twists and turns. Every now and then, Tristan would look back to make sure we were keeping up.

"Sabiiina," Cain's voice was taunting now. It crept through the narrow corridors like poisonous gas. Cold sweat and fear seeped through my pores.

Lowering my head, I dug in and pushed harder. Tristan's vampire led the way. Next to me, Adam's thumping pulse was a visceral sensation in my solar plexus. I focused on counting the beats to distract myself from the fear. I tried to remind myself that Cain didn't have the magical skills of a mage or the preternatural speed of a vampire. In the end, he was simply a man.

"Why can't you guys just flash us out of here?" Giguhl demanded after we'd run for what felt like miles.

"I won't leave Calyx and Horus behind. We'll flash out once they return," Tristan said. "Just a little farther."

The vampiress led us to what appeared to be a dead end. But then she held up the torch to show a scaffold set against the walls. A tall ceiling rose above this section of the tunnel, probably twenty feet high. She handed the torch to Tristan and started climbing.

"Where's she going?" My voice was breathless and high from fear.

"The Christians built in skylights and airshafts during construction. Many have been closed or built over from above. She's checking to see if this one is still open."

A piecing whistle reached us from somewhere above. Then thin, blue light filtered down. The rush of air that accompanied the light smelled a lot like freedom.

I leaned against the crumbling stone wall. Sweat and dirt coated every inch of my skin. Relief at losing our pursuers warred with resentment in my gut. I didn't want to owe Tristan a debt for saving my ass. Especially when my plan to blackmail him into helping us had crashed and burned so spectacularly.

"That was way too close," the female vampire said.

"Needlessly so," Tristan snapped. He rounded on me. "I thought I told you to leave Rome."

I raised my chin. "I am not yours to command."

"Well someone needs to. What the hell were you thinking?"

I frowned. "With which part, exactly?"

Giguhl snorted.

"Your teammates filled me in on your ludicrous plan."

I crossed my arms defensively. "At least I had a fucking plan. Unlike some people who are ready to surrender before the real battle's even begun."

"Your sarcasm is both unwarranted and unnecessary."

"Your existence is unnecessary," I shot back.

"Ouch," the vampire chick said. "Can we put aside family dysfunction hour for a few minutes so we can formulate a plan to get very far away from here?"

I sucked at my teeth, daydreaming about telling both of them to go fuck themselves. But I knew that was only my battered ego talking. Plus, she was right; our hideout was not safe enough.

We'd taken refuge in a farmhouse a couple of miles from the shaft we'd exited. The stone was blackened and crumbling from years of exposure to the elements. The roof, such as it was, had gaping holes that exposed the clear night sky. The first pale streaks of dawn already decorated the horizon.

Tristan nodded toward the vampire and faery, who'd come through the airshaft a couple of moments earlier. I noted that all of Tristan's people wore small golden pins bearing his sword and chalice symbol.

"Now that Horus and Calyx have returned, we need to move to the safe house up north."

"Excuse me?" I interrupted. "But how in the hell are we going to defeat him if we leave Rome?"

Tristan tilted his head. "Your ignorance is breathtaking. The trick with Cain is to stay a step ahead. If we're in Rome, we'll be sitting ducks."

My eyes flared and my fists clenched.

"Sabina…," Adam began, no doubt trying to intercept an outburst. I held up a hand to cut him off. I drew in a long, slow breath through my nose. Despite my father's crappy personality, I needed him if I was going to defeat Cain.

"Look, I'm sorry, but I've had a really shitty night," I said. "But I appreciate you helping us."

Tristan's eyes narrowed, like he expected a trick.

"Really. But how did you guys manage to find me?"

Tristan's gaze swiveled to Adam. The mancy held up his cell phone. "A little mortal magic."

I frowned. "What?"

He smirked. "Your phone had a GPS tracker."

I remembered then that Cain had my cell phone in his pocket the entire time. "Well, thank the gods for small favors."

"Speaking of," Tristan said, "before we continue, I need all of your cell phones and other means of communication."

"Why?" I asked, making no effort to hide the suspicion in my tone.

"Because from this moment on, we're going on blackout. We can't risk Cain tracking our devices like we tracked yours. Plus, I need to be sure none of you are going to communicate with anyone who might be tortured to betray our location."

His logic, annoyingly, made total sense. Besides, if we needed to talk to anyone back in the States, Adam could just flash there. Since Cain still had my cell, I looked to Adam. He pulled his phone out of his pocket and passed it to Tristan.

"Thank you for understanding," Tristan said. He dropped the phone to the ground and smashed it to tiny pieces with his boots.

"So what's the plan, people?" Giguhl asked.

Tristan shot the demon an annoyed look, like Giguhl had overstepped. He answered, but when he did, he spoke to me as if I'd asked instead of my minion. "First, we need to get out of Rome. We have a farm near Tuscany. Between me and Lazarus"—he nodded at Adam—"we should be able to flash all of us there."

"How far is it?" I asked.

"Far enough," he evaded. "If we head out now, we can reach it before sunrise."

"Does this mean you've changed you mind about working together?" I said.

Tristan's mouth hardened into a thin line. "No. It means I can't trust you to leave Rome on your own, so I'm taking you away myself."

I suddenly understood why so many people bitched about having parents. All my life, I'd longed for a benevolent parental figure to nurture and support me. But if my experience with Tristan so far was a taste of what being parented was like, I decided being an orphan was the way to go.

I opened my mouth to tell Tristan I had no intention of allowing him to hide me away while he got to have all the fun, but Adam elbowed me. Shooting him a glare, I noticed Giguhl was making cease-and-desist gestures, too. Traitors.

"I believe your friends are trying to hint that you should hold your tongue. Smart of them," Tristan said, his tone dry. "I'm well acquainted with the infamous Kane temper and I assure you it will do little to sway me."

I crossed my arms and glared at my father. Why the hell had I wanted to work with him again? Oh, right. I didn't have a choice. But I suppose he was right. Blowing up at him now might convince him to change his mind and leave us there. Besides, I'd have plenty of time to convince him to work with us once we were in a safer place.

I forced my shoulders to relax and cranked my lips up into what I hoped was a genuine smile. Judging from Tristan's dubious expression, I failed. Still, I forged ahead. "Lead the way, *Dad*."

18

When Tristan had said we were going to a farm, I expected something with wide-open fields and possibly a red barn. A few cows, maybe a tractor—that kind of thing. Instead, Tristan's "farm" was really a gorgeous villa set among Tuscany's rolling hills. The place looked like something from a sweeping period piece where the dashing Italian count sweeps his virgin bride away for a deflowering.

We materialized at the base of a hill. The villa sat above us like a genteel reminder of an era gone by. On our way up, we passed a small building on the right. From my brief glimpse, it seemed to be some sort of family chapel, judging from the small gold cross over the doorway, which was so low I'd have to duck to enter. Across the path from this squat building was a small rose garden. I'd have been charmed if I wasn't so on edge.

Tristan and the vampire whose name I hadn't gotten yet led the way. My senses were on high alert for signs of trouble. Only instead of finding any, they were overcome by the countryside's deafening silence.

Beside me, Giguhl inhaled deeply. "The air smells weird."

"You've been in the city too long," Adam said. "What you're smelling is fresh air."

Giguhl's nose wrinkled. "No, it's not that." He sniffed again. "I think it's cow shit."

Adam laughed. "Like I said, fresh country air."

"Are you coming?" Tristan snapped from farther up the hill. Obviously he wasn't as impressed by the idyllic setting. Part of me was starting to wonder if Tristan Graecus was ever impressed by anything.

At the top of the hill, we reached a gravel courtyard. Buildings surrounded the area—the manor house, a small brick structure filled with chairs and tables for gatherings, and another medium-sized building that I couldn't identify without further investigation. Beyond the building, black shapes set against the near-dawn sky implied an orchard or copse of trees just beyond.

"Now for the introductions." Tristan started at the far end of the line. "Horus and Calyx are our weapons experts."

The male, Horus, was as wide as he was tall. The hilt of his sword jutted out from behind his dark red ponytail. Both the weapon and the shade of hair told me he was probably a few hundred years old. As for the fae, she was... surprising. Most female faeries were petite. She was certainly shorter than me, but her finely muscled frame made her appear taller. A quiver of arrows was strung to her back and she leaned against a longbow. They both nodded curt greetings.

Next, Tristan turned to the female vampire, who, judging from what I'd seen of her interaction with my father, was his right hand. Once again, I was struck by her beauty—the ivory skin and clear blue eyes seemed so out of place among this team of warriors. "And this is our scholar. If you need to know about dark races history, Nyx is your gal."

I froze.

"Wait," Adam said. "Nyx?" He shot me a sidelong glance.

The female nodded and smiled. "Don't wear it out," she said with a wink.

"Oh shit," Giguhl breathed.

Tristan frowned. "Is something wrong?"

My mouth worked for a moment as I struggled to wrap my mind around the fact that the vampire Asclepius wanted me to kill worked with my father. But Adam put his arm around me and squeezed, a warning to keep quiet. "Oh, it's nothing. It's just an unusual name."

Nyx laughed. "It's a nickname. My real name is pretty pretentious, so I prefer Nyx."

I opened my mouth to ask her real name, but Giguhl piped up. "Hey, Sabina, isn't she the—"

"Thank you all," Adam said louder than necessary to cover Giguhl's potential blunder, "for your help tonight."

The mancy elbowed me in the ribs because I was openly gawking at Nyx. "Oh, um, yes. Thanks."

"Sun's coming," Tristan said. "We should all turn in. Nyx, can you show Sabina and her friends to their rooms?"

The vampire nodded. "This way, Miss Graecus."

"She's a Kane," Tristan said.

Her cheeks heated. "Forgive me. Of course. Miss Kane."

"Don't worry about it," I said. "You can just call me Sabina." I pointed to the mancy and the demon. "Adam and Giguhl," I said, finally introducing them since Tristan had rudely left them out of the intros.

She smiled at the guys. "Yeah, we met earlier."

I'd totally forgotten that Adam and Giguhl had somehow found Tristan and his team to come help me. I definitely needed to get that story from Adam once we were alone.

Nyx shook hands with each male anyway. I noticed she didn't hesitate or flinch when shaking Giguhl's claw. The fact that she treated Giguhl with the same respect she showed Adam and me was impressive. Classy move.

"If you'll follow me?"

I glanced at Tristan, who'd stepped away to speak with Horus and Calyx. Judging by their alert postures, they were talking about something important. That worked for me. I wasn't looking for some sort of warm farewell. Still, it rankled that he just handed us off to his underling and expected we'd do as we were told.

As we followed Nyx, I watched her chat amicably with Giguhl. Why in the hell couldn't Asclepius have sent me to kill anyone else but someone on Tristan's team? Don't get me wrong, I didn't have too many moral qualms about killing her. I didn't want to kill her, but I knew going into this mission I might have to make tough choices. And right then, Nyx was standing in the way of being clear and free of Asclepius's debt.

No, it was more a strategic quandary. I was pretty sure making Asclepius happy would also screw up my plans to convince Tristan to let us help him catch Cain.

Maybe if I made it look like an accident, I thought. But wait, she had that stupid vest that made her immune to magical and mundane weapons. So I also had to figure out how to get her out of it—

"Sabina?" Nyx's voice cut into my thoughts. I jerked my head up to look at her.

"Huh?"

"Everything okay?" She smiled genuinely, like she actually cared.

No. You're fucking up my plans, lady.

I cleared my throat and forced a smile. "Peachy."

*   *   *

Nyx took us the opposite direction from the villa and toward the orchard. As we walked, she chattered about the history of the estate. "This was originally Etruscan land. In fact, there's a tomb in the villa's basement."

That certainly explained the tingle of awareness I felt the minute I stepped onto the property. I hoped the existence of a burial ground wouldn't cause problems. I tended to have mishaps around graves. But maybe the fact that this particular one was pretty ancient would mean there'd be no accidental zombie summoning, like that time in New Orleans.

"…farmland until the church purchased it," Nyx was saying.

We'd already passed the outbuildings I'd seen when we arrived and continued past a small garden. Hearty rosemary plants still thrived despite the chill. The piney scent perfumed the air.

"The villa was originally a convent and was used as a hospital for the aged and infirm. That's why, in addition to the crypt in the basement, there's also a cemetery through there." She pointed toward a field on the right. She turned into the olive grove and waved us along. "Eventually a noble family bought the land and turned it into a country estate. But after a couple of centuries, the family fell on hard times and had to sell. Tristan got the place for next to nothing."

She looked at me, as if waiting for me to confirm that Tristan was clever. I sent a lukewarm smile and nodded. "I'm surprised it's so well maintained. When Tristan mentioned coming here, I had the impression it was deserted."

"When you called Tristan a few days ago, he sent me ahead to get everything ready. I went back to join them after Tristan found out you weren't…" She drifted off.

"Maisie," I said.

She nodded, her expression apologetic.

Adam cleared his throat. "Forgive me, but how did you all survive when Cain woke?"

I paused, realizing I hadn't had a chance to explain what few details Tristan had shared about that the night we met.

Nyx's face fell. "We didn't all survive. We lost six in the battle."

We all fell silent as that sank in. Given the strength I'd seen in Tristan's surviving team members, the fight must have been pretty fierce.

Nyx continued. "The only reason Tristan and the rest of us are alive is that we were out on a mission that night—luckily. If we'd been there, we'd be dead too. No doubt about it."

"I'm sorry for your losses." The words felt so inadequate even as they spilled out of my mouth. Having lost so many friends at Cain's hands myself, I knew the rage they all must have felt.

Nyx nodded to accept my feeble consolation. "He wouldn't have gotten so many of us if we'd seen it coming." Her eyes darkened. "When we returned later that night, we found all the bodies. Luckily the cameras captured the entire thing. Or unluckily, I guess," she laughed uncomfortably. "One second he was unconscious and the next he leapt off the table. He managed to take the guard by surprise and unarm him. Between the shock and knowing the consequences if he was mortally wounded, the team didn't stand a chance. He cut through them like a hot knife through butter." She shook her head. "The worst part is we have no idea how he managed to break Tristan's spell. Only his blood should have been able to unlock it."

I grimaced as my stomach clenched. "I do. I know how he did it."

Nyx's eyebrows rose in question.

I swallowed and quickly filled her in. "Just before he killed Maisie, he compelled her to do the ritual to break the spell using her blood."

Her mouth fell open. "Oh my gods. Since she was his daughter..." She trailed off.

We reached a small bungalow on the edge of the olive grove. Nyx shook herself as if dispelling a shiver. "Tristan will be interested to know the specifics. It will aid him in crafting a new spell when we try to trap Cain again."

I bit my tongue at this. I'd already told Tristan that Maisie broke the spell, but I'm sure he'd want every last detail I could remember. But if I had my way, I'd be changing Tristan's mind about his plans to capture Cain on his own the next evening.

Nyx used an old-fashioned key to unlock the door. Throwing it open, she flipped the light switch. "Here we are."

The walls of the living area were light blue and painted with faded murals of nymphs and fauns. A low wood-beamed ceiling hung over the space, giving it a cozy feel. Off this area was a small kitchen with a wooden table and a tiny fridge.

We all spent a few minutes wandering through the space, checking for security measures. As it turned out, there were shockingly few in place. The doors had only simple locks—easily broken in by a well-placed boot. Adam said he'd set up some wards before we turned in.

"I guess I'll leave you to it, then," Nyx said.

"Thanks." Adam smiled at the vamp.

She paused, looking restless, like she had more to say. She bit her lip and then finally spoke. "Listen, Sabina, I know it's not my place, but we're all really glad you're here."

I laughed. "I'm not sure your leader agrees."

She waved a hand. "Oh, Tristan's all bluster. You'll get used to it once you get to know him."

I forced a smile. No use telling her I wasn't there to get to know anyone. The fact that Tristan was my father didn't matter. He was just someone I had to work with to get the job done.

After Nyx left, Adam, Giguhl, and I gathered in the comfy living room for a postmortem.

A fire crackled in the hearth, but I was having trouble relaxing despite the surroundings. Giguhl stood next to the hearth, looking unfazed by the crazy turn of events. Had it really just been a few hours earlier that we'd set out to trap Cain?

"Where to start," I said with a sigh.

"We can start with Nyx." Adam nodded toward the door the vampire had just walked through.

"Yeah," Giguhl said. "When are you gonna kill her?"

"Giguhl, don't be ridiculous," Adam said. "She can't kill Nyx now."

I chewed on my bottom lip. "Not yet anyway."

"Sabina," Adam said, his tone full of censor.

"What?" I shrugged. "I don't know yet. I mean, obviously I can't just take her out in the middle of everyone. But maybe if I staged an accident?"

A frank male stare greeted that statement.

"Hey, I'm not saying I want to kill her. I mean, she seems nice and all. But weren't you the one who said I shouldn't screw around with a god?"

The mage sighed and fell back against the couch cushions. "Normally, no, you shouldn't. But I'm thinking that assassinating one of your father's team won't end well for any of us. Especially when we need him to stop Cain."

I scrubbed my hands through my hair. "Look, I don't have to make a decision right now. I'll just see how things go."

"Fine," Adam said. "Just promise me that you'll discuss it with us before you act."

"Of course," I said.

"Okay, now that that's settled," Giguhl said, "what the hell went down with Cain? I heard you try to summon me, but nothing happened."

I grimaced at the remembered pain. "He had his goons stab me in the back with a brass stake."

He curled his claw into a fist. "I'd like to shove a stake up that bastard's ass."

Adam's lip curled. "Remind me not to piss you off."

The demon raised his brow. "Trust that shit, mancy."

"Anyway," I said. "I want to know how you found Tristan and convinced him to help rescue me."

"After you disappeared with Cain," Adam began, "I flashed back to the apartment, grabbed Giguhl, and we went straight to Dicky's bar."

I frowned. "Why Dicky?"

"I didn't trust him when he said he hadn't had any contact with Tristan."

"Dude, you should have seen Adam," Giguhl jumped in. "He threw the mage up against the wall in front of everyone and threatened to burn the bar down if Dicky didn't get Tristan on the phone."

"Holy crap! What did Dicky's pals do?"

Adam waved a hand. "Not much. They were too busy trying not to piss themselves in the presence of a huge, angry demon."

I grinned at them. "I wish I could have seen that."

"Hells yeah," Giguhl said. He held up a claw for Adam to high-five. The mancy halfheartedly tapped it back.

"Anyway, once I convinced Dicky I was serious, he had no problem getting Tristan on speakerphone."

"And boy was he pissed," Giguhl said. "When he found out you were still in Rome, he almost crawled through the phone."

I glanced at Adam. "How'd you convince him?"

The mancy smiled. "After he stopped yelling, I simply reminded him that even though he didn't believe you were the Chosen, you were still his daughter. I also might have mentioned that if he didn't help and you died, I would hunt him down and kill him myself."

"Holy shit!"

Adam didn't crack a smile. Obviously, he'd been dead serious when he threatened my father. "He demanded my name. When I told him, he said he remembered my father. And of course he knew Aunt Rhea pretty well."

"Wait, you threatened him and all he did was ask your name?"

Adam nodded. "I get the impression your father isn't a stranger to threats. Anyway, I guess something I said changed his mind because next thing we knew, he appeared in Dicky's office with his posse."

I blew out a breath and leaned back. As grateful as I was that Tristan relented and helped Adam and Giguhl, it irked me that their acquaintance was what changed his mind. My life being in danger didn't sway him, but the fact that Adam's aunt was a bigwig mage did? Nice. But none of that was Adam's and Giguhl's fault. "Thanks, guys."

Adam's jaw clenched. "I'm not letting you more than arm's length away from me for a good long time."

I realized then just how hard it must have been for him to watch Cain disappear with me. I squeezed his hand. "I'm sorry."

He lifted my hand and kissed my knuckles. "Don't ever scare me like that again."

"Bael's balls, it suddenly smells like Cupid farted up in here." Giguhl yawned and stretched. "I'm gonna turn in before you two scar me permanently with your sexings. Try to keep the grunting down."

I raised a brow. "You too," I shot back.

"Seriously, G," Adam said. "One of these days you're going to sprain your claw."

"Don't talk about Darlene that way." He flexed the digits of his claw. "She's a gentle lover."

Adam looked at the demon like he'd just spoken in tongues. "You named your claw after a woman?"

Giguhl rolled his eyes. "Don't judge." With that, he turned and headed toward his room. On the way, he grabbed a bottle of olive oil from the countertop. When he shut the door behind him, I turned to Adam.

"Are you as disturbed as I am by what we just witnessed?"

"Are you referring to the fact that your demon is about to seduce himself less than twenty feet from where we're sitting?"

I nodded.

The mancy took my hand and helped me rise. "I say we drink an entire bottle of wine and never speak of this again."

19

*T*hat night I had the most delicious dream. Adam and I were on a moonlit beach. The waves licked the sand languidly. The waters were calm, peaceful.

Adam held my hand and stared out at the moon. The bright white orb was heavy, fecund. It rose high above, blessing us with its light.

"Is this the future?" Adam asked in a hushed tone.

I turned to look at him. "Maybe it's the present. The calm before the storm."

In the distance, a bolt of lightning cracked through the sky. There was no sound, but it flashed ominously, like a warning.

"The storm's far away," he said. "We have right now. Just you and me and the moon."

He kissed me then. A sweet, slow kiss. I closed my eyes. Flashes of light from the far-off lightning made the veins in my lids glow red. But I ignored them and surrendered to the moment. Adam's sandalwood scent mixed with the air's salty tang, leaving me thirsty for him.

He lowered me to the sugary sand. Ran his hands over

my skin. I sighed happily and wound my fingers through his hair, pulling him to me for a kiss. This one hotter, deeper. I flipped him over and went to work on his zipper. Soon, but never soon enough, he sprung free, hard and ready.

I slicked my tongue over the salty skin of his neck. His pulse beat fast and hot. He swallowed and bucked his hips. "Take it."

He thrust into me at the same moment my fangs pierced his throat. His blood filled my mouth, his sex my core.

"Yes," he hissed.

I was so lost in the taste, the feel of him, I didn't notice the pulling sensation at first. But then it grew in intensity, tugging at me.

I grabbed Adam's shoulders tighter. Grasped his hips with my knees. But the irresistible force ripped me away.

"Sabina?" Adam shouted, sounding far away.

He lay far below me on the sand, his arms outstretched and his mouth wide as he screamed my name. My body launched through the air, away from the safety of his arms, like I'd been shot from a catapult.

My landing was not gentle or graceful. I hit something hard and tumbled ass over ankles. Pushing my hair from my eyes, I realized I'd fallen at someone's feet. Feet encased in familiar sandals.

"Shit." I scrambled back, my eyes rising up the white robes to meet the fierce scowl of Asclepius. "Did anyone ever tell you your timing really sucks?"

He crossed his arms and said nothing. Uh-oh.

I rose awkwardly, surveying my new surroundings. He'd brought me to the Crossroads in the Liminal. Eight roads created the spokes of the wagon-wheel pattern. In the center, where we were, a tall pole was topped by a red flag.

A chill crept down my spine. The last time I'd been in the

Liminal was the night Cain murdered Maisie. I had a feeling Asclepius hadn't chosen this spot to deliver happy news.

"Why is Nyx still alive?"

I held up my hands. In my head, I tried to read his expression for any clue he already knew I'd found her. If he was unaware Nyx was a member of Tristan's team, I didn't want to be the one to tell him. But instead of outright lying, I went with vagueness. "There are some...complications."

He made a disgusted sound. "I grow impatient with your excuses, Mixed-Blood."

I held up my hands. "I'm doing the best I can here."

"I know you have found her."

My stomach flip-flopped like a fish choking on air. "How?" No sense denying it. "I thought you couldn't see her?"

"I can hear, Sabina. You have spoken her name numerous times tonight. That tells me you've made progress."

"Look, what do you want from me? I've got Cain on my ass and my father just showed up out of the blue after fifty-odd years. And on top of that the chick you want dead is his friend." I shook my head as stress threatened to overwhelm me. "Thanks for forgetting to mention that little detail, by the way."

He smirked and offered a careless shrug. "If I told you Nyx was an ally of your father's, it only would have complicated matters prematurely."

"And by that you mean I would have refused to take the deal."

"Precisely. But you took the deal and now you must see it through or suffer the consequences."

"Can't I just kill her after I take care of Cain? If I kill her now, Tristan won't help me."

"Not my problem."

I scrambled to think of a solution. There had to be a way to appease Asclepius without ending any chance of getting Tristan's help. "What if I can convince her to give me the vest? That's what you really want, right?"

The god pursed his lips. "If I just wanted the vest, I would have said so. No, Nyx must be punished for her treachery."

I threw up my hands. "I can't do it now! If you can just hold on until I figure out this Cain situation, then I can take care of Nyx. Otherwise, it cannot and will not be my priority."

"I could easily make it your first priority." The threat in his tone made goose bumps spread over my skin. "Did you know Cain thinks you're still somewhere in Rome?"

I just stared at him. Inside, I was bracing myself.

"Perhaps Cain would kill Nyx for me. He is, after all, He Who Kills to Get Gain." The god tilted his head. "I figure it wouldn't take much to buy his services. Just a simple address."

I clenched my teeth. "You wouldn't do that."

He smiled. "Wouldn't I?"

"If it's that easy to sell me out to Cain, why haven't you already?"

His expression became thoughtful. "Because watching you amuses me. Also, I am no fan of Master Mahan, as you'll recall."

I nodded, remembering that Cain and Asclepius fought each other in the Liminal when the god tried to help Maisie at my request. "Then how can you even consider helping him?"

"I am a fair god, Sabina. I believe in chances, which is why you have had three opportunities to make good on your promises."

I snorted. "Yeah, you're a real upstanding guy like that."

"Silence yourself before my good humor flees." He shot

me a glare that would make lesser women cry. "Because I am so reasonable, I will give you seventy-two hours. If Nyx is not dead and the vest is not in my possession by then, I will go to Cain."

"You are a real bastard, you know that?"

He smirked. "I do."

I sighed. "Okay, fine."

He looked surprised by my easy acceptance. "You're going to kill her?"

"What choice do I have?"

He banged his staff three times into the packed dirt, just like he had when we'd made our original deal in New Orleans. His way of sealing our contract, I guessed.

"I'm relieved that you're being so practical, Sabina. It'd be such a pity to unleash Cain on you when you're so close to achieving your goal."

I tilted my head. "What do you know about it?" I asked carefully. I didn't want to act too eager and give Asclepius something else to hold over my head.

"Stay on your course and you'll get your chance."

"What does that even mean? I'll get my chance to kill Cain?"

The god shrugged in an infuriating manner. "We'll see."

I made a disgusted sound. I was so sick of vague prophecies and the god's love of verbal chess.

"All right, then," Asclepius said. "Off with you. Don't forget—you have three nights."

A flash of lightning tore through the Crossroads, blinding me. When I opened my eyes again, I was in bed. Adam snored quietly with his back to me. I sat up slowly so as not to wake him. I tiptoed to the bathroom and splashed some water on my face. When I looked up into the mirror, I stared hard at my reflection.

It had been months since I killed someone. Even longer since I'd killed someone who hadn't tried to kill me first. While I was eager to kill Cain in the most painful manner possible, Nyx didn't deserve to die. Sure, she'd jilted Asclepius out of a favor, but in my mind that just proved she was cleverer than I'd given her credit for. It was the god's own fault for not collecting before giving her the means to hide from him.

But the fact remained that Asclepius was serious about his threat to reveal my location to Cain. Dead serious. If I didn't kill Nyx, Cain would kill everyone anyway and then force me to take him to Lilith.

I ran a hand over my damp face. Sometimes my recently discovered conscience was a real pain in the ass. The old me wouldn't have thought twice about removing Nyx as an obstacle. But the new me? Felt like the entire situation wasn't just needlessly complicated, but also unjustified. Even if I could convince myself to kill an innocent being, I couldn't get over the harshness of Asclepius's punishment. Did anyone deserve to die just to soothe the ego of a god?

Also playing into my resentment was the fact that Asclepius had backed me into a corner. If he'd known me better, he'd understand that blackmail pissed me off more than it intimidated me. No matter how this all played out, I was now determined to make the god pay for putting me in this position—that is, if I survived long enough to deliver the just desserts.

I groaned and pulled away from the mirror. Despite my qualms, the consequences of not killing Nyx were worse than the ding my conscience would take doing it. So, unless the moonrise brought one of Adam's miracles with it, it looked like I would have to add murder to my To Do list.

20

The next evening, I woke alone. For once, I was relieved Adam had already risen. After I'd fallen back to sleep following Asclepius's ultimatum, my subconscious had become a nightmare realm.

The fright fest had featured all the greatest hits: Maisie calling me a murderer, Cain taunting me with promises of pain, and Tristan telling me I was a huge disappointment.

Maisie and Cain I could handle. I didn't have to face them that evening. But Tristan was waiting for me not a hundred yards from the safety of my bed. I had no illusions that convincing him to see me as more than an inconvenient guest would be easy. But I refused to take no for an answer. I wasn't sure if I was the Chosen, but I knew I was the most motivated to do whatever it took to end Cain.

Including, it appeared, murdering Nyx.

I'd hoped that sleeping on the issue would present some sort of new solution, but I just couldn't figure out a way around it. I still needed to talk to Adam, but I had a sinking feeling he wouldn't be able to offer me a viable solution either.

I sighed and forced myself from the warm covers. My feet slapped the cold hardwood a split second before Giguhl rushed in.

"Oh good, you're up."

I rubbed the sleep from my eyes and yawned. "Barely. What's up?"

"Nyx already came by. Said Tristan was getting antsy waiting for you."

The vampire's name made my stomach cramp. To cover my reaction, I glanced at the windows. It was already full dark. "Shit. What time is it?"

"Seven."

I started rushing around looking for clothes. "Why didn't you wake me?" Freaking great. I'd planned on going in strong and forcing him to listen to my reasons for teaming up. Now he'd have the advantage because I felt rushed and guilty for sleeping in.

"Adam said you needed the rest," Giguhl said with a shrug.

I pulled on a pair of jeans. "Where is he?"

"He went to check on the security for the rest of the estate."

I tossed on a long-sleeved T-shirt and ran a comb through my hair. "Okay." I blew out a breath. "Let's go."

"Um, Red?"

I stopped. "What?"

"Shoes."

"Shit."

Instead of leading me to the villa, the demon made a right to enter one of the other buildings I'd spied the night before.

A simple wooden door opened into a large room. Judging from the massive, map-strewn table in the center, this was mission control of Tristan's operation. And speaking of control, Tristan stood at the head of the table bent over a large map of Italy. Nyx was by his side, eagerly listening as my father spoke to Horus.

When we entered, a few eyes strayed in our direction but were quickly averted to refocus on tasks. Tristan, however, kept his eyes on the map. Instead, it was Nyx who came over to guide us toward the lord and master.

She reached for me with a smile, but I shied away. I didn't want her kindness muddying the waters. Not when I'd likely be betraying it so soon.

If Nyx noticed my coldness, she didn't react. She simply left us at one side of the table and went to rejoin Tristan. We stood nearby long enough that I was starting to get twitchy. Apparently, no one interrupted Tristan Graecus until he was good and ready.

"...when Calyx gets back from hunting," Tristan was saying to Horus.

I cleared my throat loudly. Tristan paused and shot me an annoyed look.

Horus's eyes shifted to me, his expression clearly implying I'd made a breach of etiquette. "Yes, sir." His response was so enthusiastic and dripping with respect I expected him to salute. As he rushed off to do Tristan's bidding, my father finally turned to acknowledge us.

"Glad you finally decided to join us," Tristan said. "Since we didn't get a chance to discuss it last night after the rescue, I need you to debrief Nyx on how exactly you managed to let Cain kidnap you."

Oh, he was good. Shame me for my lateness and then follow it up with a topic guaranteed to put me on the defensive. If my father knew me better—or at all—he'd have known I knew his games better than he did. I'd been raised by the master of power players—Lavinia Kane.

"If your spell to bind him had been better, Cain wouldn't have had the chance to kidnap me or anyone else."

All the air was sucked out of the room. Tristan's people froze like statues. Giguhl's gaze swiveled between Tristan and me, as if trying to figure out who would punch first.

Tristan, however, laughed. "I see the apple doesn't fall far from the tree."

Adam walked in the door. He immediately saw all the tense postures and the anger hovering in the air like a bitter fog. He shot me a questioning look, but I was too busy glaring at my father.

"What the hell does that mean?" I demanded.

"You get that bitchy streak from your mother's family."

I slammed a hand down on the map. Tristan crossed his arms. His cool, unruffled demeanor made me see red. Once I was sure I had his attention, I spoke in a low, hard voice. "Do not presume to know me."

Tristan stood up straighter. "You don't like it? You're free to leave."

Godsdamn him. He knew I wouldn't—couldn't—leave.

"Actually," he continued, "why are you here? Oh, that's right." He snapped his fingers. "Because you didn't listen to me and got yourself captured by your enemy. You're impetuous and stubborn, and one of these days it's going to get you killed. You don't want to get as good as you give?" He pointed to the door. "Good luck."

The weight of several stares pushed down on my shoulders. My cheeks flamed with shame. He made it sound like I was some spoiled child.

Luckily, Adam cleared his throat and stepped in before I

could prove him correct. "Maybe we need to take a deep breath here. We're all on the same side."

Tristan looked at Adam. "Who invited you into this discussion?"

A muscle in Adam's jaw went rock hard.

"I invited him," I said, barely containing my anger at his rudeness. "Look, you're right. I made a mistake. I thought I could handle Cain but I couldn't. But you know what? Neither could you."

Tristan's face hardened. I held up a hand to stall another flare-up.

"That's why we need to band together. We're clearly not getting anywhere separately. Maybe together we can prevail against our common enemy."

A muscle worked in Tristan's jaw. I had him and we both knew it.

"So drop the bullshit dictator routine and let's get busy."

He snorted. "Get busy doing what? My plan involved the Chosen."

I raised a brow. "What makes you so sure I'm not her?"

"Let's just say I have it on good authority."

Giguhl snorted. "Oh, that's convincing."

Tristan raised a brow at me. "Do you always allow your minion to question his superiors?"

"Giguhl is a member of my team. He's free to speak his mind." I crossed my arms. "As for you being superior to him in any way? Not fucking likely."

The demon puffed up.

My father hesitated, like he suspected I was fucking with him. "You treat your minion as an equal? Seriously?"

I crossed my arms. "As a heart attack."

"Interesting." His tone clearly indicated he was adding that to my list of faults.

"Whatever," I said. "You were about to tell us who told you Maisie was the Chosen."

"I have a source inside Lilith's court."

"Who?" Giguhl asked. He knew more about the power players in the demon world than anyone.

"I highly doubt a fifth-level Mischief demon would know a member of Lilith's inner circle."

The demon raised a scraggly black brow. "Try me."

"Or better yet," I said, "bring this mysterious source here so he can tell us."

"She," Tristan corrected. "And I don't see why summoning her is necessary."

"Actually, it's a good idea," Adam said. "After all, Maisie herself believed Sabina was the Chosen."

"Predictions from Oracles are notoriously slippery," Tristan said.

"And demons are notorious liars," I countered. "No offense, G."

The demon shrugged. "It's true."

I found it hard to believe I was arguing that I was the Chosen. After all, I'd used the same logic Tristan was throwing at me when Maisie and Rhea tried to convince me I was supposed to be the New Lilith. According to them, New Lilith was supposed to rise up and unite the dark races, ushering in an eternity of peace for everyone.

As nice as that sounded, I prefer free will over fate, and the very idea some path had been picked for me grated. However, back then, we hadn't known that the Chosen could kill Cain. If that was true, I'd wear a crown and sash with "Chosen" written in gold glitter if that's what it took to convince my father.

"Look, you said only the Chosen can kill Cain," Adam

argued. "Don't you think it's pretty important we're absolutely sure it can't be Sabina before you dismiss the only chance we have to kill him?"

Tristan sighed. "Fine, I'll summon her. But only so you'll drop this nonsense once and for all."

A puff of purple smoke erupted in the circle of salt Tristan had cast. The scent of brimstone and a high-pitched whine filled the room.

"Tristy!"

At the same moment I recognized the voice, the smoke cleared, revealing a six-foot-tall golden skinned demon with a peacock's tail.

My stomach pitched and rolled. "No fucking way."

"Oh shit," Adam breathed.

Both our gazes swiveled to Giguhl. He looked like he'd been sucker punched. "Valva?" he whispered.

The Vanity demon froze, her blue gaze locked with the Mischief's. "Schmoopie?"

Giguhl whimpered.

"Keep it together, G," I said.

A bead of sweat crept down Giguhl's temple, just below his horn. "Wh-what is she doing here?" he said, his voice panicked.

Tristan frowned. "What do you mean? You asked me to summon my informant."

Either Valva got tired of waiting or she couldn't contain her excitement a second longer. Totally ignoring the salt circle, she leapt across the room and launched herself at Giguhl.

"Sugar lump!" She jumped up and wrapped her legs around Giguhl's stiff frame. "I've missed you!"

My minion looked shell shocked as the Vanity demon rained kisses all over his face.

Adam and I exchanged a worried look.

"Red?" Giguhl whimpered. "Help."

I almost refused. It was one thing to support my friend. It was something else entirely to try to peel an amorous Vanity demon—and her thrusting pelvis—away from the reluctant object of her affection. So instead, I took the middle road.

"Ahem! Valva?"

The smacking sound of her kisses filled up the room. It was so loud, everyone else averted their eyes from the display. Tristan's arms were crossed and he glared at me like it was all my fault.

"What the hell is going on?" he demanded.

I held up a hand to tell him to hold his horses. My priority was saving Giguhl.

When the Vanity didn't respond to my voice, I tapped her very hard on the shoulder. Some might call it a punch, but potayto, potahto.

She paused her kisses and turned her head, a fierce scowl on her face. "Oh. Sabina. It's you."

I executed a little wave. "Hey, V. Listen, do you think you could pull yourself away from sexually assaulting Giguhl long enough to explain what the fuck you're doing here?"

She snorted. "I'm not assaulting him."

"Giguhl?" I asked, keeping my eyes locked with Valva's glare. "Do you want Valva to keep dry humping you?"

"Yes! No! I'm so confused!" he wailed.

I snapped my fingers and pointed at the demoness. "You, down."

She opened her golden lips to respond, but a quiet command from Tristan shut her down. "Now, Valva."

According to the laws of demon–mage relations, since he'd summoned her, he technically controlled her. But I knew from experience Valva wasn't your typical demon.

The demon rolled her eyes and, with obviously reluctance, dismounted from Giguhl.

"Now," I said to Tristan and Valva. "Explain yourselves."

"I'm as confused as you are," Tristan said. "I had no idea your minion was acquainted with Valva."

"Oh, I'd say from the looks of things, they're a little more than acquainted," Nyx said, tongue firmly in cheek.

Back in New York, not long after I'd arrived and met Maisie for the first time, Giguhl had started fighting in Slade's Demon Fight Club. Surprisingly, my Mischief demon turned out to be a fierce fighter in the ring and quickly became the demon to beat—that was, until Valva strutted into the ring. A few flicks of her blue peacock tail and Giguhl was a goner. Not only did he refuse to fight her, but he also declared his love for her the very same night.

Long story short, my twin had taken custody of Valva. It wasn't Maisie's choice since the Vanity demon bound herself to my sister, but the arrangement seemed to work out well for both of them. At first.

It was only later, after our grandmother had kidnapped Maisie, that Valva had shown her true colors. The drama went down in a vampire strip club in Los Angeles. We'd gone there to seek the help of an old ally in finding my sister. Unfortunately, the Vanity demon didn't understand the meaning of the phrase "low profile" and had jumped onstage to work the pole. In addition to starting a riot among the vamp strippers, she'd also made such a scene that the Dominae's guards found us.

Once we'd narrowly escaped the bar, Valva had turned on us when we tried to make her understand why we were angry.

First she called me a controlling bitch. Then she'd turned on Giguhl, the demon she supposedly loved. She broke his heart and flashed out like she couldn't wait to be rid of us.

But now we found out that she'd been helping Tristan. And I wanted some answers.

"Valva?" I said, raising a brow. "You want to explain yourself?"

She dusted off her tail feathers. "Not particularly."

"Too damned bad," Adam said, crossing his arms. "Why do you keep popping up? First you show up in New York and now you're an informant for Sabina's father. We deserve an explanation."

She shrugged. "It's simple. Since I can move between Irkalla and the mortal realm, Mom sometimes asks me to do little jobs for her."

I rolled my eyes at her use of the word "mom." I had a hard time imagining Lilith, the dark goddess and Great Mother, as anyone's mommy.

"Little jobs like manipulating people?" Adam said.

The demon's eyes shifted left. "Maybe."

Tristan crossed his arms. "Will someone please tell me what you're talking about?"

While Adam filled Tristan and his group in on our past experiences with Valva, I sidled up to Giguhl. "You okay?"

He kept his wary gaze on the Vanity. She was too busy interrupting Adam and adding her own version of the story to notice Giguhl's regard. "I don't know," he said. "I just... didn't think I'd ever see her again."

"You and me both." I patted him on the arm. "Don't worry. With any luck we won't have to deal with her for very long."

He nodded absently but didn't look as enthused about her eventual exit as I'd hoped.

"So basically what I'm saying is that given her history of deceit and manipulation, I'd suggest you seriously reconsider trusting any intel she's given you," Adam said to Tristan.

"Hey!" Valva squeaked. "I never lied to you guys."

I glared at her. "Whether you spoke any lies or not doesn't matter. You led us to believe you were Maisie's minion and then you fucked us over in Los Angeles."

She threw up her hands. "I didn't have a choice! Mom called me back to Irkalla. I had to make a clean break from you guys."

"Really?" Giguhl said finally, his tone hard. "You call that clean?"

Valva's cheeks reddened. "I didn't want to hurt you. But don't you see? You wouldn't have let me go if I hadn't said those things."

Adam, Giguhl, and I simply stared at her with pitiless expressions. She'd told Giguhl he had a small dick and was a lousy lay. Hardly necessary or fair. Because Valva was a Lilitu, the race of demons spawned directly from Lilith as opposed to the Shedim demons like Giguhl who were bound to Irkalla unless summoned by a mage, she could flash between the worlds at will. Therefore, she could have just disappeared without saying anything. Instead, she'd pillaged Giguhl's heart and TNTed any chance of us ever trusting her again.

Valva's lip started to tremble. "I'm sorry."

"Save your tears, okay?" Giguhl said. "They won't work on me. Not anymore."

Valva made a little choked sound and ran out of the building. Nyx called after her and followed, presumably to comfort the demon.

Tristan sent a fierce frown at the demon. "That was unnecessarily rude."

I snorted. "Whatever. She's a Vanity demon, Tristan. Those tears aren't real. Valva doesn't care about Giguhl or any of us. You'd be a fool to trust anything she says."

"Look," Tristan sighed. "I'm sorry if you had a bad experience with her. But I trust her."

I threw up my hands. "How can you say that?"

"Because she saved my life."

I realized I'd been so thrown off by Valva's sudden arrival that I hadn't gotten the story on why she told Tristan that Maisie was the Chosen. "How?"

Tristan sighed, clearly impatient with the entire situation. "I'll tell you but you'll have to come to my room. There are some things I should show you."

I exchanged a look with Adam. Would we finally start getting some answers now? "Lead the way."

*T*ristan led us through the manor house and down into the basement. On our way there, we saw no sign of Nyx or Valva. Probably they'd locked themselves in one of the villa's rooms so the demon could whine about how mean we were.

Calyx and Horus had stayed behind to do tasks Tristan had given them. Giguhl had bowed out of joining us, saying he needed some alone time. Upon hearing this, Adam and I shared a tense glance but otherwise kept our mouths shut. No doubt there'd be a big discussion about Valva's appearance later, but for now we needed to focus on getting answers from Tristan.

He led us through the villa and down a set of rickety steps to the basement. The instant my feet hit the ground, an overwhelming wave of death energy consumed me. "What the hell?" I gasped, swaying.

"Oh, it's the Etruscan tomb over there." Tristan pointed to a low opening in the wall. "I find it stimulating."

I swallowed the bile that rose. "That's one word for it."

"Hmm," he said. "Obviously you haven't had very much training in your Chthonic powers."

My mouth dropped open. "Yeah, my Chthonic father should have trained me but he disappeared before I was born."

Tristan grimaced and turned away. He threw open a door and entered without another word. I closed my eyes and took a couple of calming breaths and willed the power in my solar plexus to equalize. Adam's hand touched my shoulder. "You okay?"

I opened my eyes and nodded. "Yeah."

"Nice comeback, by the way. Did it make you feel better?"

"It did." My lip twitched. "Thanks."

"Let's go." He kept a hand on the small of my back as we entered. I felt fine, but I appreciated the connection.

Tristan's room resembled a monk's cell. A single twin bed sat in the corner. Little more than a mat on a spring frame with a single, thin blanket. No pillow. In keeping with the ascetic theme, his few possessions were organized with military precision. Shoes lined up neatly along one wall. A small chest with a pair of pants neatly folded on top. A single shirt hanging from a hook.

In fact, books were the only embellishments. Behind the table and chair in the "office," the entire wall was covered in bookcases. Most people intersperse knickknacks among their books, but these shelves were filled top to bottom with tomes. Row after row of perfectly aligned books, arranged by size. The table was similarly organized. Tidy stacks of papers rested on either side. A pen was perfectly aligned across the top of the leather pad.

Adam and I stood next to each other across the desk from Tristan. The minute we'd entered, he'd beelined for the bookcases. With his back to us, he scanned the cracked leather spines lining the shelves.

Finally, he made a sort of *aha* sound and pulled out a single large volume. Its weight thudded on the desk, upsetting the orderly layout. Instead of opening it, he took time to right the pen and the blotter and align the books perfectly before he looked up. He was so methodical in this exercise I started to wonder if he had a little obsessive-compulsive disorder. Either that or he was buying time before he presented his evidence.

He came around the desk and leaned back against it with his head down and his arms folded. When he looked up, his expression was grave, like he was about to deliver bad news. "How much do you know about when I disappeared?"

I hesitated. I hadn't expected him to start at the very beginning. "Enough. Rhea filled me in on some of it."

"Rhea? I thought Orpheus would have told you."

"He spoke of you some but"—I tilted my head—"he died before any of us knew you still existed."

Tristan paled. "Yes, a great loss for all of magekind. Who is leading the Council now?"

"Rhea."

Tristan's eyes flared. "A wise choice. She'll make an excellent leader."

Adam cleared his throat, clearly uncomfortable with Tristan's familiarity with his aunt. "So Orpheus knew you were alive?"

"Yes. He helped me escape to Europe when it became clear my life was in danger in the States." Tristan shook off his sadness and switched back to business mode. "But I'm afraid after a time, circumstances dictated I cut all ties. It was safer for everyone that way. My biggest regret is that I never had time to explain everything to Orpheus before he died."

I clenched my teeth. Nice that his biggest regret wasn't abandoning Maisie and me.

"What circumstances?" Adam asked.

"We'll get to that in a moment." Tristan shook his head. "Nyx told me what you said about how Cain broke my spell." His expression tightened into anger and I had a feeling it was mostly directed inward. "I had no idea he was accessing the Liminal through his subconscious. If only I'd figured it out sooner, Orpheus and Maisie would still be alive."

I sighed and moved closer. I didn't want to feel bad for my father. Not when the promised explanation hadn't arrived. Not when it was indirectly his fault Orpheus and Maisie were dead. But he suddenly sounded so...defeated. "Look, I'm the last person who wants to excuse you. Trust me on that. But 'if only' won't change anything." I paused. "All we can do now is move forward."

Adam shot me an ironic look. I paused. Huh. Maybe I did need to take that advice myself. I certainly had done my share of that kind of talk since they died, too.

"You're right." Tristan cleared his throat and stood straighter. "So you asked how Valva saved me. But to get to that, I have to admit some uncomfortable things." He paused and took a deep breath. "After I escaped the assassins who were sent after me, I went to California to find your mother. But Phoebe wasn't in Los Angeles."

I nodded. "Lavinia hid her in Muir Woods near San Francisco." I'd met the faery midwife, Briallen Pimpernell, who'd hosted my mother during most of her pregnancy.

Tristan nodded. "By the time I found that out myself, your mother was already dead."

"Wait, you went there?"

He nodded. "Yes. Briallen Pimpernell told me what happened."

My mouth fell open. Adam was similarly shocked. "Wait, Briallen knew you were alive?"

He nodded. "You have to understand. I was inconsolable when I found out Phoebe was dead. I'm ... not proud about this, but I threatened the fae. Told her if she told anyone I was alive, I'd come back and murder her."

I pictured the plump, friendly faery and frowned. I'd rarely met a more gentle spirit than the midwife, and the very idea of Tristan threatening her like that lowered him even further in my opinion. "Did you ask her about us? About Maisie and me?"

His eyes shifted left and he shook his head. "Honestly, I was so insane with grief I didn't care."

My gut twisted. "Nice."

"Sabina, I know how it sounds, but it was a long time ago. Besides, she did manage to tell me that my mother and Lavinia had each taken one of you. I figured you'd be well cared for."

I snorted and crossed my arms. But I didn't want to get into a discussion about my shitty childhood. I didn't need his pity or his apologies. I just wanted answers.

"When I left Briallen, I asked Orpheus to help set me up with a new identity in Europe. I had to get as far away from Phoebe's memory as possible." He shrugged in a self-deprecating way. "I became the cliché of the self-sabotaging mourner. I drank myself silly. Got into fights. Almost got killed a time or two. Then, once I'd move past my anger, I went into a deep well of depression."

"How long did all that last?" Adam asked.

"About five years."

My jaw dropped. A year I'd understand. But five? Jesus. "So what happened once you recovered?"

He looked up then. Dark memories haunted his gaze. "What makes you think I've recovered?"

I looked away. I didn't want to consider that my father

was still in pain. It would be harder to maintain my distance then. "Anyway, you were saying?"

"Five years after your mother died, I decided to try and access Irkalla through the Liminal. I figured I'd just go down there and either steal Phoebe or stay with her." He shrugged self-consciously. "Like I said, I was a little...off. Before I met Phoebe, Ameritat—your grandmother?"

I nodded to acknowledge I knew of her.

"She and I had been experimenting with my magic in the Liminal."

"Yeah, Rhea found Ameritat's journals. She seemed to think you abandoned the experiments because your mom thought it was too risky."

He nodded. "We did. Or rather, once I met your mother, I lost interest." He smiled wryly. "Anyway, I got it in my head that I'd find the entrance on my own. I started going into the Liminal regularly. It was risky, just like we thought. I almost didn't make it back a couple of times."

"Yeah," I said. "It's fucked up."

"You've been there?" He looked both surprised and impressed by this news.

"Twice. Once by accident and the other to find Maisie. It's like an extended horrific acid trip."

He looked at me for a moment. "Yes. That's it exactly. It's bad enough that the landscape constantly changes. But it also messes with your head. Mirages appear. Labyrinths."

"Did you find the entrance to Irkalla?"

"No."

My eyes widened. "No as in not yet or no it doesn't exist?"

"No as in I stopped trying. I went into the Liminal hundreds of times over the years and never found it."

"You just gave up?" I asked.

"No, I woke up. Thanks to Valva."

"Explain."

His face took on the intensity of someone looking deep into the past. "I was lost. Utterly and totally. There was this damned labyrinth. The walls were made of body parts— thousands of corpses. Arms jutting out, sightless eyes." He shivered involuntarily. "I don't know how long I tried to find my way out, but it almost cost me what remained of my sanity." He paused, his eyes looking into the middle distance, clearly lost in the memory. "But then I turned a corner and there she was."

"Valva," Adam said.

Tristan nodded.

I tried to imagine my father, half crazed, lumbering through a labyrinth of bodies and then seeing a six-foot-tall golden demon standing there. It's a wonder he didn't just lose all his marbles right then. "That must have been quite a shock."

He laughed a little. "It was. After she convinced me she was real and wasn't there to kill me, she said she had a message from Lilith. She said that I was wasting my time looking for a door that I wasn't meant to find. She also said I'd be reunited with my Phoebe eventually, but first I had a job to do."

"What kind of job?"

He sighed. "She said that as the father of the Chosen, I had to ensure Cain didn't bring about the end of the dark races before the Chosen had a chance to fulfill the prophecy."

"So that's why you've been so obsessed with Cain?" Adam said.

Tristan grimaced. "Not entirely."

Judging from the reluctance in his tone, I knew I wouldn't like the next part of the story.

He turned to me. "This might be hard for you to hear, but I need you to listen."

I frowned at him. He made a move, like he wanted to take my hands, but I folded my arms against my chest. "Okay?"

His hands fell uselessly at his sides. "When I met your mother, I was in California on a diplomatic mission. Ameritat wanted to negotiate some new provisions for the Black Covenant with the Dominae. I went out with a group of Pythian Guards."

"Was Orpheus there?" Adam asked. In addition to leading the Hekate Council, Orpheus had been the head of the Pythian Guards in the years before his death, but back then he would have just been a member of the special force that protected the Council.

Tristan nodded. "Yes. Anyway, the discussions were going surprisingly well. Lavinia and the others seemed open to the discourse. We'd been there about five nights when Phoebe arrived. She'd been away at one of the estates your grandmother owned, but that night she came home and we all met her. Her beauty struck me immediately. But she was the daughter of Lavinia Kane. I wouldn't have dared incurred her wrath. Besides, I'd been raised to hate all vampires; the idea of becoming romantically involved with one didn't interest me in the slightest, no matter how attractive."

"But you were there on a diplomatic mission."

"Sure," he said, "but that didn't mean I trusted them. Far from it. I slept with an applewood-handled knife under my pillow every night."

"So you didn't dig her immediately," I said. "What changed?"

"It was odd. I'd barely spoken but a few polite words to

her over the course of a few days. She seemed equally uninterested. But then, one night, after a large state dinner, we both ended up in one of the gardens at the Dominae estate. Maybe it was the way the moonlight hit her hair or the music coming from inside the house, but I suddenly found her quite beautiful." He shook his head. "Then we started talking. About books, music, silly things. We didn't have a thing in common, but we talked so long that eventually her maid came looking for her. Before she left, she asked me if I'd meet her again the next night to continue our discussion." He waved a hand. "Anyway, that's how it all began. Once we confessed our feelings for each other, I never questioned how it came about. Or why."

I frowned at him. "What do you mean? Isn't that normal? You spend enough time with someone and feelings sometimes just happen naturally."

"Sabina," he said, his tone frank. "There was nothing natural about it."

I stared at him, confused. "What do you mean?"

"That's what Valva told me in the Liminal. Phoebe and I didn't fall in love because we wanted to. We fell in love because Cain had one of his Caste of Nod mages cast a love spell on us."

I stepped away from him, as if it could protect me from what he was saying. "But why? Why would he do that?"

He raised his hands. "Don't you see? If my negotiations with your grandmother had continued to go well, then Cain would be that much further from his goal. He needed to do something to ensure that lasting peace was never achieved. What better way to do that than to orchestrate a forbidden star-crossed love affair between the daughter of the Alpha Domina and the son of the Hekatian Oracle?"

My breath whooshed out as if he'd punched me.

"Once I found out that all our suffering was based on a lie, making Cain pay became my sole purpose for living. The irony is Cain's plan backfired because his love spell led to the birth of the Chosen. And according to Valva, the Chosen is the only being capable of killing Cain without repercussions."

I'd fallen silent as I tried to absorb the concussions of his bombshells. Only instead of getting all introspective and considering how this information changed my view of myself and my purpose on this earth, I gathered my rage like a lightning bolt in my midsection.

"So to summarize," I said, keeping my tone even and cool, "a Vanity demon showed up when you were crazy and drunk and told you a story where the father of the vampire race forced you to fall in love and make babies with the wrong chick. She also told you not to feel too bad about it because eventually one of those kids would make sure the revenge you craved was carried out. You, naturally, latched on to this explanation because it was easier than accepting that you had any responsibility in the situation."

"No," he said, his voice rising. "It wasn't like that."

I slashed a hand through the air. "You know what?" I said, my voice trembling. I hated that I couldn't hide my anger. "You could have just admitted that you didn't want us." I shrugged but my hands were trembling with rage. "Maybe the thought of being around Maisie and me would just remind you too much of Phoebe. Maybe you'd never wanted kids period and it was more convenient to pawn us off. Whatever. It wouldn't have been easy to hear, but at least it wouldn't have been as insulting as that bullshit you just fed me."

"I know you are angry. It's probably well deserved. However, it doesn't make the facts less true."

"That's funny," Adam snapped. "I haven't heard one fact yet."

"Then maybe you'll believe this." Tristan turned and retrieved one of the books from his orderly desk. "This is a ledger listing members of the Caste of Nod."

Adam and I exchanged looks and practically ran around the desk.

"How the hell did you get it?" I demanded.

"We confiscated it when we managed to bring Cain down a decade ago. It lists members of the Caste going back centuries. If you flip to the 1950s era, you'll see a mage named Birch Jericho listed."

Adam's head snapped up. "Birch? I remember him. He was a friend of my father's."

Tristan nodded. "Yes, I remember you back then. You were what? Five, six when all this happened?"

Adam swallowed. "Yeah. Birch would come visit me every now and then after my parents died and tell me stories about them."

The mancy continued scanning the page. His finger scrolled down the names for a moment before he stopped. "I'll be damned." He kept his eyes on the page while Tristan started explaining.

"Birch was the highest ranking Pythian Guard under Orpheus at the time, so he was with us in Los Angeles." He sighed. "The night I was attacked, a vampire showed up on my doorstep. This was shortly after Lavinia discovered my affair with Phoebe, but of course I didn't know we'd been found out yet. The fighting was furious but I somehow managed to kill him.

"I ran, figuring Lavinia had sent the assassin after me." His hands tightened on the desk. "I ran into Birch on my way to find Orpheus. At first he pretended to want to help, but the instant I turned my back he attack me. After I killed him and dumped his body in the Hudson, I ran. Eventually Orpheus found me, but I was convinced he was there to murder me, too."

"Why?" Adam asked.

"What would you think? Birch was a friend of mine. The only thing I could figure was that Lavinia and Ameritat had decided to kill both Phoebe and me as punishment for breaking the Black Covenant."

"You thought your own mother wanted you dead?" I asked.

"Once Orpheus convinced me he was on my side, he swore I was wrong and said that maybe Birch had gone bad. I didn't believe him and demanded he help me escape to Europe." He nodded. "It was only later that I realized the vampire was sent by Lavinia but that Birch worked for the Caste."

Adam scrubbed his hands over his face. "Okay, so maybe Valva wasn't lying about what happened in the past. But we have no way to know if her predictions for the future are accurate. You said it yourself—prophecies are slippery, and in our experience, so is Valva. Not to mention, how can we be sure Lilith wasn't just fucking with you?"

"Why would she do that?"

I crossed my arms. "Because deities are assholes. They enjoy screwing with our lives and watching us squirm."

"What do you know about deities?" Tristan demanded.

I glanced at Adam. He shook his head. I knew he didn't think this was the time to tell Tristan about my deal with Asclepius, but the perverse part of me wanted to. After the bombshells he'd dropped, I wanted to share one of my own. However, if I told him now, it'd be impossible to convince him Nyx's death was an accident later.

"Because," I began, and paused. Adam shot me a worried look, but I ignored him. "The gods are always manipulating things behind the scenes. So when you tell me that Valva brought you a message from Lilith, I'm immediately suspicious about her motives."

Tristan fell silent. He watched me with a speculative glance, as if he was questioning my motives, too. Finally, he said, "Let's assume for a moment that you're correct."

"She is," Adam said.

Tristan ignored him. "What's our move? Cain is still out there."

"First," Adam said. "We need to get Rhea here. She needs to know what's going on. Besides, she also believes Sabina is the Chosen and I have a feeling you'll trust her word more than ours."

My father sighed. "Okay." There was a phone on his desk. He lifted the receiver and handed it to Adam. "This line's secure. Get her here ASAP. The longer we delay making a plan, the more the risk of Cain finding us."

Adam nodded and dialed. While he spoke to Rhea, Tristan turned to me. He opened his mouth to say something, but a female voice interrupted. "Tristan?"

We both looked up to see Nyx and Valva standing at the top of the steps. Valva's eyes were red rimmed and puffy. She wouldn't look directly at me, which was fine because my gaze was glued on Nyx. And Tristan's narrowed gaze was on Valva.

"Valva has something to say to you."

Adam hung up the phone. "Rhea's on her way. She'll manifest in the courtyard."

I nodded, but my eyes were still swiveling between Tristan and Valva.

"Tristy...," Valva began.

He looked away from her. "Sabina, why don't you and Adam go meet Rhea. We'll all convene in the living room upstairs."

Without comment, Adam and I made hasty progress to the door.

As we approached Nyx and Valva, the demon glared at me. Dismissing her, I glanced at Nyx and saw something golden wink from the V of her shirt. My eyes widened, realizing I was seeing the top of the magical vest. I jerked my gaze away as if staring too long might singe my corneas.

Something in my gaze must have startled Nyx. Her smiled faltered and she stepped aside, pulling the edges of her shirt together. I nodded as I passed but couldn't look her in the eye.

Asclepius's deadline hung over both our heads like an executioner's ax, but only one of us was aware of the danger. But I couldn't do anything about that situation until I had a chance to talk to Adam so we could figure out all the angles. In the meantime, I prayed Rhea would be able to convince Tristan to listen to reason.

22

*I*f Rhea felt one ounce of relief or nostalgia at seeing Tristan in the flesh for the first time in almost fifty-five years, she didn't betray it. Instead, she marched onto the scene like a short, silver-haired general.

We were in the meeting room, which I'd taken to calling the War Room. Tristan tried to take the reins of the meeting early on, but Rhea was having none of it. "Adam, tell me what you know."

What followed was an hour-long rehash of recent events interspersed with bickering and shouting from both our side and Tristan's team, as well as the occasional whine from Valva.

Finally, Rhea executed an ear-piercing whistle. "All right," she said once everyone shut up. "Valva?"

The demon crossed her arms and raised a bitchy brow.

"Are you certain that the Chosen can kill Cain?"

"Yes. Mom also said that we needed to be sure Cain didn't kill Tristan's progeny because then we'd be stuck with Cain for eternity."

"Did she say 'progeny' or did she speak of Maisie by name?"

Valva squinted, trying to remember.

"You told me the Chosen would be capable of powerful magic, remember?" Tristan prompted.

Valva frowned. "Yes, but I never used Maisie's name."

"You did," Tristan said. Then he paused and frowned. "Didn't you?"

She shook her head. "No. Mom just said I should reveal that you are the father of the Chosen. She didn't tell me which twin would fulfill the prophecy."

Rhea turned to Tristan with an incredulous expression. "Wait, are you saying you just assumed it was Maisie?"

Everyone turned to stare at Tristan. His cheeks burned but he crossed his arms and frowned at Rhea. But I could see the guilt, the doubt in his eyes.

"I don't believe this." I threw up my hands. "Do you have any idea how much time we've wasted because of your fucking assumption?"

"Sabina," Rhea said in a low, warning tone.

"Now hold on," Tristan said, his voice rising. "Just because she didn't use Maisie's name doesn't mean she wasn't the Chosen. I may not have been in Maisie's and Sabina's lives, but I am not unaware of their histories."

I frowned. "What? You spied on us?"

"I prefer to think of it as benevolent observing." He nodded to his team. "And based on the information my team gathered, I believe that of the two of you, Maisie was more likely to be the Chosen."

I crossed my arms. "Based on what, exactly?"

"Sabina, your sister was a respected leader of her race. In addition to her skills as an Oracle, she was an expert diplomat and powerful in several magical disciplines. She was trained by my mother, who was one of the most beloved leaders of the mage race for almost two millennia."

"That's all true," Rhea said. "But Sabina is a Chthonic mage. I trained her myself and some of the feats she's managed far surpassed Maisie's own powers."

"Which she's had only, what, six months to develop? Before that she spent all her time carrying out Lavinia Kane's death orders," Tristan said. "I'm sorry but I'm hard-pressed to believe the Chosen is someone who spent her life shedding the blood of those she was destined to rule."

I opened my mouth to argue, but he wasn't too far off base.

"Yeah," Horus chimed in. "Remember what she did to poor Thomas."

I frowned. "Who?"

"Thirty years ago, I tried to have my team gather intel on you. I sent Thomas, a mage on our team, to follow you and snap some pictures. One night, you caught him spying on you and challenged him."

"When?"

"It was just after you finished Enforcer school."

I shook my head. "I don't remember."

"I'm fairly certain you didn't take the time for proper introductions before you shot him."

My mouth fell open. "I . . . I don't know what to say."

Tristan tilted his chin. "There's nothing to say. He got careless and you caught him. Given your profession, he should have been more careful. But needless to say, I didn't want to risk any more of my people trying to find out more about you. I already knew enough."

Silence descended over the room as we all absorbed this information. I glanced guiltily at the rest of Tristan's team. Nyx's expression was solemn but free of judgment. Calyx wouldn't meet my eyes. Horus looked like he wanted to punch me.

"But don't you see?" Adam said finally. "It's precisely because of Sabina's former profession that it makes more sense that she'd be the one who'll kill Cain. Gods keep her, but Maisie didn't have the stomach for murder."

I jerked my head in time to see Adam's face flush. While he wasn't wrong, we were both remembering how easily murder came to my sister under Cain's influence.

"Killing Cain is only the final test of the Chosen," Tristan said. "Once that test is passed, the Chosen will become the New Lilith who will unite all the dark races. Which I think we can all agree would be a challenge for Sabina given her history of anger issues and the fact that she's created enemies in every dark race in existence with her killing."

I'd had it. I wasn't going to stand there and try to convince this man of my worth. I had a job to do and I was going to get it done with or without Tristan's help. Time to throw down an ultimatum.

"Like it or not, Maisie isn't here. *I* am." I thumped my chest with my thumb. "I survived all of Cain's attacks thus far. I have the Chthonic magic, the weapons skills, and the combat experience." I paused to let that sink in before I delivered the ace up my sleeve. "And I am the one who bears the twin stars of the Chosen on my back."

Tristan raised a brow. "Are you willing to bet your life on the chance you're really her?"

That stopped me. I'd spent so many months denying any suggestion I might be the prophesized New Lilith. I hated the idea that fate could chose my path for me. On the other hand, I wanted Cain dead more than I wanted to be the mistress of my destiny or whatever. In fact, in a way, I decided that pursuing the idea of being the Chosen felt a lot like grabbing fate by the throat and forcing her to meet my needs. "I'm willing to do anything to end Cain," I said. "If that means proving I am the Chosen to you and to Lilith and to anyone else who demands it, then I'll do it."

Tristan laughed, a harsh, mocking sound. "Tough words. One wonders, though, if you have the skills to back them up."

"Sabina is a total badass," Giguhl said. "She's got more skill in her pinkie than anyone in this room."

Calyx snorted dismissively and Horus cracked his knuckles. I ignored them and held Tristan's challenging gaze.

"Well, Sabina? Are you willing to put your money where your demon's mouth is?"

I raised my chin. "You throwing down a gauntlet, old man?"

He didn't answer immediately. Just kind of watched me for any signs of doubt or weakness.

"That's an excellent idea, actually," Rhea said.

My gaze jerked to my mentor. "Huh?"

"A test," Tristan said, his tone speculative. He looked at Rhea. "What do you have in mind?"

Rhea nodded. "Whatever it takes for you to believe Sabina is the Chosen."

Part of me—the proud part—was insulted by the very idea. But the perverse part loved the chance to surprise him. Tristan Graecus needed to see I was a force to be reckoned with. The more I thought about it, the more I loved the idea of seeing the look on his face when I forced him to admit he was wrong.

Tristan crossed his arms and pinched his bottom lip methodically as he considered her suggestion. "It won't be easy."

I flashed my fangs. "I'd be insulted if it was."

23

$\mathcal{A}$n hour later, we all gathered in the courtyard for Tristan's first test. When the idea had been proposed, I'd assumed there'd just be a single test. However, after disappearing into his office with Valva and his team for half an hour, they'd emerged to announce that I would have to undergo two tests. I had to pass both for Tristan to agree to move forward with the mission.

"Your first task will be to defeat Horus in hand-to-hand combat."

I laughed. "You're not serious."

Tristan crossed his arms. "I assure you I am."

"But you already said you were aware of my fighting skills. Why waste time making me embarrass Horus?"

The massive male vampire laughed and crossed his arms.

Tristan sighed. "I am well aware of your exploits, Sabina. This first test is just to get a baseline of your combat skills."

"Whatever. Just don't blame me if Horus gets hurt."

"In your dreams, little girl."

I gritted my teeth at the insult. The truth was, Horus was not going to be an easy opponent. First, he was older than me by at least a couple of centuries. Age meant strength and experience. He also had the weight advantage with his height and all those muscles. Normally I would have used his weight against him, but he had a warrior's posture and surprising grace that hinted at agility. But his attitude pissed me off, which would definitely work against him.

"You may proceed," Tristan said.

I went back across the clearing to where Rhea, Adam, and Giguhl waited. Everyone else stood on Horus's side, including Valva, who kept casting forlorn glances at Giguhl. The way everyone circled the fight area gave me a sense of déjà vu. Then it hit me. This was starting to feel more and more like one of Giguhl's Demon Fight Club set-ups. I shook off the feeling. Surely my father intended for this to be a friendly little sparring match. A demonstration more than a brawl.

"Okay, Red," Giguhl said, putting his hands on my shoulders. "I want you to go for his 'nads."

I shrugged his hands off my shoulders. "Relax. I've got this."

"I'm just sayin'."

Adam glanced uneasily toward Horus. "He looks like he's ready to get serious, Red."

I looked over my shoulder. Tristan was coaching Horus, but the vampire's eyes were locked on me. I frowned at him and turned back around. "Whatever. I can take him."

"Just don't get overconfident," Rhea warned.

"Stay light on your feet and don't let him corner you," Adam coached. "With his size, you might be able to wear him down before he can use his superior weight against you." He kissed my lips quickly for luck. "Now go kick his ass."

Behind me, Tristan clapped his hands and walked to the center of the courtyard. Horus came up behind him and I joined them there. My father stood between us like a ref.

"All right, you two. No weapons." He shot me a glare. "No magic. Fangs are allowed, of course. First to tap a vein wins."

My eyes jerked from Horus to Tristan. "Seriously?"

"What's wrong, Mixed-Blood? Scared?"

"Dude, what's your problem?" I snapped.

"Easy now, save it for the fight," Tristan said.

"I hope you fed tonight," Horus said, ignoring Tristan. "I'd hate to injure *the Chosen*." His mocking emphasis on the word indicated his opinion on my suitability for the role.

I cocked a brow and laughed. "You're funny. Did anyone happen to mention I used to be an Enforcer for the Dominae?"

"Did anyone mention I was, too?"

I stilled. "Seriously?"

"Back before you were born, girl."

"Well, then. I hope you fed well, too, old man."

He tossed back his head and laughed. "This is gonna be fun."

"If you two are quite finished, we'll begin." Tristan held his hand between us. Paused, building the tension. Horus's gaze bore into mine, promising pain. I smirked back. "Aaaand... fight!"

Tristan backed quickly out of the way and went to join Nyx at the sideline. Horus and I each fell back into fighting stances. I balanced on the balls of my feet, ready to pivot for his attack.

Behind me, Giguhl and Adam clapped and called out encouragement. Behind Horus, Nyx and Calyx did the same.

Horus was absolutely still, but his shrewd eyes were assessing me for vulnerabilities. I was patient, waiting for the attack I knew was coming. He was too eager for this to let me get in the first hit. I decided to hang back, let him take the lead, get cocky.

Calyx grew bored as Horus and I took each other's measure. "Are you guys just going to stand there or—"

The fist exploded against my jaw like a sledgehammer. My teeth slammed together, sending vibrations of pain through my head as it snapped backward. Stars danced in my vision. I shook it, pivoted, and delivered a roundhouse to his midsection.

Horus stumbled back two steps. Only two. I'd kicked him hard enough that his ass should have hit the dirt. But he didn't grunt or even twitch an eye.

I raised my brows. Damn, this dude was tough.

As if to prove that point, he ran at me with his head down like a stampeding bull. His shoulder crashed into my diaphragm like a battering ram. The air whooshed out of me and my body slammed to the gravel. I brought my knees up and flipped him back over my head before he could settle his weight on top of me. I kicked my legs up and gained my feet just in time to receive a backhand.

Blood flew from my mouth and pain streaked through my jaw. I wiped the trickle of blood from my chin and licked it off while he watched. His eyes widened. I smiled.

He came at me with a flurry of fists. I ducked and weaved, delivering jabs to his stomach as I avoided his punches.

Adrenaline surged through my veins like a drug. Like cocaine and whisky and sex. It'd been far too long since I'd had a good old-fashioned fight, and I was enjoying the hell out of myself.

But his abs were like concrete and before long, the knuckle of my right forefinger cracked. Giving up on the jabs, I reared back and kicked. My foot slammed into the center of his chest. A loud crack as a couple of ribs broke. He flew back and crashed into the facade of the manor—twenty feet away. Plaster broke off from the wall and fell on his head.

Horus jumped up and shook the dust from his hair. He ran forward, executed two impressive handsprings, and landed in front of me with a wink. I stood my ground despite my shock. No one that large should be that agile. He bounced on his toes in front of me like a prizefighter. "Okay, I'm warmed up now."

I laughed. "I hope so, Grandpa." As I spoke, I lifted my leg to kick his chin. He caught my foot and brought his elbow down on my knee. A loud pop as the joint surrendered. An explosion of fire. I fell to the ground and grabbed my destroyed joint.

"Hey!" Adam shouted.

"Leave them be," Tristan snapped.

Horus backed away to preen in front of his fans.

"Bullshit," Giguhl said, and started to intervene with Adam. Rhea grabbed their arms.

"No!" I held up my free hand. The joint hurt like Hades, but it'd heal soon enough. Besides, one little injury wasn't enough to make me surrender.

Adam, Rhea, and the demon stilled on the sidelines, their expressions part panic and part disbelief.

Using my hand for leverage, I got my good leg under me. I tested my right leg and winced. My blood was already working on the injury, but it'd be a while before I had full range of movement.

"Hey, asshole," I yelled. "Anyone ever tell you not to turn your back on an opponent?"

Horus turned slowly, a cocky grin on his lips. He flashed a little fang. "You want more?"

"The man said it's not over until someone taps a vein. And I suddenly find myself parched."

Horus executed an it's-your-funeral shrug. "Suit yourself."

He ran at me again, his head down. Major miscalculation. At the last second before he impersonated a wrecking ball, I jumped out of the way and pivoted on my good leg. I grabbed his shoulder and used his forward momentum against him. He went down hard. I followed, slamming both my weight and my good knee into his back. He slid into the dirt face-first. My injured knee wouldn't bend, so I balanced precariously on his back. Acting quickly before he could recover, I grabbed the vamp's hair and jerked his head back. Just as I was about to slam my fangs into his jugular, he executed a death roll.

I crashed into the gravel.

And Horus crashed into me.

His hand found my knee and squeezed. I gritted my teeth to keep from screaming. Cold sweat bloomed on my chest. Horus lowered his face into mine.

"Scream for me." His fingers tightened. My fangs ground together and I writhed under his grip, but I didn't make so much as a whimper.

From far away, males shouted. An argument. I blocked it out and focused all my attention on Horus. My right hand was pinned under his body, but he was so sure the pain he was inflicting would unman me that he hadn't bothered with my left. I worked it down until my fingers wrapped around the twin targets.

He stilled. I squeezed. He paled.

I smiled despite my own pain. "Scream for me."

We lay there like that, him putting insane pressure on my knee and me squeezing his balls like vise. A hush fell over the courtyard. Who would break the stalemate first?

I twisted my fist. He whimpered. His eyes watered and he started to tremble. But the stubborn bastard didn't release me.

"What's it gonna be, Horus? I can handle a permanent limp, but do you really want to be stuck singing soprano?"

"Fuck. You." His face had gone red now. He lifted his face to the sky, whether to pray or escape the evil smile on my lips, I didn't know.

After that, it was over quickly. I clenched my fist one last time, applying a little English to his testicles. He yelped. I released.

He was so relieved he eased up on my knee. I reared up and snapped my fangs into his jugular.

I didn't indulge, though. The instant I broke the skin, I pulled back. No sense adding more insult. He'd fought dirty but he'd fought well.

I fell back into the gravel, panting against the throbbing pain in my knee. Horus curled up into the fetal position, cupping his bruised balls.

The courtyard was silent for a couple of beats. A few seconds later, the rhythmic sound of slow clapping filled the clearing. I raised my head to see Rhea, Calyx, and Nyx applauding. All the males were too busy shielding their pelvises with their hands and averting their gazes.

Except Giguhl, who threw me a thumbs-up. "Told ya to go for the 'nads!"

I let my head fall back to the gravel. A quick assessment told me that in addition to the knee issue, I also had a broken finger, at least one black eye, several contusions on my jaw, and a broken nail.

In other words, I felt freaking awesome.

When Adam finally got over his fear for his own testicles, he came over and kneeled next to me. I knew it was him without looking because his sandalwood scent preceded him. I opened my eyes and smiled.

"How you doing?" His hands ran over me, checking for broken bones. When he reached my knee, I hissed. He released it immediately and shouted for someone to bring ice.

"Don't worry," I said. "It'll be right as rain in no time."

He glanced over to where Calyx and Tristan were helping Horus off the ground. "He probably needs the ice more anyway." He looked back down at me and smiled. "Remind me not to pick a fight with you—ever."

I glanced down at his pelvis and grinned wickedly. He grimaced and held out a hand to help me up. Giguhl rushed over and got my other arm and wrapped it around his shoulders. "Dude, you were awesome!"

"Thanks, G."

"Seriously, it was great to see you back in action."

I smiled. "It felt good." I winced as I accidentally put too much weight on the knee. "Mostly."

"Sabina!" Tristan snapped.

We all stopped and hobbled around so I could look at him. "Yeah?"

"See to your wounds. We'll proceed with the next test tomorrow at dusk." He looked at Rhea. "A moment?"

Rhea nodded and went to follow him after shooting me a thumbs-up. Nyx followed them in, but Valva lingered.

"Someone's in trouble," Giguhl singsonged.

"Whatever," I said. "I only did what he asked me to do. You'd figure he'd be glad I could hold my own."

"Ah, don't let it bother you," Adam said. "You did good, babe."

With that, he turned to guide me toward the bungalow. Giguhl started to go with us, but Valva called out. "Giguhl? May I speak to you for a moment?"

Adam and I shot Giguhl a concerned look. He sighed and waved us on. "I'll be there in a sec."

"Are you sure?"

He blew out a breath. "Yeah. Might as well get this over with."

I patted his arm. "Be strong."

24

I sat on the couch with my injured knee propped on some pillows. Adam had insisted I sit still while he checked over my wounds. Really all I needed was some blood, but I felt weird asking him for it. I didn't want him to think I saw him as a convenient blood dispenser. Besides, I was kind of enjoying his ministrations.

He sat on the coffee table with my injured hand in his lap. Fashioning a splint out of a stick and some tape, he started wrapping my broken knuckle. "So, the first test went well, I think."

I nodded. "I have a feeling that was the easy one, though."

Adam glanced up. "You think he's going to ramp up the difficulty since you hurt Horus?"

"Nah. He doesn't strike me as that petty. But I do think he'll want to test my magic."

"So?"

"Tristan's a Chthonic. I'm thinking he'll want to make sure my skills are up to snuff."

"Sabina, your Chthonic skills are wicked."

"When I'm in danger, sure. But they've never been tested by another Chthonic in a controlled environment."

"Ah," Adam said. "You're nervous about impressing him."

I shifted uncomfortably. "No, I'm not."

He shot me a dubious look. "Red, it's only natural you'd be worried. I mean, I know you say you don't care that he's your father, but part of you has to want to prove yourself to him."

By that time, he'd finished wrapping the finger. I pulled it away, pretending to inspect his handiwork. "The only thing I want to prove is that I am the Chosen so I can kill Cain."

"Whatever you say." His tone clearly implied he wasn't buying it.

"I mean it. I don't care what Tristan Graecus thinks about me. Especially when he's made it clear he's already made up his mind."

"Sabina—"

I waved my uninjured had to cut him off. "Don't Sabina me, Adam. You heard him. He thinks I'm just some hotheaded killer."

Adam checked the ice bag on my knee. "No offense, but given the information he had to go on, I don't blame him for that."

"Thanks," I said in an injured tone.

"Stop," he said. "You know what I mean. All he knew before three days ago was that you killed his informant in L.A. and you worked for the Dominae. Tristan may have fallen in love with a vampire, but mage ways die hard. You lived as a vampire and were raised by Lavinia. Who, by the way, tried to kill him. I'm not saying his prejudices were right, but I understand where he's coming from."

"Yeah, well, I've got one more test to get through to try and undo those prejudices. I just hope it's enough. Every moment we're wasting on these tests gives Cain a chance to track us down." I paused, realizing I hadn't had a chance to fill Adam in on the new developments with Asclepius. "Adam?" I started slowly. "There's something I have to tell you."

He set down the bottle of antiseptic. "That doesn't sound good."

I cringed. Smart guy, that Adam. "Asclepius made another appearance last night. He's pissed it's taking so long for me to off Nyx. Especially since he somehow figured out I've found her."

Adam cursed and lowered his head into his hands.

"It gets worse. He's decided to up the stakes. If I don't kill Nyx in the next three nights"—I blew out a breath for courage—"he's going to tell Cain where we are."

Adam's head jerked up. His face was pale. "Sabina, you have to tell Tristan about this."

I threw up my hands. "I can't! Best case, he'll kick us all out of here and we'll lose our chance at Cain. Worst case? He and his team turn on us and we're suddenly fighting for our lives."

"So what are you going to do? Kill Nyx in cold blood?"

I shook my head. "I don't want to, but I don't see another choice."

"Sabina, there's always another choice. You know that. Promise me you won't kill her until we've had time to consider all the angles."

"I just wish we had more time."

"We have tomorrow night and the next, right?"

"Yes," I said slowly. "But I really don't see how that's going to make a difference."

"A lot can happen in two nights, Red."

I blew out a long breath. "Okay, you're right. I won't kill her. Yet. But you need to prepare yourself for the possibility. If it's a choice between saving you and Giguhl or sparing Nyx, you know what I'm going to do."

"Let's just hope it doesn't come to that." He patted my good knee. With a sigh, he rose to put away the supplies. I glanced at the clock and realized Giguhl had been gone for more than an hour. Way too long in my opinion for him to tell off the Vanity demon.

With a groan, I pushed myself off the couch. Adam's gaze jerked toward me. "What do you think you're doing?"

I could have told him I was worried about Giguhl, but that would only earn me a lecture about staying out of the demon's personal business. So instead, I told him the other issue I wanted to go check on. "I'm going to go look for Rhea. By now she has to have more information about tomorrow's test."

Adam watched me for a moment. I could practically see the wheels spinning in his gorgeous head. Weighing the pros and cons of trying to talk me into sitting my ass back down and resting. I also saw the moment he realized he'd just be wasting his breath. "Fine, but I'm going with you."

I shrugged casually. "Fine by me."

He frowned. My easy acceptance made him more suspicious of my motives than not arguing. He held up a hand. "After you."

Despite the twinge in my knee, I managed to walk to the door without a limp or a grimace. In truth, I was feeling a ton better than I had when he'd helped me back to the house. But I'd feel even better once I knew what the hell was keeping Giguhl and got the lowdown from Rhea on my father's tests for the next evening.

*   *   *

The demons weren't in the courtyard. Adam had no idea I was looking for them instead of Rhea, so he strode right through the area and made a beeline for the villa. I limped behind him, figuring the demons might have taken their discussion inside.

We made it to the second floor and were halfway down the hall toward Rhea's room when a grunting noise reached me from inside a door. I paused and listened. A moan joined the groaning. Either someone was injured or there was some serious sexing going on in there. I pursed my lips and considered my options.

As I stood there undecided, Adam turned back with a frown on his face. "What are you doing?" he whispered.

I shushed him. "Something's going on in there."

Adam tilted his head and listened. A high-pitched squeal cut through the door. We jerked back and exchanged shocked looks.

"C'mon," I said.

Adam grabbed my arm. "What? You can't just barge in there."

Time to come clean with my suspicions. "What if it's Giguhl and Valva? Adam, he could be making a huge mistake. We have to stop him."

He sighed the sigh of the martyred. "Seriously, Red? You don't even know if that's Valva's room. Besides, I don't know about you, but I'm not real eager to witness those two making the beast with four horns."

I chewed on my lip, undecided. "Adam, we can't risk Tristan finding out. You saw how protective he is of her. If he sees Giguhl nailing her, he's going to freak and we might lose any chance of him helping out."

He sighed. "All right, but I'm keeping my eyes closed."

He reached past me and pushed the door open slowly. It was dark outside, but the inside of the room was deep midnight. Only a slim stream of light peeked from the cracked door across the room.

More groaning and the sound of squeaking springs assaulted my ears. Adam nudged me from behind, his hand on my shoulder. I glanced back and true to his claim, he had his eyes clamped shut. What a baby.

I crept in farther. "Giguhl," I whispered.

The only response was male grunting on the other side of the door.

Adam nudged me. "Even I could barely hear that. If you're gonna do it, put some volume on it so we can get out of here."

I swatted him away and stood straighter. "Yo, Giguhl!"

The sex sounds cut off. Panicked scrambling. A whispered argument.

"Guys, we know you're in here," Adam called. "Might as well come out."

I crossed my arms and prepared to deliver a lecture to the demons. Except the body that ran by the cracked door wasn't green or gold. It was flesh colored. I also thought I caught a flash of red hair.

My stomach dropped with embarrassment. "Oh." I breathed. "Sorry, we thought—"

The door flew open a foot or so and a head emerged. This one had no horns and the hair was black. A second later, I recognized my father's enraged countenance.

"Oh shit!" Adam yelped.

Nyx's face appeared over Tristan's bare shoulder. When she saw Adam and me standing there with our mouths open, her cheeks flamed red. "Sabina!"

Tristan's initial surprise quickly morphed into outrage. "What the hell are you doing here?"

"I . . . I . . . I—"

"We're so sorry," Adam said smoothly. "We thought you were someone else." Then he put his hands on my shoulders, pivoted my body, and pushed me out the door.

I stumbled over the threshold and into the hall. "Keep walking," Adam warned, pulling me along now.

He guided us down the stairs, through the villa, and into the courtyard. He didn't stop until we were in the olive grove behind the bungalow. A small sitting area had been set up around a fire pit. He pushed me onto one of the benches.

While I sat in shock, Adam busied himself lighting the fire.

"Adam?" I said finally.

He looked over his shoulder from his kneeling position. "Yeah?"

"You know how some things can't be unseen?"

His lip twitched. "Yeah."

"Was my father really naked?"

"I'm afraid so."

I shuddered and scrubbed my hands over my face. "Jesus. It's bad enough to have to witness that, but with Nyx? Am I the only one who finds it weird he's with a vampire?"

"Yeah, why would a mage be into a hot vampire chick?" He cocked an ironic brow at me.

"That's different. You aren't with me because of some unresolved psychosis from a past love affair that may or may not have been orchestrated by a psychotic human. Face it, Tristan has issues."

"The same could be said for the fact you're with me." He leaned toward me and whispered, "Daddy issues."

I tilted my head and shot him a look. "I do not have daddy issues!"

"Riiight." He rose and brushed his hands on his jeans. Behind him, the fire roared to life.

"Because that guy isn't really my father. He was a sperm donor. That's it."

"So the fact that he was alive all this time and didn't try to find you doesn't play into this at all?"

I crossed my arms. "Absolutely not. It's just that... he's...he's being unfaithful to my mother's memory."

Adam's mouth fell open and a sharp laugh escaped. "Oh please. Sabina, your mother died almost fifty-five years ago. Surely you don't expect a male to be celibate for five decades. Especially after he found out about Cain's love spell."

"Um, hello, she didn't just die. She died giving birth to the kids he knocked her up with. Then he just disappeared." I shook my head. "It's not right and I'm not buying the whole 'males have needs' line of bullshit."

Just then, the crunch of approaching footsteps reached me. I sat up straighter and looked toward the noise. I groaned audibly when I saw Nyx approaching.

"Awkward," Adam said under his breath. He must have also realized Nyx had been close enough to hear our conversation.

I blew out a breath. "Hey, Nyx."

She walked up with a solemn expression. A few tense seconds passed as we each tried to think of things to say. She rubbed her arms against the chill. "Sabina, may I speak with you privately?"

Adam raised an eyebrow. "I need to get more wood for the fire, anyway." As he passed, he squeezed my shoulder. I wasn't dumb enough to believe this was a comforting gesture. Instead, he was warning me not to kill my father's girlfriend.

"What's up?" I said, trying to feign a casualness I didn't feel.

"May I?" She motioned to the space on the bench beside me.

I shrugged and scooted as far over as I could without falling off.

Once she was settled, she leaned her head back and looked up at the night sky, as if collecting her thoughts. "I love it here," she said. "In Paris, you can't see the stars."

Okay, I thought. *She wants to ease into this. I can handle that.* "Oh yeah? Is that where you grew up?"

She nodded, her eyes still heavenward. "My family lived there until I was about seventy."

In my head, I was calculating the fallout if I took advantage of the lack of audience and fulfilled my promise to Asclepius. On one hand, clearly my father would be really pissed if I killed his fuck buddy. On the other, if I made it look like an accident, I could mark it off my To Do list.

I didn't have anything personal against Nyx, not really. If she wanted to bump uglies with a bitter mage, that was her business. But Asclepius was too serious a threat to ignore, despite Adam's advice to wait and see. Still, he couldn't have foreseen that this perfect opportunity would present itself so soon after our conversation.

To buy myself some time for more internal debate, I played along with her conversation. "Where'd you all move after that?"

She dragged her gaze from the celestial display to look at me. "We didn't move anywhere. I escaped after Cain murdered my mother and father."

My mouth fell open. That must have explained why Georgia's friend had met Nyx in Lyon. She'd been on the run. "I'm sorry to hear that." Shit. I didn't want to sympathize with her. "Do you know why he killed them?"

"I have theories, but it was a long time ago." Her tone told me she just didn't want to get into it. "After it happened, I moved all over Europe. Part of me was terrified he'd come after me, too. I spent more than a century always looking over my shoulder. It takes a toll on a person. The constant fear. And the soul-crushing loneliness." She shrugged, as if she were telling someone else's story. "I suppose a psychologist would claim I was depressed, and I guess I was. Anyway, there's this bridge in Budapest—the Chain Bridge. Have you heard of it?"

I shook my head, wondering where all this was going. I looked around quickly. The assassin I used to be was weighing the variables. We were very alone. If I could woo her into taking off the vest, my problems would be solved.

"It's glorious at night with its light reflecting off the dark waters of the Danube. Buda Castle is nearby and the bridge offers a breathtaking view of its towers and crenellations." She sighed wistfully and then shook herself out of her reverie. The longer she talked, the harder it was to work up the nerve to just off her and be done with it.

"It was the perfect setting for my suicide."

Even though the fact that she sat right next to me proved she hadn't gone through with it, my stomach cramped. I'd had my share of troubles, but none so horrible I'd be willing to kill myself. I couldn't imagine what kind of agony she had to have been in to make that decision. More than that, though, I didn't want to sympathize with her. "But vampires can't drown."

Crap, what are you doing? my vampire self yelled in my head. Her having a death wish could work in my favor. *Don't be an idiot*, the other side of me replied. *You know it's wrong.*

Besides, Adam will never speak to you again. And with good cause—you're not that cold-blooded killer anymore. Right?

Nyx smiled. "They can if they eat the forbidden fruit first." I couldn't stop the gasp that escaped my lips. She rubbed her hands together as if trying to get warm despite the fire's heat. "It's silly now, in retrospect. But I spent hours at the market looking for the perfect apple. Did you know the forbidden fruit comes in hundreds of varieties? So many shapes and colors. Different flavors—sweet, tart, everything in between."

I frowned and shook my head. Despite my own immunity to the forbidden fruit, I hadn't ever really considered sitting down and actually eating one.

"But finally I found a ripe juicy red one after staring at the apple cart for nearly an hour. The salesman thought I was crazy." She laughed at her younger self.

"Jesus, Nyx."

She patted my leg. "Don't worry. I didn't jump." She winked.

"What stopped you?" I asked her.

The vampire on my shoulder yelled, *What's stopping you?!?*

"Your father." She let that hang in the air for a moment before she continued. "Thirty years ago, he was just starting to put together our little army. He spent several years tracking down rumors of other beings who'd lost loved ones by Cain's hands. One by one, he convinced each of us to join his cause." Her eyes got this faraway look and a ghost of a smile flirted with her full lips. "He looked so handsome that night. So angry, too. He pulled me away from the railing and yelled at me. I cried, of course. Not because he yelled or even because he stopped my plan."

"Why, then?"

"Because I was so relieved. Him showing up to stop me? It was a sign from the Great Mother herself. She sent Tristan to give me a reason to go on living."

I blew out a rush of air. "Wow."

She smiled. "Yes, wow. It wasn't hard for me to decide to join his cause. It's not that I had some hunger for revenge. I knew I'd never get my family back. But I was so tired of being alone. It didn't take long for our group to become my new family."

"I'm sure your attraction to him played a role, too." The minute the words left my mouth, I felt horrible. She'd just trusted me with such a personal story that she didn't deserve judgment from me. "I'm sorry," I said quickly. "That was unfair."

She shook her head. "No, it's true. I was quite taken with your father from the beginning. In addition to admiring his looks, I saw him as my savior. A potent combination for a lonely girl." She nudged me with her shoulder, as if I'd been there myself. Honestly, I hadn't, not really, but I forced a laugh anyway. "But Tristan wanted nothing to do with me besides ordering me around. I didn't have any talent for weaponry, but I'd always been a bookworm. So I was put in charge of researching and documenting everything I could find on Cain. Looking back, I think sticking me in dusty old libraries was Tristan's way of keeping me out of trouble."

"So what changed things?" I asked, motioning vaguely in the direction of the villa.

"I finally wore him down. I was quite determined in my pursuit, but still it took most of two decades." She smiled broadly then.

"Damn. Twenty years?" I laughed despite myself. It was too easy to forget this was my father we were talking about.

"Oh yes, but some males are worth the wait."

"Why are you telling me this?" I said.

"Because I need you to understand that our relationship isn't just a fling."

I stiffened. "I never thought that."

She nodded, accepting that. "But I also want you to know that even though Tristan has been my lover for ten years, he is still in love with your mother."

I squirmed. "You don't have to say that—"

"Don't I?" She raised a brow.

"No. I didn't know my mother. And until a week ago, I thought Tristan was dead. I have no emotional attachment to either of them. So save your breath if you're worried I think he's betraying Phoebe." I paused, remembering what Tristan told me earlier. "Besides, Tristan believes he was manipulated into falling in love with my mother. I find it hard to believe he continued to carry a torch for her once Valva told him."

"Your father is a complex man. Believe it or not, he feels things deeply—so deeply he shoves the emotions down and refuses to analyze them. If you asked him, he'd probably say he never loved her. But I know he did—and still does. Every time we make love, I see her ghost in his eyes."

I sighed deeply. "I already told you, Tristan's life is none of my business."

"If you really think that, why are you here?"

"I'm here because I need his help to avenge my sister's death," I said, squaring my shoulders. "The sister he had no interest in beyond helping him pay Cain back for that fucking love spell that set us all on this collision course."

"Is that what you think?"

"It's what I know, Nyx. He had fifty-four years to find Maisie and me, but instead he chose to hunt down the boogeyman."

"He tried to keep up with your lives. With Maisie it was simple at first because of Orpheus."

Remembering what Tristan told me, I nodded. "Orpheus kept him updated on her. At least until Tristan stopped communicating with him."

"Tristan knew that if Cain found out he still had ties to Orpheus, he wouldn't be safe. So he cut off all contact to protect his friend. You have to understand that."

On some level I did. Still, it didn't make the truth hurt any less. Someone was watching over Maisie while I fended for myself against Lavinia.

Nyx grimaced. "But after he lost Orpheus as a contact and you killed Thomas, he still tried to keep up with both of you. He's even got a photo album filled with pictures."

"Whatever," I said. "An album doesn't make someone a father."

"That's true. But I'd like to ask you to give him a chance to do that now."

"Why should I?"

"Because it may be the only chance either of you will have."

"Look, Nyx," I said, rising and brushing my damp hands on my jeans, "I appreciate what you're saying, but it's not that easy."

She took my hand and squeezed it. "It's not that easy for him, either. I know he's...difficult. But he honestly believed he was doing the best thing for both of you." The conviction in her eyes made me feel sorry for her. She was clearly in love with Tristan, but from what I'd seen, he treated her like shit. What's worse, she didn't even realize that he was as driven by the need for revenge as I was—more, given how long he'd been going after Cain. He wasn't trying to protect Maisie or me. He was biding his time until he could use one of us to make Cain pay for fucking him over.

Kill her, that seductive voice whispered. *Put her out of her misery before she finds out Tristan doesn't care about her. Before he uses her like he wants to use you.*

A white-hot spot of pain bloomed in my temple. My conscience, probably. A warning, definitely. Killing Nyx might erase my debt to Asclepius and prevent Cain from ambushing us, but I wouldn't escape with my soul intact. Maybe I'd lost my edge, but I also was shocked to realize I didn't miss it all that much, despite the ramifications.

I removed my hand from her grasp. "I need to go."

Nyx sighed and stood. "Thanks for listening."

I nodded and turned, but I felt that to just turn my back on her now would be cruel. I stopped and said, "Not that it makes much difference, but I'm glad you never ate that apple."

She stilled. "I never said I didn't eat the apple."

My stomach sank. "What?" I whispered. If she was telling the truth, that meant Nyx was no longer immortal.

Which would explain why she needed Asclepius's vest. As the pieces clicked into place, relief flooded me that I'd won the battle against the old, bloodthirsty voice in my head.

Nyx nodded. "Tristan found me after I'd eaten half of it. He didn't stop me from becoming mortal. He just stopped me from becoming dead."

I blew out a long, slow breath. I might regret my next question, but part of me wanted to hear her side of the story Asclepius told me. "How have you managed to stay alive all this time? I mean, no offense, but your lifestyle isn't exactly safe." I tried to keep my tone curious, light, but it came out sounding all squeaky.

A twinkle appeared in her eye. "Remember how I told you Tristan put me in charge of research?" When I nodded, she continued. "I ran across this ancient rite to implore the god of healing for help. I did the ritual and he made me this." She opened the top three buttons of her blouse to reveal the vest. The golden chain mail winked in the firelight. "As long as I wear it, I am immune to all weapons." She ran a hand over the golden links. "Isn't it beautiful?"

My heart picked up speed. "What did the god ask for in return?" I prayed she'd offer some explanation that would prove Asclepius was lying so I'd be off the hook.

Her eyes skittered away from mine. "A simple blood sacrifice, nothing more."

My heart sank. Dammit. So Asclepius had been telling the truth about Nyx running out on her bill, so to speak.

"Dealing with the gods is dangerous, Nyx."

"Sabina," she began, her voice serious, "I was ready to die that night in Budapest, but your father showed me that I could channel my sadness and use it for the greater good. Stopping Cain is worth any price paid to the gods, or anyone else for that matter."

I should have warned her. Should have told her that Cain wasn't the only enemy looking for her. But instead, I took the coward's way out. "I need to go find Adam. Good night, Nyx."

The glow in her eyes dimmed and a disappointed grimace turned down the corners of her mouth. But she nodded and said quietly, "You too, Sabina. Please don't tell Tristan about our conversation. He can be quite...fiercely protective of his privacy."

Not a problem, I thought. The last thing I wanted was to have a heart-to-heart with Tristan Graecus. I nodded. "Understood."

With that, I turned and walked away from my chance of getting Asclepius off my back. But at least my conscience was clear. Now that the decision was made, I felt lighter somehow, clean.

Ironic that the first time I'd ever walked away from a kill also marked the moment I might have ensured all our deaths. Because unless we figured out a way to stop Cain before Asclepius's deadline, he was coming for us.

25

I walked back into the bungalow with my shoulders slumped. Adam stood in the kitchen, drinking wine from a bottle.

"Oh gods," he said, his tone defeated. "What did you do?"

I squinted at him. "What?"

"Nyx. Did you do it?"

I shot him a give-me-a-break glare. "Of course not."

He perked up. "Really?"

I briefly considered acting affronted, but he'd see right through it. "Don't get me wrong. I thought about it. But then she told me this sob story about her dead parents and how Tristan saved her from committing suicide."

Adam frowned. "Wha—"

I waved a hand. "Long story. Anyway, I couldn't do it. She's so...nice," I said bitterly. "And as much as I hate to admit it, you were right. There has to be another way to get Asclepius off my back."

Adam sighed and set down the wine bottle. "Come here." He opened his arms.

I walked into them and went limp against his sturdy weight. "We're doomed."

He pulled back and tilted my chin up. "No, but you do have to tell Tristan what's up."

I groaned. "Like I said, doomed."

"I know Tristan's not exactly easy to talk to, but he's easier to reason with than the psychotic killer who wants to kidnap the Queen of Irkalla."

"True." I sighed. "Okay, I'll tell him tomorrow. When the time is right."

He shot me a dubious look.

"What? It's not like I'm going to blurt it out before the test. 'Hey, Dad,'" I mocked, "'a healing god wants your girlfriend dead or he's going to sell us out to your mortal enemy.'"

Adam chuckled. "Okay, maybe you have a point."

I nodded and looked around, realizing we hadn't been interrupted by a certain demon's snarky commentary. "Where's Giguhl?"

He opened his mouth to reply, but the door flew open and the Mischief stomped in. Judging from his thunderous expression, the talk with Valva hadn't been friendly.

He stomped across the room and dropped into the armchair adjacent to the couch. "Well, that sucked ass."

"What happened?" I asked as gently as I could.

The demon leaned forward and put his horned head in his claws. "She wants me back."

Adam and I exchanged a worried look. "And?" the mancy prompted.

Giguhl looked up, his expression tortured. "And I told her no way. Been there, done that, have the scars to prove it."

"Good for you," I said.

He grimaced. "Don't get too excited. She told me a lot of

stuff. About why she had to break it off with me. About how she still wants my body. I don't know"—he scrubbed a claw over his face—"she sounded pretty convincing."

"Of course she did." I rolled my eyes. "She's an excellent actress."

"Yeah, but part of me wants to believe her."

I was pretty sure I knew exactly which part he was thinking with. "Well, don't listen to that part. It only gets you in trouble."

Giguhl shot me a bitch-please look. "I was referring to my heart, gutter brain."

I rolled my eyes. "Sure."

"Okay, I'll admit she still makes the Pitchfork vibrate, but it's not just about sex. I loved her."

"It's only natural you'd be having doubts," Adam said. "She broke it off with you without any explanation. Of course you'd want to believe she was forced into it. But you have to use your head here, G. If she's telling the truth and you get back together with her, how long until Mommy Dearest calls her back again?"

The demon stilled. "I hadn't thought of that."

"Well you should. Do you really want to risk her breaking your heart again?"

He sighed and shook his head. "No."

I relaxed a fraction. "Good."

Giguhl flopped back against the chair with a groan. "I don't understand females at all."

"Amen, brother," Adam said with a wry smile.

"Hey!" I protested.

The mancy shrugged. "What? It's true. It's like you know from birth how to fuck with our heads. Back before you succumbed to my charms, I didn't know what the hell was going on."

"It's true, Sabina. You were a major tease. Just like Valva."

My mouth dropped open. "Take that back!"

The Mischief demon grinned at me. "Truth hurts, don't it?"

I crossed my arms. "Whatever. I'm just glad you're not getting back together with her. You can do way better."

"I don't know, Red. Before she ripped out my heart and stomped on it with her stilettos, I couldn't believe my luck that such a megababe was with me." The demon sighed and rose. "Anyway, I'm gonna hit the sack."

After we'd said our good nights, he lumbered toward his room with drooping shoulders. Seeing it made me want to find the Vanity demon and kick her ass. How dare she show up and screw with his head like that?

"Whatever you're thinking, don't."

I shot Adam an innocent look. "Who, me?"

"Sabina, I know you care about him, but you can't get in the middle."

I crossed my arms and glared at the floor.

"He's a grown-assed demon, Red." He patted my leg and stood. "Anyway, I'm sure nothing will come of it."

I prayed he was right, but I'd seen the doubt in Giguhl's eyes when he said he didn't want to rekindle things with Valva.

I dreamed again that night. Only this time no gods or nightmare versions of my relatives appeared. In fact, I didn't remember anything about it. But one second I was asleep and the next I opened my eyes as the dream dissipated like vapor.

I tried to sit up, but I couldn't. I tried to open my eyes but found it impossible.

Paralyzed.

A heavy weight slammed into my chest. The weight crushed my lungs. Panic rose in my throat like bile. I tried to scream, but my mouth wouldn't work. I willed my hands to move, to hit Adam so he'd wake and help me. But my arms lay frozen and heavy on the mattress.

Breath on my face. Crushing pressure on my chest. Soft laughter. "Don't fuck me over, Mixed-Blood."

Through the haze of panic, I recognized Asclepius's voice.

I tried in vain to fight him off, to dislodge his weight. Hands closed around my throat, icy cold. I choked and screams lodged in my throat like shards of glass. "Because if you do, the vengeance I will unleash on you will make Cain look like a choir boy."

The hands tightened, cutting off my air. Veins throbbed, desperately searching for oxygen. With every last ounce of strength in my body, I sucked in air and pushed it back out in a mighty whoosh. "Adam!"

The weight lifted, disappearing as suddenly as it had appeared. Air flooded my lungs. Feeling returned to my limbs and brought with it a thousand pinpricks of needles. I reared up, gasping and sweating.

"Sabina?" Adam said, reaching for me in the dark.

I scrubbed a hand over my face and tried to calm down. Swallowing was easier than it should have been given I had just been choked. "I... I'm okay."

I ran my hands over my throat, my arms, my chest. I really was okay. No pain, no swelling, no bruises. Only the shadowed echo of terror lingered.

"Bad dream?" he asked. Adam was used to my nightmares now. Ever since Maisie died, I had them almost nightly.

I nodded. "I think so." Now that I'd gotten my breath

under control, my brain was starting to function again. Obviously, Asclepius hadn't appeared in my bed to choke me. It had been some sort of lucid dream.

"Tell me?" Adam asked, yawning.

"I thought Asclepius was choking me. I couldn't move. Couldn't yell for help. His weight was like an anvil on my chest."

Adam sat up then, rubbing my back. "I've had dreams like that before. Rhea calls them the Hag."

I turned to look at him, rested my chin on my upraised knee. "The Hag?"

"The old legends tell of a night hag who sits on her victim's chest while they sleep and sucks their life force away. But Rhea said that there's a more scientific reason. When we dream, our bodies go into this state of paralysis. The Hag dream happens when we wake up too soon and our brain hasn't switched out of dream mode fully. It's freaky."

I sighed. "To say the least. I was terrified."

"Given your experiences in the dream world, I'm sure it was. Besides, it's not out of the realm of possibility that Asclepius forced it to happen. What did he say?"

I briefly described the choking sensation and Asclepius's final threat.

Adam leaned back toward the pillows and pulled me with him. Soon I was snuggled up against his side. He kissed the top of my head. "You've had some major shocks lately. Not surprising they'd manifest in your dreams."

"Yeah," I said. "But the Asclepius stuff wasn't just a dream."

"True. But what can you do? Once we tell Tristan about the deadline, everything will sort itself out. In the meantime, you've got to get your head straight for the test tonight."

"Bael's balls, you guys! I'm trying to get my beauty rest here."

I sat up and peered over the side of the bed to where Giguhl slept on the ground. He'd appeared at our door just after dawn. Apparently, his interaction with Valva had freaked him out so bad he couldn't stand to be alone. We refused to let him get in bed with us but had agreed to let him crash on the floor.

Adam groaned and threw a pillow at the demon. "You could pull a Rip van Winkle and it wouldn't do any good."

"Don't be bitter, mancy," Giguhl shot back. "It's not my fault you aren't getting any action."

"Yes, actually, yes, it is."

I laughed and got out of bed. "All right, boys. The sun's almost down and we need to start getting ready."

Two male groans followed me to the bathroom. I didn't bother looking in the mirror. I knew what I'd see. A stressed out chick with pale skin and carry-on luggage under her eyes. What I needed was a long shower, a gallon of coffee, and a major dose of confidence before I faced my father's next test.

I got two out of the three, but beggars can't be choosers. Even if the beggar in question might be the Chosen.

26

*T*hat evening, we all stood in the middle of the small graveyard on the western edge of the property. A crumbling stone wall surrounded the plot, and time hadn't been much kinder to the grave markers. By the entrance, green moss covered a statue of the Virgin Mary like a shroud. The instant I entered the place, the death energy tugged at my diaphragm with a heaviness that felt like dread.

"You've proven you're strong and an adequate fighter," Tristan was saying. He still hadn't looked directly at me, which I assumed was an unfortunate result of seeing him naked the night before.

Speaking of awkward, across the way, Horus crossed his hands protectively over his crotch. He'd healed completely thanks to his vampiric blood, but I had a feeling he'd be giving me a wide berth for a while yet.

I narrowed my eyes at Tristan's characterization of my skills. Adequate? I'd show him fucking adequate.

"However," my father continued, "in Irkalla, you will not be facing corporeal beings who you can punch or shoot.

You will be facing spirits. Including, I am sure, many who you put there yourself."

I nodded. He was probably right. I'd killed hundreds of beings from several of the dark races over the last fifty-odd years. Chances were pretty good I'd run into a few of them once I reached Irkalla.

"Therefore, tonight's test will measure your Chthonic skills, or more precisely, your ability to control spirits."

My stomach clenched. Naturally he'd chosen to test the one area I had the least experience with. Sure, I'd summoned some zombies a couple of times, but one of those instances was a mistake. "I'm ready," I lied.

Tristan nodded. "Let's begin."

When Tristan said he wanted to test my Chthonic spirit-controlling skills, I figured he'd just make me summon a ghost and ask it some questions. I have never been more wrong about anything in my life.

After I announced I agreed to Tristan's test and everyone had their reactions—some excited (Giguhl and Rhea), some far less enthusiastic (Horus and Calyx)—Tristan had ordered everyone out of the graveyard. Rhea, Nyx, and Adam had stayed but were ordered to stay outside of the graveyard at all times and to not interfere no matter what happened.

Once we were alone, my father turned to me. "Brace yourself."

He threw his hands in the air and started chanting. The energy rose so quickly it left me disoriented. Black energy rolled into the graveyard like a tempest, swirling with frigid wind and overwhelming power. I put a hand to my head and tried to regain my equilibrium.

I couldn't see anything. A thick black mist had settled over the graveyard. I waved my hands to clear it. "Tristan?"

No answer. I thought I heard Adam shout something, but he sounded far away. He was only about ten yards, though, so the distortion had to be part of Tristan's spell.

I shook off every external sensation. Closed my eyes, swallowed the rising panic, and tried to center myself.

A loud cracking sound echoed, like the earth ripping apart. My eyes flew open. My heart thumped a warning. I spun around, desperately searching the mist for some clue about what was happening.

The clue arrived in the form of a skeletal hand. It exploded from the ground and grabbed my ankle like a vise. I fell to my ass on the grave.

"Godsdammit!"

I grabbed a knife from my boot and hacked at the wrist. The fingers tightened, cutting off blood supply to my foot. Because the hand was already rotted to the bone, it didn't take long to cut through the desiccated ligaments connecting the wrist to the arm. The hand broke away still attached to my leg. I uncurled the bent phalanges and chucked the dead hand across the graveyard.

I scrambled back until my shoulders hit the grave-marker. Using the stone for leverage, I jumped up. Keeping my eyes on the grave, I waited for its resident to emerge from the soil.

That's when I heard them. Low moans crawled through the mist. The dark energies permeating the air were filled with a mosaic of emotions. Malevolence, confusion, unbearable sadness. The scent of rot filled my nostrils. A cold chill scraped down my spine.

Revenants. Lots of them.

I'd summoned and controlled the reanimated dead

before, but I'd never fought any that someone else had summoned. However, I knew from experience that taking their heads off would kill them. Or rather, rekill them.

I ducked low and took stock. Down there the mist was lighter and I could see several pairs of feet shambling my way. What I didn't see was a weapon. Besides the small knife in my hand, I had a gun in my waistband, but it would only slow them down. I needed a sword or a scythe or some other large, sharp instrument.

The fog started to dissipate, revealing a slow but determined undead army. Each Revenant's appearance was more horrific than the last. Rotted faces exposed grayed teeth in sinister smiles. Muscles hung from yellowed bone like beef jerky. Shriveled and blackened eyeballs rattled in sockets. But the worst were the skeletons. One lacked leg bones and dragged itself across the ground by its sharp, bony claws. Another wielded its own arm like a club.

And then there was the moaning—the terrible, soul-jarring moans.

The cloud had retreated until it was a black wall surrounding the graveyard. It blocked my view of Adam and the others—probably to protect them as much as to reinforce Tristan's order not to interfere—but I could finally see Tristan standing by the entrance. He leaned with his arms crossed against the statue of the Virgin Mary.

"Tristan?" I shouted.

"Yes?" His tone too casual.

"I hate you so much right now."

He chuckled. "Good to know. Focus, please."

The circle tightened around me. I did a quick count. Dread was a frozen stone in my gut. One to three I could probably manage, but there was no way I could hack my way through twelve Revenants with nothing but a small blade and a gun.

"How in the hell—" I started to shout. But then a new thought occurred to me. Tristan had said that the purpose of this test was to see how I handled my Chthonic powers. That meant he expected me to use magic to win, not brute force.

So despite the tarry ball of fear in my gut, I blew out a long, calming breath.

Okay, Red, I said to myself. *Think dammit!*

I was in a graveyard, which meant my Chthonic powers would get a nice boost from the death energy. Graveyards were also liminal spaces, so that would help, too, since the goddess Hekate, patron goddess of magic and Chthonic energy, loved a good transitional space. And what was more transitional than the soil where mortal bodies returned to the earth?

I pulled out my gun just in case one of the Revenants lunged at me and closed my eyes. I could feel them closing in, but I focused on calling my powers. The ground beneath me trembled, but instead of signaling another animated corpse, it announced the arrival of the primal Chthonic energies that gave me my power.

Magic snaked up my legs in black tendrils. Wrapped around my torso, my arms. Rushed through my veins and filled my senses with the taste of blood and the overpowering scent of soil and iron.

My lids flew open. My vision was tinged red as if someone had dipped my pupils in blood. Power throbbed through me like a second pulse.

The Revenants stopped ten feet back. Whether they were confused or merely curious I didn't know. But I didn't intend to give them time to get over it and attack.

A woman in a tattered lace gown that had probably been white at one time but was now brown and yellow took a

hesitant step forward. The zap of magic flew from my eyes
like two black lasers.

She exploded in a fiery pyre. Her horrible screams cut
through the night like shards of glass. The other Revenants
shied away and hissed, like animals witnessing fire for the
first time.

The scent of burning flesh filled my nostrils. I smiled.
One down, eleven to go. From the corner of my eye, I saw
Tristan stand straighter. But instead of looking impressed
by my display, a furious frown turned down the corners of
his mouth.

I froze. Shouldn't he be in awe of my amazing Chthonic
powers?

"Sabina?" Rhea called. Her voice was muted because of
the veil of fog, but I heard her.

"No!" Tristan yelled. "You cannot help her. She has to
do this on her own."

I frowned at him. What was I missing? Surely he didn't
expect me to just stand there and let the undead feast on my
brain.

Another Revenant began a shambling attack. This dude
wore a dusty black gown with a white collar.

"Oh, come on!" I yelled. "A fucking priest? Really?"

I might not be a mortal and I might not worship the
same god as the sons of Adam, but even I knew killing a
man of the cloth was bad juju. I paused, looking around the
circle as something Nyx said the other night flashed into
my head. She'd said these grounds had once been owned by
the church and served as a hospital for the aged and infirm.
So basically, I was fighting a zombie horde of priests, nuns,
and fucking invalids.

I gritted my teeth and shot a death glare at my father.
Luckily for him, I had enough control over my powers now

that my anger didn't manifest as an actual death ray; otherwise he'd be toast. "You want me to kill a bunch of devout do-gooders?"

Tristan cocked a brow. "Who asked you to kill them?"

There it was. Everything clicked. Somehow I had to figure out how to take control of them and send them back to eternal slumbers without rekilling them . . . or becoming an all-you-can-eat brain buffet.

I took the gun and fired several rounds into the ground at the feet of the zombie priest and a few others who looked like they were about to make a move. The noise and the muzzle's flash had them cowering back into formation.

Good, I needed time to think.

I knew a couple of things about Revenants. You had to cut off their heads to stop them. They were afraid of fire. And, if you were the one lucky enough to summon them, you could command them at your will.

That last part meant that Tristan was currently controlling everything these guys did. I frowned and sucked on my teeth as I considered my options. I sent out an experimental stream of Chthonic magic—not a zap, but a gentler tendril of energy. Maybe if I could interrupt Tristan's power over the Revenants, I could wrest control from him.

The feelers spread out through the graveyard. It wove over headstones and around statues. Sunk low into the earth, combing the soil for the roots of his control. I closed my eyes to focus on the feedback. Earthworms wriggled against the energy as it crawled past them. I smelled rich, fallow soil fertilized with the remains of so many bodies. My power crawled under the feet of the Revenants, seeking the magical source. And there, finally, throbbing under Tristan's feet was a ball of bright light buried deep in the earth.

The instant my powers touched the sphere of energy, a

painful zap zinged back through the ground and hit me like a bolt of lightning. Stars danced in my vision. My teeth rattled in my head. I groaned and shook myself. Time to try again.

On the periphery of my consciousness, I felt Tristan staring at me. Could feel his hold on his powers and his surprise that I'd figured out the trick.

This time, I was braced for the counterattack. I absorbed the pain and used it to fuel my spell. The tendrils of my dark energy curled around Tristan's spell and hung on tight. Now I could feel Tristan's emotions as he struggled to maintain hold on his own powers.

The Revenants started moaning again, this time in confusion. I dug down deep, calling on all my reserves to destroy Tristan's hold on the Revenants. My left shoulder throbbed. I ignored it. I already knew I was in trouble without the physical warning.

The spell wouldn't budge. I put everything I had into it, but Tristan's power was too strong.

Blood.

The single word echoed through my head like a whisper. I paused. Was that the key? I knew from past experience that blood amplified a spell. But could it also help overcome another Chthonic's magic?

I shrugged. What the hell? It certainly couldn't hurt at this point.

Without further hesitation, I bit into my wrist and held my trembling hand over the earth. The instant my blood hit the soil, the ground shifted and roiled. It forged a deep furrow under the dirt as it sought the target. The effect was like throwing water on a grease fire. My power flared up, engulfing Tristan's spell in flames. The earth under my father buckled and he fell to the ground in a lump.

The instant the spell was broken, my eyes flew open. I watched Tristan fall. The instant he hit the dirt, the fog surrounding the graveyard disappeared. Adam, Rhea, and Nyx all stood on the other side of the wall, looking pale and worried. "Tristan!" Nyx called, moving toward the gate.

"No," he called. "I'm . . . I'm okay."

"Sabina?" Adam shouted.

"I'm fine! Stay back." He looked unconvinced, but I didn't have time to explain. I also didn't have time for a victory dance. Because the zombies were suddenly on the move. Toward me. With their arms outstretched and their jaws gaping and hungry.

Despite the magical fireworks they'd just witnessed, they stared at me with dead eyes. I swallowed hard against the pressure rising in my throat. When I raised them, my hands trembled from the excess of power. "Go back to your graves. Your work here is done."

A couple of the Revenants blinked, but none of them stopped. Frowning, I tried again, raising my voice. "I *said*, go back to your graves. Now!"

Again, nothing. They moved closer. The fetid stench of their coffin cologne made me gag.

"Sabina," Tristan called. He still lay on the ground. A grimace of pain contorted his face and his hand cupped his right ankle. For a moment, guilt cramped my stomach. Had I been too rough with my spell?

I shrugged off the guilt. He deserved it for the shit he'd pulled.

"What?" I called, my eyes on the zombies. Four feet now.

"You forgot to take control of them."

"Oh shit," I squeaked. In a flash, I whipped my powers back up and used them to surround the horde. I tried to recall the invocation I'd used the last time I'd summoned

Revenants in the graveyard in New Orleans. "Sprits of the Loa, Hekate, Great Mother Lilith, I summon and invoke thee to send these restless spirits back to their graves!"

The air popped. Thoughts that were not my own flooded my brain—memories combined with outraged cries and pitiful whimpers. My head throbbed and I grabbed my temples to buffer against the cacophony. Bile rose in my throat. I breathed through my nose as I struggled to grab the tangled threads of control. I opened my eyes and froze.

Not two feet from me in a complete circle, eleven Revenants bowed at my feet. Relief flooded me, cooling the hot panic piercing my skull. My voice shook when I spoke. "Your work here is done. I release you. Rest in peace."

As a group, the undead turned and shambled back to their graves. Their retreat was accompanied by the loud popping of joints and the papery crackle of decayed skin. Across the graveyard, Adam, Rhea, and Nyx watched in mute awe. Tristan had risen from the ground and was favoring his right leg. His expression was dark but unreadable as he watched, too.

My heart hadn't stopped pounding since the skeleton hand had grabbed my ankle. And it didn't calm until the last Revenant disappeared beneath the soil. Only when the mound had stilled did I release the powers. Normally I tried to expend the energy slowly, but this time I pushed them out as fast as I could. I felt hot and dirty and...disgusted. As rotted as the organs of those corpses.

The energy swirled into the soil like a vortex, like a spectral vacuum sucking the filth away. Once every drop of Chthonic energy was gone, I sagged into the headstone behind me.

A hush fell over the graveyard, but the echo of spent magic made the air throb.

Tristan spoke first. "Well," he said, "normally I'd lecture you about being careless, but all things considered, the results were…" He paused as if searching for the right word. I held my breath. "Satisfactory."

The air escaped me in a rush of bitter laughter. "Fuck you."

He raised a brow. "It appears that in addition to working on your anger management issues, your cockiness, and your impatience, we'll also need to address your total lack of respect."

I started to tell him where he could put his respect, but then what he said hit me. "Wait, does that mean I passed the test?"

He executed a curt nod. "Yes. Now, come along. We have a lot to do and not much time to do it."

He turned and started shouting orders at Nyx. The vampire scrambled over to help him limp back to the villa. I watched them go as warring emotions duked it out in my gut.

On one hand, I was psyched that we could finally get moving on our plans to stop Cain. But on the other, I was disappointed that he couldn't spare more than a lukewarm compliment, which was quickly erased by his judgmental assessment of my many and varied character defects.

Footsteps approached and I looked up to see Rhea and Adam bearing down on me. The mancy arrived first, grabbing me in a hard hug. "No offense, but I really want to kick your father's ass right now."

I pulled back to reward him with a smile. "You and me both."

"Now, now, children. Tristan's methods might be a tad…unconventional, but they're also very effective. Gods, Sabina! You were amazing."

"I just wish I hadn't screwed up on the last part."

The silver-haired mage waved away my concern. "The true test was being able to break Tristan's spell."

"It was pretty breathtaking," Adam said.

I shot him a you're-just-saying-that look.

"Seriously. How did you know how to do that?"

I shrugged. "I have no idea. Instinct, I guess."

"Well, whatever it was, it worked. And now we can finally put the next phase of Operation Kill Cain in motion."

I blew out a deep sigh. I knew I should be excited, but the truth was I had some doubts. When I'd thought about going to Irkalla, I'd figured I'd have to do some fighting. But Tristan's little test had proven that when it came to battling spirits, I had no idea what I was doing. Give me a gun or a knife and I could kill a man seven ways to Sunday. But when it came to matters of the spirit, I was a total newb.

"What's wrong?" Rhea said, shooting me that look that told me she already knew and had an answer ready.

I shook my head. I was in no mood for a rah-rah speech about how I could do this if I only believed in myself and trusted fate. Whatever Irkalla threw at me, I'd take it as it came. "I'm just hungry," I said.

Two doubtful looks greeted this statement. It wasn't a lie, exactly. All that magic had worked up a crazy appetite. "Hey, controlling a zombie horde is hard work. I'd punch a nun for a cheeseburger right about now."

They both leveled me with arid glances. Finally, Adam put an arm around me and propelled me toward the gate. "You've been spending way too much time with Giguhl."

27

*W*hile I was raiding the fridge in the villa and filling Giguhl in on what had happened in the graveyard, Tristan had been busy. We found him in the meeting room with maps and old books spread out on the tabletop—all perfectly aligned, of course.

When we walked in, Tristan didn't look up to acknowledge our arrival. Nyx and Valva stood next to him, discussing a map Nyx was holding.

"Hey, guys," I said.

Nyx looked up and smiled. "You look better."

I felt better, too. After I'd finished with the Revenants, I felt like I hadn't slept in days. The food had helped, but I'd be needing some of Adam's blood soon to recover completely. "Thanks." I looked around. "Where's everyone else?"

"They're getting supplies ready," Tristan said in a clipped tone.

I watched him spread a large piece of paper across his desk and wondered if he ever laughed. Then I immediately frowned. What did I care if he was ever happy?

"Sabina?"

Jolted out of my thoughts, I jumped to go around the desk to stand beside him. The paper he'd spread was a large map, which had been hand-drawn on thick vellum. Judging by the yellowed color and rough edges, it was quite old.

"What's this?"

"This is Irkalla." He waved a hand over the map.

I leaned down to get a better look. Unlike maps for most countries that showed the land from a bird's-eye view, this one looked more like a cross section with several levels. At the top, someone had written in elaborate curling script, *Irkalla, the Infernal Lands*.

"Where did you get this?" Rhea asked, leaning in closer.

Nyx spoke up. "We found this in a collection owned by an eccentric billionaire mage in the Netherlands. He claimed a demon he'd summoned gave it to him in the eighteenth century."

I looked up at Giguhl. "What do you think, Giguhl? Is it accurate?"

The demon leaned over the large vellum map. "For the most part." He pointed a claw to a rendering of the Adamantine Gate near the top of the map. A snarling three-headed dog lay next to the black archway. "Except that bitch, Cerberus, is way uglier in person than this picture shows."

"Irkalla is divided into regions for each of the dark races," Nyx said. "Valva, do you want to explain?"

"After I show you the secret shortcut to Irkalla through the Liminal, the real tests will begin." The golden demon sounded surprisingly businesslike.

"Hold on," Adam interrupted. "Is there a reason why Sabina can't just have Giguhl, or you, for that matter, flash her in and skip all the tests?"

"There are impenetrable wards set into the borders of the Infernal Lands. They're there to keep the living out."

"And the dead in?" I asked.

She nodded. "Anyway, pretty much the only way in—in the case of the living—or out—in the case of the dead—is through guarded access points. If I tried to take Sabina through with me, she'd hit the barriers and be locked out."

"So why can demons move between realms?" I asked. "You guys are alive."

"Because Irkalla is our home," she said simply. "Plus most demons—except for the Lilitu, like me—can't leave Irkalla without magical intervention."

She was telling the truth. Only mages could summon demons from the underworld, and once they reached the mortal realm, they could only stay if they were under the control of that mage or if he or she transferred control to another mage. I guess it was some sort of preternatural checks and balances to ensure demons didn't flood out of Irkalla and take over Earth.

"But Giguhl took Clovis to Irkalla," Adam pointed out.

Giguhl spoke up. "Clovis is half demon, so he can pass through the wards, and Sabina—a mage—sent him there magically using me."

"So the gates are something any alive being would have to go through to get to the palace, right?" Adam asked.

Nyx stepped up. "Yes and no. Because Sabina will be trying to prove that she's the Chosen, the tests were specially devised by Lilith to help weed out pretenders. Only someone who could actually be the Chosen will pass through all the gates."

"So, for example, if Tristan had managed to find the secret entrance all those years ago, he wouldn't have faced the same tests to get through the gates?"

Valva nodded. "Right. He would have just had to pay special tolls in the forms of magical items, but that's why we make the secret entrances so hard to find. Mom and Dad don't want to be bothered by every yokel with a hard-on to prove himself with a quest to Irkalla."

Tristan grimaced. "Thanks, V."

"No offense, Tristy." She cringed. "The truth is that if Mom hadn't sent me to stop you, you would have eventually found your way in."

His eyebrows shot up. "Really?"

She nodded. "But if you had, it would have set off a chain reaction that would have led to Lavinia Kane wiping out the entire mage and faery races. If that had happened, Mom would have had to destroy all her earthbound kids."

"Which means if I'd found that doorway, we'd all be dead right now," Tristan said, connecting the dots.

The room fell silent as we all absorbed that information. Her reminder that fate had plans for us that we couldn't begin to understand was sobering.

"Okay," Adam said, finally changing the subject. "To summarize: Getting through the gates is really just the first part of Lilith's overall test. If Sabina fails at any of them, it will prove she isn't the Chosen."

"Right," Nyx said.

"As I was saying," the demoness continued, "in order to get to my mother, you've got to get through gates located in the dark races realms." She pointed a metallic fingernail at the second level of the map. "After you get through the Adamantine Gate—the main entrance—the next one is here in the Hekatian Fields."

"That's where mages are punished?" I asked.

Tristan shook his head. "Unlike the mortal hell, Irkalla isn't concerned with punishing the sinful. Instead, it's an afterlife residence for all the dark races. There's certain areas devoted to punishment, but they mainly exist in the demon realms."

Nyx picked up the explanation. "The mage realm is first because it's sacred to Hekate and it's closest to the Adamantine Gate and Cerberus, both of which she also rules."

I nodded. "I guess that makes sense. She's the goddess of Liminal spaces and dogs."

"Right. Moving on," Valva said. "After the mage area is the Fae Realm. It's home to the Unseelie Court." At my questioning look, she explained. "They're the exiled dark faeries who tried to wrest control of the fae from Queen Maeve in the early days of the race. But don't worry about them. They're all terrified of Queen Maeve."

I'd met Queen Maeve on several occasions, and while she could be a first-class ballbuster, I found it hard to believe the Unseelie Court would be scared of her. "Why is that?"

Nyx looked up and shrugged. "She's a demigod. None of the Unseelies can compete with her powers."

My jaw dropped. "Maeve is a goddess?"

"Demigoddess," she corrected. "But yeah, a deity."

That certainly explained how she escaped being poisoned by my sister when she took out Orpheus and Tanith at the treaty signing. It also explained how she went through four stages of woman each year—child, maiden, mother, crone. I tucked that in my back pocket for examination later.

"What's this here?" Within the region marked for the fae, there was a small section labeled *Lupercalium*.

Nyx took that one. "The werewolves aren't numerous or powerful enough to get their own level, so the fae allow the were dead to live in a small area in their lands." Nyx moved her finger lower. "Vamps are next. They live in the Bloodlands."

Of course they did. While the other races all had somewhat poetic names for their final resting places, the vampires had picked a forbidding name. Typical. "Is there a reason for the order of the realms?" I asked.

Nyx looked at me with a speculative glance. "Very astute of you. Much like on the earthly plain, the fae and weres act as a buffer between the mages and vamps."

Considering the mage and vampire races had been mortal—or immortal in the case of the vampires—enemies since Hekate created the mages, it made sense to keep them separate.

"The Bloodlands are relatively small compared to the others since vampires don't die so easily," Valva explained. "Which, of course, you know all about."

While it was true vamps weren't easy to kill, I'd personally offed three hundred twenty-seven vampires in my time as an assassin for the Dominae. But I didn't think it was smart to remind Tristan about my checkered past as an assassin. "I'm sure I have lots of fans there."

"I wouldn't be so flippant about it if I were you," Tristan said. "Chances are good you'll be running into old enemies as part of the tests."

That shut me up. In my head, a list of potential enemies appeared. In addition to the ones I'd killed for the Dominae, there were countless others of every race.

Tristan cleared his throat. "Past the Bloodlands are the demon areas. The lower-level temptation demons such as Nasties, Greedies, Lusts, Vanities, and Mischiefs"—he nodded at Giguhl—"live here in the Gizal region."

"What's it like there, Giguhl?" Rhea asked the demon.

"A total shit hole."

"It's true. Low-level demons get the worst real estate." Valva nodded. "The more serious demons—Anarchies,

Blasphemies, Vengeances—live here in the Zigal region. Much nicer digs, but technically it's more like one large realm divided into two neighborhoods."

"Yeah," Giguhl said. "Gizal is what mortals would call the wrong side of the tracks. The snobby Lilitu demons got the prime real estate of Zigal."

I looked closer at the map and saw that on the border between Gizal and Zigal there was a dark pit drawn between the two sections of the demon region. The area around the hole looked just like a Hieronymus Bosch painting with lots demons stabbing various sharp instruments into the orifices of sinners. "Let me guess—the Pit of Despair?"

Tristan nodded. "Stay away from there."

"No problem."

Valva waved a hand. "Oh, it's not so bad. I've spent a few epochs partying by the Pit. The weenie roasts were totally fun."

All the men grimaced at the demon. She shot them a clueless look. "What?"

Tristan cleared his throat. "And of course all this leads us to the lowest level and Asmodeus and Lilith's palace."

I squinted at the large black fortress drawn on the very bottom of the map. I read the wording out loud for everyone. "The Bone Palace."

"Cheerful."

"Sounds like the name of a strip club, if you ask me," Giguhl said. "I don't know why Asmodeus hasn't changed it. It's kind of a joke among the Shedim demons."

Valva looked at him in shock. "Really? I'll have to tell Mom."

Giguhl grimaced. "Please don't."

Tristan cleared his throat, so I switched back into student mode. "Okay, so there are what? Six regions?"

"Yes. But five gates. The entrance to Irkalla. And these." He pointed to the Adamantine Gate, one in Hekatian Fields, another in the Fae Realm, and a final one in the Bloodlands. "Once you make it through the gates, you'll still face Lilith's final exam."

"So how does one get through the gates?"

We all looked at Valva. She shrugged. "Some will demand a toll of some sort; others might force you to answer a riddle or perform a task before they'll open the portal to the next realm."

Adam glared at the demoness. "So basically you don't know?"

"Hey," Tristan said in a warning tone.

"I'm with Adam," I said, crossing my arms. "Her answer isn't exactly inspiring confidence here."

"Valva already told you these aren't the normal tests because Lilith herself created them to test the Chosen," Tristan said, his tone heavy with censure. "While the information we have may be incomplete, we're lucky to have Valva's assistance. You'll remember that when you speak to her from now on."

"Sorry, Valva," I said with a saccharine smile. "I didn't mean to be a controlling bitch again."

The demon crossed her arms.

Tristan shot me an annoyed look. "Sabina, your humor is brave but misguided. This isn't a game."

"You think I don't know that?" I raised my chin.

Finally, he sighed and said, "So your first task is to come up with a list of enemies. Chances are good some if not all of the gatekeepers will have it out for you."

I chewed my lip. "Okay. I'm going to need a pen or three...and lots and lots of paper."

Tristan sighed. "Sabina—"

Giguhl spoke up. "She's totally not joking about that part. She's got a shit ton of enemies."

Tristan looked at Adam and Rhea for confirmation. They both shrugged and nodded.

"When are we going in?" Calyx asked.

Tristan glanced at Nyx. She took over. "There's a new moon in three nights. I think that's the best time to go in. What do you think, Rhea?"

Rhea stroked her chin, looking from the map to me. "I agree."

As much as I'd love three nights to prep for this mission, I didn't have the luxury of that kind of time. I glanced guiltily at Adam. He grimaced and nodded.

Looked like the time had arrived to come clean about Asclepius's deadline. "Actually, we might have a slight... wrinkle."

Several pairs of eyes swiveled toward me. The weight of their stares bore down on me. Not until that moment did I realize how stupid I'd been to wait so long to tell them about Asclepius. No doubt they'd be suspicious about my reasons for holding back. And they'd be right.

"Oh?" Tristan asked, crossing his arms. "And what might that be?"

I chewed on my bottom lip. Crap, this was hard. I glanced at Nyx, who looked more curious than alarmed. I hated that in a few seconds that expression was going to harden with either fear or, the more likely option, hatred.

Unfortunately, my hesitation gave Valva time to butt in. "She's talking about how Asclepius wants you dead."

My stomach dropped with dread. Nyx gasped and went pale. "How in the hell...," I began. But then I realized how Valva knew about all that. I swung around and pinned Giguhl with a glare. "Really, Giguhl?"

My minion blushed and stuttered for a moment. "I…I couldn't help it. She forced it out of me."

I shook my head at him. "Unbelievable."

"How…why?" Nyx stammered.

"I owe Asclepius a favor and he asked me to hunt you down." I held up my hands to show her I meant her no harm. "That was before I knew you personally."

Nyx's fangs flashed. "Try it, murderer."

"Hey!" I said, wounded.

"Calm down," Giguhl said. "If Sabina had wanted you dead, you'd already be a pile of ash. She had a chance last night and didn't take it. Right, Red?"

Adam closed his eyes like he was praying for patience. "You're not helping, Giguhl."

Tristan's eyes narrowed as the implication of the demon's comment sank in. I rushed ahead to try and do some damage control. "That's what I was going to tell you. Asclepius appeared in my dreams two nights ago. He figured out that I've located Nyx and wanted to know why she was still alive. I convinced him I still intended to go through with it."

Nyx bared her fangs again and tensed.

"He gave me seventy-two hours to make good on my promise. But that was"—I looked at the clock on the wall—"almost forty-three hours ago." Sighing, I braced myself. "He said if I didn't prove I'd killed her by then, he's going to tell Cain where we're hiding out."

"Godsdammit!" Tristan yelled.

My mouth snapped shut. It was the first time I'd heard my father curse.

"Sabina," Rhea said, "you should have told us this yesterday."

I threw up my hands. "I know! But I was worried if I did

that Tristan would kick us out before I had a chance to convince him to help us stop Cain."

"What makes you think he's not going to do that now?" Nyx said with a raised brow.

"Because," Rhea retorted, "you need Sabina as much as she needs you."

Nyx snapped her mouth shut. Tristan stood with his arms crossed, glaring at all of us. Rhea's words hung in the air like smoke.

"Look," I said finally. "I'm sorry I didn't tell you earlier. But I've thought about it and realized we can still make this work. We just have to go into Irkalla earlier."

Rhea shook her head. "Asclepius resides in the Liminal. If you try to get to Irkalla through the in-between, he'll know you're trying to screw him over."

My stomach dipped. Shit, I hadn't thought of that.

Tristan blew out a frustrated breath and sank into a chair. "We're defeated before we even got a chance to begin." He shot me an accusing look. "I knew I should have trusted my instincts about you."

My chest tightened painfully. His words were like a dagger that hit too close to the mark.

"Actually," Valva said, "the Liminal isn't the only way into the Infernal Lands."

We all swung our shocked gazes to the demon. "What do you mean?" Rhea asked.

Valva shrugged. "Some of the gods created back-door entrances so they wouldn't have to deal with going through the Liminal."

Hope bloomed in my chest, easing the ache of Tristan's disappointment. "Where?"

"The closest one is in southern Italy. There's a cave that

used to belong to the Oracle Sybil. One of the goddesses has an entrance there."

Tristan stood slowly. "So if we can convince the goddess to allow Sabina entrance—"

"We could avoid Asclepius altogether," Rhea finished.

Valva nodded.

I looked at Valva. "Which goddess?"

"Hekate."

I nearly swooned with relief. Because I was a Chthonic mage, Hekate was the goddess I called upon for aid most often. I'd never met her personally, but it had to be a good sign that she'd lent me her powers several times in the past.

"Good gods, it just might work," Rhea said.

I looked at Adam, who smiled. "Miracle number three."

28

$\mathcal{A}$ kitchen was the last place I expected to spend my last night before rushing off to meet my fate. But once Rhea found out that I'd have to summon Hekate in the flesh in order to gain entrance to Irkalla, she'd announced that we had some baking to do.

She and I stood on either side of a large wooden island in the middle of the room. The wood was smooth and dark from years of use.

"Tell me why you suddenly got an urge to make baked goods?" I asked.

She opened the stainless-steel fridge and started gathering ingredients while she explained. "Summoning a god involves bribery. Remember how we used those honey cakes to sweeten Asclepius when we asked for help?"

I nodded. "Yeah, but can't you just summon whatever we'll need?"

She peeked her head from inside the fridge to shoot me a look. "Sabina, what was the first thing I taught you about magic?"

I pursed my lips. "That it should be used judiciously."

She nodded. "Right. I also told you that taking the easy way out decreases the potency of the plea. You have to work for a god's favor."

"Okay, so we're making honey cakes?"

She placed a bottle of milk, a few eggs, butter, a couple of lemons, and a container of ricotta on the butcher block. "No, we're making cheesecake." She turned and disappeared into the small pantry. When she continued, her voice was muffled. "In ancient times, the Greeks would leave offerings called Hekate Suppers at crossroads. They usually included things like fish, eggs, and garlic. But there was also a sacred cake called *amphiphon* that was ringed with candles, like our modern birthday cakes."

"And this *amphiphon* was a cheesecake?"

"Of sorts." She came back out carrying flower, cinnamon sticks, almonds, and a large jar of honey. "The recipe has been passed down through my family since all the women in my line were priestesses. We make them for every event sacred to Hekate."

"Um, Rhea?" I said.

She was busy pulling out bowls and utensils. "Yes?"

"I've never really cooked before. Like ever."

She waved a hand. "Don't worry. I'll walk you through it. It's not so different from when I taught you potions in my workroom."

I wiped my suddenly-moist hands on my jeans. "Okay, what's first?"

She put me in charge of cracking eggs into a glass bowl while she measured out the dry ingredients. I managed to get more shell than yolk in the bowl on my first effort, but soon got the hang of it. We fell silent for a few moments as we worked.

In truth, it wasn't so hard, this cooking stuff. But part of me wished I were with Adam. After the meeting with Tristan, we'd all split up. Adam and Nyx had headed into town to gather some supplies, Giguhl and Valva had been sent to scout for plants and herbs for amulets and potions, and Tristan went to fill Calyx and Horus in on the plan. We'd decided to send the vampire and the faery ahead to Lake Averno to scout the area. The next day, we'd join them at sundown to proceed with the summoning ritual.

While I knew we all had important jobs to take care of, I longed to be doing something more productive than baking. But if Rhea was right—and she always was—these cakes would help gain Hekate's favor, and the fact I was making them myself would earn me extra brownie points.

After I'd finished cracking the eggs, Rhea instructed me to beat them to form stiff peaks, whatever that meant. I went to work frothing the eggs, but after a few moments, I couldn't stand the silence.

"Hey, Rhea?"

"Hmm?" she said, taking a pull from the brandy she'd used to marinate the raisins.

"Do you thing this is going to work?"

She looked up. "Put a little more wrist into it."

I paused, realizing she was referring to my whisking technique. "No. I mean, do you think our plan will work?"

"Yeah, I knew what you meant." She sighed. "Honestly? I don't know."

My stomach dipped. If there was any time I needed her to lie to me, now was it. But one of the things I loved most about my mentor was her no-bullshit attitude. "You don't know if we'll be able to convince Hekate to help or you don't know if I'll be able to prove that I'm the Chosen?"

"Stir faster." Once I sped up, she answered my question.

"I don't know about any of it. Do I think it's possible to convince Hekate to help? Yes. Do I think it's possible you're the Chosen? Definitely. But at this point there's no way to know what fate has planned."

I glared at the foamy eggs. "Fate."

"I know you have this prejudice about fate, but at a certain point you just have to leap off the cliff and trust that things will work out as they're supposed to."

By this point, the eggs were thick and creamy. "Good?" I asked.

She took the whisk from me and tested the consistency. "A little more."

I started stirring again, keeping my eyes intent on the task because I couldn't look at her when I asked my next question. "But what if fate's plan means we're all going to die?"

Rhea put a hand on my wrist. I stopped stirring and looked up.

"Sooner or later, everyone dies."

"Vampires don't."

She raised a brow. "In theory, but how many vampires have you known who are no longer on this earth?"

I paused and thought about it. Besides Alexis and my old friend Ewan, I thought about all the vampires I'd killed personally. Not to mention all three of the Dominae were dead and they were supposed to be the strongest vampires on earth. Looked like immortality wasn't the guarantee against death I'd always believed it to be. "I guess you're right."

"Of course I am." She patted my wrist and sat back with her arms crossed. "But my point is that few beings get to choose their last acts. Too many die by accident or as a result of poor choices or simply because they consorted with the wrong friends. But if fate decides that you'll die tomorrow, at least you'll go out fighting the good fight."

I fell silent as I pondered these words. Hadn't I argued pretty much the same thing when Erron urged me to give up and run? Still, it was one thing to face my own demise. Something else entirely to realize that if I failed, everyone I loved would die, too.

"Look," she said after a moment. "I know what you're thinking and you need to stop. We all know what's at stake. We all know how it could end. And we haven't left you yet."

I smiled at her despite the strange stinging sensation behind my eyes. "That just proves none of you can be trusted to make healthy decisions."

Rhea looked me in the eye. "No, it proves that we trust you. That we believe in you. You're ready, Sabina, and we'll be by your side until the end, be it bitter or sweet."

I cleared my throat to dislodge the gravelly emotion that choked me. "Are my peaks stiff enough now?"

Rhea smiled a wobbly smile. She didn't bother even looking at the eggs before she answered. "I'm proud of you, Sabina."

I shifted my eyes away. "They're just eggs, Rhea."

"Look at me."

I sighed and raised my gaze to her face. "More than anything, I wish I could be there for the moment you claim your birthright." We'd all decided it was safest for her to go back to New York and make sure the mages were on red alert in case the plan went south and Cain took retaliatory action. The sincerity in her gaze almost made me lose it. "But since I won't, I'll say this now. You have every tool you need to succeed inside you. Believe that. You're ready for this."

I swallowed hard and tipped my chin in a jerky motion.

But before I could say something dumb and ruin the moment, she nudged me out of the way with her hip.

"Now, enough of that." She wiped at her eye with a dish towel. "Grab that ricotta and honey. I'm gonna show you how to make a cake so good, Hekate will worship at *your* feet."

29

A couple of hours later, my stomach was full and warm from the cakes Rhea and I had sampled. Once we'd declared the batch fit for a goddess, I'd left Rhea to go check in with Tristan to go over any last-minute details. I didn't expect a long discussion since the mission was fairly straightforward and his people had proven to be efficient and well prepared, but I also wanted a chance to study the map of Irkalla some more.

When I knocked on the door to his basement room, he didn't respond. I tried the knob and was surprised to find it unlocked. I opened it slowly, rapping quickly on the panels again. "Tristan?" I called. Again no answer.

I let myself in, figuring I'd just study the map of Irkalla and Nyx's notes while I waited for him to come back.

I took another look around the room. I'd noticed the spartan décor before, but now I realized what bothered me about it. Most people have some sort of personal items in their living space. Photos, mementos, souvenirs—something. But Tristan's room was completely bare of anything that might indicate he had a personal life at all.

Of course, from what I'd seen from him thus far, the lack of personal items shouldn't have surprised me. While I'd witnessed camaraderie among the rest of his team, Tristan seemed to be always an arm's length away. Even with Nyx, who had shared his bed.

I scanned the room for the map. Not seeing it, I realized it must still be in the meeting room where we'd talked earlier. I turned to leave, but a book on the desk caught my eye. It stood out only because it was the one item in the entire room that wasn't perfectly aligned. The leather-bound volume lay at an odd angle, as if it had been dropped hastily onto the surface. I normally wouldn't have thought anything of it, but given my father's love of order, it made me curious.

The cover was cracked brown leather. Nothing fancy. But the weight of the volume told me this wasn't just a normal book. I opened the cover and realized it was, in fact, a photo album. I paused. Was this the album Nyx had mentioned? The one Tristan kept to record Maisie's and my progress over the years?

A flip of the page confirmed my suspicion. I knew immediately that the baby in the black-and-white print was Maisie instead of me. Why? Because she was smiling.

I stared at the image for a long time, memorizing every detail. Only a few strands of hair were visible on her smooth head. Because the image was black and white, it was impossible to know if her hair showed the signs of her mixed blood so young. She lay in a bassinette, swaddled in white cloth. Her big, bright eyes dominated the shot. Maybe I was projecting, but those young eyes seemed to contain too much knowledge for an infant. Her mouth was open in a gummy grin. Her milk fangs were hidden behind those gums so that to the ignorant observer, she looked like any other adorable infant.

Seeing my sister as a baby made something inside me crack open. Five decades later, that innocent being was dead, but at that moment, she had been perfect. Unsoiled by conflict or the vagaries of fate. Back then, the world was nothing but potential for my twin. She had no idea of the mother who'd died shortly after giving birth. Or the father who ditched her to be raised by his relatives. Or the sister who wasn't strong enough to save her.

My chest tightened with regret. I didn't bother trying to staunch the tears stinging my eyes. There was no use. I flipped farther into the book to poke at the wounds a little more. Might as well get it all out now. Dragging out the process of watching my dead twin's happy life in pictures wouldn't make it hurt any less.

The second shot was Maisie as a toddler. She wore a simple white outfit. Two chubby legs held up the bulk of her round body as she stood. One dimpled hand rested against a female knee. The image cut off the female above the thigh, but I assumed it belonged to my paternal grand-mother, Ameritat. In the background, a magic workroom, similar to the one belonging to Rhea, only larger and more elaborate, confirmed the identity of the female. Ameritat had been revered as the Oracle of the Hekate Council for two millennia. Her healing powers were renown.

The facing page showed Maisie as a girl. She held a wil-low branch in her hand—a magic wand for a fledgling mage. She wielded the wand proudly with a determined frown on her small face. Far too serious for one of her tender age.

The photos were blurrier now. Tears gathered in my lashes, spilled down my cheeks. A couple of drops fell onto the image of my twin. I started to turn the page, but a creak on the stairs stopped me. I looked up to see Tristan staring at me.

"What are you—" he began in a harsh tone.

I dropped the book and hastily swiped at my eyes. But it was too late. He'd seen the tears.

"Sabina?" he said. This time his voice wasn't gentle, but it held a note of concern I'd never heard from him before.

I shook my head and sniffed. "Sorry, you weren't here so I thought I'd wait." Another swipe of the eyes. "I didn't mean to pry."

He came forward then. "No, it's all right. That's your history."

I laughed. "Maisie's history, you mean." I wasn't exaggerating. Thus far, I'd yet to see one image of me.

Tristan frowned and came to stand beside me. Reaching past me, he grabbed the book. "No, you're in here, too."

He flipped several pages—past more images of Maisie, the pictures slowly filling with more color as the years passed—to one about halfway through the book. The one he stopped on was definitely me.

I stood next to a statue of the three Dominae in the estate's garden. My profile was upturned, as if I was gazing up at their faces with admiration. Along the edge of the image, someone had written simply *Sabina*.

"That's one of the few we managed to get of you in Los Angeles. Do you remember what you were doing here?"

As I studied the image, my mind flew back to that night thirty years earlier. I considered telling him I didn't know, but why? He seemed genuinely interested, and besides, it was the past. It couldn't hurt me now.

"I do, actually. I think that was the night Lavinia informed me I wouldn't be allowed to become an acolyte to the Temple of Lilith because she was sending me to Enforcer school." I swallowed against the flashback of pain that memory brought up. "I'd escaped into the gardens because I knew if I was around her one minute longer, I'd kill her."

His eyes widened. "I didn't realize you wanted to enter the priestess caste."

I nodded absently and ran a finger over the plastic sheet covering the picture. "I was naïve to think they'd ever allow a mixed-blood to join the temple."

He didn't respond. He was quiet so long, I looked up. He was watching me with new eyes.

"What?" My tone was more defensive than I'd meant it to be.

He shook his head. "Nothing. I just realized there's a lot I don't know about your early years."

"There's not much to tell," I said bitterly.

"I doubt that very much," he said quietly. "I knew Maisie was well protected and loved, so I assumed it was the same for you. But maybe I was the naïve one."

He was getting a little too close to the truth for my comfort. I didn't want to have a heart-to-heart with this man about my fucked up childhood. Especially when he'd done nothing to stop it.

I cleared my throat and turned to the next page. This one had been taken more recently—within the last six months.

"I was so relieved when I found out you'd joined Maisie in New York," Tristan said. "By that time, I had dozens of photos of Maisie but only that one shot of you."

I nodded, studying the picture. I was walking down the street in New York. A deep frown wrinkled my brow and my fists were clenched.

"You look like you want to kill someone in this one. Any idea who?"

I chuckled. "Any number of beings."

He must have sensed my internal steel doors were

locked tight now because he cleared his throat and turned more pages. I felt itchy, like I wanted to claw my way out of my skin. As he flipped, the images blurred into swirls of color. Pictures of me fighting a werewolf pack in Central Park. Me coming out of Slade's bar. Adam and me holding hands. And just then, he turned one more page, and my heart skipped a beat. My hand slammed down on his to prevent him from turning the page.

"Wha—" he said.

Ignoring him, I grabbed the book and brought it closer to my face for inspection. This was the first image in the books that showed Maisie and me together. It had been taken at the Crossroads, the mage estate north of New York. Maisie and I were side by side, walking through the grounds together. We leaned into each other, like we were whispering secrets. Our red and black heads were so close you couldn't tell where my hair ended and hers began.

Whoever took the picture had obviously used a zoom lens. There was no way they'd be able to get that level of detail without me sensing their presence. Maisie was laughing and had her hand on my arm. I smiled back at her, clearly enjoying myself. My chest tightened. I felt embarrassed to have an unguarded and private moment exposed.

Anger rose up suddenly. Tristan didn't deserve this picture. He didn't deserve the right to pry into our lives. He didn't deserve to intrude into the few private moments my sister and I had shared.

Without thinking about what I was doing, I ripped the plastic sheet back and pried the picture from the sticky backing.

"Hey—" Tristan began.

I swung around. Whatever he saw in my face had him backing down. I glared him down as I stuffed the picture into my back pocket. "You had no right," I said, my voice low and hard.

His face paled. "I know."

I turned back to the album and flipped to the last page. The final image was of Adam, Giguhl, and me. We were walking through the French Quarter together. If I had to guess, it was taken our first night in New Orleans. The night Lavinia appeared to ambush me near Jackson Square. I'd been so angry. So fueled by rage. By the desire to get Maisie back so we could all return to normal life. Whatever that was.

Little did I know that just a few short months later, Lavinia and Maisie would be dead and I'd be in Italy with our father. The only constants in that entire fucked up story were Adam and Giguhl. Tristan didn't deserve them either. I pulled that picture out, too.

"Sabina...," he began haltingly. "I know this is painful for you."

I laughed, a bitter sound. "Don't act like you care." I held up the book. "Besides a handful of crappy photos, you don't know the first thing about who I am or how I feel."

"You're right." He met my anger levelly. His frankness made me pause. "I knew a lot about your sister. Between Orpheus's updates and the research of my team, I felt like I knew her—a least a little bit. But you?" He sighed and ran a hand through his hair. "Were always a bit of a mystery."

"I didn't have to be," I said, raising my chin.

"Didn't you?" He raised a brow.

"Please, you only had one shot of me in Los Angeles and it was taken long before I could have killed your spy. Admit it, you never made much of an effort with me because you believed Maisie was the Chosen."

Tristan sighed and crossed his arms. "I'm sorry. I admit now there's a chance I might have been ... wrong."

"A chance?" I said, my voice incredulous. "Well, that makes me feel so much better."

He shot me an impatient look. "If I were you, I'd spend my time between now and tomorrow night getting my ego in check. Your fight with Horus was a perfect example. If you allow cockiness and anger to guide you tomorrow, you're destined to fail."

I ignored the fact that I knew very well I'd been showing off. Some perverse part of me had wanted to prove to Tristan that I had skills. But that was neither here nor there as far as this conversation went. "So, what? You figured you'd stick a pin in my overinflated ego? Make me insecure and scared before I head off to the fight of my life?" I huffed out a breath. "Jesus, it's like you want me to fail."

"That couldn't be further from the truth. The fact is, I— and everyone else—need you to succeed. You're our best and only shot at finally killing Cain. But you won't be able to stroll blithely into the underworld like you own it. A little humility and common sense will serve you better than that chip on your shoulder."

"Oh, that's rich! You want to know why I have a chip on my shoulder?" I stared him down. "You put it there. You and my mother." His mouth fell open, but I steamrolled ahead. "While you were off chasing windmills and Maisie was being adored by the mages, I was hidden away in the Dominae compound because Lavinia was ashamed of her mongrel granddaughter. She forced me to give up my dream of going into service to the Great Mother because no mixed-blood could possibly be allowed such a revered position in the vampire race. Then I was forced to become a killer because in Lavinia's eyes it was the perfect job for an abomination like me. I killed for her for thirty years and I was good at it.

"After I woke up and got away, I used those skills to defend myself against beings who wanted me dead because I was a freak. I used that pain and anger to spur my resolve to get stronger, faster, more powerful. And I did. My killing skills combined with my Chthonic magic make me the best fucking shot you've got to get the revenge you want. So forgive me if I'm a little angry when you tell me to be humble." I threw up my hands. "Humility is for martyrs. And I don't plan on dying for your cause any time soon."

"That's not—" he began.

I cut him off. "Fair? You're right. It isn't fucking fair. I don't want this to be my life. I don't want everything to be messy and hard, but it is. Whether or not I'm really the Chosen doesn't mean shit to me right now. All I care about is the mission and making sure Cain dies. I'll do whatever it takes to make that happen."

He opened his mouth, but I wasn't done.

I lowered my voice. "But if you think I'll ever forgive you for making me pay for your sins, you're wrong. Dead wrong. You can blame Cain for bringing you and Phoebe together, but he didn't force you to abandon me. He didn't force you to wait until I finally was useful to you to introduce yourself. You can look at those pictures and think you know me or my sister, but you don't know shit." My throat felt tight and scratchy. Tears stung the backs of my eyes, but I didn't let them fall. "You should be ashamed of yourself that you never got to meet Maisie. She was amazing."

Tristan swallowed hard. He was quiet for a moment. But his stricken expression didn't earn him an ounce of sympathy from me. He couldn't just stroll back into my life and tell me I needed to be less me. "Are you done?" he said finally.

I nodded, blowing out a long breath. I felt lighter now having gotten those painful words off my chest.

He crossed his arms. "You can go now."

That threw me for a loop. I'd been expecting some sort of retort. Maybe an apology. An attempt to mend fences. The last thing I expected was nothing. Although, given Tristan's track record, I should have known better. As far as I could tell, he was very talented at sidestepping confrontation and not taking responsibility for his actions.

"Fine." I turned to go. My hands were shaking from the emotional hangover of my rant. I clenched them into fists so he wouldn't see. When my foot hit the bottom step, he cleared his throat.

"Oh, and, Sabina?"

I paused and looked at him. Part of me was relieved. The other part prepared to feel vindicated. "Yes?"

"Be sure and close the door behind you."

I watched him for a moment, like I was waiting for him to laugh or something. But he didn't. He just looked at me expectantly. Finally, I executed a jerky nod. I ran up the steps and slammed the door behind me. And with it, I slammed my heart against any hopes I'd secretly held that Tristan Graecus and I would ever be a real father and daughter.

30

I marched across the courtyard with the angry words Tristan and I had spoken nipping at my heels. Gravel crunched loudly under my boots in sympathy. I was half-way to the bungalow when Adam called out.

"Sabina!"

I kept walking.

"Red?"

I finally paused and turned. Nyx was with Adam. They'd obviously just returned from town. They each carried card-board boxes filled with supplies.

"Uh-oh," Adam said as they got close enough to get a good look at my face. "What happened?"

I crossed my arms and shook my head. No way was I getting into this in front of Nyx. As it was, she was eyeing me suspiciously, like she expected me to attack her at any second. "I'll tell you later. How was the supply run?"

Adam shot me a speculative glance but said, "Good. I wish we'd been able to find some fresh mandrake root, but we got everything else. How are things here?"

"Rhea and I got the cakes made. I haven't seen the demons."

"Where's Tristan?" Adam asked.

I waved a hand as if I couldn't care less. "Last I saw him was in his office."

Nyx nodded and said to Adam, "I'll go update him on what we found." She rushed off like she couldn't wait to be out of my presence.

Once she disappeared into the villa, Adam turned to me. "What happened with Tristan?"

I raised a brow. "What makes you think—" He tilted his head and gave me a frank appraisal. I sighed. "Oh, fine. We had a fight."

"You had a fight as in you told him off or you had a fight as in you killed him?"

I nudged Adam's arm with my elbow. "Give me a break. The guy's an asshole and I wouldn't have minded introducing him to my right hook, but give me a little credit."

Adam bumped me with his shoulder. "Let's put this stuff in the bungalow and you can tell me all about it." His tone implied he wasn't looking forward to the rehash.

"Don't worry about it," I said. "It was just some stuff that probably needed to come out sooner or later. It'll be fine."

He looked at me. "You sure?"

I nodded. "Yeah. The mission's still on, if that's what you're worried about."

"I'm not worried about the mission. I'm worried about you. You have a lot of shit to process over the last week."

I shrugged. "Look, I don't want to spend what might be our last night together talking about Tristan Graecus."

We opened the bungalow door and walked straight into a scene from demon porn. Apparently, while I was telling my father off, Giguhl and Valva decided to get each other off.

"Gah!" I shouted. "Jesus, you two!"

The scrambled apart like two teenagers caught by their

parents. "Sabina!" Giguhl said, his voice high with panic. "I didn't expect you back so soon."

I crossed my arms. "I can see that." I picked up a pillow and threw it at him. "Among other things. Cover yourself."

Valva pulled a throw off the arm of the couch and covered her bare breasts. She eyed the door like she was planning her escape route. Giguhl stood, holding the pillow in front of his pelvis. "Please don't be mad."

Was I mad? I wasn't so sure. Shocked? Sure. Grossed out? Definitely. But mad? I sighed and leaned against the door. "I just don't understand. Last night you said—"

Giguhl waved a claw. "I know what I said last night. But tonight, while Valva and I hunted down the herbs for you guys, something changed." He glanced at the demoness with a warm look. "Our eyes met over a patch of stinkweed and I suddenly knew. None of it mattered. Not the past. Not the future." He stood straighter and grabbed Valva's golden hand. "All we have is now."

I looked at Adam. His eyes were suspiciously shiny. I swallowed hard. I didn't want to waste another moment worrying about anything or anyone else. Because Giguhl was right. All we had was now, and I intended to use it showing my mancy how much I loved him.

"Just do us all a favor and get a room," I said finally.

Giguhl's jaw dropped. "You're not going to yell?"

I shook my head and grabbed Adam by the hand. "Have fun, you two. I know we will." With that, I pulled the mancy after me and locked the door behind us.

I took the box of supplies out of Adam's hands and set them by the door. He smiled at me like I'd just done something brilliant.

He didn't say anything. Just waved a hand. The room lit up with a hundred flickering candles. I raised a brow. "Nice."

He came forward and ran a hand down my face. "Beautiful."

Adam and I generally came together in a heady rush of adrenaline and desperate passion. But that night called for slow, lingering lovemaking. Taking the time to savor, revel in each other.

I leaned forward and kissed him softly. The contact, the taste of him made a rush of heat flood my chest—desire and need and love. The warmth radiated through my limbs and swirled in my core. I wrapped my arms around his broad shoulders. His sandalwood scent enveloped me. My own shoulders relaxed as I left my worries behind and focused totally on this beautiful man, this perfect moment.

His hot tongue entered my mouth and explored languorously. The warmth in my stomach blossomed into heat. I gripped his hair in my hands, pulling him closer, but never close enough. His hands sneaked under my shirt and calloused palms created delicious friction against my skin. Needing to touch him, too, I pulled his shirt over his head. Placing my hand over his heart, I felt its reassuring thud against my palm.

I pulled away from the kiss to gaze on the muscled planes of his chest, the hard ridges of his stomach. His Hekate's Wheel mark winked at me from under his waistband. The mark was bracketed on either side by the indentions of his hip bones, pointing to the Promised Land.

I lowered myself to my knees before him and unclasped his jeans. I kissed the mark that identified him as one of the goddess's children. Laved my tongue over the hot, smooth head of his sex. His hips bucked and he groaned.

"Sabina." His tone held the reverence of a man in prayer.

I raised my hands to grasp his hands and his fingers tangled with mine. Taking him fully in my mouth now, I stroked him with my tongue. The air filled with the breathy sounds of arousal.

My fangs throbbed against my gums, signaling their imminent growth. Normally they don't extend until I'm in the throes of serious arousal, but pleasuring Adam and hearing his sounds made them make an early appearance. I pulled back, not wanting to hurt him.

He cupped my chin and tilted my face up. "Hungry?"

I nodded, unable to speak. I wasn't sure if he was asking if I was hungry for him or for his blood, but either way the answer was yes. Emotion and a spark of something mischievous, something distinctly Adam lit his eyes. He pulled me up and urged me back toward the bed. "Let's see what we can do about that."

He laid me out on the bed and took his time removing each item of clothing. He worshipped every inch of skin he exposed with his mouth. Then, finally, he spread my legs open before him like a banquet.

I was impatient for his mouth and feverish with the need for his blood. But instead of lowering himself between my thighs, he climbed onto the bed. Leaning over me, he placed a lingering kiss on my lips. "I want to try something new," he whispered.

I swallowed hard. "Okay."

He spread out next to me with his head at my hips. "Now we can both satisfy our hungers."

It took me a moment to catch his meaning. But once it hit me, I dove in like a starving woman. The same instant his tongue found my core, my fangs found his femoral artery. His blood flooded my mouth. Unlike the jugular's deoxygenated blood, this rich brew directly from the artery packed a heady punch. His passion added a flavor to the blood, like dark spices, and the unselfish offering of the gift made it taste all the sweeter.

As a reward for his brilliant idea, I encircled him with my palm, stroking in time with the lapping of his tongue, the pulls of my mouth on his thigh. The world swirled in a kaleidoscope of sensation. The tension of my approaching climax, the flavor of Adam, the sounds of his moans, the pulse of his hot flesh in my hand, the musky perfume of sex and sandalwood and blood.

But the feast of the senses paled in comparison to the feeling of complete connection with Adam. This man who'd stood by my side through countless battles and heartbreak. This man who'd seen me at my worst and loved me anyway. This man who taught me that loving someone didn't make you weak or vulnerable. I'd never felt stronger or more invincible than when I was with this incredible man.

My heart felt impossibly large for my chest to contain. My skin throbbed with sensation. My breath hitched as the frenzy reached a fevered pitch.

The entire world held its breath. Adam groaned. My legs went rigid. We plunged into the chasm.

Together.

Hours later, the sun was already rising when we finally fell to the bed in sweaty heaps.

"Damn, woman," Adam panted.

I laughed and curled into him with feline movements. "Damn yourself. I feel drunk."

He stroked a palm down my chest and settled it on my stomach. "Are you saying I'm intoxicating?" he teased.

I placed a palm on his cheek and looked him in the eye. "You are." I placed a kiss on his lips. "I love you."

He sobered instantly. He pulled me toward him until we lay face-to-face. "I love you," he said in a fierce tone. "I know that we need to sleep, but I don't want to. Not yet."

I stifled a yawn. "Me neither."

"Good, because I need to talk to you about something."

Something in his tone told me that our little bubble of intimacy was about to burst. I wanted to hang on to it for a few moments longer. "Can't we just talk tomorrow? I just want to hold on to you for a while."

He shook his head with a solemn expression. "No. It has to be now."

I cleared my throat and braced myself. "Okay," I said slowly.

He licked his lips and looked away. Adam wasn't one to get nervous easily. Uh-oh.

"Just tell me whatever it is fast."

He blew out a deep breath. "Sabina, I . . . I know that neither of us knows what tonight will bring." He paused to collect his thoughts. I nodded impatiently. "But I prefer to believe that we'll somehow figure out a way to win."

"Of course."

He shot me a look. "I won't get through this if you keep interrupting."

I bit my lip and nodded for him to continue.

"But even if we don't win and the future doesn't exist for us past a few more hours, I need you to know that I love you."

I opened my mouth to say that I knew that. Of course I did. But he held up a hand. Then he turned away. The movement caused a rush of air to cool the skin he'd been touching. With the loss of his heat, my stomach sank. I slammed my eyes shut.

"Red? Look." His tone was soft, almost pleading.

I stilled and opened my eyes. It took me a couple of blinks before I realized what I was seeing. In the foreground, a silver circle shot through with blue. In the background, Adam Lazarus stared at me with his heart in his eyes.

My heart fluttered. "What's this?"

With his free hand, he lifted my right hand. He slid the ring over my middle finger—the same one mages wore their handfasting rings on. The heaviness of the ring echoed the weight of the moment.

"Look at me," he whispered.

I blinked back the tears that gathered at my lashes and forced my gaze to his dear face.

"You are the most frustrating, stubborn woman I have ever met. You are also the bravest and you have the biggest heart. I don't know what tomorrow will bring or if there will even be a tomorrow, but you would make me the proudest male alive if you agreed to become my soul mate."

I looked up, confused by the word. "Soul mate?"

"It's what mages call their spouses. We believe that the union of two people is a conscious and deliberate joining of souls."

My fingers trembled as I looked at the ring. "Where did you get this?"

His lips tightened at my delay in responding. "I bought it in town tonight. It's just silver and lapis." He shrugged. "If I'd had more time—"

I shook my head, cutting him off. "It's beautiful." I let out a long shuddering breath. My heart pounded in my ears. Never in my life did I ever think I'd be so lucky. "I don't deserve you, you know."

"Sure you do. We deserve each other—that's why we're so good together."

"Yes," I whispered. "Yes, I will be your soul mate."

He tackled me and suddenly I was too busy sobbing. And kissing him. And saying quietly to myself, "Miracle number four."

*T*all pine trees rose like old gods from primordial soil. The air was scented with the dark perfume of damp earth, pine needles, and the pleasing brackish tang of lake water. Silence reigned except for the occasional soft lapping of water against rock.

Lago D'Averno was located in southern Italy, near the town of Pozzuoli. According to Nyx, the lake was sacred to the Romans, who believed it to be the entrance to Hades, their version of the underworld. "But the modern history of the area is interesting as well. Last year, the Italian government seized the lake from a private owner because of Mafia activity."

"Oh?" Giguhl piped up. "Like what?"

"It was a hideout for their hit men and their drug-fueled parties. They also found evidence of several executions on the site."

"That's pretty awesome," Giguhl said, shooting me an excited look.

That certainly explained the heavy death energy in the air. I hefted the bag of supplies higher on my shoulder. "Let's get moving."

Because it was the new moon, the night was spectacularly dark. But instead of feeling like a bad omen, it felt…comforting. I suppose it should. After all, in addition to being a Chthonic mage, I was also a vampire. Night was my kingdom.

Recent rains left the earth muddy and our feet sank into this ooze, masking our footsteps. Tristan led us through the tree line and we emerged on the banks of the lake. The body of water was formed in an old volcanic crater and was almost perfectly round. I stopped, listening for signs of trouble, but the area was quiet. Too quiet.

"Why is it so calm?"

"*Avernus* means 'without birds.' It's believed most wildlife avoids the lake because of volcanic fumes," Tristan said. "But I think they avoid it because they know this place is full of dark, heavy magic."

"Where's this grotto?"

He waved a hand over his shoulder to indicate we should follow him. We climbed down the banks of the lake and trekked a couple of miles. Probably this area was a draw for tourists during the day, but now it was closed and we had the run of the place.

Eventually, we found the entrance to the grotto. It stood at the end of a pathway lined on either side by towering trees. Cut into a tall rock wall, the entrance looked like a large keyhole—or the entrance to a womb.

When we reached the opening, Tristan held up a hand to still us. "Sabina must go in alone. She will summon Hekate and make the proper offerings. Once they have set off, we will follow."

"Wait." I shot Tristan a panicked look. "I thought you were going with me?"

"We'll be behind you," he said. "But only you can open the gates." He motioned to Giguhl. "She'll need the bag."

Not for the first time, I wished Rhea were with us. She'd said her good-byes in Tuscany before we'd headed out. She'd wanted to come, but we'd all decided that if the worst should happen, she needed to be alive to lead the mage race. The good-bye was tearful and hard, but I was relieved that she, at least, would be safe.

Giguhl came forward quietly and handed over the sack containing all the items we'd collected for the rites. His face was solemn as he surrendered it to Tristan.

I forced a smile. "Thanks, G." He laid a massive claw on my shoulder and squeezed.

"If you run into trouble, summon me. Remember that."

Part of the plan was to send Valva and Giguhl ahead to the demon realms to wait for us. It would be too much of an energy drain to maintain our hold on them in the nondemon areas, since their bodies would be pulled back to Gizal and Zigal like magnets.

I blinked against the sudden sting in my eyes. "I will."

He hugged me hard. "I'm ready."

I pulled back with a sniff and looked at Valva. "Stay with him."

She smiled and put her arm around Giguhl's waist. "Absolutely. We'll see you in Gizal."

I took a deep breath and muttered the incantation to send Giguhl back to his home. The instant before he disappeared, he winked at me. Valva disappeared a split second after Giguhl. Since she was a Lilitu demon, she could move between the mortal realm and Irkalla of her own will.

"Adam," Tristan called. "Come help her prepare while I help Calyx and Horus set up a perimeter." The faery and vampire had met up with us the instant we materialized in the forest. They'd spoken quietly to Tristan to let him know the coast was clear but otherwise had remained silent. "We don't want any nasty surprises interrupting the rites."

I blew out a long, deep breath. We'd gone over all this at the estate before we flashed to the lake. But now, facing the reality, I realized how unprepared I really was for what was coming. After all, Tristan had based his instructions on vague theories and arcane bits of information. The truth was, none of us really knew what was waiting for us in Irkalla—that is, if we could get there at all.

Adam came forward, taking the bag from Tristan. "How you doing?" he whispered.

I choked on an ironic laugh. "Peachy."

He placed a warm palm on my suddenly cold cheek. "You're gonna do great. Soon this will all be over and we can go on a nice long vacation. Just the two of us."

"You promise?" The tears were more insistent now. Neither of us expected to come through this intact. We'd danced around that issue, but neither of us had spoken the words out loud. I'd never met Lilith in person, but her reputation didn't leave me feeling very confident I'd escape this confrontation unscathed.

He looked me dead in the eye. "Sabina Kane, I promise with every fiber of my being that we will be together. Nothing above or below this earth will keep me from you." He kissed the ring he'd given me the night before.

His vow caused a shudder to pass through me, like a spell had been cast. I returned his clear-eyed stare and repeated the words. "Adam Lazarus, I promise with every fiber of my being that we will be together. Nothing above or below this earth will keep me from you. Even if death separates us, I will always be yours."

His eyes flared at my impromptu addition. "If death separates us, I will always be yours," he echoed in a whisper.

I grabbed him and pulled him to me. More than anything, I wanted his words to be true. More than that, I needed his strength against me. Needed my last sensation on this mortal realm to be his scent, his heat, the taste of his lips.

Despite our promises, we kissed like we'd never see each other again. "I love you," I whispered against his lips.

If Tristan or the others were uncomfortable by the display, they didn't react. No uncomfortable clearing of throats or shuffling of boots or claws. Eventually, though, Nyx whispered gently, "It's almost midnight."

I pressed my lips against Adam's once, twice, three times to sanctify my vows. Then, with tears blurring my vision, I pulled away so he could dress me. As he bent to open the bag, his free hand swiped at his eyes. I didn't bother trying to remove the tears from my eyes or face. Salt and strong emotions were great conductors of magic. They'd strengthen the ritual. And I needed every advantage I could get.

The gun belt had been a gift from Nyx. The twin pistols had mother-of-pearl inlaid in the handles. Adam had provided the apple bullets. Next, he added a few protective amulets. They clinked against the priestess necklaces and the lodestone necklace Zen had given me. I suddenly felt like Mr. T, but I wasn't about to reject any of the magical weapons.

Finally, Adam finished loading me down with weaponry. "You look like a warrior queen."

The corner of my mouth lifted. Truthfully, with each new item, I felt my resolve strengthen.

"Here goes nothing." I took a deep, calming breath. Ahead, the entrance to the Oracle's cave yawned open like a demon's maw, waiting to swallow me into the abyss. A hush had fallen over the crew, their tension palpable against my skin. I accepted a torch from Tristan, as well as two unlit ones to use later, which I stuck in my pack. He offered me a facsimile of a reassuring smile but said nothing. What was there to say, really? Good luck? Hope you don't get killed?

"Don't fuck it up," he said finally.

I bit my tongue against an angry retort. "Yeah, thanks."

I stepped into darkness alone. The air here was musty, noticeably colder. My footsteps echoed off the ancient stone walls in time with my thudding heart. Every dozen or so steps, an opening in the wall let in a breeze off the lake. The air whistled through the corridor, like dire predictions from Sybil herself.

One opening led to a small, dank room. Steps down took me to a natural bridge made of stone. Dark, oily water stood on either side. Time and moisture had promoted algae, which spread across the top like a cancer. I realized this must have been the ritual cleansing area Nyx had warned me about.

As the vampire had instructed me, I dipped my fingers into the water. It was thick and smelled terrible, like sour dishrags and mold. I ignored my gag reflex and touched my fingertips to my forehead. As I did, I whispered a prayer to Sybil, thanking her for allowing me to enter her sacred space.

I exited the bathing chamber and continued down the corridor. At the end, a large room opened up. High, arched ceilings rose overhead. Besides the main space, two side niches were bathed in shadow. Low stone benches had been carved into the walls. But straight ahead, a conspicuously bare space must have once held the Oracle's throne.

Just in front of the empty spot, in the center of the main room, sat the charred remains of an ancient fire. I lowered the torch for a closer look. Among the burned wood and ashes, small animal bones bore evidence to past sacrifices. A shudder passed through me. Would Hekate demand a sacrifice? If so, it was a good bet that the powerful goddess would demand something more powerful as a tribute—a blood sacrifice.

I seated the torch into a rusted metal bracket on the wall and began removing supplies from the pack Adam had given me. First, I spread out a black cloth in front of the old fire pit. On that I placed the *amphiphon* cakes Rhea and I had baked. I removed the black candles and placed three in each cake. Once they were lit, I laid out a flagon of red wine and a plate of almonds. I placed a yew twig, sprigs of lavender, and fragrant verbena along the top and edges of the cloth. Last, I removed the three large black pillar candles. These I poked into the earth, each flame representing the points of a triangle.

My preparations made, I retreated toward the doorway and sat. Crossing my legs into lotus position, I placed my upturned palms on my knees and closed my eyes.

"Sovereign Goddess of Many Names, Goddess of Magic, Queen of Crossroads, Lady of the Underworld, Hekate, I invoke and implore thee, reveal your almighty form to my undeserving eyes."

A hot wind swirled through the chamber. The air echoed with warped whispers from another plane. I swallowed against the pressure building in my chest and continued my prayer. "Goddess of the Gateway, hear my prayer, heed my call, accept my humble offerings. Torchbearer, light my way, show me the entrance I seek. Hekate, I invoke thee three times three."

The wind blew faster, harder. Even as the barometric pressure dropped, magic rose. At first, a prickle against my skin, then deeper. The blood in my veins sizzled, my stomach cramped, my heart galloped. My breath came in short bursts as my lungs struggled against the pressure. The power thrust up through me, forcing my eyes open.

A cyclone of black light formed in the center of the candles. The fires danced in the wind. Then, as quickly as the winds rose, they died. My ears buzzed from the sudden silence. I blinked and stared at the empty space between the flames.

I looked around, wondering what I'd done wrong. Had I angered the goddess? Forgotten a step? I looked right first, into the shadows of the side niche. Nothing. A low screech echoed through the chamber. A chill crawled over my skin. Turning my head slowly left, I saw two red eyes starting at me from the darkness.

I froze. Dear gods, what had I summoned by accident?

A large white owl flew out of the darkness. My heart stopped.

"Stryx?" I whispered. With achingly slow movements, I rose, not wanting to antagonize the vampire owl.

"Relax, Mixed-Blood. The owl means you no harm."

If power had a voice, I'd just heard it. The tone was low but resonated with unmistakable authority. The owl stopped its circling and landed on a stone perch near the ceiling. I watched it out of the corner of my eye.

Twin lights ignited inside the niche.

I fell to my knees.

Snowy hair rose and swirled around her head like the halo of a fallen angel. Just above her brow, a crown depicting a full moon and waxing and waning crescents glowed. A black Hekate's Wheel—like the one all mages bore on their bodies—was branded into her forehead. Her irises were full black, like ebony marbles. She wore black robes and carried a black lacquered staff covered in arcane symbols.

I'd summoned this goddess's powers on many occasions. I knew the dark potency of her energy. Yet, seeing the goddess in the flesh terrified me. This was no minor god, like Asclepius, that I could outsmart or challenge. Hekate could end me with a passing thought.

"Rise, child. You were brazen enough to invoke me. Do not lose your nerve now."

I rose unsteadily to my feet. My knees felt loose and watery, but I forced myself to look directly at her. "I'm sorry."

She didn't acknowledge my apology, either finding it unnecessary or too pitiful to accept. "Her name is Sophis."

I frowned. "Who?"

The goddess nodded toward the owl. "You called her Stryx. But her name is Sophis."

I paused as relief flooded through me. Stryx had been a familiar of Cain's. Even though I'd accidentally gotten Stryx killed back in New Orleans, when I'd seen this owl, I was convinced Cain had somehow found me. But now that I'd calmed down somewhat, I remembered that many of the sources I'd read about Hekate had mentioned she traveled with an owl to symbolize her wisdom.

"What's this?" Hekate pointed her staff at the black cloth and the feast I'd laid out.

I paused. Was this a test? "A humble offering."

She snorted. "Quite humble, yes." She walked over to the cloth and poked at the items with the staff, as if she wouldn't lower herself to touching them with her skin. While she prodded my offering, Sophis flew down from her perch to sniff the food. The goddess waved a hand to give the owl permission to feast. The bird pounced, devouring everything—the cakes, the flagon, the twigs, and even the cloth.

While the disconcerting sound of a binging owl filled the cave, Hekate looked at me. "What else do you have?"

I looked up quickly. "Excuse me?"

"Are you hard of hearing, girl?"

I tilted my head. "No."

She sighed like I'd disappointed her. "If you seek entrance to Irkalla, you're going to have to do better than cake and cheap wine."

I paused. "I...I'm sorry, but I thought those were the items you required."

"For simple requests, yes." She shrugged. "A breech birth or perhaps a simple blessing of crops." Her gaze bore into me. "But you seek entrance to Irkalla. Therefore, I'll require a more valuable offering."

Ah, I thought. *Here we go. Gods and their demands for blood.* "Where do you want it?"

"Excuse me?"

"My blood. That's what you want, right?"

She threw back her head and laughed. "Child, I have no need for blood. What I need is gold."

I frowned. "You want me to...bribe you?"

She pursed her lips. "If you want to be tacky about it. I prefer to call it a tithe." She held up a finger. "But not just any gold. Only items of true value will appease me."

Sophis finished her feast and hopped over to the corner to rest. I felt those red eyes on me and knew that despite the relaxed pose, the owl would tear me apart with one word from her mistress.

I racked my brain, trying to remember all the information

I'd read in Tristan's dossier of the goddess. I knew she liked dogs, yew trees, and honey. She was best summoned in liminal spaces or crossroads with three spokes. Her symbols were torches, cauldrons, rings, and ... crowns.

"Wait!" I grabbed my knapsack and dug around until I found the item I was looking for. When my hand curled around the cold metal, I let out a little whoop. I held Persephone's crown high. "Here you go."

I held the crown out to her. She merely looked at it. After a moment, my triumph faded and was replaced by confusion.

"You dare offer me a crown worn by Lilim?" she said, referring to the fact the crown had belonged to all the Alpha Dominae of the vampire race. As the goddess of mages, she was obviously offended to be offered an item from a being who worshipped Lilith.

I dropped my hand. "Shit—I mean, sorry. I wasn't thinking."

Her eyes lowered to my chest. "Your necklaces have been consecrated by those loyal to me. I will take those."

My heart clenched. I looked down at the priestess of the Blood Moon amulet Maisie had given me. Her own matching necklace was hidden under my shirt. Mine I didn't mind handing over, but Maisie's? I had so little left of my sister; I couldn't imagine surrendering it. I glanced up at the goddess, prepared to pretend I hadn't heard her use of the plural.

"You may have it," I said, removing my amulet.

"The other as well."

Still playing dumb, I started to remove the amulet Zen had made for me. Hekate arched a brow.

"Do not insult me, child."

My stomach clenched. Of course she knew about Maisie's necklace.

"How badly do you want to access Irkalla, Mixed-Blood?"

I looked behind me, where the long corridor stretched back to where everyone waited. I didn't want to part with anything of Maisie's, but I wasn't willing to let my sentimentality ruin our chance at gaining access to Irkalla.

I turned toward Hekate again. "If I give you both, do you swear you will open the gate to Irkalla and permit me and my friends to enter?"

Sophis screeched in the corner. The sound made the hair on my arms stand on end. Hekate's eyes narrowed. "Did you just demand I do your bidding?"

With every second of delay, it became more difficult to keep my impatience at bay. "Look, I'm sorry if I offended you, but this amulet means a lot to me. I need to know that giving it to you will appease you enough to fulfill my request. Otherwise, I won't part with it."

She smiled. Only instead of looking friendly or reassuring, it was creepy. Someone really needed to talk to Hekate about her people skills. "I will allow you and your friends to enter the realm of the dead if you give me both necklaces." I opened my mouth, but she held up a hand. "You will also agree to pet Cerberus on the belly when you see her at the Adamantine Gate."

My mouth dropped open. "Sorry, did you just ask me to pet the three-headed hell beast that guards the entrance to the underworld?" I knew I was treading in dangerous waters, but I couldn't help myself.

The goddess narrowed her eyes. "Are you mocking me, Mixed-Blood?"

I waved a hand. "Never mind. Fine. I accept your terms."

She held out a hand for the amulets. My fingers found the chain of Maisie's necklace. I looked down at the

Hekatian symbols and ran a finger over the moonstone. I slowly raised it to my lips. "I'm sorry, sister."

I pulled off the necklace. The instant it left my skin, I felt hollow. I knew the tests ahead would be worse, harder to handle emotionally. But the guilt weighing on me then felt like an anvil on my shoulders. I knew it was just a necklace. A stupid hunk of gold and stone, a symbol. The love I had for my sister still existed whether I wore her symbol or not. But I had a real sense that Hekate—for all her might and power—didn't deserve to own it.

Still, what choice did I have?

I handed it over. The goddess took both necklaces with a smile. I braced myself to watch her put them on, but instead she put it between her teeth and bit down. I wasn't sure whether to be annoyed or offended she thought I'd give her a fake bauble. Satisfied I hadn't, she slid them around her neck and looked down to admire them. "Do you really want to do this?"

I knew she wasn't asking about the exchange. She was asking if I was sure about entering Irkalla. I blew out a big breath. "Yes."

She looked up, met my eyes. "Once I open the gate, you will proceed through four more. I warn you, your journey will not be easy. Sacrifices larger than these"—she fingered the necklaces—"will be required."

I raised my chin. "I'm ready."

She tilted her head. "Are you? We shall see." With that cryptic remark, she turned. "Sophis, open the portal."

The owl rose, shook itself. Spittle flew from its beak and where the drops landed they sizzled like acid. It stilled, raised its head, and sang.

The sound wasn't unpleasant. Sort of a melodic hooting. I frowned at it, wondering what this had to do with opening the gates to Irkalla. But then, just behind Hekate, where the three torches still burned, the air started to shimmer. Instead of turning to watch, the goddess kept her eyes on me. I focused on the opening portal, but I felt her gaze weighing me. What did she see—a heroine or a fool?

Regardless, once the portal had fully opened, she stepped aside and held out a hand. "A word of advice before you go." I dragged my eyes from the portal to look at her. "Your enemies will know the instant you cross this threshold."

My stomach clenched. "Asclepius?"

She nodded. "And he's inviting an unwelcome guest to the party."

Ice chilled my skin. "Cain?" I whispered. *Godsdammit!* "Where is Asclepius's entrance?"

"I can't tell you that, but Cain will have to go through the same gates you do. You will have to stay on the move or he will catch up with you."

My heart thumped like a drum of war.

"Remember, Mixed-Blood," Hekate continued, "if he succeeds in kidnapping Lilith, the dark races are doomed."

I swallowed hard. "I understand."

"Gods speed."

I nodded and blew out a breath. She'd said if I moved fast enough I could stay ahead of Cain. That meant I didn't have time to panic or to worry. The time had come to grab fate by the throat. "Will it stay open? So we can get back out?"

"Your optimism is charming." She smiled ruefully. "But, yes, it will remain open until you leave or…" She trailed off, waving a hand.

I appreciated her not vocalizing the "you die."

"Sophis will guide you to the first gate."

"Got it. Thanks." I turned and yelled over my shoulder, "We're in!"

When I turned back around, Hekate was gone. But before I had a chance to regret not asking her more questions, Sophis zoomed through the portal. I didn't have time to wait for the others, although I could hear their boots pounding against stone. I didn't want to chance losing the owl's trail and get lost in the underworld.

"And so it begins," I breathed. I stepped through the threshold from the mortal realm into the Infernal Lands.

32

*P*assing through the portal into Irkalla felt a lot like jumping from a hot tub into an arctic ocean. Goose bumps exploded on my skin and my teeth chattered. My eyelashes clung together from the frost. I rubbed at my eyes with a shaking hand and tried to keep a visual on Sophis.

The owl flew ahead, a pale blur in the dense gray air. I squinted and saw the silhouette of something large and dark in the distance.

I stumbled forward. The fog created a buffer that insulated me from sound. In fact, the only thing I could hear was my harsh breaths and my boots crunching on the ground. I looked down and realized I wasn't stepping on rocks but millions of bones. The grisly sight was all the encouragement I needed to pick up the pace.

I broke into a jog. Soon, the fog dispersed and gave way to a riverbank. A black metal bridge spanned the silver waters. The closer I got to the river, the more I felt it tugging at me, like it had its own gravitational force. My eyes teared and a deep sense of melancholy filled me. Each step took a Herculean effort. I realized then where I was: Acheron, the river of woe.

As I pushed myself across the bridge, I noticed a boat bobbing in the water. A bent and gnarled male in tattered gray robes stood on the prow—Charon? He caught me looking and nodded as if to say, *I've been expecting you.* Then he threw back his head and cackled.

Spider legs crawled up my spine. I pulled my eyes from him and focused on reaching the end of the bridge. I had to get away from the river before its depressing energy wore me down.

At the end of the bridge, the bone ground cover started again. On either side of the makeshift pathway, skeletal trees contorted over the path to form an archway of sorts. At the end of this tunnel, the red sky opened up above. And just beyond, the Adamantine Gate loomed like a sentinel.

Based on the myths I'd heard about the infamous gate into the underworld, I'd expected it to be forged from black metal with deadly spikes and perhaps a few bloodstains. However, this towering structure was actually...pretty. Large columns rose high above me and were made from a clear crystal or perhaps diamonds. The light was dull and flat so there was no spectacular prismatic show. Instead, the clear panes of the columns reflected back like mirrors. My face refracted back at me from a million angles.

Sophis landed on top of the gate and screeched. A trio of low growls responded.

Cerberus.

The dog was as large as a grizzly, and its three heads bore three sets of razor-sharp teeth. Six pairs of black eyes promised despair. Three long tongues lolled out of three gaping maws. Its one butt slammed onto a pile of skulls at the base of the gate's columns.

My mouth went dry. Giguhl had told me once that Cerberus was a bitch—literally and metaphorically. "Good girl," I said, my voice shaking. She stood and bared her teeth. Hackles stiffened on her back like porcupine quills. Her snake tail rattled ominously. "Easy."

I moved forward with halting steps. My hands were extended in front of me in what I hoped was a calming gesture. The three muzzles sniffed the air. The beast moved forward for more. Three cold noses dripping with snot snuffled my palms. I held my breath and prayed that the hell beast would find my scent acceptable, but not appetizing.

The heads pulled away with a snort. I braced myself for the mauling I expected. Instead, Cerberus lumbered to the ground and, with a sigh, exposed her belly to me.

My heart slowed to a mildly panicked pace. Hekate wasn't kidding when she told me I'd have to rub Cerberus's belly. Only the goddess hadn't mentioned the three rows of grayish green teats. I threw up a little in my mouth. But Hekate made me promise to do this if I wanted to gain entrance to Irkalla. Plus, I figured the hell beast wouldn't take too kindly to rejection.

I took a deep breath and knelt next to the dog. Her three faces watched me expectantly and her legs lolled back like a whore at a gangbang. I decided to just suck it up and get the petting over with. As quickly as I could, I ran my hands over Cerberus's stomach.

Never had I been so close to vomiting as when I touched the cold, clammy teats of the hell beast.

Luckily, the whole thing was over quickly. I wiped my palms on my jeans and stood. The sets of obsidians eyes shot me bitch-please looks at my lackluster petting skills. I crossed my arms. "You want more?" I nodded toward Charon across the way. "Ask Ichabod Crane over there to help you."

The dog sniffed and padded on its lion's paws toward the gate. It stood there expectantly, as if to say, *Be gone with you*.

"That's it?" I said. "I just walk through?"

The three heads yipped back in the affirmative. I glanced through the columns, trying to see what waited for me on the other side. But I couldn't see past the reflections from the mirrored surface. From what Valva had told us, just beyond these gates was the Hekatian Fields. The closest thing to allied territory I'd find down in the underworld.

I took a deep breath. Raised my foot to take the first step—

"I wouldn't do that if I were you."

I froze and turned to look over my shoulder. Charon stood right behind me. I hadn't heard him approach and finding him so close unnerved me. Well, that and the gruesome face peeking out from the folds on his hood. He looked like the love child of Iggy Pop and Marty Feldman, complete with bulging eyes and heroin cheekbones.

I stepped back, careful not to cross the invisible plane created by the columns. "Why?"

"You have to pay the toll."

I frowned. "Hekate didn't mention a toll."

He shrugged and pointed a gnarled finger back across the bridge. Adam, Tristan, and the others all stood on the other side. They were yelling and jumping up and down, but I couldn't hear them. "Your friends cannot enter unless you pay the toll."

I sighed. "How much?"

"Not how much—what."

I crossed my arms. His deadly halitosis made brevity a necessity. "Okay, what do you want?"

"Answer a question."

I huffed out a breath. "I don't have time for pop quizzes!"

"Take it or leave them behind."

I narrowed my eyes at the ferryman of the underworld. "Fine, but this better not be a trick."

"What is your goal?"

"That's it? That's the question?"

He nodded.

"If I tell you my goal, you'll let them in?"

"No, if you answer wisely, I'll let them in."

I hesitated. On the surface, it was a simple question. But too much rested on the outcome of my answer to throw out a flippant response. My first instinct was to claim revenge against Cain. It's what had driven me and brought me to this specific moment. But was that really my ultimate goal? Once Cain was dead, what did I want? Happiness seemed too trite. What was happiness anyway? I'd never heard a convincing definition. And peace sounded too much like an answer a pageant contestant would give.

"I'm waiting," Charon prodded. His taunting tone set my teeth on edge.

"Give me a minute."

What I really wanted was to stop struggling all the time. For as long as I could remember, I'd been at war with myself. On one side of the battlefield was my vampire side—the vicious, bloodthirsty, selfish Sabina. On the other side was her opponent, the more thoughtful, contemplative mage Sabina. Every decision I made ever since I'd opened myself up to my magical roots required debate. It was exhausting. It prevented me from fully accepting love as well as offering it. So, maybe, in the end, my ultimate goal was to find the sweet spot between those two. Maybe then I'd finally be happy.

That might be the actual answer, but would it appease Charon? Only one way to find out. Letting out a here-goes-nothing breath, I looked the ferryman right in the eye. "My ultimate goal is to find balance."

A hush fell over the clearing. Even Cerberus seemed to hold her breath as we waited for Charon's verdict. Finally, he said, "Interesting."

"Interesting as in it's the right answer or interesting as in I'm shit out of luck?"

His lips spread into a creepy smile that revealed crooked, gray teeth. "There was no right answer, Mixed-Blood. There is only your answer."

With that cryptic remark, he disappeared. The air popped and I blinked at the empty space where he'd stood. The sound of running feet reached me and I looked up to see Adam and the others barreling across the bridge.

"Thank the gods." Seeing those friendly faces acted like a balm on my frayed nerves.

Adam tackled me with a hard hug. "I thought—" He swallowed hard.

Behind him, I saw Nyx try to grab Tristan's hand, but he shrugged her off. His gaze rose up, taking in the Adamantine Gate. Nyx shied away, shooting hurt glances at my father. Horus and Calyx stood behind all of them, their weapons drawn in case of attack.

Cerberus had lain back down on the ground, looking bored by the new arrivals. Sophis hooted and rose off her perch to fly back toward the portal and Hekate.

"It's okay," I said, raising my voice so everyone could hear. "I just had to haggle with Charon a bit to let you guys in."

Adam blew out a breath. "What's next?"

Tristan pulled his gaze from the towering mirrored gate. "Hekatian Fields."

33

*H*ekatian Fields looked like the land that winter forgot. Liquid, warm sunlight—or something like it since we weren't on Earth—rained down on our faces. A long road made of smooth river stone wound down the hill and through the crater leading to mountains in the distance. Below, a lush valley spread out below us like open arms. Simple houses dotted the slopes of the surrounding hills.

The valley itself was a patchwork of color. True to its name, the mage lands had been subdivided into several fields of colorful flowers and herbs.

"There's the meeting house." Nyx pointed to a large building that resembled an ancient Greek temple on the far side of the valley. "The next gate is inside."

With that, we set off down the road. As we walked, several mages came out of their homes to watch us. They wore Greek chitons, just like the ones the Hekate Council wore for ceremonies in the mortal realm. Some waved and others simply stared. But I never felt threatened. In fact, I had to keep reminding myself that these weren't living mages at all, but their souls.

"Stay alert," Tristan warned. "This may be friendly territory but there will still be a test."

I nodded and adjusted my knapsack. Adam walked next to me, his posture alert and his eyes missing nothing.

The road had looked long when we'd set out, but in no time, we'd reached the temple. The road branched off to the left and we followed it.

A hundred steps rose to the entrance. I looked up and saw two figures standing at the top—one female and one male. I gasped as I recognized the guy.

I took off running before anyone could stop me. Adam didn't even try. He'd seen Orpheus, too, and was keeping up with me. But Tristan, who'd been Orpheus's best friend, held back and called out for us to be careful.

By the time we reached the top, we were both panting for breath. We stopped three steps below where Orpheus and the female stood. Actually, now that we were closer, I realized Orpheus stood several feet behind the chick. And when we reached them, he wouldn't look at us.

"Orpheus!" Adam called. "Ameritat!"

I froze. My gaze moved back to the female—my paternal grandmother. She had long black hair that stood in startling contrast to the deep blue of her eyes. Now that I looked at her more closely, I realized I should have known she was my father's mother from the instant I saw her. In addition to inheriting her coloring, he'd also gotten his omnipresent frown from her.

But Ameritat's eyes weren't on me. Instead, she stared intently at something behind me. I glanced back and saw Tristan frozen on the steps.

"You have some explaining to do," she said. Her tone was icy and hard. Hardly the warm mother–son reunion one might have imagined.

Tristan trudged the rest of the way up the steps. "I know," he said. "But there's no time."

She crossed her arms. "Oh, yes, your fool's errand."

"Hey!" I said.

It's one thing to observe those blue eyes when they're not looking at you, but something else altogether to receive the full force of them after you've mouthed off their owner. I instantly regretted my tone. She was my grandmother, after all. But given my somewhat jaded past with my other grandparent, well, I couldn't help myself.

Speaking of family reunions, I looked around, bracing myself to see my sister exit the shadows. When I realized Orpheus and Ameritat were alone, I asked, "Wait. Where's my sister?"

"Hello, Sabina." A reproach weighed down the greeting. Clearly my blurted question had been out of line.

"Hi." I waved lamely. "Maisie?" I prompted.

Ameritat grimaced. "She is not in this realm."

Adam frowned and stepped forward. "What do you mean? Where did she go?"

My grandmother shook her head. "I do not know where exactly, but I know her soul passed into Irkalla."

Adam and I exchanged tense looks. Part of me was disappointed and worried not to find my twin's spirit resting peacefully among her kin in Hekatian Fields. But the other part, the selfish part, was relieved not to have to face her and my own guilt when so many other immediate challenges demanded my attention. I swallowed my conflicting emotions and focused on the situation at hand.

"Anyway, what did you mean about the fool's errand?"

"I meant exactly what I said. Turn back now and leave this place before you get yourself and everyone else killed."

I raised my chin. "Pardon me, but that's bullshit."

Her eyes widened. "I suppose I should expect such churlish manners from one raised by the Dominae."

My hands hit my hips. "Considering you're the one who agreed to that arrangement, you have no one to blame but yourself."

"Sabina," Tristan said in a warning tone. "Enough." He moved up to the same step Adam and I stood on and faced his mother. "If you know why we're here, then you also know why I didn't come to you when you were still alive."

She dipped her chin. "I do. But that doesn't excuse the fact that you're leading your own child to her death."

My stomach dipped. Normally, I'd just write off her dire prediction as a case of the Chicken Littles. But Ameritat, when she was alive, had been the Hekatian Oracle. Predictions were kind of her thing. "Are you saying that you've seen my death?"

She looked me in the eye. "Yes."

Adam shifted uneasily next to me. "You have seen the possibility of her death," he said. "We all know prophecy is not a guarantee."

"Lazarus," she said. I'd forgotten Adam had known my grandmother when she was alive. "I am glad to see you have grown into such a strong man. But you allow your love for my granddaughter to make you blind."

Adam's jaw hardened. "Orpheus?"

During our conversation, the former leader of the mage race had kept his eyes downcast. But when Adam called to him, he looked up. The pain in his gaze made my chest contract. "Listen to her," he said. "There has been enough bloodshed."

I threw up my hands. "Excuse me, but you seem to be forgetting that as long as Cain is alive, blood will always be shed."

"There has to be another way," Orpheus said, stepping forward. "Magic—"

"Failed," Tristan snapped. "We tried magic and it failed. You know that."

Orpheus met his friend's challenging gaze. "My friend, it warms my heart to see you again. One day, when it is your time, we have much to discuss. But for now, I am begging you to turn around and leave."

"Hold on," I said. "This is a test, right? You predict my death to scare me and see if I run away. Well guess what? I'm not running."

Ameritat shook her head sadly. "This is not a test. This is your grandmother and your friend promising that you will not survive this."

I raised my chin. "Well this is your granddaughter and your son telling you we will see this through."

Ameritat sighed. "As you wish." She turned sideways and swept an arm toward the golden doors of the temple. "Your test awaits."

I glanced sideways at Tristan. He stared at his mother for a few moments. I could feel his indecision. But finally he nodded. "Do it."

Adam and I started to pass my grandmother, but she shook her head. "No, she must face this alone."

I paused and looked at Adam. He looked ready to argue, but I put a hand on his arm. "I'll be okay."

He reached up and squeezed my hand. I shook myself and blew out a breath. As I passed Orpheus, he shot me a regretful smile. One that said he fully expected me to be right back here in no time—as a ghost.

The golden doors were warm under my hand. They creaked open to reveal a cavernous room with a high, domed ceiling. Statues of Hekate and other magical gods littered the space. At the front of the room, a female and male waited for me. She wore a golden chiton and her long, black hair was tied back in a simple braid. He wore a silver chiton and had cropped black hair. However, their faces were so similar, I guessed they were probably siblings, if not twins.

Frowning, I approached carefully. I didn't recognize them, but the power came off them in waves.

"Are you prepared," the female said.

"To face your test?" finished the male.

I nodded. "Yes. But if I may? Who are you?"

She smiled kindly. "This is my brother, Museos."

"And that is my sister, Circe."

I blinked. Holy crap. I was standing in front of the first mages. Literally, the first. Circe and Museos were the twins born from the union of Hekate and Hermes that spawned the mage race.

"Before you may proceed into the other realms," said Museos.

"You must make a sacrifice to demonstrate your devotion to your task," said Circe.

I nodded quickly. Given my experience so far, I figured they'd either want a trinket or to ask a question. "Name it."

"Because you have refused to heed the prophecy of the Oracle, you will now sacrifice your powers."

My mouth dropped. "What?"

"You will now sacrifice your magic," repeated Circe. "That is, unless you have changed your mind?"

I held up a hand. "Wait, all of my magic?"

They nodded in unison. "As well as the magical items you bear." They pointed to the various amulets given to me by Adam and Zen.

The magical trinkets I could part with, but my magic?

For the first half century of my life, I got along just fine without any magic at all. But in the last six months, it had come to symbolize more than just my ability to destroy or heal. It symbolized a new side of myself. One free of the demands of the Dominae's authoritarian demands. Coming into my magic had brought me closer to Adam and many other beings I considered my family. If I let the magic go, would they still want me around?

I glanced back at the closed doors. On the other side, Adam waited for me to dispense with this test. What would he say if he knew that the next time he saw me, I'd be powerless?

On the other hand, what would he say if I gave up just because I was afraid I couldn't cast spells anymore?

I looked back at the twins. The truth was, this wasn't up to Adam. I wanted to believe that he and everyone else would still accept me if I lost the part of me that made me a mage. But in the end, did the possibility they wouldn't accept me outweigh the benefits of making sure they were all safe?

No. It did not.

Besides, if they had a problem with it, I'd just kick their asses until they accepted me again.

"Okay," I said. "Take them."

I lifted the necklace Zen gave me over my head and handed it over to Circe, along with the few protective amulets Adam had created for the mission. She nodded and set them on the floor. Museos lifted his foot and, with a mighty stomp, crushed them to powder. A puff of smoke lifted from the debris as they expended their energy.

Next, Circe stood in front of me and Museos fell in behind me. "This might sting," she whispered.

I gritted my teeth and braced myself. "Just do it."

They clasped hands on either side of me and started chanting in Hekatian. I closed my eyes and tried to will my heartbeat to slow. Tried to convince myself this wasn't a big deal.

But then the pain started. It began as a hot cramp in my stomach. The heat spread quickly, exploding through my veins like fire. I gasped and trembled. My heart lurched and then beat triple time. Sweat broke out on every inch of my skin. My insides felt like they were boiling. I might have screamed, but I couldn't hear anything over the pounding in my ears. A sucking sensation pulled me in two directions at once. The pull was so intense it felt like they were trying to rip the skin from my muscles and the muscles from my bones.

I started to sag but their joined hands caught me under my arms. Supported my weight even as they weakened me.

I don't know how long the agonizing process took. But when they finally finished, I felt like a discarded burlap sack. Opening my eyes took more effort than it should have. Through the slits between my lids, Circe was glowing from inside. Heat at my back told me Museos probably was, too. They hadn't just taken my magic; they'd absorbed it.

I wondered if this was how Erron felt when the Hekate Council removed his healing powers. No, I decided. This was worse. Erron was a Recreant, but he still had power. He was still a mage. But I was…

What was I now, exactly?

"It is done," they said in unison. "Go in peace, vampire."

A vampire? I blinked because that was all the physical reaction I could muster. I knew they'd taken my magic, but it hadn't occurred to me that the loss would leave me fully Lilim. The irony was I'd spent so much of my life wishing to be a full-blooded vampire. Prayed so many nights to Lilith to take away the curse of my mage blood. But now that it was gone, I felt...hollow.

The golden doors opened behind me. Running footsteps echoed, but I couldn't turn to look. I was barely able to hold myself upright. Adam came around and put his hands on my shoulders. His eyes searched my face for a moment and then he froze.

"Jesus, Red, what did they do to you?"

A male curse sounded behind me. Tristan. "Gods protect you."

"What?" I rasped.

"Your hair," Nyx whispered.

With effort, I raised my hands to my head. I don't know what I expected to feel exactly, but it still felt like hair. But then it hit me. They'd removed all traces of magehood from me. "It's all red now, isn't it?"

Adam nodded, his eyes wide.

"You may pass through the gate," the twins said.

Adam rounded on them. "What did you do?" he shouted.

I swallowed hard. "Adam...I'm okay."

"Like hell you are," Tristan said, coming closer. "You look like shit."

"Thanks." My tone, weak as it was, dripped with sarcasm.

"We did not harm her, Adam Lazarus," the twins said. "She sacrificed her magic willingly."

Adam turned slowly toward me. His face was pale and his eyes were frightened. "Sacrificed your magic?"

I nodded. "It was the only way."

Ameritat and Orpheus joined us then, their movements hurried. "You must go!" my grandmother shouted.

Something in her voice told me this wasn't an idle suggestion. "What's wrong?"

"Asclepius opened his portal into Irkalla," Orpheus said.

"What?" Adam said.

I'd totally forgotten to tell them about Hekate's warning.

"He dares not enter the Infernal Lands himself, but he has granted entrance to a malevolent energy."

"Cain?" Tristan asked, his tone dark.

Ameritat leveled her son with a withering glare. "Yes."

"Shit!" Nyx gasped. She had just as much reason as me to be worried. After all, Asclepius only helped Cain to get to her. That meant Nyx was also on Cain's hit list.

"Where is he?" Adam asked.

"Nearing the Adamantine Gate as we speak. Hurry and we will try to delay him as long as possible."

"Wait, can't you just close the portal behind us?"

Orpheus shook his head. "Not if you want to be able to escape later."

I turned to the others. "Move!"

The twins chanted an incantation. The far wall of the temple shimmered and swirled, opening the gate into the Fae Realm. Adam put my arm over his shoulder and helped me run. At the opening, I stopped to make sure everyone got through. When I did, I saw Tristan speaking with his mother and friend. "Tristan, let's go!"

He tried to hug Ameritat, but his arms moved through her spectral from.

"Good-bye, my son," she said wistfully. "I hope we do not meet again for many years. Now, go!"

Tristan cast one last regretful glance at his mother and took off running. He grabbed my hand and together we jumped through the portal.

34

The Fae Realm resembled the Blue Ridge Mountains area where Queen Maeve had established the Seelie Court in the earthly realm. We ran through lush forests filled with both conifers and hardwood trees, sparkling brooks and deep pools, medicinal plants and flowers of every variety and color. For a long time, we didn't see any beings. But occasionally, a flash of wing would show behind a bracken-covered log, or the top of a blond head would peek around a giant toadstool.

Eventually, the forest gave way to a clearing with a pool in the center. The water sparkled with iridescent light and tiny sprites buzzed over the surface like dragonflies. Tall redwood trees circled the clearing and a thick carpet of moss covered the shore of the pool.

Reaching this spot, we all slowed. Even though losing my magic had temporarily weakened me, my vampire side had stepped up and renewed my strength quickly. But I was thirsty, thirstier than I'd ever been. I needed blood, but I knew I wouldn't find any here and Adam needed all his strength, too, so feeding from him wasn't an option. So I settled on approaching the pool. I knelt down and cupped my hands to lift the water to my lips. The water sparkled in my hands like liquid moonbeams.

"Red, I'm not sure that's a good—" Adam began.

"Stop!" a female voice squeaked.

I looked up quickly. On the opposite side of the pool, a female in a green hooded robe stood. She was short—not a surprise since she was probably a fae—and two delicate hands jutted from the wide sleeves of the robe.

Behind me, Horus's sword sang as it exited its scabbard. Calyx aimed her deadly bow at the intruder. Nyx, Adam, and Tristan fell in behind me protectively.

"Anyone who drinks from the sacred scrying pool will die instantly."

The water trickled between my fingers. "Thanks," I said. I wiped my hands on my jeans. "Who are you?"

Only her mouth was visible through the hood's opening and it spread into a smile. "Have you forgotten me so soon, Sabina?" She pushed back the hood.

I gasped and stumbled back. Adam caught me and steadied me. "Vinca?" I whispered.

She dropped the dire tone and waggled her fingers at us. "Hey, guys!"

My heart clenched. The last time I'd seen the nymph was when Adam and I delivered her body to her family for burial. She'd died at the hands of a vampire named Frank back in the winery the Dominae used as a cover for a mage bloodletting operation. We'd won that night but had paid huge personal costs to gain the victory.

Vinca's death had hit me hard. She was the first female friend I'd ever had and the first person whose death I gave a shit about. I suppose I should have expected that I might run into her spirit in Irkalla, but with all of Tristan's talk about running into people who wanted me dead, it never occurred to me I'd see old friends, too.

Adam and I stood in shocked silence for a few moments. Vinca's smile faltered the longer the silence drew out. "Guys?"

I shook myself. "I'm sorry. I just…didn't expect to see you."

She shrugged. "I know. But when I heard you were coming, I volunteered to be the one to lead you through the Fae Realm."

"You did?"

"Of course," she said. "Why wouldn't I?"

I glanced away. "Because it's my fault you died."

From the corner of my eye, I saw her hands slam down on her hips. "No, it was not, Sabina Kane. You know damned well I begged you to be on that mission. I knew the risks. I just didn't watch my back."

"I should have been watching it," I argued.

"How? If I recall, you had your hands full fighting Clovis," she said, referring to the half vampire, half demon who'd double-crossed us. "Now stop feeling guilty and come give me a hug!"

I rounded the pool in a flash and threw myself at her. Only instead of touching her, my arms passed through her. So did my body, except for an odd sort of catching sensation, like a thread snagging on a splinter, before I stumbled toward the tree line. She giggled. "Whoops. Sorry, I keep forgetting I'm totally dead now."

I shook myself. The cold sensation of passing through Vinca's spirit clung to me like frost. "What was that weird little friction there?"

She shrugged. "Spirits are naturally attracted to corporeal forms. I'm afraid that was my soul trying to hitch a ride in your body. Sorry about that."

I waved a hand. "No worries. It just caught me off guard."

Adam and the others had come around the water now, too. I waved off Vinca's apology. "It's just good to see you."

She smiled. "Ditto, sexy hexy." She noticed Adam's hand on the small of my back. "Hey! Are you guys finally together?"

Adam and I exchanged rueful smiles. When she'd been alive, Vinca fancied herself a soothsayer, but her predictions usually were about as accurate as those of late-night TV psychics. Except, apparently, in the case of her predicting a love connection between the mancy and me. "Yes, ma'am," Adam drawled. "She couldn't resist my charms."

Vinca pumped a tiny fist in the air. "I knew it!"

Nyx cleared her throat, bringing the nymph's attention to the rest of our group.

"Now, are you going to introduce me to your friends?"

I quickly made the introductions. When I got to Tristan and introduced him as my father, her eyes widened and she shot me a questioning glance. "Long story," I said.

She seemed to accept that. "And where's Mr. Giggles?"

"He's waiting for us in Gizal," Adam said.

The mention of the demon realm sobered everyone right up. After all, as nice as this little reunion was, we couldn't afford to hang out. Not with Cain on our tail.

"Vinca," Adam said. "It's so good to see you, but we're kind of in a hurry. Can you point us to the next gate?"

She frowned. "You've already found it." She pointed to the pool.

"I thought you said it was a scrying pool?" Tristan asked.

"It's both. In order to pass through to the vampire realm, you'll have to accept the vision the pool offers."

"What kind of vision?" I asked.

"It's different depending on the viewer. Could be anything, really."

Given the tests so far, I had a pretty good idea the scrying pool wasn't about to offer up a happy vision.

Before I could respond to Vinca's explanation, a voice called out through the forest. "Sabina!" Cain's singsong call made my heartbeat stumble.

A chill passed over me, like someone walked over my grave. I looked around to see if anyone else heard it. Everyone except Nyx and Horus—the other vampires in the group—just watched me. Their expressions were tense as they waited for my answer but otherwise untroubled. But Nyx paled and sweat beaded on her brow. "He's coming," she whispered. Beside her Horus white-knuckled his sword.

"What? Who?" Calyx demanded.

"Cain," I said simply. Without wasting time explaining further, I turned to Vinca. "How do I do this?"

"Just clear your mind and gaze into the waters. It will take care of the rest."

While I ran to the edge of the pool, I heard Nyx explain to the others what we'd heard. Our vampire ears allowed us to hear things from very far away. Our only hope now was to get the portal open ASAP and jump through before Cain descended.

Tristan started barking orders for everyone to spread out to guard the perimeter. I placed my hands on the soft moss and blew out a long, slow breath. I cleared my mind and focused on the glowing water. I stared until my eyes unfocused. The water went blurry but didn't change.

"Saaabiiiinaaaa!" Closer now. A couple of miles and closing in fast. Muttered curses reached me as everyone else finally heard Cain's call.

I blinked and shook myself. "Come on," I said to the water. "Show me already."

The surface warped and stirred, then began swirling. Then it stilled, calm and clear as a mirror's surface. At first, I couldn't make out any discernible symbols or images. I leaned closer, bending out over the water.

Smoke rolled across the surface. When it cleared, I saw myself crying. My hair was blond and hung around my face like a shroud.

"What the hell?" I whispered as I watched the scene unfold.

In the vision, I looked up as doors burst open and Cain rushed into the room with an army of spirits. I could smell their bloodlust, their hatred.

The shot widened and revealed a raven-black woman looming over me like death itself. Lilith.

"Your answer?" she demanded. "Quickly!"

I looked up at her, my hair falling back to reveal blood-shot eyes totally lacking in strength or hope. In a voice as dead as the ghosts in Cain's army, I whispered, "It's too late."

"Saaaabiiinna!" Cain's voice cut through my brain like a blade, severing my connection to the pool. He was closer. Too close.

The pool released me from its thrall. I fell back on my ass on the moss-covered shore.

"Red?" Adam called. "Getting anything?"

Hands trembling, I pushed the hair back from my eyes. My stomach felt like a nest of vipers.

"Sabina?" Tristan called when I didn't answer Adam.

"Yeah?" I said absently.

"What'd you see?" Adam again.

I looked up and realized everyone was staring. With the

exception of Vinca, they all looked curious and tense. I quickly decided to keep the vision to myself. I wasn't so easily swayed that I'd let one incomplete hallucination destroy my resolve.

Besides, even if my initial interpretation was right, I was fully prepared to die as long as I took Cain with me. But this wasn't a debate I wanted to have with Adam or anyone else.

I swallowed the residue of shame left over from watching myself cower. "It showed me Maisie's death."

Adam's face fell. "Oh gods, Red."

I shrugged. "It's okay."

Vinca cleared her throat. I glanced at her and froze. The nymph's expression was so grave that I had to believe she knew I was lying. Had she seen the vision? I pleaded with my eyes for her to keep it to herself. She nodded subtly.

"So how do we open the gate?" Tristan called.

"Sabina has to place a drop of blood in the water."

I licked my lips. After seeing my own death, a small blood sacrifice was hardly worth a second thought. I bit the tip of my finger and milked two large drops of blood. When they hit the pools, the waters boiled like a cauldron and swirled.

"The gate is open," Vinca called.

"He's here!" Calyx shouted from the perimeter.

"Everyone jump in! Now!" I shouted. I ran to Vinca and stopped myself just in time to keep from falling through her again. "I'm sorry to leave you like this."

She laughed through a sob. "What's he going to do? Kill me?"

"I didn't deserve you as a friend then and certainly don't now, but I'm relieved as hell you're too stubborn to do what's best for you."

My friend raised a hand and touched mine. An icy chill spread through my muscles and bones, and once again, I felt the friction of her soul trying to attach to mine. The spectral contact was as close to a high five as she could give me. "Give 'em hell, my friend."

"Sabina!" Adam yelled from the bubbling pool. Vinca pulled her translucent hand from mine. The loss of her coldness was both a relief and a disappointment. With one last smile at my friend, I turned and ran full-tilt toward the water. I grabbed Adam's hand and together we leapt into the swirling vortex of water the instant Cain burst into the clearing.

35

*E*ven though we'd jumped down into the scrying pool, we emerged up into a stark, alien landscape tinted black and red. Instead of the clean, iridescent waters of the faery realm, this underground lake was filled with blood.

"Ugh!" Adam groaned, leaping out.

Tristan was less vocal with his disgust but beat a hasty exit as well. Meanwhile, Nyx, Horus, and I took our time. I even swallowed a few mouthfuls of the stuff as I glided toward the edge. The blood tasted pure, like the hemoglobin equivalent of a clear mountain spring. When I finally reached the edge, Adam held out a hand to help me climb out of the crater.

"Well, I think it's safe to assume we made it to the Bloodlands."

I shook myself off like a wet dog. "Everyone look alive. I have more enemies here than I can count."

Horus snorted. "You're not the only one."

I stilled, remembering that he'd once been an assassin for the Dominae, too. "Let's just pray word of our visit hasn't spread here."

Nyx was looking around. "Hey, where's Calyx?"

We all exchanged worried looks. "Shit, I thought she came through with us?" Adam said.

I shook my head. "Last time I saw her, she was running toward the forest. I figured she'd jump in after us."

We all fell silent as we processed that information. "Vinca will help her," Adam said. "After all, Calyx is a faery."

"We need to go back," Horus said, stepping toward the pool.

Tristan grabbed his arm. "We can't. Most likely she's busy being a pain in the ass to Cain to give us a head start. If we go back now, her sacrifice will mean nothing."

Horus stared intently at the red pool, as if willing Calyx to emerge. A few tiny bubbles popped on the surface, but no one emerged.

"Horus," Tristan said, his tone quiet but authoritative. "We need to move."

When the vampire looked up, his face was composed. I knew that giving up on Calyx cost him, but he was a seasoned soldier. He'd see the mission through and use his emotions to fuel him in battle. "Let's go."

"What did Valva say to expect here?" I asked Tristan.

He shrugged. "I believe her exact words were 'It's creepy as shit.'"

Looking around at the black volcanic rock that made up the walls of the cave, I found myself agreeing. "Let's get out of this place. Maybe outside looks better."

I led the way to the mouth of the cave. Outside, the sky was dark like midnight. I guess this shouldn't have surprised me, but since the mage and faery realms were both covered in blue skies, I'd assumed the Bloodlands would be the same. But I guess it made sense that vampires would be most comfortable in a nocturnal setting even in death.

The landscape outside wasn't much different than the cave. A blood river ran through the center of a deep cavern formed by porous cliff faces. Only the golden leaves of a few apple trees broke up the red and black theme. Limbs heavy with the forbidden fruit, the trees clung to rocky crags like they were about to plunge to their deaths in the river below. Only instead of the common red apples of the mortal realm, these had black skin.

"Apple trees?" Adam asked.

I shrugged. "They can't hurt them now, I guess." In order to kill a vampire, you had to first remove their immortality with a dose of the forbidden fruit's toxic juice. Now that they were in Irkalla, the dead vamps could indulge in apples for eternity.

I approached a low-hanging limb and plucked one. Using the knife from my boot, I cut into the flesh. The inside was as red as a rose and the crimson juices dripped over my hands like I'd shived someone. I raised my hand to lick away the drops, but Nyx grabbed my wrist.

"No!" she yelled.

"Nyx, I'm immune to the forbidden fruit."

She shook her head. "These aren't normal apples. I didn't know they really existed before now, but according to my research, they're fabled to make any immortal being mortal. Any."

"Even gods?" Adam asked.

She nodded solemnly.

Adam raised his brows and stuck a couple of the apples into his pack.

"Shit, thanks," I said to Nyx.

She took the apple from me and threw it. It splashed into the blood river where it burst into flames. "Consider the scales between us balanced."

I wasn't so sure they'd needed balancing. After all, it's not like I saved Nyx's life. I'd simply refused to end it. Still, I smiled at the vampire, relieved to put that nasty business behind us. "Deal."

"Let's keep moving," Tristan snapped.

We followed the river for a mile or two until we saw a large castle set high on a cliff. The place looked straight out of old Hollywood versions of Count Dracula's eerie abode.

Tristan pointed to the building. "Who wants to bet the gate's in there?"

"Of course it is," I said with a sigh. We followed a winding path leading up to the cliff. The higher we went, the more I could see of the Bloodlands. From this bird's-eye view, I finally saw the souls of several vampires. Or rather, I saw the shadows of several bent, dark creatures. Instead of the swaggering monarchs of the night they'd been in the mortal realm, here they resembled wraiths.

The shadows crawled over the banks of the blood river and lapped up the liquid like animals. As I watched, one soul strayed too close to another. The vampire whose territory had been breached turned on the other with fangs flashing. They fell on each other like two lions battling over a prime watering hole. The battle was brief but fierce. The loser skulked away into a cave to lick his metaphorical wounds. The victor started to resume drinking from the river, but something caused it to stiffen. Its head jerked around to look up at me.

I froze. The feral face belonged to Alexis Vega.

I shuddered.

"Red?" Adam whispered. "You coming?"

I pointed a shaky hand at Alexis. "Adam, look."

The spirit that used to be Alexis snarled and turned her back on us. Adam let out a breath. "Jesus."

Is that what I would become when I finally died? A bloodthirsty wraith forced to scrape and fight for a meager slice of territory for all eternity?

I tensed to go help her, but Adam grabbed my shoulders and turned me back toward the path. "No, Red. We can't do anything for her now. We've got to keep moving."

I shook off the horror and guilt of seeing my old ally turned into little more than an animal. Her fate was sealed. Ours were not. With a regretful last glance at Alexis, I turned and continued up the hill.

By this point, we'd almost reached the top of the cliff. Two vampires stood guard at the black gate. They each held spears, which they crossed to bar our entrance. "Who seeks entrance to the Dominae's fortress?"

"David?" I said. "Ewan?"

David Duchamp was an old friend who I'd killed back in Los Angeles after the Dominae told me he'd been feeding information to their enemy, Clovis Trakiya. I later found out David had been innocent, and I carried the guilt of that decision like a lead yoke ever since.

He'd reappeared to me in spirit form several months earlier in a New Orleans City of the Dead and gave me some information he claimed was from Lilith, so I guess we were kind of on not friendly terms, but less adversarial ones.

"Sabina." David spat my name out like a mouthful of venom.

Or not.

"What are you doing here?"

"Thanks to you, Lilith handed me over to the Dominae."

I blinked. "How is that my fault?"

"I told you too much when I visited you in New Orleans."

Actually, he'd scared the hell out of me by showing up in a graveyard like the Ghost of Murder Victims Past. He'd spouted off a bunch of dire-sounding but completely vague nonsense.

"It pissed off the Great Mother," he continued, "so she threw me to the dominatrices to be their slave."

"Look, dude, no one forced you to tell me shit. So if you got into trouble, it's your own damned fault."

"Sabina," Tristan warned.

I shot him a glare. He didn't know my history with David. "Whatever," I said, dismissing David's presence altogether. "Ewan?"

Ewan was another vampire friend from Los Angeles, but I hadn't been his killer. That dubious accomplishment belonged to my grandmother. Ewan had been a bar owner and information broker who Lavinia had murdered for fucking information out of one of her Undercouncil members. While David looked like he wanted to kick my ass, Ewan looked like he didn't recognize me at all.

"It's me—Sabina."

"Your presence is expected in the Dominae's fortress," Ewan said in a monotone. Considering he'd been a gregarious and smooth bar owner when he was alive, the change in personality creeped me out. It was like he'd been lobotomized as well as murdered.

I glanced at Adam. I hadn't given much thought to who might be waiting for us in the castle. But now that they'd identified it as the home of the dead Dominae, I realized it made perfect sense. The leaders of the vampire race had led the living vampires with steel fists. Why should dying change their approach?

But that also meant I was about to come face-to-face with my grandmother, Lavinia Kane.

I'd expected to run into Lavinia at some point on this quest, but that didn't help with my anxiety. I hadn't seen my grandmother since the night Maisie killed her in a New Orleans cemetery. Of course she'd be waiting for me inside. Lilith couldn't have chosen a better—and by better, I mean more fucked up—person to conduct my test. No doubt about it, getting through this next gate would be the toughest test yet.

Ten minutes later, Twiddle Bitter and Tweedle Dumb led our not-so-merry group into the main hall of Castle Dracula. At the front of the room, seven thrones had been erected on a dais. In each, a different female sat, each more intimidating than the last. Some quick math told me these were all the Dominae who'd ever existed. Back in ancient times, a singular female ruled the race before the new laws requiring three heads of the race were instated, which explained the female in the center. Her skin was so pale she practically glowed and the dried blood shade of her hair indicated her ancient age.

To her right sat the Dominae who had been the first triumvirate to lead the race. And to her left, three thrones were filled with Persephone, Tanith Severinus—who'd died the same night as Orpheus—and Lavinia Kane.

The edges of the room were lined with the males who served these ancient, powerful females. They wore collars around their bowed necks and didn't dare look directly at any of their owners. The Dominae had always been violently matriarchal on earth, and it seemed those practices extended to their afterlife as well.

When we'd entered, Nyx and Horus had fallen in beside me with the others bringing up the rear. Since this was vampire territory, we'd have to be careful about protocol, thus the three vampires in our group needed to be the most visible.

As we approached, my eyes were on Persephone and Tanith. While I wouldn't say they were exactly allies, they were the closest things I had in the room besides those who'd come with me. Besides, I could feel Lavinia's hot glare on my forehead and I wasn't ready to face her yet.

I felt Adam's presence at my back. No doubt his eyes were on them, too. Part of me wondered if Tristan felt like a lamb being led into the wolf den but didn't chance a look back to confirm this.

But while Tanith met my gaze steadily, Persephone's attention was to my left, on Nyx. Now that I saw them together, I realized why Nyx had looked so familiar when I met her. She looked just like…

My steps faltered. My eyes swerved back to Nyx. She didn't look shocked to see Persephone. If anything, she looked in awe to be in the presence of so many powerful female vampires. I shook my head; maybe I was just imagining things. But, damn, they really did look alike.

I finally chanced a glance at Lavinia. The hatred I expected was in her eyes, but so was confusion. No doubt she was puzzling over my new hairdo. I wondered if seeing me as a full-blooded vampire would soften her disposition toward me. Then I laughed at myself. The only thing that would soften my grandmother would be an exorcism.

"Sabina Kane." The speaker was the ancient female in the center. I wracked my brain to try and remember the lessons I'd learned as a child about her and remembered that her name was Inanna. I shifted my gaze to her but was careful not to look her directly in the eye. To do so would be a direct challenge, and I didn't want to start this conversation off with her feeling the need to put me in my place.

I stopped twenty feet back from the dais and bowed my

head. The show of respect cost me some major pride points, but I had a feeling this group wouldn't find any sign of rebellion amusing. I dipped to my knee and touched my right hand to my forehead. "Protectors of all Lilim, the blessings of the Great Mother upon each of you."

On either side of me, Nyx and Horus mirrored my movements.

"You may rise," Inanna said. As we stood, she continued. "I see you have survived your tests thus far. I'd say it's nice to see you have finally embraced your vampire side, but do not for a moment think this will aid you in the coming test."

"Don't worry," I said. "I know better than to expect any mercy from this group."

She smiled. Her fangs were brilliant white and sharp as razors. "Excellent." She kept her eyes on me. "Domina Kane, you may proceed."

Lavinia rose. Her spectral form still wore the same ruby ball gown she'd had on when my sister ripped her head from her body. As she came down the steps, she smiled like a snake ready to strike. "What have you done with your hair?"

As far as opening salvos went, it lacked that certain menacing quality I'd been expecting. Still, it put me on edge. I raised my chin but said nothing. I wasn't about to explain to her that the shameful mage blood she'd abhorred had been removed. Besides, she probably already knew and was just trying to put me on the defensive.

"I see you've brought friends," she said, looking over my head. "Tristan Graecus, I'm surprised you dare step foot in Irkalla."

"Why?" my father shot back. "You tried to send me here yourself."

Her face tightened. "Yes, that's what I get for not doing the job myself." She waved a hand. "No matter. You'll be here permanently soon enough."

"Enough," I said. "Just get on with it."

Her shark's eyes glittered menacingly. "I wouldn't be in such a rush if I were you."

I crossed my arms. "Try me."

She smiled then, a cold, self-satisfied expression that sent a chill of foreboding down my spine. "Since you are fully vampire now, your test is to prove you're worthy of that pure blood."

I tilted my head. "How?"

She opened her mouth to continue, but a sound from outside made her stop. I turned toward the doors, where several fists pounded against the wood. Muted shouts filtered through. I could only make out a few words but my name and the word "revenge" stood out like neon.

"Oh good, right on time," Lavinia said.

"What the hell is that?" I demanded.

"That, my dear, is the sound of hundreds of vampire spirits demanding your blood. Three hundred and twenty-seven to be exact."

Cold sweat erupted on my chest. My hand automatically went to grab my gun, but then I realized that bullets were useless against spirits.

"You have two choices," Lavinia continued. "If you refuse to endure one of these tests, you will have to fight your way through that mob to get back out."

No way in hell would I be able to fight off that many angry spirits. Even with the help of two mages and two vampires, the odds were too steep. There's no way we'd all survive. And even if we managed, Cain was still out there somewhere.

"Are you ready to hear the options?" Lavinia's tone had a singsong quality to it that told me she was enjoying this too much. I looked around at my friends. Their tense faces stared back at me and I knew that there was no way I'd be able to risk them like that. So whatever the test entailed, I'd do it.

The banging at the door intensified.

"Yes!" I yelled.

Lavinia snapped her fingers and the banging stopped instantly. I blew out a relieved breath.

"Your first choice is you must select one of your team and drain them of every drop of their blood."

My stomach cramped as if she'd punched me. A hush fell over the throne room.

I briefly considered changing my mind and battling through the horde, but I knew it wasn't possible. If I drained one of the team, then only one would die. If I chose to fight, we all would.

"What is the other choice?" I asked, praying in vain it would be easier.

Lavinia licked her lips. "You renounce all ties to your vampire blood."

"What does that entail, exactly?" Adam asked.

Lavinia shot him a venomous look for daring to address her directly. She looked back at me as if I had asked the question. "You will surrender your fangs and your immortality." Her tone was too giddy. This was the choice she was hoping I'd make.

I chewed on my bottom lip, considering the possibility and sorting through possible loopholes.

"Sabina, no," Tristan said, coming closer. I turned to face him. "You can't give up your vampire powers. You still have more tests to survive. You already gave up your magic; there's no way you can survive the remaining challenges without any powers at all."

I raised my hands in a futile gesture. "What choice do I have otherwise? Are you going to pick which one of you I kill?"

Tristan raised his chin. "Me."

I stared at him in shocked silence. "What?"

His stare didn't waver, but he said nothing more.

"I second that selection," Lavinia said with a shit-eating grin.

Ignoring her, I gaped at my father. "Why would you do that?"

"My life has been dedicated to one purpose: stopping Cain. If surrendering my own life will aid you in that mission, I will give it gladly."

"Tristan, no!" Nyx gasped. "Sabina, kill me." She started to undo her shirt to remove her vest. "It's the only way to convince Asclepius to leave you alone."

"Stop!" Persephone yelled.

We all turned to stare at her. She rose from her throne and came down the steps. Her gorgeous face was pale, like she was terrified. "Nicolette, I will not allow you to sacrifice yourself."

Nyx blanched and gaped at the Domina. "How do you know my real name?"

Persephone raised her chin. "Because I named you myself." She rounded on Lavinia. "Before *you* forced me to abandon her."

"I ordered you to kill that child!" Lavinia shouted.

A hush fell over the room as we all watched the drama unfold. Persephone and Lavinia faced off with fangs flashing. Nyx looked like someone had slapped her, but she opened her mouth to say something. I grabbed her hand

and shook my head. If Lavinia and Persephone threw down, we might just get a chance to escape making the impossible choice I'd been given.

"I could not kill my own child," Persephone said. "You of all of us should understand the pain of losing your own blood." Lavinia's scowl faltered. "So I gave her to a family in France, far away from your notice. My greatest regret is that I did not find her myself before I died."

Nyx was trembling now. "I ... I don't believe you."

Persephone turned to look at her daughter. "Your adopted parents' names were Antoine and Josephine. I threatened to kill them if they ever revealed your connection to me."

"Well, you didn't have to worry. Cain killed them before they had the chance."

"This is all very touching," the ancient one said. "But let's get back to Sabina's choice, shall we?"

I shot at glare at the ancient bitch. Persephone and Nyx were unaware of anything but staring at each other. Tristan turned to face me.

"I know when I met you I said that I didn't believe you were the Chosen. I am still not positive on that account."

"Gee, thanks," I said.

"But," he continued as if I hadn't spoken, "based on the valor you have exhibited tonight, I believe in my gut you will find a way to pass Lilith's tests." I cringed, knowing he was wrong. "If sacrificing myself allows you that chance, then so be it."

My eyes stung suddenly and my throat tightened. As much as I'd resisted the idea that I needed Tristan Graecus's approval or respect, hearing those words opened something inside me. Something that felt a lot like ... pride. But if he thought I was going to murder him now, he was an idiot.

I poked a finger at his chest. He jerked as if I'd slapped him instead. "You listen to me now," I said, my voice thick. "Don't think you know me. Because you don't. At all."

"I know that and not having the privilege of watching you grow into the woman you've become is one of my greatest regrets. But now I have a chance to make up for it."

"Shut up," I said. He frowned. "And stop interrupting me or I won't be able to get through this." He clamped his lips together and nodded. "I've done a lot of sick shit in my life. Things I'm not proud of. Things that make me capable of killing you right now and not giving it a second thought."

Nyx gasped behind me, but a low murmur from Horus followed, indicating he was preventing her from intervening.

"However," I continued, "I've learned a few things in the last six months. Things about family." I looked toward Lavinia. "Things about love." I glanced at Adam. "Things about myself. Things you couldn't possibly know because you haven't been around." My father grimaced but stayed silent. "One of those lessons was that good friends are hard to come by. And when the shit comes down, your team is all you've got. So, no, I won't be killing you tonight. Because I may not need a dad, but I sure as hell need all the friends I can get."

The corner of Tristan's lips lifted into an ironic smile. "If we're going to be friends, we really need to work on your flagrant use of profanity."

My lips twitched in response. "Fuck you."

He grabbed me and pulled me into a hug. It was the first time I'd ever hugged my father. I realized I didn't care if we'd never have a normal father-daughter relationship. It just felt damned good to know he was on my side.

"Enough!" Lavinia's shrill voice cut through the air like lightning. "Have you made your choice, then?"

I turned, standing shoulder to shoulder with my father. "Take them," I said. "Take my fangs, my immortality. Take every trait that ties me to your poisonous blood."

Lavinia chuckled. "Such brave words. One wonders how brave you'll be in the demon realm when you're as weak as a human."

I cocked a brow. "While you're at it, take this fucking red hair, too."

The remaining Dominae rose and started toward me. Adam grabbed me for a quick, hard kiss. "I love you," he whispered. Then he walked away to join the others, leaving me alone in the center of the seven most powerful vampire females ever created.

Persephone refused to take part in the ceremony. Instead, she came to stand next to Nyx. No doubt there'd be repercussions for her once we moved on, but for now I appreciated her solidarity—late as it was.

The five remaining younger Dominae joined hands. Lavinia didn't look too happy to be touching Tanith. Not a surprise given Tanith had conspired with the Hekate Council to kill Lavinia. However, my grandmother's desire to officially erase me from her race must have overridden her hatred of the turncoat Domina.

The two ancients came forward then. One held a black apple like the ones I'd seen outside. The other held a pair of silver pliers.

The first burst of cold fear slammed into my gut. I'd assumed it would be like the mage rite to remove my magic. But I should have known better. Vampires enjoyed making others suffer. They'd make this as painful as possible.

The ancient who hadn't spoken once since our arrival

stepped forward and handed me the apple. "Do I have to eat it all?" I asked.

She smiled like a serial killer after a particularly gruesome murder. "One bite."

I raised the apple to my lips. The shiny onyx skin glistened in the light. I glanced left toward the solemn faces of Adam and my father. I looked to my right at Lavinia's eyes, which were wide with anticipation. The instant I took the bite, I'd be mortal. Not mage or vampire, just Sabina.

And that scared me more than the threat of pain.

Whether "just Sabina" would be strong enough to weather the remaining tests, I didn't know. But there was only one way to find out.

My fangs broke the flesh. The taste of copper and iron filled my mouth. I chewed the mouthful of mealy fruit and swallowed quickly. The bite scraped the inside of my throat like I'd swallowed shards of glass.

Pain unlike any I'd experienced in my life exploded in my gut. Worse than getting shot. Worse than a demon's spell. Worse than any poison.

The apple slammed to the floor. Two seconds later, my body joined it.

My vision dimmed and blurred. My fists clenched. The blood boiled in my veins. I felt each individual cell in my body explode. Smoke belched from my nose and ears and mouth. Wretched dry heaves forced me to roll onto my stomach. I somehow managed to rise up on my trembling arms and knees despite my weakened state. My throat burned and my stomach cramped as my body tried to expel ... something. Gagging, suffocating, writhing.

Oh, please, gods, make it stop.

I fell into a trembling, sweaty heap on the floor. My mouth flew open and I vomited a pool of bright red blood.

Shouts erupted but sounded far away. Someone stood over me. Rough hands flipped me over onto my back. Too weak to resist, my hands were pulled to the side and pinned by someone's knees.

"Open wide now," the head ancient said. She knelt over me, the pliers flickering in the light like an Inquisitor's tool of torture.

I ran my tongue over the sharp tips of my fangs for the last time. Funny, after burning from the inside and vomiting gallons of evil, having my fangs ripped out with pliers wasn't so bad.

The worst part was the blood that pooled in my mouth. The dirty penny flavor made me want to vomit all over again. Instead, I rolled to the side and spit several times. The effort cost me because I couldn't move another inch.

Someone nearby said, "It is done. Open the gate."

"No," Lavinia cried.

"Enough! She passed the test. Step aside, Domina Kane." A pause and then, "Collect her and be on your way."

A few moments later, gentle hands grasped my arms and helped me up. My head lolled to the side. The comforting scent of sandalwood surrounded me. Thank the gods, too, as I couldn't stomach the smell of blood for one more second.

A loud whooshing sound filled the chamber. I blinked my eyes open and saw a swirling black vortex behind the thrones on the dais.

"Nyx! Come on!" Tristan yelled. I was jostled and lifted from the ground. "Take her," Tristan said to Adam. He ran off to collect Nyx.

A sucking sensation pulled at my body. I moaned. "Easy, now," Adam whispered. "Almost there."

Trusting the mancy would get us through, I relaxed into

his hold. The air changed from the wintry cold of the Bloodlands to a dry, searing heat scented with brimstone.

"Well it's about damned time," a familiar voice groused. "Holy shit! What the fuck happened to her?"

I'd never in my life been so happy to hear Giguhl bitch at us.

36

This way," a deep male voice said.

"Are you sure about this, G?" Adam's voice rumbled in his chest. My head was pressed against the broad expanse. He was obviously running judging by the severe jostling I was receiving. But I couldn't work up enough energy to complain about the roughness of the ride.

"He's right," Valva's high-pitched voice replied. "It'll help her."

"Either way, we need to hurry," Tristan said, farther away. "By the time Nyx and I jumped through the gate, the Dominae were freaking out."

"Why?" Giguhl said.

"Because Cain had entered their lands. They were very excited to have the father of their race visit. So I'm pretty sure they won't be delaying him like the mages did."

My eyes popped open at this. I moaned and tried to sit up. Adam shushed me and bent over to whisper, "Relax. We're making a pit stop to restore your strength."

"Is she awake?" Giguhl demanded.

I raised my head and looked over at the demon.

"Hey, G." My voice cracked. My throat felt like I'd gargled nails.

"Bael's balls, I leave you alone for a couple of hours and look what happens. Nice hair, by the way." His tone dripped with sarcasm.

I tried to raise a hand to touch my hair, but it fell useless by my side. "What's it look like?"

"Don't listen to him," Adam said. "The blond will just take a little getting used to."

I gasped. "What?" If he was telling the truth, then one detail from my vision at the scrying pool had just come true.

"And, no offense, but it's kind of dull and lifeless, too. If you survive, you should seriously consider a hot-oil treatment," Valva offered.

Leave it to the Vanity demon to focus on what's really important. While I absorbed the fact that my hair was lacking in both color and healthy shine, the gang was jogging through something out of a nightmare. The demon realm looked very much like the paintings I'd seen of the mortal hell. Lots of fire and brimstone. Souls being tortured in increasingly bizarre and painful ways.

"Where are we?" I asked.

"Gizal," Giguhl said. "We're near the Pit of Despair."

Well that certainly explained the prevalence of hot pokers.

"Ah, here we are," Giguhl said. "Set her down on that rock, will ya?"

Adam gently lowered me to a boulder. I forced a smile at him, even though the simple movement had left me nauseous. He touched his hand to my cheek before turning to Giguhl.

"Okay, Horus, go get some water. There's a clean stream on the other side of those rocks."

"Is it safe?" Adam asked. He nodded to Horus, who ran off.

Giguhl nodded. "You and Valva spread out and look for a flower with black leaves and purple petals."

"What are you going to do?" Adam asked.

"I'm going to make sure none of my relatives bother our girl."

Adam and the others ran off. Giguhl came to sit next to me on the rock. He put a heavy arm around my shoulders. "So," he said conversationally, "you're mortal now."

I nodded. "I guess so."

"Ah, don't look so glum. You've still got us. You still know how to use a gun. And I bet Zenobia could even teach you some of the mortal magic she knows."

As long as I'd known him, Giguhl had never been a glass half full kind of demon. Granted, his form of pessimism was usually hilarious, but I wouldn't exactly describe him as an optimist. It was one of the things we had in common. But I appreciated his words nonetheless. "Thanks, G."

He rocked into me. "No problem. I'm just glad you're still here."

"So what's the plan?"

"There's a flower that grows here. It's got healing powers that rival just about any medicine on earth. You're gonna eat some of it, rehydrate, and then go face your destiny."

A shocked laugh escaped me. "You make it sound so easy."

He shrugged. "Hey, what's up with Nyx?"

I glanced over his shoulder to where Nyx and Tristan stood. They were close together, whispering about something. "She just found out that her mom was one of the Dominae.

He gasped. "Shut up! Which one?"

"Persephone."

"Dude, that's awesome news."

I shot him a look. "Does she look like she agrees?"

He looked at the vampire, who was sobbing. "No, but it's good news for you."

"How?"

"Red, if she's Persephone's daughter, you're off the hook. She can lead the vampires."

I stilled. "Holy shit, you're right."

Giguhl patted my shoulder. "See? Everything's going to work out just fine." His tone was jovial, but I detected a fine thread of tension that made me wonder which of us he was trying to convince.

Just then, Adam and Valva ran back over. In the Vanity's hand was a clump of purple flowers. "Found them," she called triumphantly.

Giguhl took them from her. "Okay, just eat some of these petals."

I took them from him and sniffed. The noxious odor made me jerk my hand away. "It smells like ass."

"Yep."

"What is this exactly?"

"They're called Demon Tears. They're created when demons spill their—" He cut off quickly. "Never mind that. Eat up!"

I grimaced, imagining several scenarios, each less appetizing than the last. "Are you sure this will help?"

"Red, would I steer you wrong?"

I cocked a brow.

"Please. Give me some credit."

"He's right," Valva said. "They're very healing."

I traded a worried glance with Adam. He shrugged. "I trust him."

I brought a small petal to my mouth for a nibble. A flavor not unlike crotch sweat exploded in my mouth. "Ack! It's disgusting."

"Quit being such a baby." The Mischief demon shoved two more petals between my lips and held my nose closed until I swallowed them. When he released me, my eyes were stinging but I managed to swat him.

"You're a shitty nurse," I bitched, grabbing the canteen Horus offered. The water tasted fresh and sweet after the disgusting Demon Tears. I gulped down the entire container.

"How do you feel?" Adam asked.

I paused and took inventory. I was still weak, but my mouth had stopped throbbing where the devil's dentist had removed my fangs. I probed the wounds with my tongue and cringed. It was like applying my tongue to a battery. A brief flare of vanity made me wonder if regular teeth would grow in their place, but I pushed that thought aside. I quickly took stock of the rest of my body and realized that despite the obscene taste of the flowers, my stomach had settled. "A little better," I admitted reluctantly.

"Ha! Told you."

Raised voices cut through Giguhl's moment of victory. We all looked over and saw Nyx and Tristan were full-on arguing now. "What's their problem?" Adam asked.

"Hey!" Valva called to the couple. They cut off mid-yell and looked over. "Adam wants to know why you're fighting."

Adam rolled his eyes. "Thanks, Valva."

"It's nothing," Nyx said quickly.

Tristan shot her an annoyed glance. "Like hell."

The vampire looked like she wanted to strangle him. "Don't you dare," she said through clenched teeth.

"Anyway," Tristan said. "We were arguing about whether she should give you her vest. She says yes; I say no."

Everyone fell silent.

I rose from the boulder slowly. I was surprised to find my legs could support my weight. Giguhl sent me a superior look, which I ignored and walked over to Nyx. Putting an arm around her, I said, "Thanks for your concern, but I agree with Tristan."

"Sabina!" Adam's tone was angry.

I turned to face him and everyone else. "There is a reason the tests required me to be weakened. If I cheat, how can I prove to Lilith I am serious about proving I am the Chosen?"

"Um, guys!" Valva shouted. "No time. We've got unfriendlies hotfooting this way."

My heart clenched. "Shit, is it Cain?"

Giguhl jumped up on the rock, nearly knocking Valva off. "Oh shit! He's got an army of vampires with him. Let's move, people. The Bone Palace awaits!"

37

*D*espite having a totally lame name, the Bone Palace was the scariest fucking building I'd ever seen. The walls were crafted entirely of skulls. Their empty eye sockets and wide, gaping smiles welcomed us to the house of horrors.

A blood-filled moat surrounded the fortress. For the first time in my life, the scent disgusted me. But not more than the bridge made from live bodies. In order to reach the entrance, we had to walk on faces, arms, buttocks, and pelvises. The way their flesh gave with each step was bad enough. But it was the screams that made my skin crawl. They sounded so terrified... and hopeless.

I'd been half expecting some sort of inappropriate joke from Giguhl as we picked our way across the human bridge, but even the Mischief looked unsettled.

In comparison to the decidedly grisly entrance to the palace, the interior was downright mundane. Walls of black marble and fixtures forged from iron. I guess even a demon king and the Great Mother of the dark races needed a break from the death imagery.

Valva walked in like she owned the place. "Mom! I'm home!"

Adam and I exchanged an anxious look, both of us not quite trusting the Vanity. Giguhl stood between us and looked worried for a different reason. "I'm so nervous," he said. "What if she hates me?"

I frowned at him. "Who?"

"Lilith," he whispered. "I want to make a good impression."

"For fuck's sake, Giguhl. Priorities!"

He shot me a pursed-lip glare but said nothing.

Adam grabbed my hand around the demon. "Be strong."

I swallowed and nodded. "Be ready for an ambush."

The mancy cracked his knuckles. "I was born ready, babe."

I certainly hoped so. Because if my vision was right, one was coming. "Listen, Adam," I said, taking him aside. "No matter what happens in there, I love you."

"I love you, too," he said slowly. "But why would you say that now? Do you know something you're not telling me?"

I shifted my eyes left as I recalled the vision from Vinca's pool. "It's just . . . I don't know if we'll all survive."

He planted a kiss on my forehead. "Maybe not, but at least we'll put up one hell of a fight, right?"

"Come on, guys!" Valva waved us to follow her.

I turned to Tristan, Nyx, and Horus. "Stay close and watch your backs."

Valva led us through a large entryway dominated by a curving staircase carved from smooth black stone. We went under the stairs and emerged into a gigantic open-air . . . something. Tall walls built from charred bones and ash spread out from the entrance in a broad circle. But the center was a lush botanical garden. Overhead, there was no ceiling but a starlit sky dominated by a huge full moon.

"This way," Valva said. She stepped onto the packed dirt and ducked under palm fronds and darted around huge, foul-smelling flowers. "Watch your step—most of these plants are carnivorous."

As she spoke, a huge Venus flytrap snapped six inches from my head. I jerked away, bumping into Giguhl. "Easy," he said, steadying me. "It'd be super embarrassing if you got eaten ten steps away from your destiny."

Valva forged ahead through the dense foliage until she finally parted two huge elephant ears to reveal an open-air throne room of sorts. The thrones were huge and made from human skulls painted bloodred. The marble floor was a refreshing change of pace from the body part theme, but otherwise everything was blood and bones.

I looked around, expecting to see Lilith or maybe Asmodeus lounging indolently on one of the thrones. Instead, a familiar face grinned at me from next to the stone blood fountain to the side of the throne.

"Oh shit," Giguhl breathed. "What's *he* doing here?"

"Sabina, darling."

I gritted my teeth. "Clovis."

Clovis Trakiya both had and hadn't changed much in the months since Giguhl dragged his ass down to the Pit of Despair. His auburn hair was a tad longer and he wore a black robe instead of a business suit. Clovis was half vampire and half demon, and when I'd known him in the mortal realm, he'd appeared in his urbane, vampire form. But now he was flashing horns and his skin was red and leathery. Despite his demonic makeover, his smarmy grin was the same.

"Welcome to Irkalla. I'm sorry I didn't have a chance to

greet you personally when you arrived, but, well, the Great Mother had me preparing some surprises for your arrival."

"I bet she did," Adam said.

"Lazarus," Clovis sneered. "I'm surprised to see you."

Adam crossed his arms. "And why is that?"

Clovis picked an invisible speck of lint from his shoulder. "Figured Sabina would grow tired of your pedestrian appeal by now."

"Cut the shit, Clovis," I said. "Where's Lilith?"

Clovis stood straighter and grinned. "She'll be here shortly." He leaned forward and whispered, "She likes to make an entrance."

"What are you doing out of the Pit?" Giguhl demanded. "Last I saw you, you were receiving some sweet back-door attention from a gaggle of Lust demons."

A shadow passed across Clovis's face. "Let's just say I convinced the Great Mother I could be more useful to her as an assistant. Better than that pussy David Duchamp."

I crossed my arms. No doubt David blamed me for Clovis taking over his position, since it was my fault the asshole was in Irkalla in the first place.

As for Clovis's success in manipulating the situation to his benefit, well, I wasn't really surprised. Despite his many and varied faults, Clovis could be exceptionally charming when he wasn't double-crossing me or conspiring to take over the dark races.

"Is this going to take much longer?" I demanded. "We're kind of in a hurry."

Clovis raised a dark brow. "If I were you, I'd curb my tongue when she arrives. She doesn't respond well to demands."

As if he'd summoned her with his warning, Lilith arrived in a dazzling display of pyrotechnics. Black smoke and flame flared up from the floor and when they disappeared, the Great Mother herself struck a pose in front of us.

I've known a few powerful females in my time—priestesses, leaders of entire races, goddesses—but even Hekate's awe-inspiring appearance paled in comparison to Lilith's dominating presence. It saturated the air like ozone after a lighting bolt.

I fell to my knees. All around me, my team did the same, dropping like flies to the floor.

I didn't dare look directly at her. My hands trembled. It was one thing to think about meeting the Great Mother. In theory, I knew she'd be powerful and intimidating. But kneeling before her felt like . . . straying too close to a black hole.

"Look at you. Trembling like a child." Her voice was as dark as midnight. "It pleases me. Rise, Sabina Kane."

The unbearable weight of her gravity made standing gracefully impossible. I kept my eyes on the ground.

"Look at me, child."

I licked my suddenly dry lips and took a deep breath. And looked into the face of the Great Mother.

My vision at Vinca's pool hadn't done her justice. The air escaped my lungs in a hiss. Turns out my black hole analogy hadn't been so far off, after all. It was as if the mortal's god had molded her out of night itself. Two massive black-feathered wings unfurled behind her, kicking up a breeze every time they twitched. Her hair reached the floor and in its black mass, shifting shapes appeared like holograms. Her eyes were obsidian marbles. Her skin was ebony, dark and perfect and cold. Black iron fangs flashed when she smiled. The only color on her face at all were two luscious red lips that explained a lot about the origins of lust.

"Why have you come?"

I froze. Was this another test? The final test? I cleared the butterflies from my throat. "I have come to prove that I am the Chosen."

The mother of the dark races threw back her head and laughed. The sound reverberated through the air, making the ground shake. Nearby, Horus made a choking sound, his hand flying to his throat. Black veins exploded on the surface of his skin and smoke escaped his ears. His body twitched and convulsed. The more Lilith laughed, the worse his suffering became until he was convulsing on the ground with bloody froth escaping his blackened lips.

"Stop!" I yelled.

Lilith's eyes cut to mine and the laughter cut off abruptly. While she held my gaze, she snapped her fingers and smiled at me.

Horus's body burst into flames. The conflagration was intense but brief. In no time, Lilith's spell consumed him completely, leaving not even a scorch mark on the marble.

The silence that followed pulsed in my ears in time to my staccato heartbeat. I wanted to demand an explanation. To rail against Lilith for her cruelty. But she'd just killed Horus on a whim to prove she could. The message was clear. She'd kill us all without remorse if it pleased her.

From the corner of my eye, I saw the stoic expressions of my team as they each struggled to keep their own reactions under control. Behind Lilith, Valva stood beside Clovis. The vampire-demon looked like he was enjoying the show. But Valva's eyes moved restlessly between the void where Horus used to be and her mother. Despite her obvious upset, it seemed even the flighty demon knew better than to challenge her mother.

"Prove that you are the Chosen?" Lilith said. Said it like

she hadn't just tortured and killed one of my team. Said it like we were discussing the weather and not the fate of all of her children. "Silly girl."

My mouth worked as I tried to form words, but Lilith wasn't done.

"You are not the Chosen." She snapped her fingers.

A door opened in the bone wall surrounding the throne room. A female with curly red hair and alabaster skin emerged. Beside me, my father gasped and took a step forward. "Phoebe?"

My mother's head jerked up and her eyes widened at seeing Tristan. At my other side, Nyx stiffened and all the blood drained from her face.

My stomach dropped in sympathy for all three of them. For Nyx, Tristan's reaction was the ultimate proof that he'd never gotten over Phoebe. And for my parents, it was the first time they had seen each other since before Maisie and I were born. What should have been a joyful reunion was instead a reminder of sadness and betrayal.

Tristan caught himself before he rushed toward her. As if he suddenly remembered that their love had been a cruel trick played by a psychotic mastermind. His posture stiffened and he crossed his arms. Phoebe noticed the change and a dark shadow crossed over her face. She glanced uneasily at Lilith, who raised a brow. "Bring her."

Phoebe nodded jerkily and reached back through the door. She led another female into the throne room. A female with red and black hair and my blue eyes.

All my concern over the tension between my mother and father evaporated the instant I recognized the surprise Lilith had invited to the party.

"Oh gods," I whispered brokenly. I fell to my knees. "Maisie?"

38

$\mathcal{M}$y gaze wouldn't leave my twin. She looked...healthy. So different from the tortured waif who'd been under Cain's thrall. Her red and black hair glowed with health and her curves filled out her black chiton.

"Sabina!" Maisie cried brokenly. She tried to break away from our mother's hold, but Phoebe held her still.

"Maisie?" Adam whispered.

"Silence!" Lilith thundered. She waved a hand and a wall of shimmering magic surrounded Maisie and my mother. Their heads jerked around and their mouths moved, but no sound escaped their prison.

Frustration rose in me like a hot wind. What game was Lilith playing? Plus, as I watched Maisie's and Phoebe's agitated movements in the circle, something niggled at the back of my mind. Something about Maisie's movements was off. I scanned down her body and gasped when I realized her feet didn't touch the floor. "She's still dead."

A feline smile stretched across Lilith's full lips. "Well, of course she is."

"Maisie?" I called.

"Don't bother," Lilith said. "The circle is just a precaution. You sister knows she is forbidden from interfering with your test."

I took a deep breath and tried to keep my head above the wave of sadness that crashed over me the instant Maisie appeared. "I don't understand. Why is she here, then?"

"It's simple really. Maisie had the potential to be the Chosen." Lilith's smile was tight, accusing. "But because of your failure to protect her, she died before she could fulfill her destiny."

Her words couldn't have hurt me more if she'd ripped my heart from my chest cavity with her fist. But Lilith had more damage to inflict.

"Without the Chosen, Cain cannot be killed. Unless…"

She let the word hang there, like a dangling spark of hope in a world gone black.

"Unless what?" My voice broke, but I didn't care. The mother of the dark races had just confirmed that my own failings had doomed us all. I'd do anything to atone for my sins.

"Unless you make one more sacrifice."

My stomach sank. She looked way too eager for this to be anything comfortable. "I've already sacrificed my magic and my immortality." I raised my arms out to the sides to show just how vulnerable I really was. "What else is there to give?"

Lilith smiled like a cobra. "You're still breathing."

My soul shrank into a cold little ball at the base of my spine. "What?"

"You can trade places with Maisie."

An explosion of movement behind me. Raised voices. Inside the circle, both Phoebe and Maisie openly wept. But I barely registered them. My gaze was glued on the dark pools of the Great Mother's eyes. Her meaning sunk into my gut like a corpse wearing cement shoes.

I swallowed to dislodge the frozen fist of fear in my throat. "If I trade places with her—"

"Then everything will be as it should."

"Sabina, don't listen to her!" Tristan shouted.

"Silence!" Lilith shouted, glaring at my father.

Through a haze, I realized I should be relieved. After all, at least one of us was the Chosen. If what Lilith said was true, then Maisie would be the one who got revenge against Cain, which had a certain pleasing symmetry.

But did I have the guts to surrender my life for hers?

The night Maisie died, I knelt before her corpse and promised to do everything in my power to avenge her death. To make things right. And now Lilith had delivered the perfect solution. In the grand scheme of things, dying seemed like an easy way to balance the scales. Easier than the constant struggle to make the right choices and battle my doubts and navigate through the labyrinthine mire of dark races politics. Easier than living.

I thought about all the beings I'd run into on my way through Irkalla. Orpheus, Vinca, David, Ewan. All the innocent people who died because of my poor decisions or my inability to prevent their deaths. Or who died just because they had the misfortune to know me. Hell, even my own mother hadn't escaped the damnation of knowing me. She'd died the instant I took my first breath.

Not to mention all the beings I'd killed of my own free will. The ones who died because I had something to prove to the Dominae. Or to myself.

I thought back to the conversation with Tristan the night he explained why he believed Maisie was the Chosen: *"I'm hard-pressed to believe the Chosen is someone who spent her life shedding the blood of those she was destined to rule.*"

At the time, I'd argued with him, but part of me, the part I refused to acknowledge in my quest to seek vengeance for my sister, knew he was right. I'd never believed I was the Chosen. Never believed someone like me was worthy of that kind of responsibility. Never believed I was anything other than damaged goods.

I took out the two pictures I'd stolen from Tristan's album the night before. The one of Maisie and me laughing together before everything went to hell. Before Lavinia kidnapped her out from under my nose and doomed her down the dark path that led to her death.

The one of Adam and Giguhl and me. We'd been through so many skirmishes together, the three of us. But now I faced the final battle alone. One where surrender was the only way to ensure victory.

With this one last act, I could make it all right. Maisie would live again and everyone I loved would survive. They'd be better off without me around to complicate their lives and threaten their existence.

My consciousness disconnected from reality. That numbing distance that had served me so well in the past descended.

Adam, Giguhl, Nyx, and Tristan ignored the goddess's demands for silence and surrounded me. Their mouths moved rapidly like they were yelling, but I couldn't hear them. I placed a hand on Adam's jaw. His eyes were red-rimmed and tears made the moss green of his eyes achingly beautiful.

If I died, he'd live.

Giguhl shouted at me. I could feel his hot breath on my face, but his words didn't register. He looked ready to tear the Bone Palace down to its foundations to change my mind. I grabbed his claw in mine and felt the pressure of his pulse on my palms.

If I died, he'd finally be free to live his own life.

Tristan pushed them out of the way and grabbed my chin. I felt the bite of his fingers in my skin. His expression was tense and his mouth moved more slowly, more deliberately. Probably, he was laying out a rational argument, but whether he was trying to convince me or dissuade me, I didn't know. Didn't care. I'd made up my mind.

I brushed past him like he was a ghost. My eyes were on my sister. Her head was bowed, as if she couldn't stand to watch me struggle with this decision. She needn't have worried.

I took a step toward Lilith, ready to give her my decision. But my arm was jerked roughly from behind. The momentum swung me around and pain cracked across my cheek.

The protective barrier I'd erected between me and reality evaporated. All the emotion and sensation I'd been buffered from hit me like a sonic boom. I staggered back from the weight of the oppressive pain and anger aimed at me.

"Don't be a fucking fool!" Nyx screamed in my face. It had been her hand that slapped me out of my trance. "She's tricking you!"

I shook my head to clear the fog of emotion. "What?"

"Aren't you the one who always said the gods are fickle and can't be trusted?"

I shook my head again. "This is different."

Tristan stepped forward. "Is it?"

I threw up my hands. "Of course it is! Don't you see? This is my chance to fix everything."

Tristan shook his head sadly. "No, Sabina. Martyring yourself is never the solution. Remember back in the

Bloodlands?" His hands tightened on my arms. "I was ready to martyr myself, too. You know why?"

"Because you were being noble."

He shook his head. "No, I was being selfish." My eyes widened in shock. "I'm tired, Sabina. Tired of struggling and scraping. Tired of being scared and unsure about every choice. Part of me felt that sacrificing myself was the right choice, but now I realize it was merely the easiest choice."

"But look at me!" I held my hands out in a futile motion. "I'm weak and useless. What would I have to offer any-one now?"

"You magic and your strength were nice. But they didn't make you who you are. Don't you see? You were both things, but they were not you. What really matters is here." He placed his hand over my heart. "You might be mortal now. You might feel defeated. But you, my daughter, have the heart of a warrior. That's why all of us have followed you here. You have to stand and fight. And you have to let us help you."

"I don't feel strong. I'm terrified and unsure and part of me just wants to lie down and surrender."

"Surrender?" Giguhl said. "The Sabina Kane I know doesn't surrender. Ever."

"Sabina." Lilith's shrill voice came from behind me. "Cain is at the bridge. You must make your decision quickly."

I turned to face the Great Mother. Maisie still floated next to the goddess with her head lowered. But now I finally noticed the spectral tears falling in a pool under her feet.

"Red?" Adam called.

I turned back around, feeling torn between the male I loved and the sister whose blood ran through my veins.

"How many times have you tried to sacrifice yourself because you thought you knew what was best for us? Remember New Orleans when you ran off by yourself?

How many times are your attempts at being a martyr going to fail before you realize you're at your best when you ask for help?"

I cringed. That stupid decision had led to Adam and me getting captured by Lavinia and almost resulted in Adam's death.

I thought back to the other times I'd tried to be noble, too. The word "martyr" had a familiar heft and taste. Self-righteousness combined with a hefty dose of self-loathing.

Was all this guilt I carried really just a way to shield myself from taking responsibility? I thought about all the deaths I blamed myself for.

"Yes, you've killed people. But the deaths you blame yourself for the most? They weren't your fault." He pointed across the room to my sister. "You didn't kill Maisie—Cain did. You didn't kill Vinca—that was Clovis's doing." He crossed his arms. "As much as you don't want to admit this, you are as vulnerable to the vagaries of fate as the rest of us. But you're so determined to control everyone and everything that you take the blame for every bad thing that happens. Lilith knows that and is using your doubt against you."

"He's right, Sabina," Tristan said. "Do you know the real reason I never sought you and your sister out?"

I shook my head, too afraid of saying something that might make him change his mind about sharing the answer.

"I was afraid. Afraid that I was too broken after losing Phoebe to be a good father."

I blinked, shocked to hear that this powerful mage had been terrified of facing his own daughters.

"But I realize now that removing myself from your lives only screwed things up more. You grew up alone and unprotected and Maisie grew up in my shadow, trying to live up to a bullshit legacy of being the daughter of a noble martyr." His tone was full of self-loathing. "Don't make the same mistake I made. I know you're afraid. I know you don't think you're up to this battle. But you are. You know why?"

I shook my head and tried to hold in the sobs that crawled up my throat.

"Because you're not alone."

I looked at the faces around me. I knew they were right. I was at my best when I allowed my team to help me. I couldn't argue with any of their arguments or pleas. But I still had no idea how we were going to get out of this.

"Okay," I said finally. "So how are *we* going to—"

Before I could answer, the throne room swarmed with hundreds of vampire spirits. I didn't see Cain among the horde. Probably he was hanging back so his army could clear a path for his grand entrance.

Shit, it was too late. My delay had just doomed us all. Just like the vision at the scrying pool had predicted.

"Sabina?" Tristan said.

"I don't have any magic left."

His eyes glistened. "I do. Let me help you."

I watched him for a moment. If I accepted his offer, I knew instinctively that Lilith's deal would be null and void. I glanced at the goddess, whose posture had gone tense and her eyes flicked restlessly toward the entrance.

The vampires closed in and flashed their fangs. Do or die time.

I nodded resolutely. "Do it."

He gripped my hand hard and smiled. "Stand back."

I moved back with Adam and Giguhl at my side. Tristan closed his eyes. The ground trembled as he called up the Chthonic powers that permeated Irkalla. It rose through his body and made the air vibrate and hum.

"*Ati me peta babka*," he said, his voice loud and strong.

Three hundred and twenty-seven vampire spirits turned in unison to look at him. "Your work here is done. Return to the Bloodlands," Tristan commanded.

As one, the entire army turned. But Tristan wasn't done. A wicked spark twinkled in his blue eyes.

"When you return, rise up against the Dominae. Even dead, you deserve freedom from their oppression."

As one, the army nodded and marched out. As they filed out, I spied Cain standing by the entrance to the throne room. His face was pale and his mouth hung open. Obviously he hadn't been expecting us to defeat his army so easily. Good.

I ran to Tristan and hugged him. He smiled down at me and I up at him. "Nice job...Dad." It was the first time I'd said that word to him without using a sarcastic tone. He winked and released me.

For the first time since I'd seen Maisie walk into the throne room, a spark of hope ignited in my chest. Tristan had been right—I wasn't alone. I had my team by my side, and for better or worse, we'd fight the good fight because surrender was worse than death.

I turned to Lilith. "My answer is no."

Her eyes narrowed. "You're certain? How will you defeat Cain now?"

Inside the circle, Phoebe's eyes widened and she threw herself at the barrier, punching at the wall of magic. Her muted screams made my skin go cold.

Behind me, a male shout. A gasp and a sickening gurgle.

The scent of blood reached my nose. An instant later, Nyx screamed.

I turned slowly. Tristan wobbled uneasily on his feet for

a moment. A rapidly spreading red stain covered his chest. A large brass spike protruded from the wound.

I scrambled across the marble, reaching him a split second after he crumpled into Adam's arms. The mancy slowly lowered him the rest of the way to the ground.

Kneeling beside my father, I touched the tip of the spike. When Tristan hissed in pain, I jerked my trembling hand away. "Tristan?" I whispered.

Adam and Giguhl knelt on either side of my father's head.

A groan crackled from his throat. I clenched my fists together and struggled to contain the sob that slammed into the back of my teeth. "You're going to be okay," I lied.

"Liar," he rasped. "Dying."

I shook my head. A tear splashed on his cheek. "Don't you fucking dare," I said. "Not now."

In the distance, I heard Nyx screeching as she kicked and clawed against Cain. The father of the vampire race grinned at me and winked.

"Love—" Tristan croaked before a wet cough shook his whole body.

"Shhh." I stroked his hair. "Just try to be still."

I met Adam's gaze over my father. He shook his head. There was nothing we could do to help him. Even if we could remove the brass spike, he'd bleed out before Adam could attempt a healing spell.

"Daughter." Tristan's throat clicked and a breath rasped out of his pale lips. I looked down through the tears I refused to let him see. "Proud." A trembling hand rose and pointed at my heart. "Stronger together."

Blood spilled from his lips. His blue eyes rolled back in their sockets. The hand he'd raised convulsed.

And fell to the ground, lifeless.

39

$\mathcal{M}$y father had stormed into my life less than a week earlier and now he was...gone.

The sob I'd been fighting finally escaped. The tears blurred and refracted the image of my father's corpse. Someone in the distance was screaming like a banshee. Muted pounding echoed in my head and the sizzle of spent magic tainted the air.

"Red?" Adam said, his tone quiet.

I shook my head and curled into myself. Heaving gasps wracked my body as the tears fell like rain.

"Sabina, look," Giguhl breathed.

I blinked and looked up. Through the veil of moisture, I saw a light escape from my father's chest. I caught my breath and watched it rise up into the sky. It hovered above the garden throne room for a moment, as if my father's spirit was taking one final look at everyone he was leaving behind. And then, Tristan Graecus's soul zoomed through the sky like a comet.

"Wh-where's he going?" I demanded, watching the streak cut across the sky.

"His soul is returning to the Adamantine Gate," Giguhl whispered. "He'll reenter Irkalla as a spirit now."

"And then he'll head to Hekatian Fields?" I asked.

Adam put his hand on my shoulder. "Probably."

I blew out a shuddering breath. But a loud whimper caught my attention. I looked over and saw Nyx drooping in Cain's hold.

Oh shit, she'd just watched the man she loved die. Telling her he would at least find comfort in the arms of my mother probably wouldn't do much to relieve Nyx's guilt or sadness.

I turned and saw Phoebe inside Lilith's circle. Her eyes were on Cain. Their depths weren't shadowed by pain or sadness but glowed poison green with rage.

I took a cue from my mother, realizing that tears wouldn't make me feel better.

But making Cain pay would.

I rose slowly. Whatever Cain saw in my eyes made him step back. But then he raised his chin and called out to Lilith. "Honey, I'm home."

Lilith's face paled. She summoned her powers and threw her hands in the air. "*Elu.*"

A shimmering wall erected around the goddess. Nice of her to protect herself and leave the rest of us defenseless against a foe we couldn't kill.

Cain laughed and stepped forward. "What's wrong, love? I thought you'd be happy to see me."

The instant Lilith's circle rose, the one around my mother and sister disappeared.

Maisie raised her head and the determination I saw there gave me hope.

"Maisie?" I said.

"Sabina," she breathed.

"Ah-ah-ah," Cain said. He opened his jacket to reveal a holster filled with more brass spikes and a gun. "No talking." He moved between Maisie and me. "Can't have you two conspiring against me."

I tilted my head. Something about his tone told me he was genuinely worried about Maisie and I teaming up against him.

"Sabina—" Lilith began.

"No cheating, dearest." Cain's tone was threatening. He kicked Lilith's circle. The barrier sparked but held firm. "Open the circle, Lamashtu."

"No!" she said.

I frowned at Cain. He didn't want Lilith helping me either. Why? If I'd failed the test and prevented Maisie from becoming the Chosen, why was he so worried?

I jerked my gaze toward my sister. She stood with her head bowed again. Obviously, her fear of Cain still lingered even though her death meant he couldn't hurt her anymore.

Cain punched the barrier now, shouting and threatening the goddess if she didn't bow to his demands. Lilith withstood every insult and name, her eyes jerking back and forth between Maisie and me.

"Sabina," Phoebe said. "Remember what Tristan said."

"Shut up, bitch!" Cain shouted. He threw a blade at my mother. Phoebe didn't flinch as the dagger flew, useless, through her spirit.

I tilted my head and frowned at her. She ignored Cain's shouts and watched me. Her eyes were pleading, as if she was begging me to put pieces of a puzzle together. "What do you mean? About being stronger together?"

"I can say no more." She nodded toward Maisie and then to me. "The rest is up to you."

Frowning, I looked at Maisie.

Stronger together.

Flashes of memory played through my mind. How Maisie's birthmark warmed whenever I was about to face danger. How I'd told Charon that the thing I craved most was balance. How Vinca's soul tried to hitch a ride with mine.

Then I thought about how my sister and I had always been two sides of the same coin. Together, Maisie and I would have made the perfect being. Her with her nurturing spirit and skills at prophecy—the powerful mage. Me with my thirst for blood and fighting skills—a vampire to the core. Her love of life and my talent for death. How together, we created a perfectly balanced dark race being.

My stomach dropped. Oh shit! Was that it? Was that the answer?

Maisie? I reached out to my sister with my mind.

No response. I wondered if she really couldn't hear me or if her fear of Cain made her too scared to respond and incur Cain's wrath.

Maisie, if you can hear me, show me some sign.

I watched my twin closely, but she didn't move.

But then, a spot on my left shoulder—exactly where her birthmark resided—began to itch. The skin warmed and tingled just like it had all those times she'd helped me.

I'm going to try something. I need you to trust me.

The heat intensified. That was as close to a yes as I was going to get.

I glanced over my shoulder and met Adam's gaze. I winked and his eyes widened. A slow grin spread across his handsome face. His mouth formed the words, "I love you." Then he leaned over and nudged Giguhl. The demon jerked and leaned down to listen. He nodded once and turned to say something to Nyx. Whatever happened, I trusted they would do what they could to help. I just prayed if everything went south, they'd also have the smarts to run like hell.

"Sabina!" Cain said. "Convince Lilith to let down the barriers or I'll kill your mage."

Adam cocked a brow. "Fuck you."

I sucked a deep breath in through my nose and blew it out of my mouth. Some might call what I did next an act of faith. Others might call it the act of a fool. Either way, I knew in my gut it was right.

"Adam," I said in a low tone. "Now!"

I ran straight for Maisie. My sister's head jerked up a split second before I slammed into her spirit.

Her soul bore through my flesh like shards of ice. I gritted my teeth and struggled to hold on to her. Caught off guard, Maisie struggled against the warm prison.

Sabina, what—she screamed in my head.

I gritted out, "Trust. Me."

"No!" Cain screamed. I heard the sounds of a struggle. Giguhl shouted something, and I knew he and Adam and Nyx were trying to subdue Cain but were not having an easy time of it.

The instant Maisie's soul was perfectly positioned, our spirits snapped together like pieces of a puzzle. The instant our essences united, a shock of energy exploded outward from my body. Our body.

The force lifted our body from the floor.

Up, up, up. We were flying.

Far below, we could see Adam and Giguhl struggling with Cain. Nyx scrambled away, chasing a gun that slid across the floor. Lilith stayed safe in her little chamber. Clovis hid behind the throne, where the coward had gone the instant Cain's army arrived. Farther afield, we saw Lil-

ith's garden surrounding the throne room. I realized then
that it was the same garden Maisie had seen in her vision.
The one she painted and showed me the night she told me I
would be the Chosen. In it, I was flying over a garden
toward a bright light in the sky.

She'd been half right. It was my body, but it was both
our spirits.

Sabina?

Shhh, Maisie. It's going to be all right now.

How do you know?

Look up.

A throbbing glow over our heads demanded our attention. It felt warm on our face, inviting. We willed ourselves
to move faster, fly higher. We raised our arms above our
head and focused on reaching the light.

So close now. We reached a hand toward the light,
yearning for it. Just before we brushed the outer edges of
this power, a deep voice echoed through our head.

Chosen.

The light spread and entered us. The force threw our
head back and filled us with its heat, its energy. Power
spread through us like lightning.

Secret knowledge filled us. A vortex of light swirled
around our skin. Filled us, glowing from the inside. Our
eyes saw eternity, our arms spread like wings, and our
heart filled to bursting. Every ounce of power that had been
taken from us returned with a vengeance—plus some. And
when we screamed, it was not from fear but from victory.

The battle cry of a goddess.

It is done, the voice said.

Our body plunged. Down, down, down.

Our eyes opened. The power coalesced around us, a
swirling golden cyclone. We heard every sound—shouting,

fists pounding flesh. The individual heartbeats of every being in the room. Every thought. Every emotion.

We raised our hand and saw our own aura. Instead of the individual red of Sabina's aura or the blue of Maisie's, it shimmered pure gold shot through with deep, royal purple.

We are the Chosen, our souls whispered in stereo.

Miracle number five, I whispered to myself.

Together, we turned toward the fight.

The instant the mage and demon saw us, they stopped fighting Cain. Giguhl's goat eyes flared and a huge smile spread his black lips. Adam paled. "Gods be praised."

Nyx stood behind Cain, her trembling hand aiming the weapon at his head.

"Nicolette," we said, our voices united into one. "Put it down."

Tears streamed down her face. "He killed Tristan," she sobbed.

"We know. But if you kill him, we will all die."

Nyx's eyes finally moved from the back of Cain's head to look at us. Whatever the vampire saw made her drop the gun. Her eyes flared and she dropped to her knees, touching her forehead with her right hand.

Cain turned around slowly. When he saw Maisie and I in our new form—whatever it looked like—his eyes went wild. Like a snake's strike, he grabbed Adam by the throat and held a brass blade to his jugular. "I'll kill him."

We smiled and waved a hand. The blade Cain held to Adam's neck dissolved. Cain yelped and jumped back. "What—"

We lowered our head, gazing up at our prey. "Run."

Cain's eyes widened. "I'm not leaving without her," he spat. "Lilith is mine."

"Dude, seriously?" Giguhl said. "You need to take a hint already."

Cain ignored the demon and raised his chin at us. "I am Master Mahan. You can't kill me."

"We are the Chosen."

"No. I don't believe it! It's a trick!" Cain's voice rose as the first hint of panic hit him. "Lilitu, tell them they can't kill me."

"Sorry, *my love*," Lilith mocked. "But you are wrong. They can and they will."

He whipped around. "But... but why? I love you. I have killed for you. I have done all of this"—he waved his hands around to indicate his grand scheme—"for us. So we can finally be together again."

"Then you are a fool. I used your seed to create the first of my children. And, yes, for a time, I fancied myself in love with you. Until your true nature, your controlling ways, your temper, your fists, proved you were unworthy of that love. You did not deserve me."

"Shut up, bitch." He punched the barrier and ignored the sizzling sound of his knuckles burning. "You're mine!"

Lilith raised an ebony brow. "You have never and will never measure up to my beloved husband, Asmodeus."

"No," Cain said through clenched teeth. "He's hidden you away in this cesspool. Forced you to bear his children. How can you be happy here?"

Lilith shrugged. "I love him."

Cain rushed Lilith's protective circle, punching and kicking. He sobbed with rage, screaming obscenities and making oaths to profane gods if they'd help him force his love to submit. The shimmering walls sparked and sputtered with each strike. Wounds appeared everywhere Cain made contact with the shield. Lilith cringed back against the other side, looking genuinely worried he might somehow succeed in breaking her spell.

Finally, the human wore himself out with his rage. His shoulders slumped and his chest heaved. When he raised his head, his expression was feral. Every meager ounce of sanity he'd once possessed had abandoned him. With a scream born of insanity and murderous rage, Master Mahan turned toward Adam, Giguhl, and Nyx.

He lowered his head and grunted like a bull. In each hand, he held a blade.

We knew his intention before he took a step. He figured if he attacked our friends, they'd have no choice but to kill him and themselves in the process. Cain had accepted he would die, but he was going to take all of us with him.

He took two running steps.

We shot out a hand. "*Usella mituti ikkalu baltuti.*"

He froze.

We raised our hands and slowly inhaled. Cain's eyes widened. The knives fell to the ground with a clatter.

Our chest expanded beyond all reasonable bounds. Our lungs were endless, hungry caverns. We watched our enemy pale and sweat break out on his skin. His body began to tremble. We enjoyed that part.

"No!" he moaned. "You can't kill me! I am Master Mahan!"

The air tasted bitter. Cain's skin began to blacken. Still we inhaled. Smoke rose from the singed patches and danced through the air. Still we inhaled. His face dissolved next. The mass of muscle and bone that remained stretched and emitted a sickening shriek. Still we inhaled.

The rest of his corporeal form dissolved into a million black particles. They flew through the air like beads of oil in water. We gulped down each acrid drop.

Once the body was gone, all that was left was a blackened aura. We consumed that, too, until finally, Cain's entire essence writhed in our belly like the serpent who tempted his mother, Eve.

We closed our eyes. Cain's dark power, his seductive energies swirled in our veins. We savored them. Images of torture, memories of his murders paraded through our head. We enjoyed them. His screams echoed in our ears. We treasured them.

"Chosen," Lilith said quietly.

Maisie and I ignored her. The high was too delicious. The power too intoxicating. The promise of conquest too seductive.

"Sabina?" Adam's broken cry burst through the haze. "Maisie?"

No, not yet. Maisie pleaded with me to hold on to the moment a little longer. *We deserve this. Vengeance is ours, sister.*

I smiled and licked my lips. Never had either of us felt more powerful, more absolutely immortal than we did at that moment. We wanted to fly. We wanted to impose our wills on the universe. We wanted to kill everyone who'd ever wronged us. And we could do it, too.

We were the Chosen. We were... invincible.

40

I thought I was invincible once, too." Lilith's voice cut through the black cocoon of power wrapped around Maisie and me. A warm hand touched our arm. "But my own hubris brought me down."

Our eyes popped open. The high of defeating Cain suddenly turned on us. Bile rose in our throat and we gagged against the bitter aftertaste of consuming all that evil. We lurched over and struggled to absorb the malevolent energy. But we were not meant to use evil as fuel. Our body lurched over and vomited black, tarry pools onto the marble. When we'd emptied ourselves of the last of Cain, the entire roiling mass was consumed by tongues of flame.

Lilith patted our back. "There, there. All gone now."

Once we'd recovered, which frankly didn't take very long given the circumstances, we stood up and wiped our mouth.

"You can separate now."

We frowned. "What?"

She waved a hand. "You only need to combine forces when you're threatened. Trust me, it's for the best. Two souls in one body is hell on the chakras."

The process of separation was harder than the joining had been. Our spirits were so thoroughly meshed inside my body that it was like ripping apart cosmic-strength Velcro. Only more painful.

I pushed, Maisie pulled. We groaned and strained, until finally my sister's spirit flew from my body. I collapsed on the ground and she slid across the marble. Maisie's exit left me feeling hollow, lonely. I'd spent so many years alone inside myself that I didn't realize how...barren it felt in there.

Adam and Giguhl ran to me. Gentle hands helped me stand. Strong arms enveloped me.

Over their shoulders, I saw Phoebe go to Maisie, comforting her.

"Thank the gods," Adam said.

"Dude, you guys were fucking awesome!" Giguhl enthused.

I glanced at Maisie and my mother again. Lilith went to speak to them. She reached out to touch Maisie's arm, and her hand went through her spirit. I froze.

"Hold on!" I called. "Why isn't Maisie back in her body?"

Lilith looked up and tilted her head. "She's dead."

I nodded and walked forward. "Yes, but we're the Chosen, right? Surely that means she can return to the living now."

The Great Mother slowly shook her head and shot Maisie an apologetic glance. "I'm sorry, but that's not how this works. Once someone is dead, they must remain so."

I slashed a hand through the air. "But she's a goddess now! The normal rules shouldn't apply."

Lilith crossed her arms. "Technically you're just demigoddesses. Regardless, there are some rules even deities can't escape. Besides, that's not how the Chosen works. You and your sister are the Chosen together because you balance each other. Mage and vampire, light and dark, blue and red." She pointed to me. "Life"—she pointed to Maisie—"and death."

I blinked at the irony. For so long I'd thought of myself as the death part of this equation.

"If she has to remain a spirit, how can she return to the mortal realm?" Adam demanded.

"You don't get it," Lilith said. "She won't be returning. Sabina will lead the dark races on Earth, and she will lead the dark races in Irkalla."

My mouth fell open. "That's bullshit!"

Lilith shrugged. "I didn't make the rules."

"Well, who did?" I demanded. "Because I want to kick their ass."

Lilith pointed up. "Elohim made the rules. Trust me, you don't want to tangle with him."

"Wait, what?" Adam said.

Lilith spread her arms. "I struck a deal with him when I married Asmodeus. Elohim was pissed that I created my own races. He wanted to destroy all my children. I promised him that if he didn't, I would retire to Irkalla and never interfere again. That's why I could not allow Cain to kidnap me from this realm. It's also why a war between all of you could not be allowed to happen. Elohim demanded that if either of those events occurred, I would have to return to earth to destroy all of you."

"But how does the Chosen fit into all that?" Adam asked.

Lilith smirked. "I knew that without firm leadership, it wouldn't take long before my children turned on each other. You're such a surly bunch," she said proudly. "So I negotiated a deal. A way to balance the scales between the two most powerful dark races. Twins born of both races who would rise to lead everyone. Elohim came up with the tests. He loves making his subjects jump through hoops."

I blinked. Was his voice the one we'd heard come from the bright light? Holy shit.

"But the catch is that there are checks and balances built into your powers. The first you've already seen when Cain's essence made you ill. The second is that you can use your powers only when you're joined together. Third is that one of you must live in Irkalla and the other on earth. Because of Sabina's Chthonic powers, she can summon Maisie to earth or come down here to visit, but the longer you're together, the weaker you'll become."

"That sucks!" Giguhl said.

Lilith shrugged. "It sucks less than it would have if Cain had succeeded."

"If we're supposed to rule the dark races above and below, what will you do?" Maisie asked.

She shrugged. "Same thing I've been doing for centuries—making demon babies, loving my man. Perhaps causing a little mischief every now and then. But honestly, I've had so little to do with my nondemon children over the last few millennia that things won't change much."

I guess that all kind of made sense, but I still had a question. "So what was up with telling me I had to kill myself?"

She cocked a brow at my tone, but I didn't give a damn. "I lied, naturally. The choice you made proved that you were worthy of being the Chosen. A true leader never surrenders."

I squinted at her. Perhaps the centuries of being alive had messed with her brain. Or maybe she'd just lived in the underworld too long. "But Maisie didn't have any tests."

"Maisie had already proven herself worthy when she died so that you could go through the rest of your quest. She'd seen everything that was coming, but instead of warning you, she stepped aside so that you could learn the lessons you had to learn."

I glanced at Maisie. "You knew all of this?"

Maisie nodded. "Some of it. I'm sorry, Sabina. I tried to help indirectly."

I nodded. "The birthmark?"

Her smile confirmed it.

Part of me wanted to be mad. At the very least, something a tad more concrete than a shoulder ache would have been nice. Just a simple, "Oh, by the way, I'm going to die, but don't worry, it'll all work out."

But I understood that even if Maisie had laid everything out for me, I would never have learned the lessons about teamwork and forgiveness and a million other things I'm sure I hadn't even realized fully yet.

I opened my mouth to deliver a response when the floor of the throne room began to vibrate. Lilith crossed her arms. "Oh, here we go."

"What's wrong?" Adam yelled over the earsplitting sound of cracking marble.

"Asmodeus is coming. Everyone act natural."

The shaking intensified until it knocked all of us to the ground. A loud cracking sound rent the air and a large chasm tore apart the floor.

A black mist rolled out of the crater and coalesced into the hottest demon I'd ever seen. Literally the hottest. In addition to a thickly muscled chest and the humongous biceps, the long blond hair, and the fallen-angel face, he also had wings made of flame. And a whip made of lightning. Not hard to see, then, why Asmodeus was the king of demons. Demigoddess now or no, I certainly didn't want to tangle with him.

Rumor had it that Asmodeus had once been in the employ of the mortal deity. An angel, I think the sons of Adam call them. But early on, not long after the mortal god made Eve for Adam after Lilith fled the garden, Asmodeus split ways with the big guy and formed Irkalla. The legend tellers say his wings are on fire because of the friction of his fall from grace.

"Lilith!" he boomed.

"Hi, honey!" she said, rushing forward.

Her husband towered over her. The frown he shot her could have leveled entire armies, but the Great Mother looked up at him with a serene expression. "What is going on here?" He looked around at all of us with a suspicious expression.

"My friends just dropped by for a visit."

He cocked his head. "Lili, I didn't fall off the cloud yesterday."

"Why are you back so soon?" she evaded. "I thought you were off training a new legion of Vengeance demons."

Asmodeus crossed his arms and heaved a great sigh. "The demon league is making noises about unionizing. I had to go bust some skulls. But imagine my surprise when Valva burst into the meeting and told me Cain was in my home. You want to explain to me how the hell your ex snuck into my kingdom?"

Lilith sighed. "Asclepius helped him."

The King of Irkalla's face looked like a thundercloud. "Asclepius!" he roared. His whip cracked through the air. A split second later, a cloud of blue smoke erupted in the center of the throne room. My jaw dropped when the smoke cleared, revealing Asclepius.

The god was in his black dog form, the one he used when he worked in the Liminal. Asmodeus waved his hands and Asclepius's body morphed into his humanoid form. He shook himself and looked up, shocked to find himself in Irkalla. His gaze zoomed around the room. Clearly he was surprised to see all of us still alive and Cain nowhere to be found. When his eyes landed on Nyx, his expression morphed into hatred. But when he saw Asmodeus staring at him with fire in his eyes, the god paled.

He fell to his knees and bowed his head. "Your Horribleness!"

"Asclepius," Asmodeus said, his tone menacing. "Did you allow Cain entrance into my kingdom through your portal?"

Asclepius's head shot up. His mouth worked as his mind tried to come up with an excuse.

"Answer me!" the king roared.

"Sire"—the god's tone became pleading—"I only did it because that one betrayed our agreement." He pointed at me.

"What agreement?" Asmodeus snapped.

"She promised to kill that vampire standing next to you and return a magical item that belonged to me. I informed her that if she failed to deliver as promised, I would contract Cain's services. She agreed to those terms."

Asmodeus's accusing gaze landed on me. "Did you agree to those terms?"

"Yes, but surely that doesn't excuse the fact that he let Cain into your kingdom."

"Doesn't it?" The demon raised a brow. "Pacts made with gods are binding. If you agreed to the contract knowing the repercussions if you failed to deliver, then you are to blame for the results."

My stomach dropped. Apparently, the demon king took promises pretty seriously. Time for some fast thinking. I cleared my throat. "Sir, actually, Asclepius isn't telling the truth about our contract. When I agreed to his demands, he said he would tell Cain our location if I failed to kill Nyx. He never said that he would allow Cain into Irkalla."

Asmodeus pursed his lips and looked at Asclepius. "Is this true?"

"Yes, but she tricked me! She decided to go into Irkalla early so Cain couldn't reach her first."

"So she bested you at your own game," Nyx said. "Not the first time that's happened, is it, Asclepius?"

"Shut up, bloodsucker!" Asclepius snapped at Nyx. "If you hadn't ignored the blood promise you made to me in the first place, none of this would have happened!"

"Enough!" Asmodeus said. He turned to Nyx. "Is it true that you made a blood oath to the god?"

She sighed. "It's true. I asked him to make me a vest that would protect me from both magical and mundane weapons. Once I put it on, I knew he wouldn't be able to find me so he could demand payment."

Asmodeus was silent for a moment. Then he threw his head back and laughed. "So she was right. Your own hubris resulted in being outsmarted not once, but twice."

Asclepius glared at the king. "They still broke their promises. I demand satisfaction!"

The demon sobered instantly. "You dare make demands in my court?"

Asclepius cowered. "I apologize, but the fact remains that sending Cain after those two was the only way to ensure I was paid for their insults."

"And what of the insult you delivered to me?" the king

said. "You helped an enemy enter my kingdom. That I cannot overlook."

The god didn't have a response to that. His face fell and his shoulders slumped.

"In addition, without Sabina and Nyx, Cain would have succeeded in kidnapping my wife. If that had happened, I would have torn your immortal body apart and posted your living body parts on spikes for all to see and taunt for eternity. So you should be thanking them for saving your sorry hide."

"So what are you going to do to me instead?" the god asked. His posture was defeated.

Asmodeus sighed and pursed his lips. "I am tempted to strip you of your powers and force you to live among humans for the rest of your short days."

Asclepius gasped.

"However, since Cain was stopped and now my love is free of her responsibilities to the children she sired with him, I'd say everything worked out for the best. I'm willing to overlook your poor judgment if you agree to forgive the debts these two females owe you."

Hope ignited in Asclepius's eyes. "Done!"

"In addition, you are banned from making deals with any of the dark race beings ruled by Sabina on earth without her permission."

Asclepius frowned. No doubt the idea of having to come to me for permission rubbed his ego raw, but what choice did he have? Surely that was better than becoming a mortal. "I agree to those terms."

Asmodeus nodded. "Now leave my sight. If you know what's good for you, you will avoid me for a few centuries until I have forgotten about this. Because I assure you I won't be so forgiving next time you screw up."

The god nodded jerkily. Sweat coated his upper lip and his skin had the pallor of a man who'd just gotten a reprieve from the gallows. "I understand."

"Be gone with you." Asmodeus cracked his whip again. The cloud rose up around Asclepius and when it cleared, the god was gone.

Nyx slumped with relief. "Thank the gods."

I put an arm around her. "In this case, I think it's more appropriate to thank the demon."

Before anyone could comment further on Asclepius's punishment, the sound of stilettos pounding on the marble filled the room.

"Sugar buns!" Valva cried. She pushed Asmodeus out of the way and launched herself at Giguhl. Unlike the first time they'd seen each other at the villa, Giguhl accepted her affection with gusto. He wrapped her legs around his waist and proceeded to kiss her with lots of forked tongue.

"Ahem!" Asmodeus didn't sound amused to be watching his daughter make out with a Mischief. "Valva, aren't you going to introduce us to your friend?"

41

The Vanity squeaked and climbed down off Giguhl. My minion blushed like a virgin on her wedding night. "Mom, Dad, this is my boyfriend, Giguhl."

Lilith pursed her lips. "A Mischief demon? Really, Valva?"

Asmodeus stepped forward, his cloven hoofs cracking the marble with each step. "What are your intentions?"

Valva stood straighter and faced down the dark goddess that mortals feared more than Lucifer and her demon husband who could destroy empires with a passing thought. "Stop it, Dad. And seriously, Mother, this isn't like the time I went slumming with that Gluttony demon." She shuddered. "Giguhl and I are in love."

I raised my brows and shot Giguhl a get-the-fuck-out-of-town look. He shifted uncomfortably but eventually nodded. "It's true. I love her."

Lilith sighed and looked at me with a martyred expression. "Kids? What are you going to do?"

"I forbid you to see him!" Asmodeus roared.

A cold sweat broke out on my chest. Adam paled. We

wanted Giguhl to be happy, but even we weren't dumb enough to challenge the King of Irkalla.

Giguhl, however, puffed up and approached his king. The Mischief had to look up, way up, to glare at Asmodeus. "With all due respect, Your Horribleness, that's bullshit."

I shot Adam a wide-eyed look. He shook his head, telling me not to interfere.

"Oh really? You're nothing but a fifth-level Gizal dweller. You don't deserve to look at my daughter, much less declare your love for her."

Giguhl raised his chin and looked the massive demon in the eye. "I not only love her, but I also want to marry her." He turned and looked at Valva with his heart in his eyes. "That is, if you'll have me."

The Vanity demon melted visibly and moved toward Giguhl. "Yes! Yes! Yes!"

"Enough!" Asmodeus shouted. "I forbid it!"

Valva stepped forward with an irritated flick of her tail. "That is enough, Dad. I have been a good daughter. Well, mostly good," she amended when Asmodeus raised a brow.

"Where will you live?" Lilith asked.

"Not under my roof," Asmodeus grumbled.

Giguhl glanced at me. "Red, can we live with you guys?"

I paused, knowing I had to be careful with my words. "Are you asking because you want to or because you don't have another choice? You need to really be sure because if you come back to the mortal realm, you'll still be bound to me but Valva won't. But if you stay here, you'll both be free."

Giguhl watched me with narrowed eyes for a moment. In truth, I was praying he'd still want to be my unofficial minion for a long time to come. But I couldn't not give him an out clause. He deserved to be his own demon for a change. To build his own life. I'd miss him like hell, but it was the right thing to do.

"I grew up in Irkalla. I have some friends here. Some good memories." The Mischief crossed his arms. "But you guys are my family. If it's okay with Valva, we'll live on earth."

The Vanity clapped her hands. "Please, I've been dying to live in the mortal realm. Irkalla is sooo boring. There's not one decent shopping mall."

"I won't have it!" Asmodeus roared.

Valva stuck out her bottom lip and glared at her father. "Daddy, I'm four thousand years old. It's time you cut the cord and let me make my own decisions."

Lilith sighed. "She has a point, dear. Besides, you know how rebellious adolescent demons are. If we say no, she'll just run off anyway."

Asmodeus pursed his lips. His fire wings twitched. We all held our breaths. I'm not sure what everyone else was thinking, but I was terrified he was about to turn Giguhl into Mischief flambé. "All right, fine," he said finally. "But I'll expect you to come home for a visit every now and then. Your mother worries."

Valva ran forward to hug her parents. Giguhl hung back, grinning like a loon, until his love called him forward to formally meet his future in-laws, the Great Mother and the King of Irkalla.

"All righty, then," Adam said, clapping his hands together. His tone was high-pitched and a thin sheen of sweat coated his brow. "Now that that's settled, I really want to get the fuck out of here."

I heartily agreed, but the thought of leaving Maisie left me torn. I walked up to my twin. "Are you okay?"

She smiled a wobbly smile and nodded. "I think so."

"So, I guess this means you were wrong."

She frowned. "What do you mean?"

"You said I was the Chosen. But it's both of us, together."

She chuckled a little, but her eyes were shadowed. "I've never been happier to be wrong in my life. It feels…right this way."

"I'm just sorry you're going to be stuck down here."

She shrugged. "Don't worry about it. I'll have Orpheus and Ameritat with me. Plus, now after Tristan ordered the vamp spirits to rebel against the Domina, I'm pretty sure I won't be bored."

I cringed. "Sorry about that."

"He was right to do it. There's no reason there can't be peace in the dark race realms of Irkalla, too. Besides, we can visit each other, right?"

I nodded. "I guess so."

"Hey," she said, leaning over to catch my gaze. "I regret nothing. You shouldn't either."

I chewed my lip to keep in the tears. "I know. It's just—"

"Sabina, it all worked out as it should. I actually kind of like it down here."

My head jerked up. "Really?"

She bit her lip and nodded. "Does that make me weird?"

I laughed. "Maisie, we're mixed-blood demigoddesses who just consumed the most evil human alive. I'd say we zoomed right past weird a long time ago."

At that point, Phoebe approached us. I'd met my mother before in the Liminal, the night Maisie had died, but this was the first time we'd faced each other like this.

"Hi," I said, suddenly feeling unsure of myself.

She smiled at me. "Hello, daughter." She winked at Maisie. "I am so proud of both of you."

The corner of my mouth lifted in an awkward, self-conscious smile. How weird was it that her pride meant so much? "So what will you do now?"

"What do you mean?"

"Well, Tristan's down here now. You two can finally be together."

A shadow passed over her face. "I'm afraid it's too late."

"Too late because of what Cain did?" Maisie asked. "With the spell?"

My mother nodded. "You saw Tristan's reaction when he saw me. I'm afraid he's convinced that what we had wasn't real."

I certainly had seen his reaction. She might be remembering when he withdrew, but I saw the joy on his face the instant he saw her. I had a feeling it wouldn't take much for her to convince him he was an idiot if he didn't believe their love had been real. "Look, I know we just met and all, but I have a feeling I got a lot of my stubbornness from you." Her lips turned up into a rueful smile, but I wasn't done. "If I were you, I'd march over to Hekatian Fields and make him stop being a blind fool."

She barked out a shocked laugh. "That would be great if I could enter Hekatian Fields."

Maisie cleared her throat. "Well since I sort of run the dark races in Irkalla now and you're my mom and all, I could probably be convinced to give you permission."

Phoebe's eyes widened. "I...I don't know. What if he rejects me?"

"Oh, I have a pretty good feeling he won't," I said. "He might put up a token resistance at first, but don't kid yourself. That man is head over heels for you still."

"Sabina," Lilith called. "It's time for you and your friends to go now."

I nodded at the goddess and turned to Phoebe. "We have to go. But next time I see you, I expect progress with Dad, okay?"

My mother laughed. "Deal. Please come back soon. I want a chance to get to know you."

Tears welled up in my eyes. I didn't bother fighting them. "I'd like that."

With that, my mother floated off to speak with Lilith.

I turned back to Maisie. "I'll see you soon, okay?"

Maisie forced a smile and grabbed my hand. I'd half expected it to wave through my skin. Instead, her hand grabbed mine as if she were made of flesh and bone rather than spirit. "I love you, sister."

I wanted to pull her against me and give her a hug, but Lilith's warnings about staying connected too long echoed in my head. As it was, the contact was draining what little was left of my energy. Instead, I squeezed her hand, ignoring the chill that crept up my arm, and looked her in the eye. "I never wanted a sister, you know." Her eyes flared. "But I had no idea how much I needed one. Thank you for finding me and showing me the real meaning of family."

Spectral tears glimmered in her eyes. "Ditto," she said, echoing the words I'd said so often in the past to avoid putting voice to my true feelings.

The corner of my lips quirked. I leaned forward. "I love you, too, Maze."

This time separating wasn't as hard. I guess with practice it'd get easier and easier.

"Red?"

I turned slowly. Adam stood off to the side, looking unsure. I held out a hand to him. Slowly, his eyes wary as he glanced at Maisie, he came over to us. Maisie's spirit shifted uneasily the closer he got.

"I think it's way past time you two had a chat," I said. I smiled encouragingly at both of them—the former best friends who'd been torn apart by the machinations of narcissistic vampire rulers and madmen.

I turned away and saw Nyx and Lilith talking over by one of the thrones. Whatever they were discussing seemed pretty serious, so I sidetracked to join Giguhl and Valva. They were talking about wedding plans while Asmodeus looked alternately bored and irritated. I tried to listen and look enthusiastic, but I kept glancing at the man I loved and my twin.

Adam's head was bowed as he listened to whatever Maisie said. Occasionally he'd nod and the light would catch the tears on his cheeks. I wasn't naïve enough to think that the events of that night would miraculously solve all of their problems. Or that it would solve all of everyone's problems. But a sense of peace descended over me. Cain's death meant a fresh start for all the dark races. We could finally stop trying to fix the past and survive the present. It was finally time to embrace the future.

"Sabina, what do you think? An autumn wedding?" Valva said.

I shook myself and looked at the demon. "That's so not my area." Then a thought occurred to me. "Hey, G. You know who would love to help you plan this?"

The demon frowned. "Who?"

I smiled broadly. "Brooks." Oh my gods, now that I mentioned it, I couldn't wait to see how Valva and the drag queen got along. Giguhl was going to have his claws full if those two started conspiring against him.

"Who's that?" Valva asked suspiciously.

Before I could get another word out, a warm hand grabbed mine. I looked up to see Adam had returned. His eyes were red-rimmed, but he was smiling. "You guys ready to head out?"

I glanced over and realized Maisie had already left. "Wh—"

He shook his head. "She didn't want a big scene. She said to be in touch once you got settled back on earth."

I leaned up on tiptoes and kissed his cheek. "You okay?"

"You know what? I think I am." He squeezed my hand and I knew he was a lot more than okay. "Red?"

"Yeah?"

"Your hair's back to normal."

Now that he mentioned it, I felt back to my old self again. Only more. Magic hummed in my marrow and—I touched my teeth with my tongue. "Holy crap, my fangs are back, too."

"Thank the gods," Adam said. "No offense but the blond and toothless look was going to take some getting used to."

I smiled at him. I couldn't imagine how pitiful I'd looked. "Where does this leave us on our miracle tally?"

He tilted his head. "What are we up to? Five?"

"Six, I think."

"Look at us. Saving the world with a miracle to spare."

"Well what did you guys expect?" Giguhl said. "We *are* Team Awesome."

Lilith and Nyx joined us then. The vampire looked a little shell-shocked, which I supposed was understandable, all things considered. "You ready?" I asked her gently.

Nyx nodded. "I think so. I'm just not sure what's next."

I realized then that Nyx hadn't just lost the man she loved. She'd also lost the team that had become her family for the last few decades. Now that her debt to Asclepius was wiped clean, she had a chance at a new life, but what that life would be was a major question mark.

I patted her on the arm. "Actually, I've got a few ideas. We'll talk about them once we're back in the mortal realm, okay?"

She swallowed hard. "Thanks, Sabina."

"Before you leave, one more small thing," Lilith said. "You can never let the humans know of the existence of the dark races. A few here and there are unavoidable, but the bulk of the Adamites in the mortal realm can never know."

I frowned. "Why not?"

"Because that was the deal I made with him." She pointed up to indicate the mortal deity. "I imagine that'll be harder once mages and vampires realize they can finally stop hating each other and get bored. But if the humans ever find out, I'll have to kill all of you. Bye now!"

I sighed. "You're a real bitch, Lilith."

If I'd spoken that insult just two hours earlier, she wouldn't have hesitated to level me to the ground with a single murderous stare. But since we were now equals of a sort, she threw back her head and laughed. "That I am, Sabina. That I most definitely am." She waved. "Don't be a stranger!"

Ha! If she thought I was going to pop down to Irkalla one a week for a fucking deity coffee klatch, she was crazier than I thought.

In the next instant, Lilith, the Great Mother of all the dark races, snapped her fingers and sent us home.

EPILOGUE

Eight months later

A full harvest moon hung fat and low in the sky. Plenty of time left before sunrise.

Not that I was worried about the sun rising anymore. Becoming a deity had ended my lifelong feud with the solar demon. But, as usual, time was still my enemy.

I rushed through the courtyard with Adam trailing behind at a more leisurely pace. "Red? Relax, it's not like they can start without you."

I shot a glare back over my shoulder. "Right, but what kind of leader is late to her own meeting? I swear, next time you suggest a quickie, I'm going to remind you of this."

He chuckled. "It's not my fault you find me irresistible."

"Yes, it is, actually."

I reached the doors to the building and wrenched them open. Inside the antechamber, two dozen security guards from every dark race pulled their weapons. I suddenly had ten guns, five swords, three bows and arrows, and several magical weapons pointed at my head.

I stilled on the threshold.

"Relax," Slade called in a droll tone. "It's just the Chosen."

All the guards holstered their weapons and fell into at-ease poses.

I shot my old friend a look. "Thanks."

He winked. "You're late. They're already in there."

I waved and ran forward, leaving Adam and Slade shaking hands. They'd follow me in, but since they didn't hold official seats on the Dark Races Cabinet, they didn't need to make an entrance.

On my way, I waved at Calyx. She took her role as the new head of security for Queen Maeve too seriously to do anything more friendly than nod. Turned out Cain hadn't gotten the fae after all. My old friend Vinca had helped Calyx escape Irkalla while we were busy in Lilith's lair. She'd been heartbroken to learn of Tristan's and Horus's deaths, but once I recommended her skills to the Queen, she took to her new role among Maeve's guard like she was made for it.

Speaking of the Queen, she'd no doubt had a few sharp words for me once I walked in those doors. I smoothed down my hair and prayed Adam hadn't left any hickies on my neck. Sucking in a deep breath, I put my hands on the handles and pulled the doors open in what I hoped was a stately manner.

"Sorry I'm late," I said as I rushed inside. Slade had been right—everyone was already seated. But the instant I crossed into the room, they all rose and bowed.

I waved an impatient hand. "Guys, we've already discussed the saluting thing. Sit down."

I took the empty chair at the front of the large, round table. Maisie's spirit hovered on my right. "Hey, sis!" I said.

"Where have you been? You opened the portal for me to come over, but you weren't there when I came through."

"Sorry, I had some . . . pressing business to attend to."

My sister raised a brow. "Pressing, sure."

From Maisie's right, Rhea leaned over. "You're late."

"Talk to your nephew," I muttered.

Rhea wore the ceremonial chiton that identified her as the leader of the Hekate Council. After we'd returned from Irkalla, the Council had taken a vote to instate her as the official and permanent leader of their government. I had to admit, I was relieved at the development. Even though Rhea never hesitated to voice her opinions on my decisions, she was fair and honest and I felt comfortable bickering with her.

The same couldn't be said for the frowning female sitting directly across from me.

"Nice of you to join us, Chosen. Do you plan on being unfashionably late to all our meetings?"

Since it was well into October, Queen Maeve was in her Mother phase of the year. A thin thread of gray decorated her dark brown hair, giving it a distinguished appearance. She wore an eggplant-colored robe and the autumn crown, which was decorated with amber acorns and metallic leaves. I had to say, I much preferred this look to her Child manifestation in the spring. It was disconcerting to argue dark races policy with a seven-year-old girl whose eyes were too ancient for her innocent face.

While the Queen seemed to accept me as the leader of the Chamber, she didn't seem too impressed with my newfound status as a demigoddess. I supposed I couldn't blame her too much, though. After all, she'd been a deity for millennia and I'd been one for only eight months. I wouldn't bow down to me either if I were her. Still, I would have appreciated a little less lip from the faery queen.

"I'll endeavor to be more punctual in the future, if you try to be less bitchy."

The Queen gasped. "Well," she huffed. Her eyes scanned the room for an ally to her indignation, but she found none among the remaining Cabinet members.

Next to me, the new vampire leader chuckled and elbowed me. "Nice one, Sabina."

I looked up and smiled. "Thanks, Nyx. Or should I call you Madame President?"

The vampire rolled her eyes. "Only if you want me to ignore you, O Exalted Chosen."

I chuckled at my friend. Over the last several months, Nyx and I had worked closely as she set up her new government in Los Angeles. Transforming the historically despotic vampire form of government into a more democratic one wasn't easy, but Nyx proved herself a strong and prudent leader.

She wore a business suit and I spied the golden rings of her vest winking from the collar of her crisp white shirt. Not for the first time, I sent a little prayer of thanks to Asmodeus for not forcing Nyx to give the vest back to Asclepius. The general vampire population was kept in the dark about her semi-immortal status, but the vest actually was probably more protection than her vampire powers would have been. Plus, she saved a ton on security. Pretty much the only backup she traveled with regularly was Slade and Georgia, but even they were more like trusted confidants than hired guns.

As for Asclepius, no one had heard from him since Asmodeus sent him away from the throne room. I guess the god decided it was better not to make deals with any dark race members than face asking me for permission. Which was fine with me. If I never saw the god again, it'd be too soon.

"Did Georgia come with you on this trip?"

The vampire nodded. "Are you kidding? She wouldn't miss the wedding for anything. She's off helping Zen set up the hall now."

I nodded. The reminder of the wedding ceremony later that night made my hands sweat. It wasn't every day a female watched her demon get married.

"Speaking of," Maisie said. "We'd better get started. Brooks will have our heads if we're not on our marks at midnight on the dot."

I picked up the silver gavel from the table and rapped it twice on the stone surface. "I now call this meeting of the Dark Races Cabinet to order. We'll begin with reports." I looked up. "Maisie, is there any news from Irkalla?"

"Yes, there's been some progress on the coup against the Dominae, but there's a holdout."

"Let me guess—Lavinia?"

Maisie nodded. "Naturally. She and one of the ancients have turned against the other Dominae and are refusing to step down. I was hoping you'd be willing to come down for a visit so we can convince dear old grandmother to cut the shit."

I pursed my lips. Part of me would love to give Lavinia a dose of humble pie, but the other part didn't relish the idea of spending more time in the Bloodlands.

Sensing my hesitation, Maisie continued. "Mom and Dad have been asking when you're going to visit again. You can even bring Adam."

I sighed. It had been a couple of months since I'd been down to see my parents and even longer since I'd checked in on Vinca. "Okay, but we can only stay for a couple of days."

My twin smiled. "Deal."

I made a mental note to share the news with Adam later.

He loved being able to visit with Orpheus when we went to Irkalla, so I was pretty sure he wouldn't have a problem.

"Alpha Romulus, do you have a report?"

As the only male in the Cabinet, Michael Romulus was hard to miss. Because it was the night of a full moon, he sent off waves of pheromones that permeated the air like musky cologne. I even caught the Queen shooting him a suggestive glance or three.

In addition to being the only male, Michael was an exception on the Cabinet because he wasn't technically the leader of his entire race. Instead, the werewolf Alphas had elected him as a sort of delegate. He reported our decisions back to the leaders and came to us with requests from individual packs. Even though we'd had our share of run-ins in the past, I actually enjoyed working with him. He could be surly and dominating, but I enjoyed the challenge every now and again.

The werewolf cleared his throat. "There's not much to report since last quarter's meeting. The Alpha of the Miami pack has had a little trouble in his sector and wanted me to ask High Councilwoman Lazarus if she'd be willing to send a few mages down to help handle the situation."

"What kind of trouble?" Rhea asked, switching to business mode.

"Some immigrants from Haiti hexed some of the weres."

"Hmm," I said. "Voodoo?"

He nodded. "I was also going to speak to Madame Zenobia to see if she had any solutions."

"That's a good idea," Rhea said. "If she can't help you, I'd be happy to send a couple of people down to look into it."

Michael smiled. "Thanks. I'll be in touch."

"Anything else, Michael?"

He paused, as if reluctant to bring up the next item. "Actually, yes. As you know, my niece Mac is expecting her first cub in a couple of months."

My stomach sank. It's not that I didn't know about Mac's pregnancy, but this topic was a touchy one for several of us in the room. Georgia worked for Nyx, so Nyx knew the whole sordid tale of how Michael forced his niece to leave her girlfriend to marry a male of his choosing. And Rhea and I had both been friends with everyone involved. I nodded for him to continue.

"The doctors believe the cub will be a female." His tone was so disappointed that I had to bite my lips to hide my smile. Served him right. "Mac asked me if you would allow her to bring the cub here for a blessing once she was born."

I frowned. "A blessing from whom? Zen?" Before she'd left for New York, Mac and Zen had been good friends.

"From you."

I blinked. I still wasn't used to the more ceremonial parts of my new role among the races. Plus, the whole thing would be so awkward. Still, Mac had made her choices and Georgia actually seemed happier since she'd been in Los Angeles. Balking about a simple blessing on a child who didn't have anything to do with the pain of her parents' joining would be pretty hypocritical of me of all people. "Tell Mac I'd love to see her and meet the baby."

Michael's eyes shifted. "Will Mac's mate also be welcomed?"

Ugh. I wanted to hang out with Logan Remus about as much as I wanted to get stabbed in the eye. But to slight him now would be a huge humiliation for the male. "He may come, too."

Michael let out a sigh of relief. "Thanks, Sabina."

I nodded and held his gaze. Michael knew I still didn't

approve of his actions where Mac was concerned, but it wasn't really my business. Even as the leader of the cabinet, I tried to keep my opinions to myself unless an issue arose that affected more than one race. I wasn't a dictator, but more of a mediator. I'd learned my lesson the hard way about trying to control people.

I cleared my throat. "Anyone else have anything to report?"

The aisle seemed so long. Longer than it should, considering the happiness of the occasion. I'd never given much thought to weddings. In fact, I'd never so much as been invited to one. But now here I was, in one.

Giguhl's green-scaled arm was linked through mine as we made the journey together. I looked over at him and found his gaze riveted to the altar, where Zen, Rhea, Brooks, and Adam already stood. I looked at the mancy and smiled. He winked back, looking both relaxed and downright sexy in his formal black chiton.

On either side of the aisles formed by the parted crowd of spectators, I spied dozens of familiar faces. Georgia and Slade on Giguhl's side of the congregation. I was so glad to see Georgia smiling. After we'd returned, she had still been in a funk about Mac and had never warmed up to owning Lagniappe. But when I'd recommended Georgia to Nyx as an advisor, Brooks had stepped up with an offer to purchase the bar from the vampire. The situation worked out brilliantly for all concerned, since Brooks was a far better bar owner than performer and his drag queen employees worshipped him.

Speaking of Brooks, he'd also done an amazing job of pulling together the demon wedding of the millennium.

After some initial bitchiness, Brooks and Valva got along famously once they'd discovered their shared love for all things gaudy. After that, the Vanity bride and the Changeling had worked together like two fabulous generals staging a rhinestone-studded battle against singledom.

The courtyard of the house Adam and I owned in the Garden District had been transformed into a sort of faery autumn garden. Tiny white lights crisscrossed overhead, creating the illusion of stars or faery dust. Valva had tried to explain the theme they were going for, but I hadn't really paid attention. Anyway, there were flowers everywhere and they'd thrown jewel-toned ribbon all over everything without a pulse. The effect was totally not my taste, but then, it also wasn't my wedding.

Giguhl and I finally reached the front of the altar, where Rhea and Zen stood side by side to officiate the ceremony. Brooks and Adam waited for us at the altar, since they were the other best men. While Adam wore a chiton, Brooks had opted for a tuxedo with a bow tie and cummerbund in Vegasy gold lamé. I took my place between them and turned back toward the audience.

Giguhl fidgeted at the head of the aisle, waiting for Rhea to give the signal. Soon, the fae musicians to the side of altar started playing a fae wedding march. The entire crowd turned in time to see Valva appear at the back of the clearing.

She looked spectacular in her magenta wedding gown, especially with the plume of peacock feathers unfurled behind her like a train. Since Asmodeus and Lilith couldn't be here for the ceremony—there'd be another one in Irkalla later—Maisie walked her former minion down the aisle.

Watching the pair approach—Valva on six-inch gold Louboutins and Maisie floating—my eyes began to sting.

If someone had told me ten months earlier that one night my ghost sister and I would be watching our minions get married, I'd have punched them in the face and told them to seek professional help. But now there was a certain poetry to this event. Everything felt like it had come full circle.

Maisie and Valva finally reached us. Rhea and Zen stepped forward. "Who gives this female to join in the sacred bond of soul mating with the demon Giguhl?" asked Rhea.

"I, Maisie Graecus, High Priestess of the Chaste Moon and Chosen of the Underworld Dark Races, do."

"And who gives this male to join in the sacred bond of soul mating to the demon Valva?" asked Zen.

I'd been so busy smiling at my sister that Brooks had to nudge me with his elbow. I stood straighter and stepped forward. "I, Sabina Kane, High Priestess of the Blood Moon and Chosen of the Mortal Realm Dark Races, do."

Zen and Rhea nodded at us to take our places next to our demons. Giguhl and Valva stood shoulder to shoulder and hand in claw. The ceremony was short but sweet. And at the end, after Giguhl slid the ring onto his demon bride's finger and they were pronounced demon and wife, Valva launched herself at her husband and proceeded to kiss the snot out of him.

When they were finally finished, a moment of shocked silence followed before the courtyard erupted into cheers.

Adam caught my hand and winked. I shot him a rueful smile. We hadn't gotten around to making our own union official. I still wore the ring he gave me that night in Tuscany and now he wore a matching one I'd had made. I guess we just felt like we didn't need other people to confirm the vows we'd already made to each other. Our souls were already joined. The fires of Irkalla had fused them in a way no wedding ever could.

Still, he liked to tease me about making me an honest woman and often referred to himself at the "kept man of a goddess."

The faery band burst into song to accompany the happy couple's procession from the altar. Giguhl jumped forward, threw up his claws, and yelled, "Let's party!"

The reception was held on the lawn beside the house. We were lucky enough to snag a double lot with lots of high walls and privacy. It had cost us a mint, but we loved living in New Orleans and the ease with which we could travel to any of the dark race capitals as needed.

Thousands of tiny white lights hung in the trees and candles floated in the pool. Colorful tents dotted the lawn and offered a variety of dishes favored by all the dark races. To cap it all off, a large stage had been erected for the band.

Speaking of the band, they'd just taken the stage and were warming up when Adam sauntered up to me bearing two flutes of champagne. He clinked his glass to mine and turned toward the stage. "I feel like our little demon is all grown up now."

I took a sip and enjoyed the cold bubbling sensation as it slid down my throat. "Don't worry. In no time he'll be back to running up our credit cards and trashing the house when we're out of town."

"Speaking of trashing houses, I'm glad Erron and Ziggy worked things out."

Erron and his new all-mage band were supplying the entertainment for the reception. Once the Recreant returned to the States, he'd made amends with Ziggy and they went about transforming Necrospank 5000 into a new, more mage-centric incarnation.

"But the new name has got to go," Adam continued.

"Oh, I don't know," I said. "I think The Foreskins has a certain charm to it."

At that moment, Erron Zorn strutted onstage. The small wedding party applauded politely. After a months' long hiatus from music, tonight would mark Erron's first public performance with his new band. He waved to his fans and pulled his guitar strap over his head. Behind him, Ziggy tapped a rhythmic beat on the drums.

"This first song goes out to the happy couple. Can we get Giguhl and Valva on the floor for their first dance as demon and wife?"

Giguhl looked so proud and happy as he led his bride onto the floor. Valva strutted ahead of him, flicking her peacock tail. Watching them, Adam put his arm around my shoulder. I leaned into him and let out a contented sigh.

I'm not sure why I expected two demons to dance to a traditionally romantic song. However, after my initial shock at their choice, I realized the acoustic version of "Super Freak" fit Giguhl and Valva better than any cheesy ballad.

"Sabina!" a female voice called.

I turned to see Georgia and the female vampire I noticed earlier at the wedding approaching. I moved forward and gave Georgia a hug.

We pulled away and Georgia turned to the female. Unlike Georgia, who was tall and had the figure of a cover model, this chick was shorter and had a short, spiky haircut. Judging from the bright red color, she was probably about a century old. "Adam, Sabina, this is Shane Bettencourt."

"Chosen, it is an honor." Shane started to kneel and touch her hand to her forehead, but I stopped her.

"Please don't. You can just call me Sabina." I stuck my

hand out. She hesitated and glanced at Georgia, who nodded. Finally, Shane took my hand and gave it a couple of hearty shakes.

"So how do you two know each other?" Adam asked after he greeted the vampire, too.

"Shane owns a bar in Los Angeles that I go to a lot."

I glanced at Georgia. Her eyes skittered away. I wasn't sure if it was because she was insecure about her new relationship or because of the obvious similarities between Shane and Georgia's ex, Mac. Sure, Mac was a werewolf, but she had the same masculine energy and had been a bar owner to boot.

"Oh yeah?" I said to Shane. "What's it called? I used to live in L.A. Maybe I've been there."

"I kind of doubt that," she said, glancing toward Adam. "It's called The Pearl Diver."

I bit my lip. "Really?"

Shane nodded. "You should come next time you're in the city."

"I think that's a fantastic idea," Adam said, earning a nudge from me.

Georgia cleared her throat. "So, Sabina, when are you finally going to make an honest man out of Adam?"

I shrugged. "We like living in sin."

"Amen," Shane said. She flashed Georgia a wink.

"Anyway," Adam said, "I don't think anything we'd come up with could compete with that." He nodded toward the dance floor.

The Foreskins had picked up the beat and now the dance floor was crowded. In addition to Giguhl and Valva, who'd switched to some pretty impressive disco moves, Queen Maeve, Nyx, Slade, Brooks, Zen, and a dozen other powerful vampires, mages, weres, and fae danced their asses off.

Even Maisie's spirit swirled and dipped among the corporeal partiers.

Considering that less than a year ago, those same beings had been on the brink of annihilating each other, it was an odd but not unwelcome sight.

"What do you say, Red?" Adam asked, holding out a hand toward the dance floor.

Two hours later, I escaped. My hair hung in sweaty ropes around my face, the hem of my dress was in shreds, and I hadn't felt so good in months. Adam stayed behind to take Zen for a spin around the floor, so I grabbed a seat at a nearby table.

Before long, Giguhl sauntered up carrying two flutes of champagne and wearing a goofy, satisfied grin. He handed me a glass and clinked his to it before taking a seat beside me.

We sat quietly for a few moments, letting the sounds of the party swirl around us. Less than a year ago, the future had been a huge, black question mark hovering on the horizon. But now it rolled out in front of us like the first rays of the sun at dawn, full of promise and hope.

I looked at Giguhl and thought about the first night we'd met. Adam had sent the demon to test my skills. Giguhl had introduced himself by way of an applewood arrow through my chest. And now I'd just served as best man at his wedding.

On the journey to becoming best friends, we'd survived countless battles, hairpin turns, misunderstandings, and tests of faith. But each of those challenges had forged our relationship with bonds stronger than blood. And I was damned proud to be his friend.

"How's it feel to be Mr. Valva now?" Apparently, demons didn't get married often, but when they did, it was customary for the male to take the female's name.

Giguhl leaned back in his chair and clasped his hands

across his midsection. "Don't have any complaints so far."
Something in the distance caught the demon's eye. "Hey,
Red? Check it out."

I turned and immediately spotted the objects of his interest. Nyx and Slade were sitting at an out-of-the-way table
with their heads close together. Something about their body
language told me they weren't talking about business. I took
a sip of my drink and decided it was a good thing. Nyx had
thrown herself into her new role in the vampire government
to distract herself from Tristan's loss, but from the looks of
things, Slade was more than happy to help her move on.

Adam approached and saw where Giguhl and I were
looking. "Good for them." He took the seat on the other
side of me and kissed my hand.

"So when do you head to Irkalla?" Adam asked Giguhl.
He and his bride would be honeymooning in the underworld.

"Tonight, just after the party. Lilith's insisting on holding a demon mating ceremony immediately to consecrate
our unholy union or whatever," Giguhl said. "Adam said
you guys are going down, too?"

I nodded. "Maisie's having some trouble with the vampire uprising in the Bloodlands, so I'm going to go help her.
We won't be there long, but I'm hoping I can fit a visit in
with my parents and Vinca."

"I'm glad your dad finally got over himself about the
whole love spell thing."

"I don't think Phoebe gave him much choice," I chuckled.
"Especially when she reminded him that love spells can only
make you attracted to someone. They can't create true love
or keep two people together. That's all a conscious choice."

Adam shot me an intimate smile. "Damn straight."

Valva came and plopped into Giguhl's lap. She planted a
loud smacking kiss on his lips. "How are you, Mr. Valva?"

"Better now," he said, pulling her closer.

"When will you guys get back from your honeymoon?" Adam asked.

"Couple months, tops."

My mouth dropped open. "That long?" I hadn't been separated from Giguhl that long since the day he barged into my life.

Valva waved a golden hand. "It would have been longer, but we need to get back to prepare the nursery."

I frowned at her. "What nursery?"

Valva didn't notice that her new husband had gone very still. "For the babies?" She rolled her eyes like I'd said something stupid.

My stomach dropped. Giguhl closed his eyes and muttered a curse.

"Who's having babies?" Adam said, shooting me a tense glance. I shook my head back because I had no freaking clue either.

Valva looked at Giguhl. "Didn't you tell them, honey?"

"I wanted to wait until after we got back, sugar knuckle."

In a voice as calm as I could manage, I said, "Tell us what, exactly?" I picked up my champagne, prepared to chug my way through this.

Valva pursed her lips and gave her husband a look that clearly indicated he would not enjoy his wedding night if he didn't spill the news. "Adam, Sabina," Giguhl said, his tone reluctant and not a little nervous. "I'm knocked up."

I sputtered a mouthful of champagne across the table. "What?"

"Wait." Adam held up a finger. "Don't you mean Valva is pregnant?"

Valva shook her head. "Gross, no."

"Giguhl?" Adam said, his tone growing alarmed. "What the hell?"

I put my head in my hands. "I'm so confused right now."

My minion took a deep breath and leaned forward. "It's true. I'm carrying our first litter."

"But how?" I held up a hand. "Wait, I'm not sure I even want to know how that's possible."

"It's simple, really," Valva said, ignoring my plea to remain ignorant of the inner workings of demon procreation. "Female demons have two sets of equipment."

Adam closed his eyes. "I know I shouldn't ask this, but I can't help myself. Do males have both as well?"

"Um, hello? How many times have you two bitches seen me in my magnificent naked form? The answer is no. The only tool I'm sporting is the mighty Pitchfork."

"Then how are you—" I stopped myself.

"Gods, Sabina, don't be such a prude," Valva said. "It's just a matter of me implanting a sperm packet in Giguhl's ass womb."

All the blood rushed from my face. Adam's face was slightly green and he swayed woozily. "Are...are you happy about it?" I whispered.

Giguhl pursed his lips, thinking it over. "You know, I kind of am. We didn't plan on it, but I think it could be pretty awesome to have a gaggle of little Vanity and Mischief demons running around."

"How many makes up a gaggle, exactly?" Adam said.

"Half a dozen, usually. We'll know more once I'm further along and my teats come in."

I bit my lip to keep in the hysterical laughter bubbling up in my throat.

Luckily, Adam had a better poker face. "And how long until these little miracles make their appearance?"

"Four months!" Valva said.

I dropped my glass.

"But don't worry, Red," Giguhl rushed ahead. "Once we wean them off the teat, they'll move back to Irkalla."

"How long?"

"A thousand years, give or take."

After the happy couple departed for the underworld and all the guests had returned to the respective centers of power, Adam and I stood on the balcony watching the sun rise.

My body was exhausted from the party but my head was buzzing. "I can't believe we're going to have six demon spawn running around here for a millennium."

Adam shrugged. "Look at it this way—they'll keep Giguhl and Valva so busy they won't have time to cause trouble."

I turned to the mancy and lifted an eyebrow. "Yes, but we'll be outnumbered."

"Not for the first time," he reminded me.

"True." I leaned over and kissed his cheek.

We fell silent as we watched the sun finally crest the horizon. "You know, it just occurred to me that the first time we met was during the last harvest moon," Adam said.

I looked up. "That's right. At Ewan's bar. You were sitting across the bar trying to look so mysterious."

He smiled. "You totally checked me out."

"Right," I said. "As a potential enemy."

"I remember the moment I saw you. You marched in with a huge chip on your shoulder, daring every vampire in the room to challenge you. Begging them to let you prove yourself."

I stilled, remembering that night. It had been only a couple of hours after I'd killed David. I'd walked into Sepulcher looking for a fight. And I'd found one. A swaggering vamp had approached me and called me out for killing his brother years earlier.

"When you killed that guy, you smiled." Adam's tone was quiet. Not judgmental, just matter-of-fact.

"I did?"

He nodded. "But you know what else I noticed?"

I swallowed hard against a rush of emotion that rose out of nowhere.

"You were standing in the middle of a packed bar surrounded by vampires who either despised you or were afraid of you. You tried to look like you enjoyed their awe, but something in your eyes caught me off guard."

"What?" I whispered.

"Loneliness."

Tears sprang to my eyes. It had been months since I'd felt that hollowed out feeling. The weight of solitude, which, along with self-loathing, had been my only companion. But now the memories flooded in and with them, the visceral pain of rejection and self-inflicted isolation.

"I guess I was pretty fucked up." Funny talking about it now—that old life felt decades in the past instead of a little more than a year.

"A little maybe," he said. "But also brave and brash and proud. I was fascinated from the moment you stormed into that room." He tilted my head up and wiped the tears from my cheeks. "And the longer we're together, the more fascinated I become."

I kissed his lips, savoring the sandalwood musk of him as it combined with the smoky scent of autumn leaves and the flavor of whisky on his skin. "You're pretty fascinating yourself, mancy."

As the sun climbed in the distance, Adam and I continued to explore our mutual fascination for each other. But I couldn't stop thinking about what a miracle my life had become in twelve short months. The road to get there had been twisty and treacherous and downright terrifying, but in the end every heartache, every cut and bruise, every tough lesson learned had been worth it.

I wasn't sure what the future would bring to us or to any of the beings I'd come to care about during my journey from burned out assassin to demigoddess, but I took comfort in knowing that whatever challenges waited, I'd never face them alone again.

A feeling swirled in the pit of my stomach. Not the foreboding, achy sense of despair that had been part of me for so many years. But something warm, glowy…pleasant, even.

It took me a moment to recognize the emotion because, frankly, I didn't have a lot of experience with it. But for the first time in my life, I was happy. For the first time in my life, I felt loved and safe and…balanced.

I smiled inwardly and my soul whispered, "Miracle number seven."

Acknowledgments

*A*s many of you know, or are about to find out once you read this, *Blue-Blooded Vamp* is the final installment in Sabina Kane's journey. I've learned so much writing this series, both about writing and about myself. Those lessons weren't always easy, but I owe a debt of gratitude to so many people for guiding me on this long, strange trip.

Devi Pillai, thank you for challenging me to always improve and for seeing the spark in this series from the beginning.

Rebecca Strauss, thank you for being an amazing agent, trusted advisor and advocate, and an all-around cool lady.

Thanks also to the entire team at Orbit in the U.S. and U.K.—Tim Holman, Lauren Panepinto, Anna Gregson, Alex Lencicki, Jack Womack, Jennifer Flax, Susan Barnes, and all of the amazing sales and marketing staff. Without all of your hard work, this series would have never found its audience.

Huge hugs to Suzanne McLeod, my stalwart critique partner. For your fast reads and brilliant insights, I will always be in your debt.

Thanks to the League of Reluctant Adults for the camaraderie and support.

To the Migues, Hughes, and Wells families, thank you for simply everything. A special shout-out to my cousin Maryam Houston, whose advice and plentiful supply of wine make her an indispensable brainstorming partner.

Emily and Zivy, thank you for believing in me. I will never stop believing in us.

Mr. Jaye, I know it's not easy being married to a writer, but your patience is the stuff of legend. ILYNTB.

Spawn, nothing makes me prouder than being your mom.

And, finally, thank you to all the readers who have stuck with Sabina (and me) through thick and thin. I hope that the culmination of her quest does not mark the end of our journey together.

Happy reading!

extras

www.orbitbooks.net

about the author

Raised in Texas, **Jaye Wells** grew up reading everything she could get her hands on. Her penchant for daydreaming was often noted by frustrated teachers. Later, she embarked on a series of random career paths before taking a job as a magazine editor. Jaye eventually realized that while she loved writing, she found reporting facts boring. So she left all that behind to indulge her overactive imagination and make stuff up for a living. Besides writing, she enjoys travel, art, history, and researching weird and arcane subjects. She lives in Texas with her saintly husband and devilish son. Jaye Wells has her own website at www.jayewells.com.

Find out more about Jaye Wells and other Orbit authors by registering for the free monthly newsletter at www.orbitbooks.net

if you enjoyed
BLUE-BLOODED VAMP

look out for

GOD SAVE THE QUEEN

Book One of the Immortal Empire

by

Kate Locke

CHAPTER 1

POMEGRANATES FULL AND FINE

ondon, 175 years into the reign of Her Ensanguined Majesty
Queen Victoria

hate goblins.

And when I say hate, I mean they bloody terrify me. I'd rather
rench-kiss a human with a mouth full of silver fillings than pick
ny way through the debris and rubble that used to be Down Street
tation, searching for the entrance to the plague den.

It was eerily quiet underground. The bustle of cobbleside was
ttle more than a distant clatter down here. The roll of carriages, the
lack of horse hooves from the Mayfair traffic was faint, occasion-
lly completely drowned out by the roar of ancient locomotives
aging through the subterranean tunnels carrying a barrage of
mells in their bone-jangling wake.

Dirt. Decay. Stone. Blood.

I picked my way around a discarded shopping trolley, and tried
o avoid looking at a large paw print in the dust. One of them had
een here recently – the drops of blood surrounding the print were
till fresh enough for me to smell the coppery tang. Human.

As I descended the stairs to platform level, my palms skimmed over the remaining chipped and pitted cream and maroon tiles that covered the walls – a grim reminder that this . . . *mausoleum* was once a thriving hub of urban transportation.

The light of my torch caught an entire set of paw prints, and the jagged pits at the end where claws had dug into the steps. I swallowed, throat dry.

Of course they ventured up this far – the busted sconces were proof. They couldn't always sit around and wait for some stupid human to come to them – they had to hunt. Still, the sight of those prints and the lingering scent of human blood made my chest tight.

I wasn't a coward. My being here was proof of that – and perhaps proof positive of my lack of intelligence. Everyone – aristocrat, half-blood and human – was afraid of goblins. You'd be mental not to be. They were fast and ferocious and didn't seem to have any sense of morality holding them back. If aristos were full plagued, then goblins were overly so, though such a thing wasn't really possible. Technically they were aristocrats, but no one would ever dare call them such. To do so was as much an insult to them as to aristos. They were mutations, and terribly proud of it.

Images flashed in my head, memories that played out like disjointed snippets from a film: fur, gnashing fangs, yellow eyes and blood. That was all I remembered of the day I was attacked by a gob right here in this very station. My history class from the Academy had come here on a field trip. The gobs stayed away from us because of the treaty. At least they were *supposed* to stay away, but one didn't listen, and it picked me.

If it hadn't been for Church, I would have died that day. That was when I realised goblins weren't stories told to children to make us behave. It was also the day I realised that if I didn't die verything in my ability to prove them wrong, people would think was defective somehow – weak – because a goblin tried to take ne.

I hadn't set foot in Down Street station since then. If it weren't or my sister Dede's disappearance I wouldn't have gone down here at all.

Avery and Val thought I was overreacting. Dede had taken off on us before, so it was hardly shocking that she wasn't answering her rotary or that the message box on said gadget was full. But in the past she had called me to let me know she was safe. She always called *me*.

I had exhausted every other avenue. It was as though Dede had fallen off the face of the earth. I was desperate, and there was only one option left – goblins. Gobs knew everything that happened in London, despite rarely venturing above ground. Somehow they had found a way to spy on the entire city, and no one seemed to know just what that was. I reckon anyone who had the bollocks to ask didn't live long enough to share it with the rest of us.

It was dark, not because the city didn't run electric lines down here any more – they did – but because the lights had been smashed. The beam from my small hand-held torch caught the grimy glitter of the remains of at least half a dozen bulbs on the ground amongst the refuse.

The bones of a human hand lay surrounded by the shards, cupping the jagged edges in a dull, dry palm.

I reached for the .50 British Bulldog normally holstered snugly against my ribs, but it wasn't there. I'd left it at home. Walking into the plague den with a firearm was considered an act of aggression unless one was there on the official – which I wasn't. Aggression was the last thing – next to fear – you wanted to show in front of one goblin, let alone an entire plague. It was like wearing a sign reading DINNER around your neck.

It didn't matter that I had plagued blood as well. I was only a half-blood, the result of a vampire aristocrat – the term that had come to be synonymous with someone of noble descent who was also plagued – and a human courtesan doing the hot and sweaty. Science considered goblins the ultimate birth defect, but in reality they were the result of gene snobbery. The Prometheus protein in vamps – caused by centuries of Black Plague exposure – didn't play well with the mutation that caused others to become weres. If the proteins from both species mixed the outcome was a goblin, though some had been born to parents with the same strain. Hell, there were even two documented cases of goblins being born to human parents both of whom carried dormant plagued genes, but that was very rare, as goblins sometimes tried to eat their way out of the womb. No human could survive that.

In fact, no one had much of a chance of surviving a goblin attack. And that was why I had my lonsdaelite dagger tucked into a secret sheath inside my corset. Harder than diamond and easily concealed, it was my "go to" weapon of choice. It was sharp, light and didn't set off machines designed to detect metal or catch the attention of beings with a keen enough sense of smell to sniff out things like blades and pistols.

The dagger was also one of the few things my mother had left me when she . . . went away.

I wound my way down the staircase to the abandoned platform. It was warm, the air heavy with humidity and neglect, stinking of machine and decay. As easy as it was to access the tunnels, I wasn't surprised to note that mine were the only humanoid prints to be seen in the layers of dust. Back in 1932, a bunch of humans had used this very station to invade and burn Mayfair – *the* aristo neighbourhood – during the Great Insurrection. Their intent had been to destroy the aristocracy, or at least cripple it, and take con trol of the Kingdom. The history books say that fewer than half of those humans who went into Down Street station made it out alive.

Maybe goblins were useful after all.

I hopped off the platform on to the track, watching my step so I didn't trip over anything – like a body. They hadn't ripped up the line because there weren't any crews mental enough to brave becoming goblin chow, no matter how good the pay. The light of my torch caught a rough hole in the wall just up ahead. I crouched down, back to the wall as I eased closer. The scent of old blood clung to the dust and brick. This had to be the door to the plague den.

Turn around. Don't do this.

Gritting my teeth against the trembling in my veins, I slipped my left leg, followed by my torso and finally my right half, through the hole. When I straightened, I found myself standing on a narrow landing at the top of a long, steep set of rough-hewn stairs that led deeper into the dark. Water dripped from a rusty pipe near my head, dampening the stone.

As I descended the stairs – my heart hammering, sweat beading around my hairline – I caught a whiff of that particular perfume that could only be described as goblinesque; fur, smoke and earth. It could have been vaguely comforting if it hadn't scared the shit out of me.

I reached the bottom. In the beam from my torch I could see bits of broken pottery scattered across the scarred and pitted stone floor. Similar pieces were embedded in the wall. Probably Roman, but my knowledge of history was sadly lacking. The goblins had been doing a bit of housekeeping – there were fresh bricks mortared into parts of the wall, and someone had created a fresco near the ancient archway. I could be wrong, but it looked as though it had been painted in blood.

Cobbleside the sun was long set, but there were street lights, moonlight. Down here it was almost pitch black except for the dim torches flickering on the rough walls. My night vision was perfect, but I didn't want to think about what might happen if some devilish goblin decided to play hide and seek in the dark.

I tried not to imagine what that one would have done to me.

I took a breath and ducked through the archway into the main vestibule of the plague's lair. There were more sconces in here, so I tucked my hand torch into the leather bag slung across my torso. My surroundings were deceptively cosy and welcoming, as though any moment someone might press a pint into my hand or ask me to dance.

I'll say this about the nasty little bastards – they knew how to throw a party. Music flowed through the catacombs from some unknown source – a lively fiddle accompanied by a piano. Conversation and raucous laughter – both of which sounded a lot like barking – filled the fusty air. Probably a hundred goblins were gathered in this open area, dancing, talking and drinking. They were doing other things as well, but I tried to ignore them. It wouldn't do for me to start screaming.

A few of them looked at me with curiosity in their piercing yellow eyes, turning their heads as they caught my scent. I tensed, waiting for an attack, but it didn't come. It wouldn't either, not when I was so close to an exit, and they were curious to find out what could have brought a halvie this far into their territory.

Goblins looked a lot like werewolves, only shorter and smaller – wiry. They were bipedal, but could run on all fours if the occasion called for additional speed. Their faces were a disconcerting mix of canine and humanoid, but their teeth were all predator – exactly what you might expect from a walking nightmare.

I'd made it maybe another four strides into this bustling

netherworld when one of the creatures stuck a tray of produce in my face, trying to entice me to eat. Grapes the size of walnuts, bruise-purple and glistening in the torchlight, were thrust beneath my nose. Pomegranates the colour of blood, bleeding sweet-tart juice, filled the platter as well, and apples – pale flesh glistening with a delicate blush. There were more, but those were the ones that tempted me the most. I could almost taste them, feel the syrup running down my chin. Berry-stained fingers clutched and pinched at me, smearing sticky delight on my skin and clothes as I pressed forward.

"Eat, pretty," rasped the vaguely soft cruel voice. "Just a taste. A wee little nibble for our sweet lady."

Our? Not bloody fucking likely. I couldn't tell if my tormentor was male or female. The body hair didn't help either. It was effective camouflage unless you happened upon a male goblin in an amorous state. Generally they tried to affect some kind of identity for themselves – a little vanity so non-goblins could tell them apart. This one had both of its ears pierced several times, delicate chains weaving in and out of the holes like golden stitches.

I shook my head, but didn't open my mouth to vocalise my refusal. An open mouth was an invitation to a goblin to stick something in it. If you were lucky, it was only food, but once you tasted their poison you were lost. Goblins were known for their drugs – mostly their opium. They enticed weak humans with a cheap and euphoric high, and the promise of more. Goblins didn't want human money as payment. They wanted information. They wanted flesh. There were already several customers providing entertainment for tonight's bash. I pushed away whatever pity I felt for them – everyone knew what happened when you trafficked with goblins.

I pushed through the crowd, moving deeper into the lair despite every instinct I possessed telling me to run. I was looking for one goblin in particular and I was not going to leave without seeing him. Besides, running would get me chased. Chased would get me eaten.

As I walked, I tried not to pay too much attention to what was going on in the shadows around me. I'd seen a lot of horrible things in my two and twenty years, but the sight of hueys – humans – gorging themselves on fruit, seeds and pulp in their hair and smeared over their dirty naked skin, shook me. Maybe it was the fact that pomegranate flesh looked just like that – flesh – between stained teeth. Or maybe it was the wild delirium in their eyes as goblins ran greedy hands over their sticky bodies.

It was like a scene out of Christina Rossetti's poem, but nothing so lyrical. Mothers knew to keep their children at home after dark, lest they go missing, fated to end up as goblin food – or worse, a goblin's slave.

A sweet, earthy smoke hung heavy in the air, reminding me of decaying flowers. It brushed pleasantly against my mind, but was burned away by my metabolism before it could have any real effect. I brushed a platter of cherries, held by strong paw-like hands, aside despite the watering of my mouth. I knew they'd split between my teeth with a firm, juicy pop, spilling tart, delicious juice down my dry throat. Accepting hospitality might mean I'd be expected to pay for it later, and I wasn't about to end up in the plague's debt. Thankfully I quickly spotted the goblin I was looking for. He sat on a dais near the back of the hall, on a throne made entirely from human bones. If I had to guess, I'd say this is what happened to several of the humans who braved this place during the Great Insurrection. Skulls served as finials high on either side of his head. Another set formed armrests over which each of his furry hands curved.

But this goblin would have stood out without the throne, and the obvious deference with which the other freaks treated him. He was tall for a gob – probably my height when standing – and his shoulders were broad, his canine teeth large and sharp. The firelight made his fur look like warm caramel spotted with chocolate. One of his dog-like ears was torn and chewed-looking, the edges scarred. He was missing an eye as well, the thin line of the closed lid almost indistinguishable in the fur of his face. Hard to believe there was anything aristocratic about him, yet he could be the son of a duke, or even the Prince of Wales. His mother would have to be of rank as well. Did they ever wonder what had become of their monstrous child?

While thousands of humans died with every incarnation of the plague – which loves this country like a mother loves her child – aristocrats survived. Not only survived, they evolved. In England the plague-born Prometheus protein led to vampirism, in Scotland it caused lycanthropy.

It also occasionally affected someone who wasn't considered upper class. Historically, members of the aristocracy had never been very good at keeping it in their pants. Indiscretions with human carriers resulted in the first halvie births, and launched the careers of generations of breeding courtesans. Occasionally some seemingly normal human woman gave birth to a half or fully plagued infant. These children were often murdered by their parents, or shipped off to orphanages where they shunned and mistreated. That was prior to 1932's rebellion. Now, such cruelties were prevented by the Pax – Pax Yersenia, which dictated that each human donated a sample of DNA at birth. This could help prevent human carriers from intermarrying. It also provided families and special housing for unwanted plagued children.

By the time Victoria, our first fully plagued monarch – King George III had shown vampiric traits – ascended the throne, other aristocrats across Britain and Europe had revealed their true natures as well. Vampires thrived in the more temperate climes like France and Spain, weres in Russia and other eastern countries. Some places had a mix of the two, as did Asia and Australia. Those who remained in Canada and the Americas had gone on to become socialites and film stars.

But they were never safe, no matter where they were. Humans accounted for ninety-two per cent of aristocratic and halvie deaths. Haemophilia, suicide and accidents made up for the remaining eight.

There were no recorded goblin deaths at human hands – not even during the Insurrection.

I approached the battle-scarred goblin with caution. The flickering torches made it hard to tell, but I think recognition flashed in his one yellow eye. He sniffed the air as I approached. I curtsied, playing to his vanity.

"A Vardan get," he said, in a voice that was surprisingly low and articulate for a goblin. "Here on the official?"

Half-bloods took the title of their sire as their surname. The Duke of Vardan was my father. "Nothing official, my lord. I'm here because the goblin prince knows everything that happens in London."

"True," he replied with a slow nod. Despite my flattery he was still looking at me like he expected me to do or say something. "But there is a price. What do you offer your prince, pretty get?"

The only prince I claimed was Albert, God rest his soul, and perhaps Bertie, the Prince of Wales. This mangy monster was not *my* prince. Was I wasn't stupid enough to tell him that? Hell, no.